# *Faithless*

*RIFTSINGER PRESS*
*PERTH, AUSTRALIA*

*Paperback Edition 2022*
*ISBN: Paperback: 978-0-6488113-4-3;*
*ePUB: 978-0-6488113-3-6;*

# Faithless

## STEVEN THIELE

RIFTSINGER PRESS

Map of
EKRA

# Chapter 1

*Faith does not guarantee safety.*

Smoke curled over the hillside as Kyra crested the rise, her gaze fixed on the scene beneath her. Her calloused hand planted an ancient staff on the ground, gripping it with the strength of a practised killer. "Finally," she said under her breath.

A hand latched onto hers, cold and clammy, but brimming with innate strength. Eli's silver eyes creased in a warm smile. "We made it."

Kyra allowed herself a moment to breathe it in. High in the wilderness, bitter wind swirled out of the mountains, whispering ancient secrets past her senses. Below, the shining city of Imbra was wreathed in golden light, Eternal Torches ringing the paths and walls, lighting the pathway home.

"I'll give the others a break," Eli said, squeezing her hand before letting go.

Her boots crunched on melting snow, over green shoots peeking through the icy covering. Kyra knelt on the ground, damp soaking through her travel-worn clothing. A shove buffeted her body and the snow leopard cub purred contentedly.

"Careful, Nix," she murmured. "You're too close to the edge." The cub paid her no heed, lolling on the snowy grass, smudging mottled black-and-white fur. Kyra smiled and brushed a hand under the leopard's chin, enjoying the brief respite. But as soon as she stopped stroking Nix, the purring stopped and ageless violet eyes fixed on her once more.

From behind her echoed an exhausted sigh, and her body ached when she twisted to look. A hulking warrior in thick traveller's garb swayed as Eli helped him down from his horse, a slumbering girl cradled in muscled arms. Monsun had pushed

1

himself hard too hard after their struggles in the mountains. His normally bronze skin was pale, and sweat beaded at his forehead. By rights, they shouldn't have even kept him moving after he was poisoned. But nonetheless, the elegant silver tattoo on Monsun's cheek stretched as he smiled wearily at the girl he carried.

The greying monk beside him groaned, instinctively rubbing the stump of his left hand. "I'm never riding again," Alsair said, his good hand switching to massaging his buttocks. As Kyra watched, Eli stepped away from Monsun and crossed to the monk, supporting the older man's weight as he sat.

"Getting old, Alsair?" Eli asked.

Alsair merely raised a bushy brow, but the gleam in his jade eyes promised trouble later. Eli's gaze turned back to Kyra, but she couldn't smile. Nothing involving Alsair could make her smile these days. Instead, she stared at her city, finally at her feet. The Eternal Torches burned without heat, sustained by the power of Nestham Himself. To touch one was forbidden. To bear one was heresy.

Heresy tasted good these days.

She shivered as her eyes landed upon the highest part of the city, contained within the interior wall, the Citadel separated from the lower city. The palace's graceful spires reached into the skyline, as did the colossal inferno of the Eternal Flame's Wellspring. And just below the roaring flame... Kyra's eyes narrowed on the Eternal Order's Cathedral, a chill creeping up her spine.

"We escaped that place before," Eli said, rejoining her at the cliff face. "We'll be fine going back in."

"You know, in some circles it's considered rude to know what people are thinking."

"I've never heard you complain yet," he said.

"When I do, you'll know." She let the smile widen, but she could already feel herself steeling the longer she looked at that city, at the joy and pain it held within. And once more, she looked at the Cathedral. The last time they'd been in that

2

building she'd been imprisoned, and Temero himself had branded Eli. A demon, the long-lost enemy of Ekra, in the body of Vindicator Cedwin. This demon was why they had returned to Imbra. They had a score to settle, and a hunt to begin.

"How can we even be sure Temero fled to Imbra?" Eli said.

"Maybe he didn't." Kyra shrugged. "After we—after Cedwin died," she flicked her gaze to Monsun, "he could have gone anywhere. But he's not dead, that's for sure. Besides, we're in no shape to hunt him now. We need support." *And I need my parents.*

He rolled well-muscled shoulders and sighed. "Just a normal day for two Marked." Power stirred in her at the mention of his magic, the physical strength and supernatural healing blending together. A Princess and a Guardian.

"Are we ready to enter the city?" Kyra asked the group, even though they'd gone over this several times. She focused in on her Vindicator. "Monsun, are you up to this?"

A flash of heavy brows hidden swiftly by royal protocol, and the warrior spoke softly, wary of the child cradled in his arms. "His Majesty dispatched me to hunt you down, but I will escort you in as companions. Keep your hoods up so they do not recognise you."

Eternal Order, Imbran Guard, nobility, peasant, demon... the list went on. Kyra nodded and was about to turn back to surveying the city when the unmistakable chink of gold rang out on their little bluff. Amora stirred, her black hair bobbing around her ears. Yes, that was several gold coins falling to the ground. And whatever melancholy had settled on her lifted as Monsun tenderly set her down. Kyra knelt by the girl, swiftly gathering the coins and stashing them back in the urchin's pouch along with whatever else she'd liberated from their time in Dawn Sanctum.

"Thanks, actor," Amora whispered, bobbing up with limitless energy.

And as Kyra stood, something prickled at her neck, a long-trained instinct combined with restored magic. She noted it, then set it aside.

"At your convenience, Your Highness." Eli grinned, with a magnanimous sweep to Kyra.

Heat bloomed on her cheeks as she rolled her eyes. Kyra patted the ancient circlet tucked into her belt, then covered it with her cloak. "I told you to stop calling me that."

# Chapter 2

The most obvious change in Imbra was the soldiers. Kyra, her face shrouded in a travel-stained hood, couldn't stop looking at them. In front of her, Monsun rode at the head of their group, tattoo and weapons on full display, while she clutched hers under her cloak. But the staff, almost as tall as she was, was difficult to keep inconspicuous. It got harder when Nix squirmed in her jacket, the cub straining the material. They marched down Royal Parade, heading straight towards the Citadel. It should have been bustling with people. Now, it was silent.

She dropped her head further and compared the guards. Imbran soldiers resplendent in clean blue tunics, their officers distinguished with white trim. Only Vindicators like Monsun wore silver. Across the street, wine and food stained the vermilion jerkins of Eternal Guardsmen. Despite their slovenly appearance, some looked lethal, their eyes alert, smiles arrogant. Each wore a medal on their chest, a dove pierced by a sword. Kyra's muscles clenched, but she regained control. No need to reveal the one they had tried to kill was within their grasp. After all, they'd nearly succeeded twice.

Beside her, tension rippled off Eli. His eyes tracked every move, hunter's instincts she'd trusted in the north. He kept his hands hidden beneath his cloak, but he tensed every time a Guardsman walked past. She stepped closer, elbowed him. The young man sucked in a breath and carried on. Nix burrowed into her jacket, the little leopard somehow understanding the need for secrecy.

At the head of their group, Amora held tight to Monsun's trim waist, cradled up against him on the horse. Behind Kyra, Alsair strode with confidence, though his Jinnam medallion remained under his robe. A robe that was too distinctive, drawing stares from soldiers and citizens alike. An Eternal Guardsman's eyes narrowed on Alsair, and Kyra reached forward—but Monsun was already glaring at the soldier, and the Guardsman quickly found somewhere else to be. But as she glanced at Alsair again, her hand cramped around her staff in memory of a stocky monk and his strangely contented smile, one who had condemned her and Eli to face Temero's proxy alone. These days, the more she looked at him, the more her headaches increased.

"Are you nervous?" Eli breathed next to her.

"Should I be?" she rasped.

He paused and held her gaze, the silver irises trapping her in endless depths, quickening her heartbeat. "Last time didn't end well." That was the understatement of the century.

"Oh, Five Hells," she cursed. "What if Trayse is here? He would recognise me as the Ghost." Jayne Farer, the Ghost, was an identity she no longer held. She was only Kyra Antarun now, Princess of Leranion, one of Nestham's Marked. She'd mastered two of the Kingdom's blessings, and her father had the third.

"We can handle Trayse. At least he's only human." Eli brushed aside that threat so easily. But Eli hadn't been in the pouring rain, kneeling over Rinna's corpse, the woman's own blood used to paint Trayse's initial into the tree. He hadn't seen lightning cracking over a slaughter of refugees and wanderers. He hadn't almost fallen for someone who was plotting to destroy him.

That night, Kyra had seen the damage one human could do. That night she had sworn vengeance. But when he had cornered Eli and her, tricking and trapping them so effortlessly, she hadn't acted. She'd frozen in fear, as helpless as when he had massacred her friends.

A gentle hand, calloused and strong, squeezed her own, and Eli's smile was a cracking light in the muddled mist of her thoughts. He abandoned caution and kissed her, and she marvelled at the scent of him, like the earth after spring rain.

6

Alsair groaned quietly behind them. "Really? In the middle of the street?"

Eli pulled back, ignoring the monk's comment. "We'll be okay," he promised her.

Her pounding heart calmed, and she threw a smile at him. They continued on through the city, avoiding the pacing soldiers. Above them, the Citadel loomed, and that was enough. She closed her eyes and summoned her magic. Dark gloves on her hands concealed the telltale golden glow of her Mark, and her senses sharpened, her balance steadied, her strength magnified.

"Feels like it's about to blow," Amora whispered. "The slums are worse, huh?"

Monsun glanced over his shoulder, stirring thick braids clasped with gold beads. "The gates of the Citadel are ahead," he said, his Biralam accent melodic and eloquent. "Remain quiet and hidden."

The looming gates overshadowed her, and the ancient carvings of snarling leopards were nothing like the ball of fuzz in her jacket. She wouldn't be able to pull this off for much longer, as Nix pressed in on her chest.

"Soon, you're walking on your own," she whispered to the cub. Nix purred, and the vibration rumbled through her torso. A smile crept over her, so she found something of great interest on the cobblestones.

"Identification, please," a Leranion soldier asked. Monsun just stared at him, cutting quite a heroic figure on the dishevelled horse. "Apologies, Vindicator. Step right through," the guard said. Monsun rumbled thanks, and they passed through. Monsun dismounted, handing the reins to his horse to a nearby Leranion guard. Kyra breathed a quiet sigh. At least that part had gone right.

"I wish we could just announce ourselves," Eli grumbled.

"Always the dramatic." She smiled. "I don't want to reveal myself until we know what the Order is doing." She tapped Monsun's leg. "To the palace, please."

He smiled at her. "That was the plan, *Highness*." Of course, he was a loyal servant of her throne. Her Vindicator had reacted well to the fulfilment of the life debt to Eli, her... what? What did they call it now? She knew how she felt, and he felt the same. Still, "courting" seemed too noble a word—when noble was definitely not Eli. Especially when the Guardian would have to hide his identity in the court lest the Order find him. Nestham above! She hadn't even considered the danger she was placing him in. She peered at him, but he was staring up at the towers of the Citadel.

Flames roared above them, the light a symbol of Nestham's blessing. One of two gifts that could reveal a Marked's power. They'd hidden their own Torch under Alsair's robe, the monk blissfully unconcerned by the power he carried.

At last, she stepped up onto the ancient stairs, and her thoughts stopped. How many times had she sprinted with reckless abandon down these very steps? With every stride, the weight of centuries bore down on her, as if generations of kings and queens, of generals and priests and heroes, were watching her.

A phantom hand caressed her shoulder, warm and motherly. One of those heroes was watching her. She hadn't seen Eshe since the day she'd killed Cedwin, the day she'd fought for her throne. But the ancient Queen protected her, guided her, just as the old Guardian Jaser Cathom watched over Eli. The thought of that prickly spirit made her blood boil.

Another step. She risked a glance up and gaped at the soaring spires she knew so well. A mighty stronghold set on a hill higher than all of the Citadel, its three towers reached into the sky as if they could touch Nestham Himself. Elegant peaks of the finest glass, set in a perfect triangle. The south-western Spire, to the front of the palace, was the Eternal Order's second sanctuary after the Cathedral. Set so the holy men could inform the ruler of Nestham's will. Of course, they needed to have her father's ear. The south-eastern Spire was the home of the Vindicators, their elite warriors and generals. Five of them, until she'd killed one a week ago. She hadn't known Cedwin, but she'd asked Monsun to tell her about him, as healing for both of them. A good man, recently appointed and burning to prove himself.

A kinder Kyra may have said the blame lay with Temero, the demon possessing the man's body, causing him to torture Eli and try to kill her. But Kyra Antarun, the Nameless Heir of Leranion, knew where the blame truly lay.

Her gaze fell on the northern spire. At the rear of the palace, it climbed above all others. The Royal Spire. Her Spire. She kept climbing, and as the wind drifted in, the waterfall's spray misted her hair. Joy bubbled up inside her, but she kept her eyes ahead and steeled herself to what she might find. When they reached the great doors, two guards in blue and white pounded their fists against their chests and let them in.

Under the palace, she knew, a great chasm ran through the hill. At least they wouldn't need the shortcut over the chasm today. Though it was faster, it still wasn't something she particularly enjoyed. Not after that incident with her friends, when they'd shut her in the lightless hole with one loud prisoner.

However, as she paced through the rich halls, every step a memory, the problem finally dawned on her. "It's too quiet," she hissed. Every servant they'd passed, every courtier, they'd all hurried on their way, never meeting their eyes. There should have been colour and light, laughter and music. But there was nothing.

Monsun nodded thoughtfully, and when the next servant girl came close, he leaned over. "Anne," he rumbled.

The young woman whipped her head around, widened eyes trained on him, a hand rising to her chest, before she smiled and relaxed. "Vindicator Monsun." She curtsied. "It's good to have you back," she said, but her pretty brown eyes blinked too quickly.

"I need you to take these two, get them cleaned up and dressed properly." Monsun pointed at Amora and Alsair. She

9

nodded and spun on her heel, flaring her lilac dress, but then Eli opened his mouth.

"Anne, what's going on?" he said bluntly.

Kyra tensed, but Anne half-turned, glancing over her shoulder before she finally looked at him, and her skinny frame shook.

"Don't you know?" she hissed. "The King is sick. Dying, some say."

Kyra's heart stopped. The world spun before her eyes, but Eli touched her shoulder, and the spinning slowed until she could see. She fought to swallow in a parched throat.

Monsun's eyes rested calmly on her until she nodded for him to lead. Alsair paused, and for a moment he stood like a rock in a wild storm, then moved on, the street urchin shuffling at his heels. Amora's narrow gaze suggested she had already calculated where to sell the valuables in this room.

"We need to find my father," Kyra whispered. She reached under her cloak and pulled out her staff, secrecy be damned. Monsun's burly figure filled the hallway in front of her, and he lengthened his stride so much that she had to half-run to keep up with him. Eli easily kept pace beside her. As she cursed at the ease of their long legs, Nix mewed inside her jacket and dug sharp claws into soft skin.

Kyra hissed at the sudden pain and touched the leopard's head, sending waves of calm through the bond. The cub still bumped against her chest, but Kyra gritted her teeth and pushed on. They turned right into the area under the King's Spire. Set furthest from the palace gate, an invading force would have to fight very far to take the King.

But she remembered these stairs, and it was like a flame caught in her heart, desperate, straining, pulsing, a twisting stream of light telling her to move. She shoved Monsun aside and charged up the stairs. A passing noblewoman clad in green looked at them strangely, and Kyra's heart lifted. She almost smiled, but refrained from saying anything. Not when she was barrelling up the remaining steps, panting for breath.

10

She didn't bother to use her magic. She deserved to hurt. Battling across the Kingdom had kept her fit, but these stairs were lethal. Until there weren't any steps left, and she was bursting onto the landing. Steel shot from scabbards and a guard in a pristine uniform barked a challenge. Monsun waved him down, and the soldier took one look at the Vindicator—and his axe—and saluted smartly.

Kyra's hand, smudged with dirt, nail beds raw and reddened, latched onto the gleaming silver handle—and stopped. Bile rose in the back of her throat, leaving a sour taste in her mouth. Her knees shook, and she stepped back. "I can't do this," she breathed. The thought of what lay beyond that door... Nix yowled from within her jacket, sensing her agitation. Kyra undid her layers and the cub sprang from her clothes, neatly landing on the floor. A gasp made her turn to the sentry stretching his chinstrap with his jaw. "Not a word," she breathed.

When she stared at that door, a steady hand latched onto her shoulder. "You can do this," Eli murmured. "I'm with you."

Kyra wrenched the door open.

# Chapter 3

The men behind Kyra were a wall of strength, keeping her from running away from that door. She had to face it, face what she'd done. *You caused this.* She had left them, left them vulnerable and grieving.

She stepped inside, just one step in worn and muddied boots. The woman kneeling by the luxurious bed rose, garbed in a brilliant red and gold gown. A simple golden circlet glittered on her brow, but it mattered not. Kyra would have recognised the high cheekbones reflected in her own face. Queen Taera Antarun, wife of King Hadrian.

"Who are you?" her mother demanded, that voice, that familiar voice cracking her heart. Taera stepped in front of the bed, her hand reaching to the back of her gown. To the Imbran tradition, and the knife concealed there.

Something in Kyra shattered for, in travel-stained clothes, with the hood up... she was unrecognisable.

Achingly slowly, she passed her staff to Eli. Her hood fell to her shoulders, and her mother fell to her knees. "Kyra."

Her name on her mother's lips was enough to undo her. The dam broke. She rushed to her mother, who was sputtering, tears leaking from honey-brown eyes. Kyra's tears left silver tracks on her face, and Taera clutched her daughter tightly, not caring for the mud and dirt transferred to her beautiful dress. The young princess couldn't speak, she just breathed in her mother's scent, felt the strength of her embrace as they knelt together on the rich floor.

Finally.

After what must have been minutes and felt like seconds, they stood together and gazed at the luxurious bed, at the motionless form atop it. Her father's face was drawn and pale, but his chest rose and fell. The strong jaw, the flaming red hair, diminished by his weakness.

"How long?" she breathed.

"Three days. The Head Healer thinks someone poisoned him."

A growl behind her, and when she turned, Eli was clenching his jaw so hard she feared he'd break his teeth. Monsun, however... the Vindicator looked ready to bring down a Cathedral with his bare hands.

Queen Taera sucked in a breath and inclined her head, reclaiming her regal elegance. "Vindicator Monsun. When your legion arrived home without you, we feared the worst, though your men assured us you were returning."

The vicious light in Monsun's eyes dimmed, and he bowed deeply, grounding the hilt of his axe on the floor. "I apologise for the secrecy, Your Majesty, but we felt it best to arrive in the city quietly," he said.

"An excellent idea," Taera said. "Yes, I imagine the Seventh remains loyal to you?"

"Always," Monsun said, slamming his hand against his chest.

"Good, good. We'll need allies. We have precious few at the moment."

A knife of panic sliced through Kyra. Already, they were making plans. Already, they were readying for... something.

"And you are?" her mother asked.

Kyra's mind snapped back to the present, and she realised her mother was staring at Eli. "Eli Serae," she jumped in breathlessly. Taera raised a brow, and the young Guardian nodded. "He's... he's a Marked."

Taera's eyes widened. "So, the rumours are true," she said. "Another Marked lives with no Kingdom."

"Yes, Your Majesty," Eli said, bowing low. At least he knew how to act in front of a royal.

"Well," Taera said with a knowing smile, "we can use all the help we can get." She shot a look at Kyra, who blushed.

When Kyra glanced at Eli, the tips of his ears flushed a satisfying red. But her heart stopped as a groan sounded from the bed. Stopped, then started pounding.

"Father?" she breathed.

Hadrian opened his eyes, and his smile stretched wide. "Kyra. I thought I was dreaming when I heard your voice."

"No, it's not just a dream. I'm back," she murmured, reaching for a calloused hand, strong with years of sword practice. But his grip was weak, his arm atrophied. She remembered him as muscular, but even that had withered away.

"Careful dear, I'm a bit sore." He chuckled.

She tried to smile. The door opened and shut until the only people in the room were Antaruns.

"How did you survive?" Taera asked her. "Where have you been all this time?"

Kyra hesitated, but these was her parents. So she told them.

She told them of the Order's attempted assassination, how she founded her team and helped refugees of the Order. How she'd trusted someone she shouldn't have. How she'd cost her friends their lives. She told them of what Trayse had done and how she had met Eli. Both her parents' eyes gleamed when she mentioned his name. And when she recounted her adventure through the mountains, a yowl sounded through the door. She smiled and opened the door to Nix, the cub looking decidedly annoyed.

Taera gasped as the snow leopard glided through the gap, fixed her violet eyes on her. Hadrian clicked his tongue, and Nix's head swung to the sound. She glanced at Kyra, almost for permission. Kyra nodded once, and immediately Nix sprung up onto the bed, snuggling up next to Hadrian. A soft purr rumbled through the room.

"She hasn't done that to anyone," Kyra breathed. Nix opened an eye and seemed to smile contentedly.

"Well done, daughter," Hadrian said. "I'm so proud of you."

"But I'm back, and you can fix this." It was almost childish of her, but she wanted to believe it.

Hadrian shook his head slowly. "I don't think I'm leaving this bed again, sweetheart."

A fresh pang of guilt sliced her heart. "This is all my fault," she sobbed.

"Lift your head up," her mother commanded with a voice of steel. "This is not your fault."

"Take this," her father said, pressing something into her hand. Her Mark flared, golden light shimmering across the room. Only two things could make that happen. One was an Eternal Flame, the other was Nesthamir. She opened her hand and found a glittering sapphire set in a ring of Nesthamir. Despite it just fitting her father, she found it slid easily on her forefinger.

"Your ring," she choked out. The ring of truth, the third of Leranion's blessings.

"It's served me for many years," he said. "Now it's your turn. I'm appointing you Regent."

Her heart stopped. "*What?*" Under what circumstances would anyone consider her a Regent? "I've just returned, I haven't seen the court in a year, I have no idea what the Houses are scheming."

"All good points," her father admitted. "But it's time we do something Finon doesn't see coming." *Oh Father, if only you knew how much Finon can see coming.* "Have Monsun summon the Vindicators," he commanded, a measure of his old strength returning. "And send that young man back in here."

She stepped out and instructed Monsun, then returned, Eli filing in behind her. He shot a questioning look at her, but she only shrugged in response. He bowed once again to her parents, armed and almost heroic, despite his ragged clothing. She shut *that* thought down quickly before it went anywhere.

"Boy, come here," her father said.

Eli swallowed and stepped to the king, tension rippling in his back. His hand rested on his sword's hilt. "Majesty?"

15

Her father reached out to Kyra and retrieved the ring. His own Mark flared, golden light dimmed by age and sickness. "Have you heard of what my ring does?"

"Vaguely, Majesty. I believe you can detect lies."

"Brilliant." Hadrian shot a smile at his wife, a cryptic language only those long-married would understand, and she sighed. "What are your intentions with my daughter?"

"Really?" Kyra rolled her eyes. "Is this the time?"

"We're about to bring this man into our politics," Taera said. "We can't take any chances."

Kyra laughed with a disdainful jerk of her chin. "This isn't about the politics, though. Where do you think I spent my last year? Sipping wine in a cabin? I can take care of myself."

Her mother glared at her, hands on her waist.

"You don't need a ring for that, Majesty," Eli smiled softly. "To protect and serve her, as she wishes. In fact, I think I made that exact oath under a life debt."

"You had a life debt?" Taera said. He locked eyes with Kyra, and she remembered words exchanged in blood-covered snow.

"And what are your powers?" Hadrian pressed.

"Similar to yours, I believe. Aside from—healing." Hope shimmered in silver eyes when he turned to Kyra. "Maybe I can heal him, the same way I healed you!"

The same hope rose in her throat and she choked back a grateful sob.

"By all means," Hadrian grunted, "do your best."

Eli hesitated, then closed his eyes. His Mark flared, ice-blue light rippling over the room, illuminating his handsome face. Kyra could only watch as he placed his glowing hand on her father's head. Her own magic surged, matching his, recognising the raw power. After a few seconds, he dropped his hand. "It's not working," he sighed. "There's something there. Something dark. It feels like—like my brand."

16

"Temero," Kyra hissed. After all her struggles, he'd take her father from her too? "Try again," she said, her voice as sharp as the blades of her staff.

"Kyra," her mother began, her face etched in sorrow.

"*Try again!*"

Eli bowed his head and flared his light, but nothing came of it. "I should go," he murmured. He couldn't meet her eyes as he filed out of the room, shoulders slumped. Nix raised her head and gazed through Kyra's breaking soul with wide violet eyes.

"Go with him," Hadrian said. "You've got a lot of work to do."

"I'm going to save you," she hissed through fresh tears, clutching his withered hand. "I promise."

"You already did," he smiled. "Now take this and go."

She forced the emotions down, took the ring, and left Nix with her father. Her serene mask dissolved as soon as she closed the door. As she collapsed on the other side of it, her parents spoke again. Curiosity warred with caution until she flared her magic, her senses sharpening until she caught the whiff of the sentry's sweat.

"You think he could do it?" her mother asked, now as clear as if she were right beside Kyra.

"I think he's the perfect one to check those names off the list." Kyra's mouth twitched, and her hand gripped her staff like it was the only thing keeping her afloat.

"He seems like a decent person. You want to use him like that?" Taera demanded.

Her father chuckled, and it wasn't out of mirth. It was a bitter laugh, riddled with vengeance, a laugh she'd never heard from him. It reminded her of Trayse. "Oh, he'll volunteer for it, trust me. Did you hear what the Order did to him and his home? He seems a good man, but I saw rage in his eyes. You can see it in the way he looks at her. He's devoted to Kyra, and he'll do anything to protect her. He's perfect."

"Do you trust him?" her mother asked. Kyra's breath caught in her throat, every part of her straining, her heart hammering.

"I detected no lie in him," her father said, and Kyra let out a shaking breath.

"That ring didn't save you, love." Her parents fell silent, and Kyra bit her lip, wiped the tears from her eyes, and went to find Monsun, waiting below. The Vindicator led her and Eli through the castle halls until they neared the chasm. Her heart hammered in her chest as they crossed the threshold into the darkness beyond.

"No prisoners currently," Monsun said.

Eli glanced at them, and she shook her head. She'd faced enough fears today. What was one more?

With that, she smiled and ventured into the roaring darkness, crossing swiftly under the castle, until they swept up into the Vindicator's Spire, hooded and cloaked once more.

* * *

"Get used to all the stairs." Kyra forced a grin at Eli.

His eyes gleamed under his hood and he smirked at her. "It'll do wonders for my figure."

She let the silence ring, made a point of holding his gaze, then tracing his body with her eyes. His cheeks flushed in the hood's shadow, and she winked at him.

A deep, long-suffering sigh echoed from the Vindicator above them, and they glanced away like scolded children. Monsun rapped once, twice, on the steel-bound door at the peak of the Vindicator's Spire. It opened immediately, gliding on oiled hinges, and a small woman emerged.

A petite face framed by short white hair beamed at him, stretching the navy blue Vindicator's tattoo across her cheek. "Monsun! Welcome home!" She pulled him into a bear hug, slapping him on the lower back several times. It seemed to be the highest the young woman could reach.

"It's good to see you too, Syl," Monsun rumbled.

"Everyone's assembled." Syl kept grinning. She seemed to exude radiance just by existing, her skin flushed with life. "Just waiting on you, and—" Her gaze swept to Eli and Kyra, still hooded and cloaked. "And who the mukk are these?"

Monsun shrugged, his heavily muscled body rippling. "The reason we are meeting." Syl merely nodded and stepped to the side, and Kyra followed Monsun in, Eli watching her back. As she passed Syl, Kyra gazed down at the polished wood, but the female Vindicator was too short for that trick to work. She peered under the hood and instantly her face drained of colour. But the warrior nodded imperceptibly and let her pass without comment.

As Kyra entered the room, as the scent of parchment and oil hit her, she forced herself to steady. For even with the power flowing through her veins, the Nestham-blessed strength, she felt dwarfed by the strength concentrated within this chamber. Contained within the two other Vindicators across the round table, its ancient surface scratched and scuffed.

The only other man stood by the glass windows with his hands clasped behind his back. His salt-and-pepper hair was elegantly combed, and he had a natural grace that rivalled a trained courtier. Tomas Pretilla, the oldest Vindicator, the General of Leranion, serving her father for many years. His tattoo was a light blue, like the sea on a cold, bright morning.

Kyra cut her gaze to the right and focused on the woman polishing her black boot on the table. She finished and, with a practised motion, flicked the cloth over her shoulder. It neatly sailed back over her and landed on the desk behind them. Raylene Oria scowled at them, her ferocity doubled by a crooked nose and blood-red tattoo. She'd rolled the sleeves of her blue and silver uniform to her shoulders. Her skill and temper were legendary, as were the stories of her adventures. Most famous was the obliteration of a Renegade fleet while working with Prince Jalek Veturan of Casalis. Grey streaked her blonde hair, tied back into a ponytail.

19

Five utilitarian chairs ringed that table, one with silver trim along the frame. Monsun took that seat, gesturing for Kyra to sit to his left. Syl sat to his right. Eli stood behind Kyra, fingers drumming on the back of her chair. Kyra's chest tightened when Raylene glared at her, spreading an icy chill through her blood. She forced herself to breathe slowly, pushing down panic. The tension eased, but she still couldn't meet their eyes, and dropped her gaze to the table for a moment, tracing over the scars on the wooden surface. A few looked disturbingly like knife scratches.

"Why did you call this meeting?" Raylene said. She fixed Monsun with a stare that stirred memories of a frozen hell and a born predator.

However, Monsun merely raised a brow, matching his stare with her own. "First, brief me on the situation here," he said, showing the world a long-held battle of wills between the two of them. Raylene just leaned back in her chair and crossed scarred, muscular arms. When the silence stretched longer, Kyra almost strained to speak, but a faint hint of dark amusement flickered in Raylene's eyes.

"The strangest things." Syl frowned, nimble hands folded on the table. Her eyes, a deep grey, kept shifting to Kyra, though she addressed Monsun. "Cedwin was acting all strange. He took your legion, tried to finish some mission the King sent you on, and then the King—"

"Did any of you do it?" Eli interrupted from over Kyra's shoulder. His voice was deeper, much deeper than usual, and the back of her neck heated.

Raylene's eyes snapped to his, the predator instantly on alert. "Are you interrogating us, boy?" she said. Eli fell silent, speech sapped by the barb.

"Perhaps Raylene merely wishes to discover who our visitors are." Tomas interposed himself into the conversation. "As you know, we never allow strangers into our meetings. Particularly ones who don't bare their faces."

He waited for a beat, and Kyra again almost answered. Too much damn power in this room. She didn't dare turn to look at Eli, but from the sounds of shifting cloth, he had removed his hood.

"My friend wasn't the most tactful, but that has never been his strength." Monsun smiled winningly. "However, he has a point. Were any of you involved in the King's poisoning?"

The chair screeched on the floor as Raylene shot to her feet, her nostrils flaring. "How dare you insult us like that? You question our loyalty?"

"Today, yes," Monsun said, and a shadow fell across his face. "Just answer. Yes or no."

"No," Syl and Tomas said together.

Raylene hesitated, then shook her head emphatically, and dropped into the chair. "No."

"Monsun," Syl said, all trace of that sparkling amusement gone, "why are you acting like some kind of gruntah?"

But the Senior Vindicator just glanced at Kyra, and she nodded. Nothing had rung a falsehood. In response, Kyra removed her hood and met the gazes of the Crown's highest warriors. Raylene's jaw dropped, all traces of anger melting from her expression. Syl went very, very still. Tomas swore quietly under his breath.

"Highness," Syl breathed. Kyra inclined her head regally, a mirror image of her mother.

"So, you're not dead." Raylene raised her brows, apparently having overcome her shock.

Kyra dropped the regal mask and shrugged, splaying her fingernails out. "Apparently not. Thanks to Nestham, skill and good friends, among whom I count Monsun highly." The Vindicator puffed with pride at the statement and Eli snorted over her shoulder.

"Why have you returned?" Tomas asked.

Kyra drew in her breath and dropped the last hailstorm. "Because I believe Finon poisoned my father, and because

Cedwin is dead." Monsun glanced at her, shame—and warning—in his eyes. She blinked an apology, for that information wasn't hers to share. Cedwin had been his warrior, his soldier, his failure.

For a long moment, none of the Vindicators dared speak, but faint tears pooled in Syl's eyes. Raylene merely clenched her jaw, that red tattoo shimmering on her cheek. "How do you know this?"

Kyra bit her lip, forcing weakness away with pain. In a room full of killers, she couldn't afford to show a chink in her armour. She'd been strong once, after all. The silence stretched longer, and she found herself scanning the room. But as she glanced out the window, a small hand waved at her, as boyish hair whipped in the wind. Amora grinned at her and disappeared to climb back down the Spire. If the urchin could climb this tower, she could answer the question. "Because I killed him."

Raylene half stood again, her hand dropping to the wicked sabre at her side, baring her teeth. Kyra refused to give ground and merely raised her hands, though her heart pounded. "A demon had possessed Cedwin, and there was no other way to free him. If I hadn't killed him, Eli would be dead."

Raylene glared at her. *But did you even try to free him?* her eyes asked.

"We buried him with full honours in the mountains. He is at peace," Monsun said. Raylene hissed quietly, and again it reminded Kyra of Nix's mother.

Tomas' grey brows drew together. "And that brings us to the other matter of importance. Who's the boy?"

*Oh dear,* Kyra thought. *He's not going to like being called a boy.*

Eli stepped closer behind her, and she didn't need to look to feel the power coursing through him. "The boy's a Guardian," he said. "I'm Eli."

"I guess you were right about the myths." Syl turned to Monsun, a slight hitch in her voice. "You never stopped believing in them."

"They were never myths, Syl." A sad smile played over his lips.

"Boy, care to enlighten us on what a Guardian is?" Raylene glanced at him dismissively, and Kyra's anger rose in his defence.

A second later, Eli's ice-blue light flickered through the room.

"He can sometimes be useful." Monsun leaned back in his chair, the commander now at ease. "If there are no objections, I'll send him to the Playground later."

"The Playground is for Vindicators only," Raylene reminded him. "But it seems like you've already decided."

"That's not how we settle matters," Monsun said. "But I would prefer if you agreed."

Raylene grunted once. It seemed to be confirmation enough.

"I will need people I can trust." Kyra leaned forward. "I don't trust Finon, and I don't think you do either. I need you on my side."

Her heart raced, and tension pulsed through the room. They flicked glances around until at last Tomas heaved a sigh. "Highness, when you vanished a year ago, I took an entire legion to find you. Failing to do so was a stain on my honour, one I want to remove. I would be proud to do so by serving you."

"If Monsun trusts you, then so do I." Syl smiled.

Raylene didn't answer, frozen anger in her eyes.

A fist hammered on the door, and Eli opened it to find a startled page clad in blue and silver. "The Chosen has called an audience. He's assuming command in the wake of the King's illness."

Kyra froze, then icy anger sharpened in her gut. Her hand skimmed the surface of the table, and the scars and scratches, somehow, gave her strength. Eli growled, and all the Vindicators rose, graceful and utterly deadly.

Kyra glanced around at her warriors and issued her first command. "We go to the throne room now." They nodded and swept past her, hands already falling to their weapons.

All but Raylene, who grabbed Kyra's wrist with a scarred hand. Kyra lifted her chin, prepared to scold her for the sacrilege, but when the princess gazed deep into brown, hate-filled eyes, she lost all words.

"I know you think killing Cedwin was a kindness," Raylene said, and she blinked rapidly, then continued. "But—but that young man was like a son to me."

"Then will you help me take down the bastard who broke him?"

Raylene bared her teeth in a fierce grin. "It would be my pleasure."

# Chapter 4

"I wish your father were here," her mother whispered into her ear. Kyra smiled but didn't dare to look anywhere but straight ahead at the looming doors. Instead, she smoothed down worn and muddied pants. At least she'd found a clean blouse in traditional Leranion blue-and-silver, fished from who knew where. This whole mismatch of outfits really didn't suit her, but it would have to do. She removed the cloak and bundled it up, then pulled out the circlet from where she'd carelessly stashed it in her belt.

"Here, let me," Taera said gently, taking it out of her hands. Soft hands made for writing placed the circlet into Kyra's tangled and messy hair, one of the few things they shared. Her mother's eyes, though a different colour, held that same intensity, that same intelligence. "This is your birthright. Every part of your life has prepared you for this. Retake your throne, daughter."

Those doors loomed. Ancient, impregnable, forbidding, they were adorned by snarling leopards in Leranion silver. But as Kyra heaved a breath, she glanced behind at her friends, her family. Her mother waited behind her, Monsun and the other Vindicators behind them. At the back, Eli waited with Amora and Alsair, and he smiled widely at her, practically glowing with pride. She winked back, and Amora grinned. Alsair's jade eyes gleamed under his new hood, and his grey beard twitched once.

Monsun barked an order and Kyra's Vindicators snapped to attention, forming a wall of muscle and steel behind her. Even Syl, small as she was, her hands hovering over the knives strapped to her waist.

That hated voice was as eloquent as ever. The master orator at work, claiming a Nestham-blessed right to the throne. Technically, the Archbishop of the Eternal Order had a right to assume Regency if the Marked was too young. Unfortunately, precedent hadn't factored in the possibility of a murderous traitor. Kyra at last allowed herself to smile at the gaping sentry. "Open it." The young man bowed and clanged the iron knocker on the door.

Once for a soldier or servant. Twice for clergy and nobility. Three times for royalty.

The doors rumbled open, and everything went still as Kyra drank in the sight. It was as if she were ten years old again, playing in this room where she'd run rampant with her friends, in the pews where she'd given away her hiding place by giggling. Rows upon rows of pews, filled with nobles and soldiers, with clergy in Order red and Musadim grey. Rays of sunlight reflected through pristine glass, highlighting blue drapes emblazoned with the roaring leopard, just like the one nuzzling her knee. On and on she looked, frozen to her core, at the massive throne on the dais. The throne of her ancestors, carved from northern stone. The hand rests were the heads of leopards. On that throne lounged a single figure, garbed in red robes, with a ridiculous hat lying on his head.

Silence fell across the throne room. Kyra's magic writhed, and she focused every inch of being on that man, that monster. Raylene and Monsun formed up at her back, the other Vindicators falling into line whilst Eli, Alsair and Amora slipped into the crowd. Kyra slammed her ancient staff on the rich floor, and the clash resounded through the room. She marched down that aisle, circlet on her head, staff in her hand, leopard by her side, ring on her finger. A Queen reborn strode to that throne, flanked by a four-person army. The sound of their boots on ancient stone resounded in the still and silent chamber. As she neared the dais, she stared into the face of that old snake and, summoning the warrior's indifference, winked at him.

*You,* he mouthed, fear flashing in his eyes before he composed himself.

Every step was an instant and yet an eternity. Until she was at the foot of her throne, and the Archbishop atop it.

Behind her, the warriors fanned out, hands on their weapons, forming a barrier between her and the silent audience. She counted the steps—one, two, three. Shabby boots on polished stone. And then she was less than a metre away from her enemy. "Get your worthless hide off my throne," she breathed. The seconds stretched out as he swallowed quietly. "*Now.*"

At last, Finon rose, and the temptation to smack him senseless ached through Kyra, her fingers clenching around Nesthamir.

His creased skin stretched around a crooked smile. "Ten thousand apologies, *Your Highness*," he smiled. His breath smelled of fresh mint. "It seems you survived the North."

"I'm very hard to kill, your *Eminence*." She smiled at him again and waited until he had stepped off the dais. Raylene pivoted closer to the Archbishop, hand wrapping around the sword at her side. Hundreds of eyes trained on Kyra as she slowly turned to face the crowd. None had moved.

"The Archbishop has overstepped himself. His precedent does not apply here," she said, face a steely mask.

"Impostor!" a nobleman yelled. He swayed on his feet, the rich robes on his portly frame edged with gold. Amber eyes dull, his face pockmarked.

Kyra stared him down and arched a brow. "Lovely to see you again, Lord Ketan, but I can assure you I am no impostor."

"Prove it!" he roared, his heavy jowls reddened with excitement. Nix snarled at him, but Kyra didn't flinch. She'd survived demons. She'd survive a drunken nobleman.

"You want proof?" she said. She didn't yell, merely sharpened her voice to a weapon in its own right. "Here's your proof!" Nesthamir flashed through the air, and she reached deep into her magic. Her golden Mark flared, brighter and brighter until the crowd gasped. "Does that satisfy you, my lord?" She swept her gaze along the front pews, so neatly sectioned up. Three men and one woman in rich clothing stared back. She didn't nod to them. They didn't nod back.

"I'm assuming command whilst my father is unwell. Archbishop Finon has no claim on this throne." The poisonous old man flashed a glare at her. She could feel the heat of his gaze prickling up the back of her neck, and her grip tightened on her staff, the magic flowing into the Nestham-blessed metal, gift from a long-dead ancestor.

Everything ached to unleash herself. Show these people what kind of warrior their princess was. But not here, not now. That wasn't her. Still...

The silence stretched longer. She pursed her lips and turned back to the Archbishop. Hate shone in those eyes, and triumph shone in her own. When Eli winked at her, it was enough to set her skin aflame. Kyra strode from the room, trumpets sounding her departure, leaving murmurs behind.

# Chapter 5

The doors slammed shut behind the princess, and Eli breathed a sigh of relief. His hand dropped from the knife at his belt—he cursed the missing sword, taken from him by the sentries, but nobody else dared move. The Vindicators were stony-faced, hands on their weapons, lethal tattoos on full display. They needn't have bothered, for the crowd of nobles and clergy sat stunned. Eli's jaw clenched when his gaze swept over the Eternal Order clerics hunched in the pews, hands folded into their robes. None had reacted to Kyra's return. Perhaps they'd been briefed by Finon.

*Finon.* Eli swung his gaze to the most hated man in Ekra. His heart pulsed in his chest, and his hand crept to his knife. So easy. So easy to end it here, with him only surrounded by a few wary guards completely outmatched by Vindicators. Raylene took one too-casual step to the Archbishop, but Monsun shook his head at the elder woman. She snarled, but fell into line. Finon spun on his heel, red robes fluttering out, and strode away, Guardsmen tromping after him. Eli contented himself with a last glare at Finon's frail back.

Monsun nodded to the rest of the Vindicators and they stalked down the aisle like myths come to life. One-by-one, the hall cleared, leaving only old men muttering amongst themselves. Eli pushed off the wall and strode to the other side of the room, his boots ringing on the stone floor. Nestham above, this very room seemed designed to intimidate. He strolled up to the lone figure in a brilliant green cloak, who had drawn several suspicious glances from the guards as the only one hooded in the entire court.

"You did well," Alsair said, his face hidden in shadow, for once with a trimmed beard.

"That was all Kyra. I just stood around and watched."

"She's been trained for this. You haven't." True. All this politics, this showmanship, it wasn't for him. Just give him something to whack and he would be perfectly happy. "What's next?" Alsair prompted him.

He thought for a moment, like it was one of Alsair's tests back in the Mount, those years spent pouring over papers. "Well, we've got the Vindicators' support, if not the court's. What can you tell me about the people here?" He flicked an apologetic grin at his mentor. "I may have forgotten some lessons."

Alsair heaved a sigh, releasing a heavy scent of coffee. "Like you forgot my ban on swimming in the stream inside the Mount."

"I got myself out of that," he replied without hesitation. He forced the quip, but instantly remembered the roar of the water, the feeling of being tossed and turned as it swept him outside and down the cliff face.

Alsair raised a brow and glanced up at him. Even though he was shorter than Eli, he seemed to project that strength, that power, that authority. "No, you didn't. I pulled you out after you went over the falls and halfway onto the plains."

"So, what can you tell me about these people?" Eli changed the subject, shifting from foot to foot. The air seemed to grow cold as Alsair smirked, his point proven.

"Lord Ketan is one of the most powerful nobles in Leranion. He's the ruler of House Ketan, one of the four great Imbran Houses. He controls the mines in the eastern part of the mountains, near the border with Amerin." He cocked a bushy brow. "It's all coming back to you now, isn't it?"

Eli shrugged and reached up for the hood. "Of course it is, but I was wondering if you had forgotten."

His mentor slapped the hand away, but Eli didn't need to see Alsair's eyes to know he was rolling them. "The other three are House Rurik, House Giara, and House Errant. Their alliances shift in an eye-blink, but normally, Giara and Rurik are close, and Ketan and Errant often ally." Alsair shrugged. "At least, that's what I've heard."

The Guardian grunted quietly and tested the knife on his belt. The hilt was well-worn, yet it had seen him through enough. "Well, we've got our work cut out for us. But what's next for you?"

"I don't know," Alsair said. His gaze turned far-off, and his face fell into shadow. "I don't think I can stay in Imbra just yet. I have something I need to do first."

The words jolted through Eli, and he blinked, shock coursing within him. "You're just going to leave?"

"You've survived without me before." Alsair grinned. "Like that trip you took a few months ago. And recently—even if I had to pull you out of prison myself." His face softened, and he placed his good arm on Eli's shoulder. "I'll stick around for another day or so. In the meantime, go follow her."

# Chapter 6

The light warred with memory's shade as Kyra staggered to her old rooms, up those endless stairs. One year. One year of fighting, of running, of living. It felt like an eternity. Only muscle memory guided her leaden legs, Nix flanking her always, until at last she crashed through her door. Nothing out of place, almost as if her parents couldn't bear to change anything. Yet a shaking finger found no dust on the shelf. The other doors leading to her study, bathing suite, and the second bedroom were all shut. Nix sprang onto the massive bed with its rich blue quilt. She curled up on the pillow, rumbling contentedly.

"You're useless," Kyra snorted before collapsing alongside her snow leopard. Ugh, an actual bed! She groaned at the luxury. *Thump.* Kyra raised her head blearily. No servant would knock like that—it was brash, almost arrogant. *Thump.* "S'open," she mumbled. Not the best idea—anyone could be behind that door—but she was too damned tired.

"It better be," a female voice yelled. And that voice—that voice—it sent a jolt of lightning through her, a spark flaring, a piece of her reigniting. No fatigue could prevent the smile that stretched across her face as she turned to face the door.

"Or what?" she shouted back.

"Try it and find out," another voice yelled. The tiredness melted from her bones and her heartbeat thrummed in her chest.

"Then get in here!" The door crashed open and two young ladies sprinted through the opening, garbed in green and white. They tackled her immediately, and she couldn't help but burst with the joy that bubbled up inside her. She hugged them so tight it seemed her magic had flared. Kyra Antarun was home.

"I can't believe you're alive," Lady Jayne Ajerst said as they sat cross-legged on the bed.

"It's so good to see you again." Kyra grinned. She had just regained something she hadn't realised she'd lost, and she thanked Nestham for it.

Lady Eislyn Ketan beamed at her. "Missed us enough to come home?"

That flicker of joy wavered, as if a shadow-kissed wind brushed alongside it, reminded her of her task. "Something like that." She forced the grin.

"Looks like you enjoyed yourself on your holiday," Jayne commented with a wry grin. Kyra shot her a warning glare as Jayne reached out a painted nail to Nix, scratching the cub on the head. Nix purred, and Kyra raised a brow. Apparently the snow leopard had improved at recognising friend from foe.

"You must tell me what I've missed!"

Jayne held up a calm hand. In anyone else, that would be near-sacrilege. "That can wait. First, how are you holding up?" she said. The Lady was not of the four Imbran houses. Her parents had fled the Plains when she was a baby, during another clash between Stallor and Fallkirk. And she had that typical Plains—no, *Amerin*—trait: her beautiful raven hair.

Kyra hesitated, eyes flicking to Eislyn. The firstborn daughter of Lord Ketan, the man who'd tried to deny her legitimacy as Queen. No doubt Eislyn would have words with her father about that. They'd been friends as long as she could remember, as they attended the balls in the city, as they learned to use the *bela,* the concealed knife all women of the court carried. Tradition—and necessity—required a young lady in Imbra to learn how to defend herself. But for Kyra, it had gone beyond that. As a Marked, she had been expected to have full control of her abilities. Her father Hadrian had learned the sword, and with his magic he'd be a match for a Vindicator. He'd had Kyra trained in the sword, but focused her training on the quarterstaff.

"I think I'm not doing too bad, first day as Regent." Kyra grinned, but it was a poor lie at best.

"You've only just returned. This last year, it's been hard," Eislyn said. *Hard for everyone, no doubt.*

"I know." A part of her wavered, that last bit of Jayne Farer holding the secrets to her chest. But Jayne Farer had been a shadow of Kyra Antarun. So she began telling her story again, except she choked when she mentioned Trayse and skipped to her time in the dungeons. But then her eyes brightened, and she mentioned her new friends. And as soon as she spoke Eli's name, their eyes gleamed.

"The pretty boy in your procession?" Eislyn waggled her eyebrows.

"He wasn't that pretty," Jayne said. "Nice jaw, though."

Kyra rolled her eyes. "He's mine."

She'd never done this before, but Eislyn smirked. "Oh, you've actually fallen for him, haven't you?" Her oldest friend leaned back, gripping the edge of the bed.

"We're working it out. We found some time amongst all the demon-killing."

"Demon-killing?" Both of them seemed very surprised about that particular comment.

"Ah, yes," Kyra said. "See, we lost track, because you two lose your minds when a man shows up."

"Continue," Jayne waved. "On with the demon-killing then."

A small part of her relished the way they sat stunned as she described the Sanctum, and the battle in the north, leaving out Cedwin and his death.

When she finished, Eislyn let out a sigh. "So, she wasn't lying about the demon-killing," she said to Jayne. "Are there more?"

"Trust me, there'll be plenty to go around if we aren't smart. Can we move onto more important business now?" They nodded, at once dead serious. "Did you know anything of what the Order was planning with my father? Anything you heard at all?" They shook their heads. And as much as she wanted to take it at face value, she couldn't. She reached into her power, magnified by the ring she now wore. Sometimes a gesture was worth more than words, and if a gesture was clear enough in its meaning, she could sense its truth just as easily as words.

Neither was lying. "Good."

"Do you want to talk about it?" Jayne pressed.

Kyra pursed her lips. "You know what? No. I'd rather just eat dinner, have a bath and go to sleep."

"Fortunately, we planned ahead." Jayne smoothed the wrinkles from her beautiful green dress, and opened the door, where Anne pushed in a tray of mouth-watering food and bowed. "Compliments of Master Chum, Highness."

"Thank you, Anne," Kyra said with a grateful smile. Anne blushed slightly as she exited.

Kyra quickly set to work, tucking into the meal.

"Mmmmf," she sighed. "S' good."

"I take it you haven't eaten that well in the last year." Jayne smiled.

"You know what else she hasn't had in a year? A bath." Eislyn turned from where she was pacing around the room.

"Is it that noticeable?" Kyra sniffed her underarm and cursed.

The blonde could barely refrain from snorting. "Very ladylike."

Kyra mimed a curtsy, but it was difficult on the bed. "Clearly, I'm no longer refined enough for you two." Nix raised her head and sniffed the air. "What is it, girl?" Kyra asked, but the snow leopard merely sighed and went back to sleep. Light flashed on the balcony, beyond the opened window. Just as she drew breath to stop her, the knife had already flashed from Jayne's hand. Kyra's breath caught in a silent scream as the source of that light brightened. Her heart stopped.

When the light faded away, Eli was standing there, a shocked expression on his face. His right hand clutched a knife centimetres away from impaling his chest.

"Jayne, what did I tell you about throwing knives at pretty boys?" Eislyn sighed.

Eli swallowed. "I—"

"Eli, come meet my friends." Kyra rushed to the balcony, hauling the young man by the arm. His muscles were stiff, as if he was stubbornly refusing to enter. After catching a knife hurled at him, he was justifiably stunned. Still, he smiled as he greeted Eislyn and Jayne, chuckling when he handed over the knife.

"Do you introduce yourself like that to everyone?" he said.

"Only the special ones," Eislyn winked. Kyra coughed and Jayne elbowed Eislyn in the ribs, even as she sheathed the knife. "What?" the blonde asked. She twigged a moment later and blinked an apology.

Kyra winced at the ladies staring at her, at *them*. "Can you two give us a moment?" Eislyn's smirk should have been painted and framed on the wall, but Jayne nodded solemnly and they shut the door quietly behind them, Jayne leaving a beautiful parcel on the bedside table. Kyra sat back down on the bed, maintaining a proper and ladylike position this time. Eli just dropped next to her, drained completely. Even exhausted, he still held that presence of pure, undiluted warrior. The Guardian.

When Kyra brushed Eli's fingers with her own, he quietly linked them together. His grip was calloused, roughened from his years of training. "Everything alright?" she asked, meeting his gaze. He idly traced her hand with his thumb, and even that made her breath hitch.

He pursed his lips. "I spoke with Monsun," he said. "He wants me to be a trainee Vindicator to replace Cedwin."

She raised her brows. "Cedwin died only a few days ago. Monsun wants to fill that gap quickly?"

"We can't appear to be weak now," he said. "I just need your confirmation." She hesitated. Was that all? "It would be a good reason for me to be here," he hurried. "Seeing as I'm not a lord, I need a reason to stay. I can't announce myself as a Guardian. Besides..." He winked.

*Don't you do this now,* she said with her eyes. He got the message, that stony glance she'd sent many times. The courtly mask dropped and she let out a sigh of utter exhaustion. "I'm just worried. You'll be painting a target on your back if you do this. Look what happened to Cedwin." It flashed through her mind, the otherworldly cruelty on the young man's face, and the sight of him standing over Eli, sword in hand.

"Kyra, you're the biggest target of all." He squeezed her hand gently. "How are you holding up?"

"That's the second time someone's asked me that in the last ten minutes." She sighed. "I'm fine." She stretched her hand, massaging it, but the tension didn't leave. Not the numbness of a drained Mark, but something else. Nix let out a quiet growl, but the cub's eyes were blissfully closed. Eli gasped softly, shifting his weight on the mattress.

"Look," he pointed out onto the balcony, pointed at the blazing sun setting over the west, at the beautiful rays stretching out over the land. He jumped up and tugged on her hand.

"Someone might see us," she protested, but Eli grinned.

"Who cares?"

*Everyone would care,* she thought inwardly. Against her better judgement, Kyra followed him out onto the balcony, leaned on the gleaming railing. He traced his fingers along her shoulder, his lips following his touch, then he braced his arms around her. Damn him. Damn him for making her feel this way. She leaned back into his warmth, felt the deep, steady thump of his heart, a strength she relied on.

"I have to say, I didn't really expect to get this far," he said, his deep voice rumbling through her skull.

"Me neither."

He shook his head and let out a low laugh. "How long have you known those two?"

Kyra raised her head off his chest, craned up to look at him. "Oh, most of my life. Court can get lonely, particularly with Leranion's nameless tradition." The name of the Heir to Leranion was never announced until their eighteenth birthday.

Superstition held that the name should be kept secret. With a demon stalking them, perhaps that tradition was warranted. "I was expected to spend a lot of time with the future ladies of the court. Eislyn's the Ketan heir, and Jayne's been my lady-in-waiting forever. It was nice to have people around that I could trust, even though they didn't know my name."

Eli glanced out to the horizon, and the setting sun gleamed in his depthless silver eyes. "So, what did they call you?"

"The court called me 'Princess,' or 'Highness'. Eis and Jayne just called me '*amica*'."

They lapsed into silence, watching the golden ball of flame disappear behind the hills. When it finally fell, leaving only glittering rays of Nestham behind, she spun and rested her head on his chest.

"I thought coming back would be easier," she said. "Now I have to play Queen as well?"

"I saw how you took on Finon. You'll be fine."

She wasn't so sure about that. "I need to tell you something." He glanced down at her, silver eyes alight with a warmth he so often displayed. She couldn't fight the shiver that swept over her. He was fire, and sometimes fire is just warmth when needed most. "Not here." She tugged him back into the bedroom, into that cradle of luxury, and frowned at the decorations. How had this room become unfamiliar? Shaking her head to clear the traitorous thought, she shut the door and paced to the enormous desk at the corner of the room. Bare, save for the spare parchment and full inkpot.

"Grab a chair," she mumbled over her shoulder to Eli, and started scribbling on the paper. Wood scraped the rug as he dragged a spare chair to the desk, lighting the little candle on the side. They scribbled, talking as they worked. Outlining enemies, allies, plans. Temero. Finon. She wrote and wrote and wrote until she came to one name, one they had avoided every time. Trayse.

"He's just one man," Eli said. "He's not that powerful."

Her quill rested on the desk and she shifted so slowly, so damn slowly, every vein like ice. "I want him gone."

Surprise flashed over his face and then he nodded. They kept working until her eyelids were drooping and the bed was looking very enticing. She slouched to her side, her head resting on Eli's shoulder.

The door rattled again, and she lurched up in her chair. Eli, startled, twisted to the side and thudded to the floor. His sharp hiss was enough proof of his injury. Kyra brushed her hair back from her face, her eyes frantically flicking to the door. She pointed at the second bedroom, and inhaled swiftly, patting herself down before her mother's voice echoed through the door.

"Kyra?"

"Coming, Mother," she squeaked, and winced. She sounded like she was eight again. When she glanced again at the floor, she found nothing. Kyra opened the door to her mother, standing there worried.

"Is everything alright?" Kyra asked.

Her mother scrunched a royal brow, honey-brown eyes narrowed in concern. "Everything is not alright," Taera answered. "I haven't seen you in a year, and then you just vanish. I still barely get to speak with you."

Kyra bit her lip. "I'm sorry, I've been—distracted." Distracted was one word for it.

Taera glared at her. "I'm your mother. You can't just shut me out like this. I have a right to know what's happening."

Kyra wasn't sure what it was, but her emotions swirled, and her shoulders curled in. All over, she shook. She hadn't felt this since Trayse captured her. Blood pounded in her head, leading to a deathly ringing that sounded like the bells of the Cathedral. "You know what? Maybe I don't need to open up to everyone!"

Her mother blinked, her face whitening to a deathly sheen. "Kyra..." she breathed.

"Just *go!*" The dam burst. Tears welled in her eyes as she choked and spluttered. "You can't help me." Kyra collapsed against the wall and threw out her hand, as if to ward off her mother. She failed, and a pair of arms enveloped her. And the ringing stopped, and she crumpled into her mother's embrace.

"I'm sorry, dearest. I just don't know what to do."

Kyra sniffed once, gaining control of herself. "I'll get there. I just need time." She forced a watery smile. "I'm used to running things on my own."

"You had Monsun," her mother reminded her.

She laughed, vision still blurred. "Monsun was under a life debt. He couldn't do a mukking thing." She clamped her lips together as Taera's brows narrowed and that motherly mask morphed into a regal glare. A faint snort sounded from under her bed and she bit her lip, praying her mother didn't hear it.

"Well, I've told the court you're resting and they will see you tomorrow," Taera said.

"Thank you."

Taera shut the door quietly behind her, and Kyra let out a sigh. The door to the other room opened, and Eli sidled up behind her, quiet as usual. He stopped a metre away behind her. "I'm not going to ask if you're okay," he said, and she let out a snort, turned and faced him.

"Just hold me." He opened his arms, and when she shuffled into them, he traced her spine with a finger. He held her for what felt like an eternity, and it still wasn't long enough. When at last she let go, she quietly left his presence, grabbing a change of clothes and shutting the door to the bathing suite behind her. The space felt too clean, and she fell still, the weight of her day pressing in on her. And as she opened the tap, spilling luxurious hot water into the tub, removing her outer layer felt like removing a second skin. She entered the bath and sighed, as the reality finally sank in. She'd survived the north, but her work was just beginning.

She emerged half an hour later in fresh clothes, the world having darkened outside. A tiny candle burned on the desk. Eli's broad shoulders hunched over where he tapped his finger on the wooden surface. "What are you doing?" she asked, not daring to raise her voice lest it crack. Lest it reveal her brokenness.

Eli didn't turn, and she was grateful. "Just reading over the notes. I don't think we can keep these around for much longer. Read them in the morning and then we'll burn them." A yawn escaped him as he stretched weary arms. "I need to get to bed, anyway. Monsun said he had a room for me near Alsair."

"You don't want to sleep here?"

The candlelight cast strange flickering shadows across his face as he turned. "Kyra, you're the Regent of Leranion. Truth be told, I don't even think I should be in this room."

She held a glare. "If you thought that, why did you come here in the first place?" He twitched, not daring to reply. "And for that matter, who I let in my room, in my bed, is my decision. And mine alone."

"Maybe not for much longer," he said.

Her glare sharpened, fury stirring and her magic roiling. "What are you implying?"

But when he flung his hands wide, her anger faded away. "Nestham above, I don't know! This is your territory, and I'm just a boy from Mount Sancti. A commoner." The doubt held like a discordant note in his voice. As if he wasn't worth more than a hundred courtiers. And he'd already given so much of himself. Even if the scars didn't show on his skin, they gleamed on his heart.

"Vindicator, you mean," Kyra smiled softly.

His eyes glowed in the dim light of the candle, and ice-blue light flickered throughout the room, as if that one word suddenly triggered all of his power. "Are you sure?"

"I can't stop you. This might help us. But I can't give you command of a legion."

Eli's smile melted her heart. "I never wanted one."

"Just get in the bed," she sighed. He practically sprang for her, and was asleep within minutes, his deep, even breathing resounding throughout the room. But she lay awake. As his living flame withered away to ash, she couldn't do anything but stare at the ceiling. This, whatever it was between them, she prayed it would last. Because he was fire, but she knew what happened to fire with nothing left to burn.

# Chapter 7

The roar of the Citadel's waterfall drowned out all noise as the cloaked figure clambered into the waiting canoe, awkwardly steering with one oar. Nestham's Shield blazed with holy fire above, his love's home glittering with starlight in a sight that always made him smile. Even on the desolate river in the silent city, he wasn't alone. The oar dipped into the water again, and wavelets lapped at the little canoe as it glided onwards. This stretch of river met up with the Kinar, and though it was too shallow for most real boats, scraps of wood like these were just fine.

Torchlight flickered on the nobles' keeps, stretching high into the skyline. Guards on night patrol, cold and bored, trudged along stone walls and private jetties. The oarsman was passing Mansion Errant's jetty as a guard tromped close. He froze, held his breath.

"What are you doing?" A voice shattered the frozen silence. The man in the canoe didn't dare move, arm locked on the oar. To flinch could be deadly.

"Sir! Checking the jetty, sir!"

"Well, get inside! There's nothing out here," the other said. Two pairs of feet thudded away, and the paddler continued on, leaving Mansion Errant behind.

He followed the Kinar until he reached the merchants' quarter, steering the canoe to an empty jetty and thudding into the wood. He dropped the paddle inside the canoe as he rummaged among the rotting planks beneath him, grasping a thin line. A dextrous hand wrapped it around the post and back again, securing the vessel to the jetty, leaving it bobbing on the calm water. As he heaved himself onto the wharf, he sighed and glanced around at the streets. Cool mist rolled off the river, a creeping fog straight off the northern mountains. No doubt it would be hard for urchins and the others on the streets, but that was an issue for another night.

He ghosted through the streets, occasionally flicking a glance to the rooftops, and the children who danced over them. Footsteps behind him, quiet breathing, and he ducked into the shadows, tugging his weathered hood over his head. He remained perfectly still, the discipline drilled into him through years of training. The runner shot past, a skinny frame with dirty blonde hair trailing behind her. A girl, maybe ten. She slowed, stopped, turned, stared right at him. Each froze, two masters of the streets examining threats.

The girl winked and sprinted off to a stack of crates by a wall, vaulted, stretching a hand to the eaves. She shimmied up and over in a heartbeat, and the shadow smiled widely. These urchins would be valuable assets as perhaps messengers or spies. The oarsman knew the Spymaster had made one of those assets into a Vindicator. Alone once again, the cloaked figure turned the corner and smiled at the stone building looming ahead, at the bright white banner emblazoned with a gold coin, the symbol of the Guild, the organisation that ran much of the industry and trade within Leranion. One sentry remained out the front, in the leather armour and blue insignia of the Imbran Guard. Volunteers, not military, but mostly good men. Approaching the light like a moth to a flame, the stranger reached into the folds of his cloak and passed across a letter. The guard frowned at the address and name scrawled on the front.

"You want to send this to Casalis Palace?" he asked the figure, who nodded. "Well, it's three gold pieces to send to Valmor, so it'll be four to send to the palace." The cloaked man swore and handed over four gold pieces. They vanished into the pouch on the guard's belt, right next to a very businesslike dagger. Only half of those pieces would be recorded tomorrow. The guard stamped the letter and dropped it into the chute by his side. "Pleasure doing business." He smiled.

"Mukking robbery," the hooded man snarled, and stalked off, shaking his head. A chuckle rang out behind him, but he had already turned the corner. Mukking expensive Guild. They already had all the merchants and many of the good healers. All the rest were Musadim and did it out of the kindness of their hearts, but the Guild paid good money for a skilled healer. No wonder they had so many. At least Hadrian could regulate their prices, so they didn't gouge everyone. Not that he did much these days.

He turned right, moving in between the alleys until he neared the noise and commotion. The slums never slept in Imbra. He crossed the little bridge into the poor quarter. All around him were the crippled, the downtrodden, and his heart ached. How could this keep occurring?

He turned down another alley and sighed. A night woman aimed to bump into him, hands on her hips and bedroom eyes already half-closed. He neatly sidestepped her, flicking a gold coin into the air that caught the light and shimmered in the mist. Painted fingers snatched it fast as a viper, and she winked at him. For once, he smiled, intelligence recognising a kindred spirit. She vanished, and he kept moving, skulking to the source of the noise.

While the rest of the buildings were almost huts, wooden shacks leaning and crumbling, one massive stone building loomed, virtually a fortress. The Leopard's Teeth didn't even try to hide its reputation, not when noise boomed from it. Not when several immense men bearing swords stood out the front, a violation of Imbra's laws. Only those in a legitimate organisation could carry them. He had left his at home, carrying only a knife under his cloak. The man shrugged and pushed into the crowd, ducking under the gaze of the guards, the noise rebounding off the walls and thudding through his skin. The men at the bottom of the pit slammed into one another, letting out bestial grunts, pummelling each other. After twenty minutes, he quickly exited, having seen enough for tonight.

# Chapter 8

A discreet knock sounded on the door, and Kyra groaned and stretched. She cast a disgruntled glance at the empty space beside her on the bed before she opened the door. "Amica."

Jayne waited in the hallway, hands gracefully held behind her back. "Miss me? You never asked for us again." Her pointed gaze brought the blush to Kyra's cheeks, and Jayne's smile widened—her point proven. Today, she wore another green dress, but slimmer, showing off her sleek form. Her hair remained in the same severe style she kept whenever she was outside her chambers.

"I didn't expect to see you this morning," Kyra said. "It's barely dawn."

Jayne glanced pointedly at the balcony, narrowing perfectly groomed brows. "Try again." Kyra turned around and found the sun not shining through the window as she thought, but high in the sky. She cursed under her breath, a word suited to the wilds, not the palace.

"Would you like me to help you get dressed?" Jayne asked, and Kyra spun straight around. Why would she—oh.

Kyra smiled faintly, awkwardly. "It's been a while. I'm used to dressing myself now."

"Yes, but you don't get to wear fun things like this when you're in the countryside. You haven't worn a fine dress in how long?"

"About a week," Kyra shrugged. "Lanmane. They had a lovely party up in the mountains." It had been lovely until *he* showed up. Her mind locked, clamped at the familiar name and earnest face of the Eternal Order spy who had betrayed her. *Trayse.* Jayne kept speaking, heedless of the change in Kyra.

"Well, you must tell me all about it someday," Jayne said. Kyra had donned her regal mask, and for the first time, Jayne didn't notice. "Besides, it's your first Council meeting."

"Oh mukk, is that today?" She hadn't prepared. She didn't know what to say, much less how to command them.

"Don't worry, it's a group of old men. You'll intimidate them without even opening your mouth—if you wear this." She strode out of view, and returned, dragging a strange contraption, a wooden frame on wheels carrying a beautiful dress. Kyra arched her brows, pretending her heart wasn't in her throat. "You want me to wear that?" she said. "It looks pretty heavy." *And heavy dresses can get you killed.*

"Oh, it's much lighter than it looks," Jayne said. "New material the Guild created in the last year, and with plenty of room for a *bela*." She spun the dress around and touched the subtle slip in the fabric at the small of the back, concealing a secret pocket. The standard accessory for any noblewoman—as hidden as possible.

"Well, why didn't you lead with that?" Kyra grinned.

It took some time, but eventually she studied herself in the mirror. The dress was a brilliant red that highlighted her skin. It cinched at the waist but somehow had enough freedom to move freely, and was much lighter than she expected. Perfect for the traditional Imbran woman. "It's amazing. I just need my—oh, *mukk*. I don't have a *bela.*" That little dagger had been beautiful, gifted by her father on her thirteenth birthday. She'd sold it for funds not a week out of Imbra.

"I have a spare." Jayne passed over a beautiful blade, a green jewel on the pommel. Kyra smiled her thanks, and sheathed the little dagger in the slip at the back.

Ten minutes later, she was standing outside the Council chambers. The sentry gaped at her, barely a hint of fluff on his chin. "Something the matter, soldier?" Kyra stared him down, using an imperious mask this time. The guard snapped his jaw shut and saluted.

His fellow sentry cringed, and Kyra had to bite back a smile. Maybe being back wouldn't be so bad. "Glad to hear it." She took a deep breath. *Am I ready?* Perhaps she would never know, but she nodded to the sentries, and they shoved open the door.

Five chairs grated on the polished oak floor and five men bowed to her, a variety of faces, clothing and professions. Monsun's tattoo scrunched in a careful smile, his fist thumping to his chest in salute. A swarthy man glared at him, fury written on every line of his face. To his side, Archbishop Finon's smile was an impeccable mask, but his eyes betrayed him. They gleamed with cunning, the old snake studying his prey.

Treasurer Rumpre lowered his goblet from a fleshy jaw, wine like bloodstains on his lips, a stain he promptly removed with the sleeve of his golden doublet. He studied her with deep-set eyes just a little too close together. She raised her brows at the purple stain on the otherwise impeccable garment.

Guildmaster Yuras openly glared at her, his arms clenching in his brown uniform. Intended to pay homage to the trades he represented, it failed miserably and separated him more from his supporters.

She stood behind her chair and tapped her fingernail on its rich wooden surface. "Gentlemen." She smirked and sat.

They dropped into their chairs at various speeds, Rumpre's chair groaning ominously. An inappropriate giggle threatened to burst forth, but she controlled it well, splaying her hands on the table and glanced around at the men watching her.

"To begin proceedings, I trust you will support me as you did my father until he recovers." *At least, I hope.* Maybe if they pretended hard enough, it would all go away.

"Highness"—Guildmaster Yuras spoke—"I, for one, am not convinced you have this Council's full support."

*That was quick.* She leaned forward, feigning politeness, but her eyes flicked to Finon again. His smile was back, stretching wrinkled lips and a greying moustache. "Oh? And why is that?"

Yuras dropped his stylish hat onto the table and adjusted the ornate bracelet over his wrist. Rumour was he enjoyed working the crafts, but his hands were porcelain, smooth and fragile. "You are still very young."

"Anything else? We've had young rulers before, even unnamed ones," she said. You're a woman, he obviously wanted to say. She could practically hear his lips straining. *Go on. Say it.*

"Oh, spare me," Hyrin the Spymaster sighed, the last one to voice an opinion. He threw his hood back from his face, highlighting a neat beard twitching under an affable grin. His deep brown eyes glowed as he spoke again. "He's uncomfortable because you're a woman." Treasurer Rumpre sucked in a breath, but a wicked smile formed across Kyra's lips.

"I'm glad to see his eyes still work," she said, and Hyrin barked a laugh. Strange how a Spymaster could be so jovial. Out of all those in the room, she hadn't expected the leader of the Veils to laugh first. Monsun openly glared at the others, but she shot him a warning glance. This was not his fight.

"Do you have any other—concerns?" she asked.

"These are trying times, Highness," Rumpre slurred, his gaze never meeting hers. He pressed a hand to his head and reached for the goblet again, a muffled curse escaping his mouth when he discovered it was empty.

Kyra's voice flattened, her strength sapped. "You don't need to tell me that." Part of her wanted to ask again for their support, but she called their bluff. "But since my father is incapacitated, these duties fall to me. I'd rather not have any issues, but if need be..." She flicked her Mark once, flashed golden light through the room, and muffled curses escaped their lips. Hyrin snorted again, and Monsun allowed himself a small smile, while hate flashed in Yuras' eyes.

"That is rather crude, Highness," the Guildmaster said.

"But effective." Hyrin chortled.

Kyra swung her gaze to Finon, the only enemy in the room who knew her truth, her joy and her pain. But she couldn't, wouldn't, reveal it just yet.

"Perhaps her Highness thinks she's playing a child's game," Guildmaster Yuras said.

*Child.* All her targeted wit vanished, and cold fury clutched at her heart. "If you think I'm playing for fun, then you have no idea who I am."

"That's the problem." Hyrin shrugged. "You vanished for an entire year and nobody could find you."

Kyra leaned back in her chair and stroked a nail along her lips. "Did you look, Hyrin? Should I be concerned that your own spies couldn't find me? Has the legendary skill of the Veils been all for nothing?"

The smile he made was bitter, sorrowful. "We searched, but it was as if you had vanished off the face of the earth."

"Suffice it to say, I was working for the greater good." But without evidence...

"Bandits had attacked her," Finon butted in.

Truth. But not the whole truth. Her blood ignited and her hand slammed on the table. Out of the corner of her eye, she saw Monsun drop his hand below the desk. Her fingers twitched, aching for the knife concealed at her spine. Monsun's eyes glowed, as she couldn't help but reply.

"Not bandits. Eternal Guardsmen." A heavy silence settled over them, and she lowered her voice, waited so they strained to hear. "Your soldiers threw me in the Kinar."

"Is this true?" Rumpre said, and Monsun immediately nodded. Finon nodded sombrely, and for all the world, he could pretend to be sorrowful. But his eyes glowed more than ever. What was the catch?

"Some of my Guardsmen had gone rogue, Your Highness. When I heard what had happened, I hunted them down, and I had them all executed promptly. That was a failing on my part." Truth and lies blended around him. *I'll bet, because you probably wanted my head in a private collection, and executed the Guardsmen to ensure their silence.* But Rumpre, the fool, allowed the excuse. Finon had outplayed her, made her play her best card and countered. He'd lured her into an emotional battle and won immediately. That wasn't how she should wage this secret war.

Kyra resumed a rigid posture, striving for that regal bearing her father had taken so many times. "Gentlemen, it seems we should adjourn and hold this conversation another time. We'll adjourn for now, but in the meantime, think about what we must do to protect Leranion."

"From what?" Rumpre asked.

She allowed the anticipation to stretch for a moment and played her second card. "From Temero."

Finon spluttered, the perfect picture of indignation. "Her Highness has finally lost her mind. First, accusing me of attempts to kill her, and now claiming a fairy tale is a threat?"

Hyrin looked at her with genuine interest for once. "Go on, Highness."

"Hyrin, have any of your agents visited Mount Sancti recently?" she asked.

Hyrin was a perfect liar, but he couldn't beat her ring. "No." Lies tasted bitter this morning. Clearly, she couldn't trust Hyrin, nor Yuras, with the hate he directed at her. Rumpre was worthless.

"In that case, I recommend looking out there. The results might surprise you. Vindicator Monsun, please dispatch a patrol to the eastern border." His eyes widened, but he nodded swiftly. If Finon was really in league with Temero... then he would decimate those soldiers. Watch and wait, she'd asked Monsun to tell the soldiers. She bit her lip and couldn't look at him. This was the game of kings, a war she waged against a demon and the man sitting across from her.

"Why is that?" Finon leaned forward casually. Immediately fishing for any information. For himself, or his master?

"There is something vitally important to protect." She smiled. Rumpre frowned, but she rose from her seat, forestalling all other questions. Belatedly, the others rose also.

* * *

The door shut behind her on oiled hinges, but the tension still didn't leave her body, passing into her left hand. "How did it

51

go?" her lady-in-waiting asked, tilting her head. The sheaf of paper in Jayne's hand matched the many crammed into the leather satchel at her waist, spilling from the bag. The other hand held Kyra's staff awkwardly.

Kyra just rolled her eyes as she took the staff, the familiar weight a comfort. "Not even remotely well. What's next?"

"Your mother asked you to attend court this morning to become Regent."

"Alright. Can you send a message to the friends who arrived with me?" Jayne nodded quickly, and she continued. "Tell Alsair he has access to the Royal Library and add him to the rolls of entry." The head librarian maintained strict access, but with Kyra's authority, Alsair could get in wherever he needed to. A shiver ran down her spine at that thought. It'd be just like the monk to need to dive into scrolls, and Kyra figured it would keep him occupied for at least some time before he started causing trouble again.

"Alsair left this morning."

She cursed under her breath. The one time she needed him... "Fine. Add him to the rolls, anyway. Can you also find clothes for a young girl, and a court-worthy tunic for Eli?"

"Where do you want me to send them?"

"Bring them to court." She hesitated, hand instinctively going to the *bela* at the small of her back. "I need you and Eis to take care of Amora."

Jayne pursed her lips and nodded. "Of course, *amica*. What are you going to do with Eli? I organised a temporary blade permit for him."

"I'll announce him to the court today as a trainee Vindicator." Kyra winked, and the slender girl rolled her onyx eyes.

"Very well, Highness." Something flashed in her eyes, too quick to recognise, but some level of formality had returned.

"I'll head to court now and deal with the nobles," Kyra said, beginning the long walk to the court.

"Be careful." Jayne fell into step alongside her. "House Ketan has grown even stronger, and I've heard it's aligning with Errant."

It was an effort not to reach for her bela. "House Ketan is with us." They had the mines and the forges secure, surely. A Kingdom without weapons wouldn't last very long.

"Eis is with us," Jayne said. "Her father, I'm not so sure anymore."

"Thanks for the warning." They parted ways, and Kyra headed for the court, just as the Lady of Amerin turned the corner, hand on that satchel of paper. Yes, Jayne was Kyra's closest friend, but she'd started as a lady-in-waiting. She was intelligent and cunning, with a keen eye for details, and had kept Kyra organised for many years, even though she was barely a year older.

Kyra made one quick detour up to her chambers and let Nix out. The cub glared at her and prowled down the stairs, sniffing every unfamiliar scent. Kyra smoothed her dress and adjusted the circlet on her head. As they made their way to court, she sensed all the looks cast her way, and Kyra smirked at the power rising through her, at the prestige she carried. Nestham above, it was corrupting.

She finally reached the doors of the throne room. Only one day ago, she'd been virtually unrecognisable. The sentry knocked three times, and the herald cleared his throat. "Princess Kyra Antarun," he announced.

She swept through, smiling at the nobles who parted for her, standing, the pews now removed. Too many refused to smile back, but she noticed Eislyn grinning back at her. Monsun stood off to the side of the throne, his silver tattoo and pristine uniform enhancing his noble bearing. The empty throne loomed before her. Her mother already occupied the smaller chair to its right. She sat and waited for them to settle before nodding to her mother.

Taera gracefully rose from her seat, and the crowd stilled. "One year ago, we were in mourning," she began. "But

53

no longer." She turned to face Kyra, and those brilliant eyes were full of life. "For our Princess has come home!"

She turned to Kyra, a wide smile on her face. "Please kneel." Her head spun, and she dropped to one knee, facing the crowd. Tradition had this ceremony in the High Language, but it was a tongue spoken only by the Marked. And her mother, not carrying the bloodline, had no translation. Jealous rulers had hunted down those who tried to decipher the ancient words.

"Who comes to claim her name?"

"Princess Kyra Antarun of Leranion," she answered in a clear, ringing tone.

"What title will bind you?"

"Regent of Leranion." Silence from the crowd, but as her knee pressed into the cold, hard stone, a strength coursed through her.

"Then speak your oath."

She looked out at her people, silent and unmoving, and spoke. "With Nestham's grace, I pledge my service to the people of the Kingdom of Leranion. I will uphold the laws of Nestham and follow the teachings of the Musadim." Every ruler in Leranion pledged to one of the creeds. For centuries, the Eternal Order had held sway with the Crown, including her father, the honorary Lieutenant. But Kyra had been drawn to the Musadim and their desire for service, to help, not hurt. "I swear to uphold justice and mercy in my judgements, in my deeds, and in my life, for as long as I shall live." *However long that may be.*

As she finished speaking, movement caught her gaze in the grey section, and a priest from the Musadim order stepped forward. As she continued to kneel, Khadim Leon smiled down at her, twinkling brown eyes wrinkled by age, and she couldn't help but smile back.

"Highness," he said. "By Nestham's grace, you have shown all requirements of an ordained Musadim, service above all." He placed his hands behind his back, shifting the pendant hanging at his chest. A simple wooden carving of a tree, it was the symbol of the Servant, the highest-ranking Musadim in Leranion. He answered only to the Elder in Amaldas, Biralam's capital.

"Considering these circumstances, we will waive the fulfilment of your service passage." The journey she'd left behind, when her Musadim escort was slaughtered by Eternal Guardsmen, when she jumped into the Kinar River, when she met Luca—

"And you have not broken the one calling of the Musadim—to do no harm to others." Mukk. Her regal mask snapped into place and she assumed a serene smile.

*Mukk mukk mukk.* How could she have forgotten this? She'd thought she was faithful. She'd trained as a Musadim, for Nestham's sake! But though she'd kept her beliefs, the teachings were ill-suited to the wilds, and she'd left them behind a year ago.

No. She could not pretend to be anything else than what she was. Yes, she'd fought her way across Leranion, but she'd done so to *help* others. She'd killed Eternal Guardsmen to save the downtrodden, she'd evacuated the persecuted from all over the Kingdom. She'd been a hero.

And that would mean nothing to Khadim Leon the pacifist. If he found out the truth about her, if he knew she was the Ghost... A Musadim could never look at a hero and see anything but a killer.

Jayne Farer was dead, murdered by Trayse, along with her friends. She had to hope her secrets were just as buried.

Her mother asked her another question, and she could barely remember the proper verse, but with her hand on the *Nesthamara*, the other clutching her staff, raw and desperate power ran through her. The Mark flashed gold, covering the hall in brilliant light.

"Nestham and the Throne confirm the Regency," her mother said, her commanding voice ringing out across the luxurious hall. "What do the Great Houses say?"

"House Errant acknowledges the Regency." A former officer in the legions of Leranion, Lord Errant's face was unyielding. He still wore a variant of the Leranion uniform, though covered in finery. Errant kept the old traditions of Leranion's warriors, but they'd always been ones to fight rather than talk. She could respect that.

"House Giara acknowledges the Regency." House Giara controlled vast swathes of fertile land east of Imbra, stretching all the way to the Plains border. Wheat and wine, that was Giara. Lord Giara wore the rich garb of most of the noblemen, gold and red combining with his unnatural paleness, living proof that not all Giarans were tanned.

"House Rurik acknowledges the Regency." Lady Rurik spoke next, the elegant head of the House in a stylish deep blue dress. Her facial expression refused to change, the glittering mask of the Ice Lady of Prian, the port city on the western coast. None would dare anger the Lady, however, not when Rurik was so close to the Guild.

All eyes turned to Lord Ketan. A vein in his neck pulsed, and he clamped his lips shut. "What says House Ketan?" Taera demanded. Lord Ketan shook his head slowly, and Kyra's heart fell. Lord Ketan turned away, but another figure was already rising. Graceful, garbed in a vibrant purple, her amber eyes shining with determination.

"House Ketan acknowledges the Regency," Eislyn said. Kyra smiled at her, and the Heir winked back.

A Princess had knelt. A Regent arose, graceful and powerful and doomed.

"My lords and ladies, I am grateful for your patience," she began in a ringing tone, already falling into the rhythms of court formality. No more plain-speak, no more bluntness, no more Jayne Farer.

"Your Highness." Lord Giara ingratiated himself with a deep bow, allowing Kyra to note the grey streaking his thinning black hair. Kyra, already growing frustrated with this damned court flicked her gaze to Eislyn. "There shall be a ball two nights from now to celebrate your return," he said.

"Such a celebration is hardly necessary." She had more important issues than a night of dancing, fun as it would be.

"I insist." He bowed again. To his credit, he was really, really trying.

"Very well," Kyra said. Maybe she could sneak in a proper dance with Eli. They hadn't been on the best of terms at the Lanmane celebration. The door opened quietly, and her fingers relaxed as three figures filed in. One was a tall and broad-shouldered man, a shock of brown hair smoothed back. The second, a young girl, darted with quick steps. The third, a young woman who could have passed for an older sister, raven hair identical to the girl. Eli wore dark gloves up to the wrists and she silently thanked him for the foresight. Best to keep one of their most powerful weapons in the dark for now, even if the silver eyes were still a giveaway that he wasn't who he claimed to be.

Eventually, the nobles grew tired of conversing with her and talked amongst themselves. Music filtered through from the stage at the side of the room, and she leaned over to her mother, seated on the smaller throne by her side.

"Is it always like this?" she breathed.

"Usually. It's got worse."

*Worse.* Worse than she remembered. "Well then, this should be interesting." She flicked a finger, and the herald thumped his heavy staff on the ground. Once, twice, three times. Kyra's fingers twitched, aching for her own weapon, and within her mind, something stirred in the aether. "Earlier this month, one of our trusted Vindicators was slain in battle." The crowd stirred, and some guards looked at her in horror. She nodded sombrely, and Monsun glanced down.

"Vindicator Cedwin was a powerful warrior, but more than that, he was a good man." Her eyes fell upon a scarred woman with a trembling lip. "In his place, I see fit to appoint a new Vindicator." Eli's silver eyes fixed on hers, wary of already drawing attention. "Step forward, Eli Serae."

The crowd muttered, but the young man straightened and stepped forth. To certain players in this game, she'd just created a new vulnerability. But others said you could tell a killer by how he walked. This wasn't just his years of training under a one-armed Jinnam. He moved like a Marked, like someone born with a wellspring of power. But in his black and silver tunic, with the sword by his side... he looked like a Prince.

When Kyra tried to swallow, she found her mouth suddenly dry again. Eli's soft boots were silent on the ancient stone steps and, with no prompting, he knelt before her. Monsun took her staff and stepped towards Eli, Nesthamir gleaming in his hand.

The Guardian's beautiful eyes locked onto hers.

# Chapter 9

Eli's stomach fluttered when Kyra glanced down at him, unspoken words he wished to say shimmering in the air between them.

"Eli Serae," Monsun said in his rich Biralam accent. "Do you swear to uphold the creed of the Vindicators?"

A month ago, he had never met a Vindicator. Since then, one had branded him and another had borne his life debt. And now he would be one of them.

"I swear," Eli said. A hand passed over his shoulder, and he sensed this oath would be unbreakable.

"Then speak your oath."

Eli remained on his knees and stared Kyra in the eyes. Monsun had prepared him for this, had told him every Vindicator created his own vows, and chose his own title. Monsun was the Shield of the North, the mighty defender of its people. "With Nestham as my witness, I pledge my undying loyalty to Leranion, to its throne, and to its people. I am Leranion's Weapon, and I will live with honour and serve justice for all my days." Eli swallowed and glanced at Monsun. "I will be the light in the darkness, the Torch of the North, long as Nestham may reign." Monsun's eyes widened, but he let a secret smile flit across his face.

"I accept your vow, Eli Serae," he said. "Live for justice."

"Die without fear," Eli declared.

"Then arise Eli, the Fifth Vindicator of Leranion," Kyra said, her ocean-blue eyes smoky, and as Monsun tapped her staff on his shoulders, it was enough to send a shiver through his body. "May you serve me well, for all your days," the Regent murmured.

"In whatever way you desire, *Highness*," he mouthed. Her nostrils flared, the only sign his comment left a mark. Heartbeat pounding, Eli rose and faced the crowd, but only sullen faces stared back at him, the hisses spreading through the gathered court.

"Get back down," Monsun muttered into his ear. "Report to the Vindicator's spire in half an hour. Wear something useful, and bring your weapons."

"Understood." Eli nodded. "Sir." Monsun's face glowed with dark amusement.

He glided through the crowds, noting how they all instinctively parted for him, like a pack of animals disturbed by humans. His hand dropped to his sword, and he glanced to the half-open great door and its constant flow of nobles. He trained his ears on the surrounding conversations, picking up snatches of words. Too many discussions were about him, the stranger ascended to Vindicator. Already, one was about him and Kyra. His heart stopped, but he gritted his teeth and moved on. Too many people in this damn room. He was built for the forest, for nature's peace. His muscles tensed and his throat closed up.

"Here he is," Amora chirped from beneath him. Instantly, the lump in his throat dissolved, and he grinned at the girl poking his leg. She wore a rich dress of green—like Jayne—and were those gems woven into her hair? The urchin could have passed for a Princess of the Plains.

"How are they treating you?"

"Not bad, gruntah. The *food...*" She closed her eyes blissfully and sighed. "Can we stay here forever?" A nimble hand latched onto his own, and he smiled. Then she held up the vambrace lifted from his arm, grinning, though a wince seemed to flash through her eyes.

"Give that back!" he chuckled and snatched it off her. Over the girl's short hair, he met Eislyn's amber eyes. "Thank you for looking after her."

She curtsied, swishing her purple dress as she did so. "Of course. We'll take good care of her. It's lovely to have someone young in this dreary old place." She sighed dramatically, pressing a hand to her forehead.

"You're not that old yourself," he said.

"Oh, he is a charmer, isn't he?" Eislyn turned to Jayne. However, the sombre lady wasn't paying attention to them. Her eyes tightened and Eislyn followed her gaze. "Oh, mukk," she gritted out. "Whatever happens, do exactly as we tell you."

"What's going on?" he protested, but a seductive purr interrupted him.

"Well, look at what the cat dragged in." A stunning blonde woman glided to Eli's right, her shapely form clad in a translucent dress.

Eislyn rolled her eyes. "Was that something your father said to you last night, Giara?"

The hair stood up on the back of his neck, and he sensed battle lines being drawn. He sidled closer to Eislyn, and a half smile spread across the newcomer's tan face. Her bedroom eyes narrowed as she turned to the three young ladies flanking her—friends? Allies? Each was beautiful, and yet malevolence spread across their faces like a bloodstain. "A new Vindicator," she said in that same voice.

Eli's heart hammered faster as she leaned even closer. "I am Antiopi Giara," she whispered, and her scent wrapped around him. He clamped his lips shut and tried to step back, but his legs refused to obey him. Her hand dropped to his wrist, and Eislyn reacted faster than a striking snake.

"Already spoken for," she retorted, linking her hand with Eli's. Her fingers were clammy, stiff. "Come on, dearest." She sharply tugged on his arm, snapping him out of the daze. Jayne ushered Amora out of the way, the girl staring with too-keen eyes as she tossed and caught a ruby, until Eislyn pulled Eli into a quiet alcove and pushed him against the wall.

"What in the Five Hells was that?" Eli hissed. She was so close—too close to him, but she just shrugged in reply.

"You really don't want to mess with her," Eislyn said. "She'll chew you up and spit you out in minutes. It wouldn't end well for you or for Kyra."

"And what were you doing?" So much had happened, and he was so far out of his depth, missed all the signs in this new battlefield.

"Did you see her reaching for her wrist?" At Eli's nod, she continued. "When a lady wants a nobleman to pursue her, she gives him a piece of jewellery, usually a bracelet."

*Oh.* "That quick," he said. So close to disaster, so soon after arriving.

"That quick." *Why hasn't Kyra given me anything yet?* "Look, we can't let everyone know yet that you're Kyra's." How did that phrase warm and break his heart? "She's already put herself in a dangerous position by appointing you Vindicator. Just give her time to establish her claim to the throne."

Eli rubbed his head, trying to clear the ache that appeared. "I don't like all this secrecy."

"You think I wanted to do that?" she hissed, and the amber in her eyes turned molten. "You think I wanted to lay claim to my *best friend's lover?* I watched you swear to serve her, but you'll be useless at court unless you learn, and quickly, or you'll put her life in danger. I lost her once, and I am not doing that again."

The bells chimed, and he winced. He was running out of time. "Look, I need to go," he said. "Can you look after Amora?"

"Yes, Jayne and I will babysit," she grated out, and when he raised a brow, she shook her head, golden tresses swaying. "Sorry. Antiopi just *infuriates* me."

* * *

The bells had long finished chiming by the time Eli arrived in the Vindicator's spire. He crashed through the door, his hand clenched on his sword to prevent it from banging against his leg. Monsun raised a brow from his seat, the picture of nobility. For the first time, Eli allowed his gaze to swing around the room. Polished glass ran around the west and south sides, allowing an unobstructed view of the city, and the setting sun would wreathe the sky in flame. Only one wall was opaque, covered with maps and parchment. Maps of Imbra, of Leranion, the Plains, and was that Biralam? Another desk rested beneath that wall, and wooden carvings stood proudly upon the parchment, like toy soldiers.

"Are you finished?" Monsun asked mildly. Eli snapped his gaze back to the Vindicator. "Your training begins now," Monsun said, without a pause, shifting from the grumpy mentor to the born commander. "Follow me." He rose like a panther and stalked down the stairs, no longer wearing his uniform, but some close-fit sparring garb, still in Leranion blue and silver. His battleaxe rested over his shoulder, strapped in where he could draw it with ease.

"Hang on," Eli called down, his voice ringing on the stone. "Why did we meet up there if we're just going back down the stairs?" Monsun just smiled and turned away, and Eli swore under his breath. As they came out on the base, he stepped away, but the larger man stopped at another wooden door. It wouldn't have earned a second glance, except for its iron bindings and gleaming lock.

"For now," Monsun said, "forget what you have learned about fighting." He unlocked the door and revealed yet another set of stairs spiralling down into the dark.

Eli reached the bottom and gasped, lost for words. A vast pit stretched out before him, perhaps a hundred paces each side. Directly in front of him was a sparring arena, with a strange-looking section of wooden platforms. A set of logs rested up in the forks of sticks, their surface gleaming in the flickering torches.

"Welcome to the Playground." Monsun grinned. Less of a grin and more a teeth-flashing, like a cat toying with a mouse. Eli pointedly ignored him and resumed his scanning of the room. Beyond, a set of obstacles made from rope and wood. They rose higher and higher until they became strands of rope hanging from the ceiling. Sunlight gleamed through parts of the roof, and a hidden breeze swirled over his skin.

"Are you going to just stand there?" a voice echoed from above and Eli's hand dropped to his sword. Musical laughter spilled from the source and moon-white hair dropped into his gaze. When he looked up, Syl hung upside down by her knees from a steel bar, her face slowly turning pink. She grunted and used her core to pull her chest back to her knees, then lowered herself back down. Eli raised his brows in appreciation, and the young woman flipped off the bar, landing with catlike grace.

"You're up for some fun, Eli," she said breathlessly.

"It looks more like torture."

"Exactly. Fun." She nodded at Monsun looming behind him.

"She's right." Monsun chuckled. He clapped a hand on Eli's shoulder, sending the young man stumbling. "If you want to be one of us, you need to train as we do."

Eli drew himself up, puffed his chest out. He still barely came up to Monsun's shoulders. "You know how Alsair trained me."

"Actually, I did not have the chance to spar with you or Alsair." The Vindicator shrugged. "Do not use any of your magic tricks." Eli hesitated, and Monsun caught it immediately. He smiled, stretching the tattoo across his cheek. "It is a crutch. When you fought in the north, you slowed down without it." He paused while Eli mulled it over. "Alsair spent ten years honing you. He taught you impressive techniques, but he didn't have all this." He flung out an expansive hand. "You will duel with me. No Marks, no tricks. Just weapons."

Eli sized him up. His arms were half the size of the boulders Monsun called biceps. "This doesn't look like a fair fight. Not if you use that thing." He pointed to the massive axe over Monsun's shoulder. The hulking Vindicator nodded thoughtfully, then glanced at Syl. The white-haired woman tossed him a sword similar to Eli's, the blade gleaming as it arced end over end. Monsun caught it neatly, a toothpick in his clenched fist.

"Vambraces off," Monsun commanded. Eli sighed and his Nesthamir guards clattered to the floor. Monsun stalked over to the sparring area, a storm in a human body, and Eli followed hesitantly. Syl's pouty lips twisted into a smirk. *This can't end well.*

He faced Monsun on a wooden platform and sidled to his right. Monsun smiled and stepped to his right, his eyes trained on Eli's. Eli took one more step and his foot fell into empty air. He hastily leapt back, heat already rushing his face.

"Take one glance. Visualise everything around you," Monsun said. "You are the eye of the storm." Eli's gaze swept around him, memorising layout, the way the planks rose and fell. He had no warning before a shoulder pushed the air from his chest and sent him to the floor.

"What was that for?" he gasped.

"You stopped watching." Monsun smiled.

Red coated his vision. "You told me to visualise everything!"

Monsun nodded thoughtfully, his black braid swaying with the motion. "I'm part of everything."

"Monsun, maybe just leave the weapons for now," Syl intervened from the side. The big Vindicator reverently placed his sword on the ground, and Eli did likewise. Monsun stepped up onto the middle platform, the highest of them all. He towered over Eli, and cast an angelic sunlit silhouette.

"Up here, boy." Monsun stretched out his hand. Eli ignored it, and instead jumped up to the platform himself, landing on all fours. He straightened and stared up into Monsun's face, refusing to back down. "Close your eyes." Eli hesitated, wary of another blow. "I will not hit you again, just close your eyes." The young man sighed and shut his eyes, reducing his world to one of blackness. He'd once lived in this darkness, when Temero had attacked him. "Now, take two steps forward." Monsun's voice seemed to be much further away.

"Monsun, I can't see."

"Good. Picture this space in your mind, however small it may be. You should be able to visualise this entire area."

Slowly, the area materialised in his mind's eye. A mishmash of wooden platforms, steps and blocks, with one musclebound Vindicator waiting on the far side.

"Take two steps forward." He stretched forward, stepping over the small gap in the middle. "One step right." He stepped to the right, instinctively throwing his weight on his left leg as his right dangled off the edge. "Jump back." He dropped off the block into a lower section, bending his knees. The calls kept coming, and Eli moved fluidly around the arena, as Monsun increased the pace.

"Forward three, back two, jump forward." Eli started moving into a trance, that perfect moment when muscles moved of their own volition, without even needing to think. "Right-three-back-one-up-left-four-forward-one—" He leapt forward and landed in front of Monsun, slowly opened his eyes. The big man beamed at him.

"We'll work on this every day. In the meantime, Syl, run him through the obstacle course." The lithe Vindicator grinned and motioned for Eli to follow. His breath heaved, and he wiped sweat off his brow, marching forward on leaden limbs.

"Fair warning," she said, "you're going to spend a lot of time winded."

"You do this often?" he gasped.

She placed her hands on her hips. "Sweetheart, we do this with full armour and weapons while fighting each other."

"...Nestham above."

She flashed a grin at him and tossed her hair. "Start with the ladder."

"What, climb up?" he asked, heart racing.

"Climb, fly, I don't care. Get your backside up there."

"Fine, fine." His knuckles whitened on the age-smoothed surface, and refused to move. "I'm not a fan of heights."

"And I'm not a fan of spiders. Now GET MOVING!" The roar lurched Eli into motion and he scrambled up the ladder. He hauled himself over the top of the ladder, onto a narrow platform of oak planks. It creaked ominously under his footsteps.

The path split ahead. Directly in front, a set of ropes hung from a log above his head. To the left, the path was merely narrow wood, less than a boot's width. Well, at least it wasn't requiring him to swing over the void. He swallowed and placed his boot on the path. Heart in his mouth, he dropped into his magic. Strength flooded his veins, wrapped around his bones, the world became infinitely clearer. But even with his supernatural balance, his knees buckled.

*Don't look down.* The phrase carried on an icy breeze swirling over a snow-covered bridge. He'd had Monsun then. He had nothing now.

"I can do this," he breathed to himself, more of a prayer than anything else. He placed his other boot on the plank. A phantom hand brushed his shoulder and he couldn't stop the smile rushing over his lips or the tingle that went down to his feet. *Imagine yourself at the centre.* He closed his eyes, and in his mind's eye, the wooden bridge stretched in front of him, impossible. And waiting for him. The world slowed down, down, down, and a voice echoed across time.

*Refuse to fear.* His eyes snapped open, and he *moved.* He glided over the platform, heedless of the drop, like the wind that roared out of the northern mountains. He skidded to a stop on the next platform, sized up the next obstacle. A single rope tied to the platform. So he grinned, yanked on the rope, and let the power sweep him away. Suspended by a rope and sheer madness. He flew, dropped, and rolled on the next platform.

"Okay, that's enough for now!" Syl's voice rang off the stone walls. Eli blinked and glanced down at the tiny woman. His gut churned, but he damped the feeling back down. Another rope hung next to him, adorned with a red cloth. "Grab the rope and slide down!" He took hold, wrapped his leg around the rope, and dropped. His pants sizzled, and a burning sensation crept along his legs. His thick gloves merely warmed in his hands, and he landed gently.

Syl's grin matched his own. "Fun, right?"

"I..." He tried to explain the feeling that had gone through him. "That was incredible."

"You'll get used to it." Her voice softened. "Remember how quickly you turned your fear into joy. To be a Vindicator is to realise fear has no power."

Monsun tossed a set of three ornate keys at him. "Those are for the Spire meeting chamber, the Playground and your quarters in this Spire." Eli nodded, still speechless.

"Oh, are we at the total obedience stage?" Syl leaned in next to Monsun, barely reaching his arms.

Monsun merely placed his forearm on her head and leaned on her, grinning at Eli while Syl fumed, wrinkling her nose. "Yes, we will need to break him of that," the Senior Vindicator said.

Eli raised a brow. "Come again?"

Syl smartly stepped out from under Monsun's arm and jabbed him in the ribs before turning to Eli. "Vindicators have a lot of power and influence in the court and military. Her Highness giving you the role will create enemies."

"Because I didn't have enough already." Eli rolled his eyes. Her grin was a little unsettling.

"You're learning," Syl replied. "We need to head back to the Spire, but keep training."

Eli nodded and moved back to practise, while the door shut behind him. Eventually, he grabbed his weapons and armour and strode from the pit, purpose lengthening his stride. He had taken two steps out the door when a messenger halted him. "Vindicator Eli. The King wishes to speak with you."

* * *

Eli wiped the sweat away from his forehead, cursing the stains under his arms and down his back. He smoothed down his tunic and coughed once as he opened the door. "Your Majesty."

He bowed low, eyes on the floor, hand on his sword.

"Come sit with me, boy." Hadrian coughed. Eli bit the inside of his cheek and lowered himself into the fine chair, studying the King as he would a wild animal. "I assume you're wondering why you're here." Eli nodded, with the subtle feeling his back was against a wall.

Hadrian's eyes were calm, despite his deathly pallor, his drawn and wrinkled skin. "I know you have feelings for my daughter." Eli blinked rapidly, his heart skipping a beat. "And no, this isn't a fatherly chat. If you hurt her, you'd never forgive yourself." The blow slammed closer than Hadrian knew. "I know you don't want to hear a dying man's words," Hadrian grunted. "But sit here a while."

Eli clasped his hands together in his lap, tracing the calluses in his palm. "I am yours to command, Majesty."

"Will you stop with the formality? That's not what I asked. Look, when I first met Kyra's mother, I was a young prince, returning from a hunting trip. I was cocky and self-assured and I marched into the throne room to see my father, and she just looked at me." His smile stretched as his eyes glanced above. "Just one look was all she needed." He stared at Eli, "And from then on I knew my task." He coughed, a wet, wretched sound, and his hand grasped for a handkerchief. When he pulled it away from his mouth, it was stained with red.

"Kyra's an incredible young woman, but she's inexperienced. She doesn't just need allies. What she needs is a shadow." Hadrian pointed at the bedside table. "Open that, it's yours." Eli reached over to the parchment, fresh with the royal seal. Just three lines. Not even lines—a list of names.

One-Eye Vera. Guildmaster Yuras. Lord Giara.

"Those people are all under the Order's control," Hadrian said. "Either by taking bribes or providing intelligence." He reached over and clasped Eli's hand. The King's skin was as cold as ice. "I wanted to use it myself, but unfortunately Finon struck before I could." His eyes fluttered, then they cleared. "If you want to destroy him, you need to force his hand."

"Sire, I am a Vindicator. Not an assassin." He'd sworn to be the Light of the North. What did that mean?

"You want to protect Kyra, and this is the best way. But be careful. There may be others who are a threat."

Eli nodded and left the King to his solitude. He pored over the parchment that night in his new quarters, his mind churning over the endless possibilities. Then he added one more name to the list.

# Chapter 10

*Boring.*

The two jewelahs had been chit-chatting for hours, but when Amora glanced at the ancient grandfather clock in their rooms—enough to feed the urchins for a week, if she could lift it—it had only been fifteen minutes. How long had it been since she'd seen the gruntah and the actor? She'd smiled when the actor had made him a Vindicator like Monsun. The gruntah was cute, like one of the little dogs that ran around the slums. And the actor had been damned impressive. Hells, she'd make a good street bluffer, if she dropped the pride from her voice. She spoke like a prissy royal, even when she wasn't wearing a dress.

And she liked these ladies, and she liked the knives they kept in the back of their dresses. Particularly when they showed her how to stash her dagger in the slip. But liking them only went so far, and now, she'd had enough. Amora abruptly stood up.

"Where are you going?" The blonde one raised a brow. The blush came naturally to Amora, thanks to Millin's lessons. Nobody ever thought much of you if you blushed, even if you cut your hair like a boy.

"Please excuse me." They'd impressed on her the importance of being polite. The gruntahs, actor and smoother hadn't been polite, but they'd been *kind.* The blonde jewelah smiled and nodded, and she rushed out the door as politely as she could. It showed she was in a hurry, but still noble. Amora hiked up the skirts of the green dress and shut the door behind her. She'd need to act fast, but Hells knew how long she'd been cooped up.

The urchins had tried to get into this old barn for years. Who knew the things she'd find in the dark, the secrets lingering there? She turned left after leaving the rooms—chambers—and strode onwards. Her trained eyes picked out the way the

71

different soldiers moved, the way the noblemen kept their eyes straight ahead. More than once she dodged away from a self-important noble—scowler, she termed him. She merely glanced down and slipped right into a dim corridor. *Finally.* The torches dimmed, and she smiled. Something fun at last.

To her left, a ladder led downwards into the dark. Her nose wrinkled at the musty smell wafting up from below, and she reached into the other pocket in her dress, pulled out the strip of fabric, and tied it over her left eye with years of practice, an old urchin trick. She stepped onto the first stair, soft slippers on stone. Not good shoes for running, but she'd make do. They seemed to serve no purpose—she should scrounge up some real shoes soon. Eventually her uncovered eye adjusted to the dark, and she opened the door at the base of the stairs. A huge tunnel stretched out into the darkness, with nothing but the sound of dripping water.

And something reaching for her, the strangest sensation, like the feeling she wasn't supposed to be here. She'd had that feeling and stolen from smarter marks, grinning as she danced away with spoils in her pocket. But this feeling—it was nothing like that.

A scream shattered all sense in her mind. A screech of pain, of suffering. What the Hells was that? A sense-stopping panic smashed through her. People screamed all the time in the slums, but never anything as hideous as that. Nothing as inhuman.

Too late to turn back now. She'd just need to remember the way back home. She cautiously stepped forward, so small in the enormous cavern. The useless slippers soaked in a puddle. Definitely need new shoes. Another growl rang off the stones and she froze, heart hammering in her chest. Fingers slid into the slip at her back and snatched her dagger, rasping steel on cloth. Sea-King steel, if the actor was right.

"For emergencies only," she had said. Wicked and curved, Amora had found it in a vault at Dawn Sanctum on one of her first nights. She'd had knives before—needed to, as a young girl in Imbra—but nothing as pretty as this. They were always cheap ones from Millin, and they rusted quickly. But the actor had shown her how to clean and keep this one, and she did it every night. Even just holding the hilt sent waves of calm through her, and she stepped through the tunnel.

# Chapter 11

Kyra's eyelids fluttered once as she unpinned the barrette keeping her hair in place. It immediately fell askew, tumbling into her eyes as she sighed into her hands. Nix's growl gave her a second's warning before the door crashed open. Kyra dropped into a fighting stance, but Eislyn and Jayne stood there, dresses awry, faces reddened and heaving for breath. And just that sight was enough to stop her heart.

"Amora," Jayne gasped out. "She's gone."

Kyra shrugged and returned to the mirror. "Amora's survived more than you think. I'm sure she'll be fine." But then a ghostly hand brushed over her shoulder, and Queen Eshe's fear seeped into her skin.

She swore, and at her command, the strength flooded her body. Golden light flashed through the room and she charged back into her wardrobe. The robe dropped to the floor, and she threw on a practical garment, belted it, strapped her dagger and slammed on travelling boots.

She whistled to Nix, and the snow leopard leapt off the bed. Kyra placed her hand on the cub's head, running her fingers through thick fur, instantly falling into her mind. The cub's boundless energy and limitless devotion slammed into her, their bond at its purest.

*Amora,* she whispered into her mind.

*Little girl,* Nix whispered back in a purr.

*Yes, little girl. Find her.* Nix blinked violet eyes once and tore off. Kyra reached for her staff, but just before she touched it, it seemed to leap into her hand. She was gone before she remembered Eislyn and Jayne and peeked over her shoulder, finding them struggling to keep up. Kyra swore again and fell into her magic, her vision sharpening, sprinting to catch the impossibly quick leopard. Nix belted along the passageway leading to the East Spire, and Kyra rounded the corner and sighed in relief. Eli glanced up from his seat and frowned.

"What's wrong?" he asked, pocketing his polishing cloth.

"Amora," was all she replied. Eli lurched up and slammed his sword back into its sheath. His vambraces hummed and light gleamed under his gloves. "Eislyn, Monsun is up in the meeting room." He jerked his head at the blonde lady.

"I should help you find her," Eislyn protested.

"No time. Get Monsun." His voice brooked no argument, and some part of her appreciated that. Eislyn nodded curtly and dashed to the staircase. Nix clawed at the next door, her gaze flicking between Eli and Kyra. Kyra met Eli's silver gaze, saw the worry reflected in his clenched jaw. Amora had wandered off before, but this time it felt different. The castle wasn't safe anymore.

"Go, Nix." The leopard butted the next door, and Eli wasted no time in opening it. They hastily formed a triangle, Nix three steps ahead, the Marked side-by-side. Even terrified for the girl, Kyra couldn't help but feel the small flicker of joy at this rightness. Being beside him, fighting beside him... she'd missed it. Nix kept her nose to the ground in the Eastern wing until there was nowhere else to go except for a spiralling stairway. The door was already ajar at the base. Eli let out a wretched cough at the smell rising from below, and she pressed her hand to her nose.

"Any idea what this is?" he rasped.

Kyra racked her brains, but it all seemed to elude her in the rising mess of her thoughts. The numbness was creeping over her again, like when Trayse broke her. No, she told herself. Never again. Laboured breathing echoed behind her and she whipped her head around, bringing her staff up to a guard position. Jayne hunched over, hands on her knees, gasping for breath, her bodice constricting all of her movement.

"You..."—she coughed—"...need to learn how to slow down."

"Stay if you need," Eli shot back. Kyra glared at him, but to no avail. He had dropped into that battle rage, that perfect storm of fury and passion beside her cool precision.

Jayne straightened and lifted her chin. "No, I need to come with you. I let her go." The world stopped, and they both stared at her.

"*You let her go?*" Eli hissed.

"Now is not the time," Kyra said firmly. "She's got the scent." Eli picked up Nix, the cub clinging to him frantically, and climbed down the ladder. Once he was out of earshot, Kyra spared a glance for her old friend. "He's right. You don't need to do this. You have nothing to prove to us." Jayne merely set her jaw and gestured for her to go on.

Kyra held her staff under her arm and dropped down the ladder. She landed with a muffled splash and almost retched at the smell. Nix yowled in the darkness, and Kyra flared her Mark. Eli, after a moment's hesitation, yanked off his glove, and ice-blue-and-gold light mingled in the caverns, Jayne gasping softly. An ancient steel door loomed in front of them.

"Sealed shut," Eli commented. "Maybe she didn't come this way."

Jayne dropped into the tunnels and swore quietly at the water. "Move aside." She shouldered past Kyra. "Honestly, men! Only thinking with their swords." She stopped and peered at the lock. "It locks by itself, but it's old. It must have been open before, and it shut when Amora moved it. But now..." Her hand drifted back to the small of her back.

"Now it's opening," Kyra said, flicking out the blades on her staff and swinging, the Nesthamir smashing the locking mechanism wide open. Eli grunted as he slammed his shoulder into the door, muscle and magic warring with iron. It screeched free of its hinges and landed flat on the ground. The Guardian stepped over it like it was a stick.

"I always like it when you do that." She flicked him a smile.

He didn't smile back. Though his face was pale, his eyes burned with silver fire. "If we need to, I'm Rifting us out of here."

"Not without Amora." She faced him, daring him to challenge her.

"Of course not."

A howl shuddered through the tunnel like an icy wind, carrying nothing but pain and horror. Jayne gasped, but Kyra merely flared her Mark brighter, and Eli slipped off his glove, their light reflecting off cold steel and Nesthamir.

Three humans and one snow leopard splashed their way into the tunnel.

Nix yowled and shot ahead. Kyra fell into a run, sensing whatever was about to happen—it would happen now. She rounded the corner. Everything stopped.

*No.*

She let out a silent scream at the small body in the mud, at the ooze spreading from it. The girl lay in the puddle, soaked in water—and blood. Kyra dropped to her knees, her pants immediately sodden and frozen, as she pressed her fingers to her neck. The girl's skin was ice, and Kyra's heart stopped. Her *world* stopped. "She's so cold," she gasped out.

"Hang on," Eli breathed, falling to her side. Radiant light flared in the tunnel and he pressed his right hand to Amora's forehead. His Mark swelled so bright it hurt to even look at him, but Kyra couldn't help but stare. His face was glowing, Nestham above, his whole *body* was glowing with pure, blessed light. The Guardian Healer. Eli kept his hand on the girl, pouring whatever magic he had into her.

Seconds later, Amora's chest rose and fell. "Oh, thank Nestham," Jayne breathed behind them. Eli shuddered once and slumped against the wall, his Mark winking out of existence, leaving spots in Kyra's eyes as his head dropped onto his chest. She enveloped them both in a hug.

"Kyra?" Amora piped.

"It's okay. I'm here," she sobbed. Amora turned her head away and retched, and Kyra fought hard to keep from doing likewise as she held the girl's hair away from her face, until the wretched sound of her vomiting ceased, and the girl tucked her head back into Kyra's chest, leaving a trail of bile down her shirt. Kyra couldn't have cared less about that.

"What happened?" she asked. The girl didn't answer, but her skin was ashen, and with the blood still drying on her, she looked like a walking corpse.

"We need to go," Jayne said. Kyra nodded and released Amora, the girl swaying quietly.

"Eli?" She shook his shoulder. "*Eli.*"

"Five more minutes," he mumbled, his head listing to the side. Another growl chilled her blood, and she turned to face the empty tunnel. Not empty anymore. In the deep dark, four glowing red eyes stared back at her. *Oh, we are mukking dead.*

Kyra slowly rose, stepping in front of the kneeling girl. She clenched her fingers, and blinked as she found cool metal there. Her staff had appeared in her hand. Nix growled a warning and slunk up to her side, sodden tail curling around her calf. Kyra never took her eyes off the red eyes.

"Jayne, get Amora out of here."

"I'm not leaving!" Amora rasped. Nestham above, what had they done to her?

"That's an order," she said into the shadows. "Leave Eli. I'll take care of him."

*Nix,* she reached into the bond. *Follow the girl.* Nix snarled once and obeyed, and Kyra felt more alone than ever. Jayne clutched Amora and rushed out of the tunnel, Nix hot on their heels. Kyra sucked in a breath and flared her Mark higher. Her mouth dried, and her gut churned faster. Dear Nestham. Four small red eyes twitched, blinking individually as they studied her. It grinned and flashed two rows of teeth set to tear her apart. The creature stood on four insectlike legs, clacking as it shifted from side to side.

"We've waited for you," it hissed.

Kyra gulped and forced down her fear, instead smiling irreverently. "You can speak my tongue." No beast could. Every follower of Nestham knew that, regardless of the colour they wore. Not even Nix could properly speak, though their connection was far beyond mere speaking. "What are you?"

The creature chittered, teeth clacking together. "We are a child of our master."

"And who is your master?" she whispered, trying to buy time before Eli would wake. The creature paused, and its eyes blinked. Once. Twice.

"You know his name."

At that, her knees quivered, though she locked them in place. Refused to do anything other than grip the staff tighter. "What do you want?" She fought to keep the quaver from her voice.

The creature—no, the demon—smiled, and waved a pincer. "I want nothing. In fact, you may leave. I have already feasted today."

The fear vanished. Blood roared in her ears, drowning out the sound of her breathing, the creature's faint hissing, Eli's groan. *I've already feasted today.* Her heart stuttered, snatched in a shadowy grasp. Then roaring fire took over, such as it never had before. "You *feasted* on her?" she screamed.

"Of course."

Kyra twisted her staff and released the blades once more, gleaming and hungry.

"A lovely weapon," it said. "Sadly inadequate."

Kyra didn't much care for its amusement. She let out a roar that shook the caverns and leapt forward, swept away by her power, speed and instinct blurring into death's perfect harmony. Her blade bounced off its pincer and the creature merely grinned and stood up to its full height. Scales covered the entire length of its body, and its stubby tail lashed in anticipation. Even its narrow shoulders stood higher than her head. Kyra fell into a guard position, heart hammering at her to *go, go, go.* But she couldn't take her eyes off the blood covering its pincer.

Eli groaned behind her, and she glanced instinctively. She realised her mistake, but the air buzzed and the creature caught her shoulder, tearing cloth and skin. Blood welled along her arm, and Kyra hacked at chitinous armour.

"Perhaps I can feed on him," it said. *No.* She let out a piercing cry and thrust forward, burying the blade in tough skin. The creature screamed, and she withdrew instantly, the rage leaving her body in droves, leaving only dizziness behind. She heaved a breath, fighting to maintain her battle awareness.

"Eli?" she said to the darkness.

"Here," he groaned.

"Get up. *Now!*" She retreated to cover him, staff raised. "Rift us out of here!" A hand wrapped around her ankle and she fell into the blackness with him. Kyra landed in filthy water, the ladder just above her head.

Eli slumped against her, dead weight again. "I didn't have enough energy to go far. I had to pick what I could remember."

"Climb!" she hissed, but he did no such thing.

"If that thing survives, we won't be able to sleep tonight," he slurred. She glared at him. Don't you even dare. He'd done worse. She risked a glimpse down the passageway, and four beady eyes fixed on her position.

"It's coming."

It slithered through the intermittent water. *Princess...*

"It's inside my *mukking mind!*" she clutched her head.

Eli stumbled up to shield her, flaring his Mark. It sputtered and died. "I've burnt it healing Amora," he gasped.

She swore again. "Get to that side"—pointing at another pillar, and he lurched over. "It lives in the dark. It may not like the light." Weak as it was, light streamed down from the trapdoor above her, and she stood in plain view, hopeless as it was. Death's smile was strangely familiar.

*Princess...*

80

The earth rumbled, and her heart shot into her throat. Tongues of flame shot out from the side and flung the creature like a discarded toy into the pillar next to Eli. Kyra leapt forward to the fallen creature. Four pain-clouded eyes blinked at her, but she didn't hesitate. Her blade flashed in the darkness, and green ooze poured from the creature's severed neck. A tongue lolled out of the fallen head and she almost retched again. On shaking legs, Kyra hauled Eli towards the ladder.

"Was that you?" he asked.

"No." Her neck prickled, but when she looked over her shoulder, she could have sworn a hooded figure crept back into the shadows.

# Chapter 12

Eli's breath rasped in his ears as he stumbled out of the sewer door, arm slung around Kyra's shoulders. Even with that support, he could barely stand. Kyra passed him her staff, and he used it in his other hand, fighting to stay upright. And, Nestham above, everything hurt.

His head felt like it was about to explode, but worse was the numbness in his hands. Nothing. No extra senses, no fire, no light, just a dull void in place of his gift. Footsteps like the thud of an army slammed to a stop, and Monsun's dark eyes bulged out of his skull. Amora's head pressed into his corded neck as he clutched her, the girl still trembling, still covered in blood. "What... Let's get you somewhere safe." He reached for Eli, and the young Vindicator clutched Monsun's muscular chest for support, Kyra moving to Eli's other side. Together, they stepped into the corridor, moonlight shimmering through glass.

"Let's keep this quiet," Kyra hiccupped. Their breaths mingled in the chilly air, and he met her gaze, a pair of battered, bloodied soldiers.

"I bet half the palace heard that explosion," Eli said.

She pursed her lips once, her only sign of worry.

Eislyn and Jayne blanched at the sight of them. Mud encrusted Jayne's dress from her splash through the tunnels, but she still carried herself like a noblewoman. Eislyn's eyes flashed at Eli when he passed her. Eli ignored her, following Monsun through empty corridors and, minutes later, they collapsed into a tiny meeting room.

Kyra lowered him into a chair, and he cradled his head in his hands. When he drew them away, blood and filth covered his skin, as if he'd walked through a war. Kyra latched a shaking hand onto his, and neither let go.

The Senior Vindicator slammed the door, and the wall shook like the palace would collapse. "What in the *five rotting hells happened?*" he hissed, clutching Amora to him. The girl didn't even raise her head. Eli growled a warning, finding strength from somewhere, but his superior took one step toward him. Just one step.

Monsun towered over his seated subordinate, with all the strength of pure-blooded warrior in that gaze. Eli didn't speak, but the bigger man's jaw was threatening to snap as he folded his huge torso into a carved chair, balancing the urchin girl on his lap. His beautiful axe thudded to the ground. Kyra still didn't meet anyone's gaze.

Eli's ears didn't stop ringing during the tense silence in the room. "What happened, Serae?" Not a question of a friend to a friend, but of the Senior Vindicator to his youngest soldier.

"There was something down there," Eli mumbled, that burst of strength fading away.

"Be specific, Vindicator." His title was a slap in the face, and a creeping heat flushed the back of his neck.

"Fine. There was a *mukking monster in those tunnels!*" he yelled. Amora let out a little sob, and Eli's breath caught in his throat as she at last revealed her face. The once-clean skin was blotched, and her eyes were bloodshot. Where they once gleamed with irreverent energy, they were now the eyes of the dead. What had it done to her? Monsun grabbed a clean towel and rubbed her face, wiped away the blood. Her blood.

Raw energy crackled inside Eli, at once strange and familiar. No. But Amora's little gasp confirmed his suspicions. Crackling power, a force as strong as life itself. The debt which bound them together. Seconds later, his heart stirred, a second bond forming. Immediately it shattered like splinters of crystal light, absolved before he could learn who owned it. He met Kyra's eyes, and she shook her head, leaving the question unanswered. Someone had directly saved them in the tunnels, then forgiven the debt. Nothing formed between Kyra and Eli, but that was no surprise. They'd saved each other too many times for the debt to appear.

Monsun slumped onto the desk and ran a hand through his braided hair. "The palace isn't safe anymore," he breathed.

A cold slice of terror shot through Eli, but he pushed it aside. "We can't leave. This is proof that Temero is here. This is why we returned to Imbra." And damn it, he wouldn't give up, monsters or no.

"Look, I don't mean to interrupt, but who the hell is Temero?" Jayne commented, and as one, they all turned to her. Eli raised his brows at Kyra. *She's your friend.*

An exhausted smile twitched the corners of her mouth. "He's a demon the Order released when they destroyed Mount Sancti."

Nothing. "What do you mean, they destroyed Mount Sancti? The Order said Nestham destroyed the Mount in an act of holy wrath."

"Oh, it was wrath all right, just not Nestham's," Eli said.

"How would you know?" Eislyn challenged him.

His voice was quiet, and filled with death. "Because I was there. It was like nothing I've ever seen. And the smell—" *Oh no.* That smell, the one that clogged his throat until it was impossible to breathe, that acrid stench of death—he'd scented that in the tunnels.

Kyra was thinking along the same lines, her brow furrowed in thought. "Whatever was used to destroy the Mount was just used in the tunnels."

"Well, that's something we need," Eli said. *Add that to the list.*

"You're talking about stealing?" Jayne jutted in.

*Nestham above...* Eli sighed. "Look, Jayne, I like you, but there's something you need to understand." He pointed a flippant finger at Amora. "Thief and former urchin, born and raised on the streets." He pointed at Kyra. "Rebel against the Order, imprisoned for helping refugees." Kyra winced, and his finger trembled on his chest. "And I'm a heretic because of

84

something I was born with. A heretic for carrying almost the same magic as Kyra. For that, an Eternal Guardsman shot me and cut my throat. So yes, I will do whatever it takes to bring the Eternal Order down and stop Temero." His voice sharpened. "So, whose side are you on?"

She swallowed, and the silence stretched out. "Yours."

"Then trust us," he said. "We've been doing this for a while now."

Kyra just squeezed his hand. Eislyn glared at him throughout, but the two ladies left together, the door clicking shut behind them. Monsun leaned forward, still keeping Amora close.

"There's a parade through the streets tomorrow," he said. "Would you like me to cancel it, Highness?"

"Huh? Oh. No, don't cancel it," Kyra said. "I'll clean myself up before that."

"See that you do." Amora clung tighter as he stalked out, cradling her with one arm.

As soon as his commander left the room, Eli slumped to the desk. A strong yet exhausted hand trailed along his shoulder.

"What now?" Kyra breathed.

"I don't know," he muttered. "Any ideas?"

Her smile was soft, promising peace and safety. "Bedtime."

\* \* \*

Eli only made it two steps into the room before he fell into the nearest chair and blinked blearily. Kyra knelt in front of him, and blood-soaked hands grabbed his own. "Stay awake," she said firmly. But those eyes were pleading with him, and her smile seemed forced. And if she could smile after what she'd seen, then he could do the same.

"I won't stay awake like this," he said, and pushed off the chair. "I'll be fine."

Every step to the window was an effort, but he stared out at the city, at the blazing Eternal Torches. Even through everything that could destroy Ekra, they would survive.

Moonlight fell across the river, a pale reflection of shimmering glory. In the window's reflection, Kyra's beautiful face grinned wickedly as she grabbed something out of her wardrobe. As she shut the door to the bathing suite behind her, he stepped out onto the balcony, breathing in the cool night air. Even with spring, his breath misted in front of him. As he braced numb hands on the railing, same as he had done not a day before, he wondered how it could all have changed so much.

The world slowed, and he finally allowed himself to drop the mask, to drop his control over his fatigue. When he'd seen Amora like that, when that thing had feasted on her, it had almost broken him. Shoulders caved in and his powerful body swayed over a lethal drop.

"Jaser," he mumbled, "if you're there... go mukk yourself." A phantom hand whacked his shoulder, and he grinned, though he doubted the old Guardian would be amused. If Jaser Cathom once had a sense of humour, it had shrivelled up and died along with his body.

Kyra stood there, a sleeveless shift carelessly draped over damp skin. His throat dried, even more when he noticed the red line along her flesh. He stepped into the warmth and sealed the outside world and its memories behind him.

"You're bleeding," he said quietly. When had that happened?

She noticed his gaze and pursed her lips. "I'll take care of it."

"Here, let me." An argument tightened on her lips, but she pointed to the dark oak box in the far corner. When he opened it, he found it full of healing supplies. Alsair had shown him the basics of patching up wounds, and first he poured honey on to stave off infection, then gently wrapped the bandage around her arm. Her skin rippled with goosebumps at each touch, and he hesitated, pretending to survey the wound closer. It wasn't deep enough to require stitches. Her eyes glimmered with too many words kept locked in, and he didn't pry.

"No magic?" her breath hitched, her lips so close.

"Tomorrow." He didn't trust his words, and stepped back, blood roaring in his ears. But he was a Guardian and her Vindicator and she was the Princess... his fingers shook in his pockets.

"No sleep until you've had a bath," Kyra said, and the moment broke.

He plodded off to the other room, but stopped dead in his tracks. How did she live in such luxury? Hot water poured out of the tap into the basin. He'd heard of places like this, but never expected to be in one. In Mount Sancti, he'd had to fill the bath himself. Eli stripped off bloody clothes and left them in a pile next to hers. Odds were they'd burn them, anyway. He reached for soap and found too many choices of oils at his fingertips.

"Rose, jasmine, lavender," he listed them off and grinned. Knowing it might not end well, but without a choice, he grabbed the jasmine soap and dropped it in the bath, washing himself all over. When he finished, the reddened water swirled away down the drain, and he found clean pants folded by the door. They fit perfectly, but without a shirt to accompany them. Well, it was warm enough inside, anyway. This entire suite was gloriously warm.

Kyra stirred, shifting the elegant gown she now wore, and he made sure to look only at her eyes. She, however, apparently had no such qualms, and her gaze swept up and down his body. His heartbeat quickened, but she merely smiled contentedly and closed her eyes again. He hopped on the bed and marvelled at the luxury she lived in as she rested her head on his bare chest. Their breath mingled in the night, and peace washed over him as he stared at the chandelier above them. The exquisite decoration seemed tacky compared to the Sanctum's crystal.

He breathed in the scent of her, the rose perfume she'd used, clinging to her even when she was in the wilds. This—this was enough for him. There were some lines he couldn't cross, wouldn't cross. Because she was the Princess, and he was her servant, her warrior, her protector. Even if she seemed intent on obliterating his self-control.

"What are you going to do about the life debt with Amora?" she breathed.

"I don't know. Absolve it, probably."

"Maybe not just yet," she said, tracing a fingernail over his chest. He tried to repress the shudder, but he could feel her smile against his skin. "It would keep her out of trouble. And you can dissolve it the moment you get into trouble, so she's not compelled."

He mulled it over. "Okay."

A second's pause stretched longer as she shifted, pressing her hand to her forehead. "Where did it all go so wrong?" she groaned. "Now we've got monsters and Finon and the entire Musadim to deal with."

"The Musadim? I thought you accepted your orders with them."

Her entire being seemed to tense. "I—I did. I was on my service trip when the Order attacked me. But one of the first tenets of the Musadim is not to harm others." She flashed a bitter smile. "Of course, they want the nobles' money, so they allow self-defence, barely. But what I was doing in the south wasn't exactly self-defence."

"You were protecting people, though," he said. "I don't see how that's a problem."

"Of course you wouldn't." She smiled. "I thought about it in the year I was gone. It was about a week after I left Imbra. Luca and I were in this little town. I can't even remember the name, but it had a lot of Eternal Guardsmen around. Some of them brought out a woman. They said she'd been a heretic, but they were going to hurt her... and I just acted." Eli's gut tightened as a tear welled in her eyes. "I killed them all."

He swallowed and just held her for a long moment. "Do you think Finon knows?"

"He would. I'd bet my life on it." She was betting all their lives on it.

"Well"—he forced the smile—"I think we need to get to work." And, Nestham above, they had so much work to do.

"Definitely." Her returning grin was watery.

But he had more grim things on his mind. "The ball is tomorrow night," he reminded her. "If that monster isn't the only one, we could be in trouble." The havoc it could wreak in an event like that.

"But that chemical—Nestham's Will, whatever they call it—it can destroy one of those. If we could get ahold of that..."

"I'm working on it."

Something in the way he said that, her far-seeing gaze snapped to him, bright and vulnerable and deadly. "You know something, don't you?"

Briefly, he thought about denying it, but it was useless. She held a truth-seeking ring, and it was *Kyra*. He could never bring himself to lie to her. "Your father gave me a list of Order supporters. He wants me to hunt them down."

She gasped and shuffled away, and the space between them was colder than a Sanctum winter. Anger burned in ocean eyes, and even though not aimed at him, it still scorched his skin. "He had no right to do that. He should *never* have told you to do that." And since then, Hadrian had barely been conscious enough to do anything else.

"I'm considering it. These people aren't good people. And if they support Finon, it's double the reason to hunt them down. One of them is Lord Giara."

Her eyes widened, and she wagged a finger in the air, lurching up. "Giara insisted on the ball—he may have something else planned. Give me a day to think about it." She may not have a day if Lord Giara was against them.

Something in his mind twinged. *Don't let her give you orders.* He shoved that voice back down in his mind. Somehow, that voice sounded like Jaser. "As you command, *Highness,*" he said, flashing a smirk.

Her cheeks flushed red before she returned his gaze. "We can have time. Just one day," she said. "One day, then we

89

can get to work." She reached over to the bedside table and grabbed a golden armlet, one he'd never seen before. Her face paled visibly, her fingers fiddling with the clasp.

"It's beautiful," he murmured, eyes dropping to the pristine piece of jewellery. She heaved a breath and leaned closer to him, eyes locking.

"I should have done this a long time ago," she said, holding out the armlet to him. "If you'd like to." His jaw dropped, his muscles slackened, *Nestham*, everything refused to work.

"Kyra, I don't know what to say."

"Then don't say anything." She pressed a kiss on his lips. When they parted, she was grinning fiercely as she slid the armlet onto his left bicep. It was a perfect fit. Eli brushed a gentle hand down her face and lifted her chin, kissing her once more, then drifted off, surrounded by enemies yet finally at peace.

# Chapter 13

Eli didn't like crowds at the best of times. When Alsair had first taken him hunting, he'd fallen in love with the simplicity of relying on skill. But now, with hundreds of people lining the streets and with duties weighing on him, hairs prickled on his neck. His left hand firmly gripped the reins of his horse, shifting under him, while his right traced the armlet above his vambrace. The cool metal washed calm over him. The sun glimmered clear over the streets of Imbra, not a skerrick of cloud across the sky, while shadows from the Citadel's walls draped him like death's veil.

Trumpets sounded. A call to stop, a call to wait, a call to hail the Regent. It matched the raven's caw, one of sorrow and death.

The procession clattered into motion as several of Leranion's finest led the way. Raylene followed them on her massive black horse. Both looked mean enough to tear his head off. Beside him, the beautiful open-topped carriage rolled along pristine cobblestones out of the Citadel. Queen Taera waved regally, her blood-red gown catching the day's rays. He nudged the horse on and flanked the carriage, shifting uncomfortably in the armour Monsun had given him. Battle-ready steel, ornate yet protective, with a strange blue half-cape sitting over his left shoulder. Out of the corner of his eye, he'd noticed Kyra flicking an appreciative eye over him and grinned to himself.

As for Kyra, she was as beautiful as ever. The sapphire on her forehead glittered along with her burning Mark. The third occupant of the carriage didn't smile, his hands clutching the massive axe balanced easily on his knees. Monsun's eyes swept from side-to-side, but he kept his usual granite face. The crowd lined the streets, their expensive silk dresses and suits flashing in the light. Soldiers in blue stood guard, holding back the wave of humanity.

Eli twitched the reins and his horse moved in closer to Kyra's carriage, Syl doing the same on the other side. The smallest Vindicator kept her back straight in the saddle, moving a little too rigidly, a far cry from the fluid movements when she ran. His gelding shied sidewards, and he instinctively leaned to compensate.

He hadn't ridden a horse in so long. His parents had owned some on the farm, and Alsair had taught him more on the plains around the Mount. Turned out those habits returned easily. Monsun glanced at him from where he guarded Kyra and Taera in the carriage. Tight eyes swept over the armour, the vambraces, the jewellery. When he noticed the armlet, his eyes glittered, just for a moment.

Eli followed his gaze and studied the armlet, weighing heavily on his arm. Amidst the swirling patterns was a snarling snow leopard, elegantly etched into the gold. His mouth twitched as he glanced back up the road. The noise got louder.

The carriage clattered past Giara Keep, then turned right to head down the hill. The sentries out the front saluted, and gold-and-red banners flapped in the gentle breeze. It seemed warmer here somehow, and sweat trickled down the back of his neck.

The cheers grew louder, yet his heart pounded in his chest. A hand brushed his shoulder, and he went rigid. Too many times he'd felt that touch. Jaser was warning him. His skin rippled, and he clutched his sword's hilt, his vambraces humming in the air.

The raven cawed again, this time directly overhead. The buildings grew less tasteful as the procession headed into the lower quarter. Citizens traded bright dresses for tough tunics, stained and torn from rough labour. Damp clothes flapped in the breeze, stretched over lines hung between the buildings.

The streets narrowed, closer and closer, until the very air felt thick. People sat on the rooftops, swaying on the tiles, craning to get a glimpse of the procession.

The crowd kept cheering. The soldiers lining the streets didn't move, their uniforms accented by a black armband, one he'd never seen before. His Mark burned under his gloves and his eyes sharpened, scanning their faces. His arms tensed as one noticed his gaze and smiled at him. The smirk was full of darkness and death.

He'd seen this man before. Eli tried to catch Monsun's eye, but the warrior for once was laughing with Kyra instead of watching the surroundings.

A shadow fell across them as the raven cawed a third time.

* * *

The shadow clutched a bow, drawn and aimed straight at the carriage, but he was too slow. An opening shot zipped overhead and the arrow buried itself in the shadow's chest. The archer screamed and crumpled to the tiles, his bow cracking on the cobbles below.

Screams punched through the air, and Eli drew his sword, his Mark burning brightly. He spared a glance at the roof behind him. Silhouetted against the skyline was Tomas in half-armour. The older man's bow was already drawn again, seeking a target.

Steel scraped on leather as soldiers and Vindicators alike drew their weapons. The screams increased, and citizens clogged the many exits, clamouring to flee.

"Retreat!" Monsun yelled. He grabbed his shield and raised it high over Taera's head, blocking her from any other arrows.

But the attackers had chosen the ambush well. The carriage couldn't move backward, and with so many people in the streets, they'd struggle to retreat. Eli's mouth dried, and he nudged his horse closer to Kyra, horribly aware of his exposed position. The princess crouched low, eyes narrowed on him.

His hearing stretched outwards, as the street seemed to still. A hundred heartbeats hammered in his ears, a hundred screams ripped at his mind, a hundred steps on the ground as soldiers and horses shifted their weight. A strange silence fell over the group.

Then the men with dark armbands snapped out of their positions and levelled their weapons on Kyra. A bowstring thrummed and one dropped immediately, an arrow in his neck.

"We're surrounded!" Syl called.

"Get their Majesties to safety!" Monsun yelled. Eli stretched out a hand behind him, staring down the soldiers. Kyra grabbed it and leapt on, slipping her hands around his waist. They spun around, but the soldiers charged.

No time to run. He heard the arrow's hiss as he twisted to face Kyra, grabbing her as he smashed his vambraces together. They fell through the Rift's twisting black, until he found what he sought and they roared back into the world, landing on the stone floor. Then the pain hit him, and his sword clanged on the floor. Eli let out a pained yell, blood trickling over his skin.

He opened his eyes with a groan.

"Take us back!" Kyra darted around the room. "We need to get my mother out of there!" Every breath was agony as she dropped low and studied him. "Dear Nestham," she gasped. He rasped a breath, blood blooming in his mouth, cold steel twisting in his skin.

"Pull it out," he hissed.

"You're going to bleed out!" she shot back.

In her panic, she'd forgotten the one thing that set him apart. What had happened to the fearless young warrior? "I can't heal with a mukking arrow in my skin!"

She blinked and focused, her iron will back full force. "This is going to hurt." Kyra yanked on the arrowhead, and with a wet squelch it slid out, tearing muscle and skin. Eli screamed again, but concentrated on his healing gift, tried to use it sparingly—but the light rushed out of him, too quickly to contain. The fire almost followed it, but with a monumental effort, he dammed it up within himself, unlike when he healed Amora.

94

Without that control, he would burn himself out completely. He grabbed his sword and focused on Kyra, her beautiful dress stained with his blood, ice glittering in her eyes.

"Don't you dare move," he said, before leaping back into the Rift. As he fell through the dark, the first thing he noticed was the noise. The Rift was always silent, but now faint screams echoed through the void. And for once, he felt like he wasn't alone.

Smoke filled his senses as he touched the ground and slashed a traitor across the chest. Blood spattered on his face, but he'd bought himself a momentary respite. The square was littered with bodies, all in Leranion uniform, about half wearing the armband. He spotted Monsun beside Taera, the troops slowly edging back towards an alley. A dead end, but something. He shifted his focus to the rest of the fight. Raylene and Syl held the front line. Raylene fought like a savage leopard, snarling as she battled three troops at once. Syl was fluid, but just as deadly.

An arrow whacked into the wood beside him, and his magic flared as he knocked a second aside with his vambraces, but they no longer hummed. Unable to Rift, unable to heal. What was left?

Years of training, a powerful gift, and five Vindicators. Eli leapt into the front lines, formed up alongside Syl. The blonde woman spared him a glance, then parried a wicked, curved blade. Eli seized the opportunity and lashed out with a cut that lopped off the would-be assassin's head.

"Draw!" the shout rang out in the square.

Eli knocked back his next opponent and frantically sought the source of the command. He didn't need to look far. On the far roof, black-robed bodies clutched bows, and a score of black-feathered arrows fell from the sky, heading towards...

"Monsun!"

"Shields!" the Vindicator roared and as one, the soldiers raised their shields to the sky, forming a temporary roof. Eli and Syl leaped back, darted to the side of the road. The arrows whined as they sliced through the air. One man screamed. Then

95

two more. Out of the corner of his eye, Tomas leaped for cover on his roof. Several arrows slashed above him.

"We're not going to get anywhere until they're dead," Eli breathed.

"Then follow me!" Syl yelled and ducked past the troops, running for cover, ducking under a buttress. Under the stone cover, arrows whined ahead, and slammed into the shields of the soldiers.

"What in the hells is your plan?" he said, clutching his sword with a shaking grasp.

"I hope you aren't afraid of heights anymore." Then she was off and running again, ducking and rolling into the next spot of protection. Eli followed, forcing himself not to fall into that rage, or the euphoria of his Mark.

"Loose!" the deadly rain fell on the soldiers. Stray shots flew at Eli, but his gift surged, and he spun, steel sparking on Nesthamir as he shielded himself with his vambraces.

Another grunt of pain, and an assassin crashed to the ground ahead, one eye sightless, the other impaled by a blue-fletched arrow. They ducked under a shop stall. A basket of berries crashed to the ground, blood-red juice oozing over the cobblestones. But now they were directly underneath the nest, pressed against the stone wall.

"How good is your climbing?" she asked him.

He didn't even ask before Monsun roared another command, and the Leranion troops responded, pushing fully into the alley. Counting on them to nullify the arrows.

"*Go!*" Syl hissed, and she jumped off to the side, where the alley narrowed into single file. She leapt up onto the far wall, paused, then turned. Eli's jaw dropped as she leapt back and forth, flowing like a waterfall in reverse. An arrow skidded next to her, and his attention snapped back to his enemy.

On instinct, he glanced at his hand, but he'd hidden his Mark. Fire coursed through his veins, threatened to overwhelm him. He didn't need to do it Syl's way. He jumped out to the side, and arrows followed him. *It must be at least five metres up.*

Eli crouched, readied his sword, and sprang, the wind roaring in his ears as he leapt up to the roof.

He landed easily, and as nineteen pairs of eyes snapped to him, Eli unleashed the Hells.

\* \* \*

Monsun's brows furrowed as he surveyed the battle, his soldiers clustered in the alley behind him. To his right, Eli engaged the archers, while Syl pulled herself up on the roof opposite the nest. With the assassins distracted, Tomas was free to divert his hailstorm onto Raylene's opponents. They fell swiftly, wounds blooming on their uniforms. The Vindicator didn't hesitate, ramming one through with her spear.

"Where's my daughter?" Taera asked him, pale yet composed, her hand trembling on her waist.

Monsun didn't turn, keeping his massive shield covering her. "Safe, Majesty. Eli got her out."

"We have to get to her!" Taera tried to push past him, but he stood his ground, blocking her exit. The Queen squared up, her jaw locked and eyes blazing in fury, so like her daughter it sent a chill down his core. "Do not deny me, Vindicator."

"This is for your protection." Monsun shifted uncomfortably, clenching his hand on his axe.

"I will not hide like a coward!" she hissed, and her hand flashed behind her, and drew out an elegant bela.

Monsun finally turned to her, raised his hand in what he hoped was a comforting gesture. "My Vindicators have this well in hand. We do not need to engage."

"Four Vindicators against twenty assassins?" she scoffed.

He turned back to the battle, telling himself he wasn't a coward for retreating. Not when he could keep the Queen safe. *But you have soldiers for that,* a twisted voice whispered.

No. He trusted his Vindicators to finish them. He swung his gaze to the roof battle, where Eli was hacking his way through the archers. On their other side, Syl sprang for the nest, blade unsheathed, and aimed for a red-haired archer. His heart thudded against his skin as the archer whirled and crashed his boot in her chest. Syl screamed as she plummeted through the air.

Monsun couldn't think, he just sprinted, all else be damned. His eyes fixed on the falling woman, white-blonde hair strung out behind her. But he was too slow—too far away.

Syl spun and rolled in a perfect crouch, up and ducking under cover immediately. He threw himself beside her, frantically checking for any wounds.

"Stop!" she hissed. "I'm fine. Get out of my face." She waved a bloodied arm, her back pressed against the cracked stone. "Get back to the Queen."

His heart stopped, and the seconds stretched out, until something caught his gaze. On a far rooftop, silhouetted against black tiles, one last figure stood, sunlight shining on flaming red hair. An assassin, unhampered by Tomas or Eli. Monsun twisted and froze as a blood-red gown flashed out of the alley. "*No.*"

The archer fired, and Taera collapsed with an arrow in her gut. Silence spread across the clearing as he laid Syl down and scrambled next to the Queen. He pressed his hands to the wound, and blood immediately trickled over his skin. And though his ears were ringing, he heard it all. He heard Tomas shoot and curse as his arrow zipped through empty air. He heard Raylene shout in victory. But the worst sound of all pierced the haze in his mind.

His Regent's screams.

# Chapter 14

They left her mother on the surgeon's table for an instant that felt like a lifetime. The room was pristine, the surgical knife freshly wiped. Kyra stood motionless, hands clasped tightly behind her back lest she lash out. Her arms shook, but she clenched her jaw and refused to blink.

"The people will need to see you're alive," Eli said behind her. She spun swiftly and impaled him with a frozen glare, but his face was just... blank.

"I'll be out soon," she said, and turned back to her mother's unconscious body. Eli's footsteps rang on the tiles, one, two, and he wrapped an arm around her shoulders. She trembled once, wanted to lean in—but she couldn't. Not now.

"The surgeon said she'll recover," he breathed.

"I'll be out soon," she repeated, spine like steel. After a long moment, he delicately removed his hand, stripping the last trace of warmth from this void she lived in. "Eli?" she called, eyes fixed on her mother, breathing so, so faintly. "The first person on that list." She tore herself from her mother and stared him down, met shimmering silver eyes brimming with fatigue, loss and sympathy, and knew there was nothing living in her gaze. "Take them down tonight."

# Chapter 15

Never had the walls of the Vindicator's Spire felt so much like a prison. Monsun stood by the massive table, Imbra's map spread out on it, their route still marked on the paper. His fingers splayed on the map as he retraced that route over and over again.

None of the others sat. Raylene alone among them hadn't bothered to change. Her armour was still blood-spattered, mirroring the tattoo on her face and the wrath in her eyes. Tomas was as calm as ever, his face refusing to give anything away. The perfect hellin's player. Footsteps echoed behind him as Syl completed yet another lap around the table. Eli leaned against the wall, yet he missed nothing. Monsun thanked Nestham none of them were armed, else this meeting could have ended in bloodshed.

"Have we debriefed all the soldiers?" he asked Tomas.

The eldest Vindicator nodded, a blink the only sign of sympathy he would show. "They've all reported in, but there's nothing to go on. None seemed to have anything to offer besides not recognising the attackers."

"They had no identifying marks aside from that armband. No jewellery or tattoos," Monsun said. All wearing new Leranion uniforms, yet none of their own troops. At least they didn't need to look for traitors. A chill went over him at the thought. "How many—how many did we lose?"

"Ten men." Tomas passed over a sheet, and Monsun didn't dare look at it. Ten men, ten broken families, ten letters to write, ten houses to visit. He closed his eyes briefly. When he opened them, nobody had stopped looking at him.

"Did anyone see the last archer?" he asked. "The one who—" He couldn't bring himself to say it.

"Tall, broad-shouldered, flaming red hair," Eli said immediately, blood draining from his face.

Monsun nodded, his suspicions confirmed, eyes narrowed on his newest Vindicator. "You've had more experience with him than anyone here, Eli. Do you think it was Trayse?"

"Absolutely. Trayse is still in Imbra," he said, locking his hands behind his back. "We should tell Kyra. She's had the most history with him. She—she deserves to know Trayse hurt the Queen."

"Do not tell her," Monsun said.

"Why the mukk not?" he shouted, as if the very mention of Trayse was enough to knock him off balance.

"Because whenever someone mentions Trayse, the Regent becomes unstable." Eli's silver eyes shuttered, and he bowed his head. Monsun glanced around at the rest of the Vindicators. "Trayse is an assassin working for Archbishop Finon. He is a master of disguise and deception." A memory resurfaced of a mountain tavern, a lovely festival and a failure of duty. "He tricked me into thinking he was Haman."

"Haman?" Raylene said incredulously. "Haman with a completely different complexion and a raspy voice?"

"Speak kindly of the dead," Tomas murmured. "Do not show Haman disrespect."

"He had me fooled, too," Eli murmured. "I brought him down for a moment, but he flipped it, took us prisoner for a night." As Monsun watched, his young Vindicator shivered, his eyes glazing over. Eli snapped back to the present. "I still think we should tell Kyra."

"This is an order, Vindicator. You will not tell Her Majesty who fired that arrow." He softened his voice. "This information does not leave this room." They all nodded. "If her Highness knows Trayse is in Imbra, she will try to kill him."

"So will I," Eli muttered.

Monsun dismissed it for now. "Syl. Tell me what you think." He daren't tell her what power he'd just given her.

She stopped pacing and studied him with calm eyes, and winter clutched his heart. No life debt had formed between him and Syl, and they hadn't ever had one previously.

"Just say it," he said.

"You should have let me fall." Syl's voice was flat, dead. "You should have trusted that I'd be fine. Even if I wasn't, you shouldn't have come to my aid."

"I reacted on instinct," he said.

"You made a choice. You prioritised a Vindicator over protecting your *Queen*." Syl's words hit him like a hammer to the gut.

"And because of that, Her Majesty is nearly dead!" Raylene cut in.

He said nothing and blinked back the traitorous tears that threatened to spill. Not again. This couldn't be happening again. But those words escaped his lips, anyway. "That was my mistake."

"By rights, the Regent could have you sacked for this," Raylene said. "They'd brand your cheek, erase your tattoo, even execute you."

Monsun wanted to reply, but he couldn't. He couldn't do anything but take the blame. Because he deserved this. Deserved it. He shouldn't have gone to Syl.

"We walked into a trap," Tomas said, cutting through the tension. "One we should have seen coming."

Monsun lifted his chin proudly, though every part of him wanted to crumble. "We will learn from this, and next time we will succeed." The sheet of ten names in front of him was proof enough of that need.

"If there is a next time," Raylene said insolently. She shifted her gaze to Eli. "What about you, boy? What do you think about all of this?"

Eli pushed off the wall, and when he slowly, steadily looked them all in the eye, a glitter of strength crept into his posture. "I think you're blaming Monsun for something he couldn't help." He glanced at Syl, accusation in his gaze. "You should be thanking him. If you hadn't been okay, you would have broken a bone, or never walked again. I might have been able to heal you, but it wouldn't have been fun. Besides, I'd burnt out all of my healing with the arrow I took earlier."

"Why didn't you stay with the Regent?" Raylene asked.

"I thought I would be more useful fighting. The Regent can take care of herself. She survived a year in the wilds without you lot." And as he spoke, it was as if the boy was more than just a Vindicator. This—this was what it had been to be a Guardian.

"I'm surprised you didn't stay with her anyway," Raylene said snidely.

"Raylene Oria, that is enough!" Monsun snapped.

The older woman glared at him. "What? We're all thinking it. Everyone can see he's obsessed with her. That could get him—or her—killed," Raylene said.

"I believe he's stronger for it," Monsun said firmly. Out of the corner of his eye, he saw Eli straighten.

"We're going in circles here," Tomas said. "Unless you have anything more to add, this meeting should end." He addressed his words to the group, ignoring Monsun. *They don't trust me.*

"Agreed," Monsun nodded. "Take some time. We will have a briefing tomorrow at the eighth bell. Lord Giara has cancelled the ball tonight, so we don't need to provide the extra security."

"This is exactly when we need to be vigilant!" Syl interrupted. "We need to protect their Majesties."

Monsun blinked. That should have been the first thing on his mind. "Five guards at all entrances to the castle, and a Vindicator to watch the King and Queen."

"What about the Regent?" Syl asked.

Eli coughed. "I can handle that." He scratched his jaw, the gold from his armlet catching the light. Monsun relished Raylene's dropped jaw.

"Dismissed for now," he said. "Tomas, I need a plan for managing a potential Eternal Guardsman crisis."

"You'll have details on your desk by tomorrow," Tomas promised him, and the others left.

"Are you going to be all right?" Eli asked. Monsun nodded, and Eli shut the door as he left.

The meeting room was cold without the others as he read the first name on the list, and scrawled on a sheet of letter paper. A standard letter of apology and condolences. It had been a while since he had written one of these.

Senior Vindicator. Commander of Leranion's greatest warriors, the highest-ranking soldier in the Kingdom. And a complete and utter failure.

Traitor. Could there really be another traitor amongst them? Nestham above, he couldn't survive another coup. Couldn't live with the consequences again.

He'd never told anyone, not even Syl. But when he walked during the night, that was when he remembered it most. Remembered the dull thud of the axe, the hundred burning fires, the death screams of men, women and children.

Remembered the way Aaliyah looked at him afterward, horror and betrayal and pain and grief and a thousand and one emotions flicking through her innocent eyes.

He scribbled his name and started the next letter.

Too often these days he woke in strange places, and nobody bothered to stop him sleepwalking anymore. He'd tried tying himself into position, but it still hadn't worked. The memories rushed at him, a constant nightmare, until a drop of sweat fell onto the letter.

He started the next letter, and wrote each of them until each apology was signed and sealed, where he would soon deliver them. But for now, he opened the southward window, too high to even measure. Leaning a powerful torso out, he snatched the thick rope attached to the roof, and swung out over the gap, climbing hand over hand until he reached the top of the Spire. The wind whipped at his braid as he sat on the stone platform, and with his back against the stone of the castle roof, he stared southward across all of Imbra. From here, the city stretched out, past the flame-touched walls all the way to the foothills. The Kinar trickled past, heading all the way out to sea. He couldn't say for how long he watched the world move past.

Failure. Coward. Traitor.

His hand drifted to his side, to the thickly ridged scar along his waist. More than ever, he missed the man who gave it to him.

"You gonna stay up there?" Syl called out. He didn't answer. Seconds later, the rope twitched, and lithe arms hauled the petite woman up onto the platform. She sat beside him, knees hugged to her chest. At least her face had stopped bleeding, though the cut was deep and might scar.

"What are you doing up in my hiding spot?" she asked.

"What does it mukking look like?" he shot back, full of a venom he'd never used on anyone. He regretted it immediately. Not even in Amaldas had he ever spoken to anyone like that. She twitched, and it was then that he realised how much of a failure he was as a leader.

Those eyes, once full of life, beautiful dancing life, were so no longer—as if they'd died in that fall.

"Well, you look like you're moping, which, sir, is pathetic."

"How dare you," he hissed. "I am your commander." Why, why did he do this? The words weren't his own.

"And now you're hiding behind your rank." She let out a pained sigh, and it sounded too much like her sigh back in Amaldas. She'd been the apple of his eye.

"What do you want me to say?" he asked, flinging calloused hands into silent space.

"A mukking apology would be nice," Syl said, "but I'd settle for some leadership. Wake up, Monsun. This isn't you."

His head bumped against the stone, and he glared at her. "I am sorry for trying to save your life. Next time, I'll just let you fall." And that brought it back, the memories of a lesson he thought he'd learned.

Her eyes burned, and she'd never looked more beautiful. "If you ever put any of us over their Majesties, you won't be worth your tattoo."

He didn't reply, and she lowered herself off the roof and back into the Spire. The wind snatched away words she would never hear. "And I would do it again."

# Chapter 16

"What are you doing?" Eislyn hissed, her face silhouetted in the moonlight. Eli swung around from the Citadel gate. He had thought she was with Jayne and Amora, taking care of Kyra in her suite. That was where he'd last seen her.

"Do you have a problem with me?" he asked. "Because it's been a terrible day for everyone. So what did I do to make you hate me so much?"

The night had already been cold, but it seemed frigid now. Eislyn could have frozen water with words alone. "I don't hate you. But I think you'll end up hurting her." Suddenly, her voice sounded a lot like Jaser's.

"You're insane. I would never let that happen. And she can take care of herself, despite what you may think."

"Oh, really?" Eislyn's teeth flashed, and she dropped her hand to the small of her back. "She had a father and a mother before you showed up."

"Finon! All of this was Finon!" He flung his hand out wide in frustration.

It didn't stop her. "And now she's all alone, and we won't let anyone hurt her. Especially not some farm boy from the middle of nowhere."

His temper almost snapped its leash, but he restrained it. Her gaze paled, and it almost seemed like she would apologise, but he didn't bother. "Then where were you when she was captured?" he breathed. When her lip trembled as the blow struck true, he continued. "I'm sorry. I don't want to fight. But ever since I found out the truth about Kyra, my sole mission has been to bring her home. I will do whatever it takes to keep her safe. I would have thought we'd be allies." She didn't answer, and he turned back towards the gate, swinging a hessian sack over his shoulder.

The gates opened for Eli once he gave his title, and he left the Citadel, joining the rest of the city. The night seemed charged with tension, Imbran Guard and Seventh soldiers patrolled the streets. He ducked into a nearby shadow and threw open the bag as the bell started clanging. A pile of cloth and some other material lay in there.

"We call it Nightweave," Monsun had rumbled. "Strong and yet lightweight. It's not as protective as steel, but if you need it, you should survive." The bell hit three, and he pulled the Nightweave shirt over his head, finding the fabric warm on the inside, a lovely fleece lining. But on the outside, it was smooth and unyielding. The pants were just as comfortable, and they tucked into soft leather boots. The bell hit nine, and when he stamped his feet, no sound echoed over the stone. Nothing. He grinned fiendishly.

He flicked the hood over his head as the bell hit eleven. The knife whispered from his belt, his sword he sheathed along his spine. Though the shirt carried more space for extra knives, he wouldn't bother with that tonight. Knives weren't his strong suit. The bell hit twelve, and he set off.

He dropped the bag, now stuffed full of his clothes he prayed nobody would take. He glanced down the empty alley, and when his Mark gleamed under his thick gloves, he moved, power now back at full strength after a meal and rest.

Thanking Syl for the time they'd worked on stealth and acrobatics, he glanced upwards, then sprang onto the roof. At least in the upper quarter, the roofs were flat, designed for summer sunbathing. He moved silently, pausing for breath, a spider in a web. Then he began running, softly hopping along the roofs, vaulting over gaps, splitting the very air of the night, flying over the streets.

Never had he experienced this kind of speed, not even sprinting through the mountains. Yet he was precise, the Vindicator training honing more balance into him. At last, the buildings became less even, less kempt, less safe. The lower quarter.

He relied more on his supernatural balance to keep him on his feet, flying over the wooden beams. A window squeaked open in front of him. He froze on quivering legs as a balding man peeked his head out. Eli didn't dare to breathe, hidden in the chimney's shadow. The man looked back inside, and Eli Rifted over the roof, jumping between his world and another.

The tributary of the Kinar River loomed before him, and he gathered his strength and leapt, like he had weeks ago. He rolled onto the filthy roof, his sword scraping along the wood, and sat in the shadows, surveying the slums. To his trained eye, several dark shapes occupied other roofs. Urchins, sentries, and Nestham knew what else.

The Vindicators kept files on all the major targets in the city, including the gang leaders, just in case they could ever catch them. One-Eye Vera would be the first on the list to fall. A couple of swift strikes from the darkness and her organisation would be finished. Why did that idea leave a foul taste in his mouth?

"I don't like the uniform change," Jaser said from behind him.

He froze like a deer caught in a snow leopard's gaze. "Really? *Now*? Is this when you want to talk? Not after everything else that has happened, but when I'm about to do something good?"

Eli's thick glove creased while the old Guardian merely regarded him steadily. "Is it good?" When Eli didn't reply, he went on. "I thought I might see how badly you mess this up."

"And what makes you think I'm messing it up?"

"Because you're perched on a roof, opposite a tavern filled with people who would love to kill you, and you're dressed like some kind of assassin."

"What, was black never your colour?" he quipped.

"It's not yours, either. This is not what a Guardian is supposed to be. You're supposed to unite the nations."

"Thank you for the sage advice. You couldn't have told me this earlier?" He couldn't believe that Jaser would just saunter in now and say this.

"You weren't ready earlier," Jaser said, rolling his shoulders in an easy manner. He bore nothing save battered armour, but he didn't need even that. He was dead.

"Oh, mukk off." Honestly, the old Guardian's pretence of wisdom was wearing on him. He breathed in and out, relishing the cool night air as the lights in the city bobbed and weaved. Life, so much life in this place. Perhaps he could find some manner of peace here.

"You carry so much anger it's a miracle you don't choke on it," Jaser said.

Eli whirled around, peace shattered. "Alright, Jaser, enough. Why are you really here?" Force down that anger, don't let him see...

"To tell you you're making a mistake," the old Guardian said.

Eli was in danger of tearing his gloves in his clenched fists. "The last time you told me what to do, you caused me a lot of problems."

"I did that for a good reason, and you still should have listened to my advice."

Absolutely not under any circumstances. He wasn't going to throw it away now. "What do you want me to do?" Eli sighed. "Let's hear it."

"Did you at least think your plan through?"

"Yes." The word was clipped, as an interrogation from a silver-eyed spirit had a habit of growing old fast.

"Then tell me."

"How about you just watch?" Eli flashed a grin he knew would infuriate the ancient Guardian. "You might learn something about being a person."

"Serae," Jaser growled. "Tell me your plan." Eli grinned and flung himself off the roof. A second later, he stalked into the *otann* den and almost retched. His heightened senses, a byproduct of spending so much time immersed in his magic, recoiled at the scent, like nothing he'd ever scented before. And nothing he'd ever want to smell again. He twitched once, eyes straining to peer through the thick haze settled on the room, visibility further decreased by the blood-red lighting throughout the chamber. This place fed on people, destroyed them. Kyra would be happy to see it gone, and he would be happy to ruin it.

A figure stepped up next to him. A slim young man, clicking his heels against the floor. "What can I get you?" he drawled. "Some coffee?" Eli raised a brow and pressed a coin into the man's hand.

"Void." The coin vanished immediately into the man's pocket, and Eli smiled blandly, fully aware he was being sized up by the attendant. His eyes had finally adjusted, and the intelligence in the attendant's gaze was plain to see. He wasn't under the effects of either of Imbra's two most popular forms of *otann*, Void and Flame.

"You sure? You look like you'd want some Flame. A man like you, dangerous. Flame makes for a wild ride." And that was when Eli stepped closer, the way he'd seen Amora do it.

"I'd like to see how much you have," he murmured, pressing another coin into the man's hand.

He pocketed it again, but greed didn't outweigh good business practice. "We don't let anyone into the cellar," the man said.

Eli flashed a conceited grin, like a cocky young noble who undoubtedly frequented this place. "Ah, but you see, I'm happy to buy your entire stock. My employer is having a small gathering, and he needs to have a large supply of Void ready." Every word tasted foul.

"Vera organises the big shipments herself," the young man said. "I just do the shopfront."

"Vera doesn't need to know." He winked. "You'd be out of here with change to spare." Heartbeat hammering, he waited, watched every flicker of emotion cross the man's face, until he smiled. *Finally. All that time with Amora has made me more devious than I expected.*

"Follow me."

The man stepped backwards and Eli followed, covering his nose and mouth with the hood on his Nightweave shirt. The attendant led him through the wooden den, past the slumped forms and the elegantly twisting dancers. Eli kept his eyes straight ahead, and they pressed on to the back of the shop, where the air was clearer. They stopped at a trapdoor, alone in the corner. A heavy brass key threaded into the lock and it clicked open.

"Thanks for your time," Eli said, and punched the worker in the jaw, instantly knocking him out. He sagged forward, and Eli caught him, lowered him into the darkness.

He shut the door behind him as he entered the cellar, barely containing his gasp. The room was perhaps twenty paces wide and filled with Flame and Void. The former was a white crystalline substance, but Void was a dark powder, rolled in paper and neatly stacked. Either way...

The cellar kept going, yet as he breathed in he caught the scent of brine, overpowering the *otann's* stench. Somewhere in the distance, water lapped against the wall. He peered into the darkness, stripped off his glove and flared his Mark. At the end of the cellar, a rickety canoe bobbed inside a channel of water, tied up along the end. Just beside it, a rusty gate.

"They must bring the *otann* through the canals." The river, and its canals, divided the slums from the rest of the city, and it seemed even criminals used it in the night's shadow. Eli replaced the glove on his hand and marched to the back of the cellar, rattled the grate. An impressive lock that he doubted he could break even with heightened strength. He pursed his lips and returned to the attendant, rummaged in his pockets. Sure enough, he found a second key and unlocked the gate. It screeched open, and he swore under his breath. Someone would notice the attendant's absence soon. He had to make this quick.

What if?

He turned back to the *otann* and smiled as an idea spread through him. He ran to the pile of Flame, grabbed as much as he could, and dropped it in the canoe. Eli moved back and forth, carrying more and more Flame and Void. All the while, his ears waited for the yells of the man waking up.

At last, the cellar was almost empty. Eli heaved the gate open fully and prepared to shove the boat out.

"*Thief!*" The screech rang through the cellar. Mukking hells! Eli gritted his teeth, flared his magic, and shoved the canoe through the gate. It jerked to a stop, and it was only then that he noticed the rope attaching it to the stone of the pier. His knife sang from its sheath and he slashed through the rope.

Footsteps rattled down the ladder. "In here!" one yelled. Eli spun and lashed out with his dagger, crumpled the guard to the ground. In a single motion, he whirled and kicked the boat, and it finally scraped out into the canals. Without him.

More and more footsteps sounded above him. He hesitated on the step, but gritted his teeth and dropped into the water. The last time he'd been in water this cold, he'd nearly drowned, at least it wasn't filthy. He spluttered, dragged down by his weapons, and gasped for breath, then dove deeper, deeper. Crossbow darts speared through the water, leaving trails of death behind them. He swam on and on through the midnight water.

Which way was up? He no longer remembered, and a silent scream escaped him, a trail of precious breath bubbling away.

Bubbles that floated upward. Eli launched himself into their path, lungs caving in on themselves. Air never tasted sweeter, and the canoe bobbed gently on the murky canal, the centre of calm amongst the chaos. Eli pushed it ahead of him, steering with the occasional kick.

In all the excitement, Vera's thugs never noticed the canoe floating along the canal. After a few minutes, he heaved himself up onto an empty pier.

From the pouch on his belt he pulled a flint and steel, sparking once, twice. A single ember fluttered onto a pile of Flame, and how appropriate that it burst into a roaring inferno. A wide smile spread across his face as orange and gold illuminated the darkened slums. When the blaze died, the solitary figure turned away. He wasn't finished tonight.

* * *

The men in Vera's pay had probably heard about the thief who brazenly stole all of her *otann* from the den. The corpse of the one who had brought her the message was still cooling in the canals, a gaping wound in his neck. Vera had guessed the thief's next target would be the Leopard's Teeth itself, the heart of her entire operation. The many guards posted on the streets, on the roofs, in every single back alley, had only one instruction. Capture the thief.

If they expected anything, they didn't expect a black-cloaked figure armed to the teeth and dripping water along the street. Eli stopped twenty paces away, a mighty sword in his hand. Ten guards held their breath. Two crossbows levelled on the figure's position. The figure sighed and charged forward in a blur of motion.

It would be some time before the guards would be able to move. Eli paused outside the entrance to the building, the guards' moans of pain filling his ears. His fists ached, and he flexed his fingers, trying to relieve the tension. "You've stirred up a hornet's nest," Jaser said softly.

"Then I'll walk right into it."

"Fine, then do so."

"You really don't want me doing this, do you?" But the old Guardian made no reply. Eli sucked in a breath, anticipating an ambush within. Even if he used only his fists, it made little difference when he threw every punch with enough force to knock them off their feet.

His power had dwindled, his strength fraying. He didn't much care. The ancient stone door loomed. Eli kicked it open and rolled through, sword coming up and out and cleaving a quarterstaff. He dropped under a punch and slammed his elbow into a stomach, collapsing his assailant.

"Everyone out!" he roared. Everyone stared at him, and fifteen men and women rose to their feet, all bearing an assortment of deadly weapons. *Mukk.* He grinned and worked his voice into a drawl, a picture of male arrogance. "I'm looking for One-Eye Vera. Anyone care to fetch her?"

"Vera's not here," said a stone-faced man as big as Monsun.

He shrugged, flippantly waving his sword. "That's the least convincing lie today, so here's my offer. You leave, and take that big box full of money I can see over there, and I won't come after you. Or," he shrugged again, "we can fight, and I can guarantee your odds aren't great. Your choice."

"You can't take all of us." But the voice was less certain, and Eli grinned.

Steel whipped through the air, and he dropped into a stance. "Are you sure?" A sigh rang across the expanse of centuries and death, and Eli smiled at his predecessor's frustration. "Fine." He twisted his wrist, loosening up the tendons. "But believe me, I'm being merciful." He shot through the air, dancing between their blades, blocking and parrying, breaking bones and knocking them out. In seconds, it was over. Several had slipped out the door in the chaos, someone carrying the strongbox.

He strode to the back of the tavern, ignoring the massive pit to his left. Nestham only knew what had gone on in there. He wrinkled his nose at the stains on the walls and floor, soot and other unspeakables.

He grabbed a staff and tapped it on the ground as he walked around, listening to the solid sounds of stone. Until the sound was hollow underneath the stained rug, and he smiled. *There it is.* He yanked the rug sidewards, heaved up the ancient trapdoor, and glanced in.

A single torch lay on the floor beside him, and he tossed it in, casting the pit into light and shadow. A woman hissed, her

115

features flickering in firelight. Her face was scarred, and her eyes—eye—glared at him.

"Hello Vera. I have some friends who would love to meet you." He turned to the writhing bodies on the filthy floor around him, and there was no compassion in his voice, nothing of the boy in the woods. "You have about ten minutes before the guard comes." The group eyed him sullenly but stumbled out. He glanced down to Vera, smiled at her under his mask. "Out you hop." He inhaled the scent of the cellar, the smell of cheap wine. And coughed. *Oh no.* The familiar acrid smell clutched at his throat and his eyes opened wide, fixed on the flame. On the barrels next to it. "*Everyone out!*" he screamed, but it was too late.

The world exploded.

# Chapter 17

"Get up!" Monsun's fist rattled on the door to Eli's room. *That boy is embarrassing me. Cedwin would never have missed dawn.* Instantly, grief and shame struck his heart, but he wouldn't let that deter him. When no answer came, he rolled his eyes and shoved the door open, but stopped like he'd hit a wall. The chamber reeked of ash and soot, just like Amaldas. Battlefields had smelled worse, but another smell lingered there, an acrid one that burned the back of his throat.

In his years listening to the Musadim seminars in Amaldas and the Order's cries in Imbra, Monsun had heard plenty of descriptions of the Five Hells. This stench was exactly the same as those descriptions, and he retched as he stepped closer to the boy. Not a boy anymore. A fugitive, a target, and someone who had held a life debt and never abused it. After he'd faced down Cedwin, Monsun had stopped thinking of him as a boy.

Monsun had appointed a Vindicator, and he'd treated Eli as such. But the man was too young to carry this kind of burden. The youngest Vindicator ever appointed, and one of the few people who could survive a *demon.*

And when Monsun saw him, ran his eyes over the young man... he was getting ready to punch someone. For he was sprawled facedown on the bed, so tired he hadn't even removed his shoes. But soot and ash covered his face, and his Nightweave was crusted with blood.

A foul curse escaped Monsun's lips, and he slammed the balcony door open, let the gentle morning breeze filter through the room. "What have you been doing, Eli?" he wondered under his breath. As if his words alone woke the boy, his Vindicator stirred and blearily opened his silver eyes.

"Good morning, Vindicator," Monsun folded muscled arms over his torso.

"Monsun," Eli mumbled sleepily. "Five more minutes?"

"Get up." Eli did no such thing, merely stretching out and rubbing a hand over his eyes. "Why are you covered in blood?" Monsun demanded. Try. Try not to give in to the roaring in his head. But that was one of his Vindicators bloodstained and half-asleep.

"I'm sorry Monsun, I can't tell you," Eli said.

"Are you ignoring an order?" He stepped closer, looming over the bed.

"You told me to stand up to you," Eli mumbled, his eyes still half-closed.

Monsun gritted his teeth and repressed the urge to slap the soldier senseless. But there was no good reason to slap a junior officer, especially a Marked. "I hope you have a good explanation for all of this."

"I do. But I can't give it to you."

Well, if he was going to play like that... "You have training today. Syl is taking you on a trip to the slums to see what's going on."

Eli's eyes snapped open. "I'm going into the slums?" A hint of fear crossed his face. Monsun nodded silently, shoving shaking hands into his pockets. "I—of course. Yes sir." He attempted a clumsy salute in bed, and failed miserably.

"Be ready to go in fifteen minutes. Wear civilian clothes and bring a knife. And get someone to wash your sheets and uniform. This room is disgusting." Monsun stalked from the room, and when he made it into the meeting chamber, he found Syl already there.

The woman turned to him, something sparking in her calm grey eyes. "Am I taking him out?"

"You could take him out with an arrow," Monsun replied. Honestly, that young man...

She raised a brow. "What's bitten you?"

"He was fast asleep, covered in soot and smelling of smoke."

"You sound like a mother hen." She laughed, and damn him if it wasn't the most beautiful sound he'd heard.

Monsun shrugged, his anger deflated. "I'm going to go check on Tomas and their Majesties. Take Eli to your rounds in the slums and when you get back, I want a full report."

# Chapter 18

Kyra opened the gilded doors and, even in her sorry state, gasped as her eyes once again swept over the rows upon rows of books climbing to the glass ceiling. Golden rays drifted down, catching on the dust floating through the air. She slowed, lingering amongst the extensive collection of knowledge, of histories, of recipes, of life and death and magic.

Every time she came here, she felt small, dwarfed by the power of centuries of learning. Imbra had been a beacon of knowledge for so long, bright as the Eternal Torches shimmering on the walls outside. And yet these were nothing compared to the Archives in Stallor, on the southern half of a broken Amerin. Nobody had heard of Amerin's relics ever since the schism.

The head librarian bustled over, peering at Kyra over ancient spectacles. "Your Highness." She curtsied. "How can I assist you?"

"I'm looking for anything on the Mark." She briefly flicked her light, glittering power on the crystal glass. Passive uses like this—the Mark, the senses, didn't burn her magic quickly. But using it actively, to move like the northern wind, or fight like a hundred soldiers, drained it horribly fast.

"Try the mystics section," she said. "I'd be happy to come and find some texts for you."

"No need," Kyra replied. "I enjoy having a look myself." The woman's smile softened in recognition and almost maternal empathy. That expression... Kyra winced.

"I'll be here if you need, dearest."

Kyra held down the shudder, turning away and heading into the mystic's section. *Why are these sections always at the back?* She went further into the library, and ran a finger along the shelves, collecting the dust as she passed. Here it got thicker and thicker, the books ancient and neglected.

Too many were missing. Removed or destroyed by the Eternal Order, most likely. Kyra paused as a phantom hand brushed her shoulder, and she knew it wasn't a coincidence she'd come here today. Not as Queen Eshe reached over her shoulder, and the greatest queen in Leranion's history guided her to the far corner. Nothing but shadows and dirt, this section falling into disuse and disrepair. But as she traced a finger down the wall, the grooves caught in her finger, and she found a small word carved there.

*Alethial.* She'd never heard of that word before in her life. Kyra bit her lip and crouched down, studying it more closely.

"Amica?" A calm voice echoed behind her. Jayne could be the harbinger of doom, could tell her there was an army on the horizon, and she'd still have that calm voice.

"Yes?" she sighed. She didn't dare turn, fingers just tracing that word.

"The Council has summoned you to an emergency meeting." And that horrible phrase, that was enough to make her head spin.

"I'm the Regent of Leranion. I don't get *summoned.*" She whirled on Jayne. The Plains woman didn't blink, and the anger drained from her bones. "I'll be there in a few minutes."

\* \* \*

Kyra touched the slip at the small of her back, running her hand over the concealed bela. She sucked in a breath, trying to muster up the energy to fight this war of words. But she just felt... drained. Where her magic roared inside her, she found only a muted shift of power.

Five men arose to meet her. One ally, two enemies and two blowing with the northern wind. "Gentlemen," she said, her voice razor steel, an impressive act.

"Let's get this over with," Hyrin sighed. The Spymaster wore all black, no visible weapon at his side.

"Very well," Finon said. "Your Highness, we are all very sorry for your situation."

"Thank you." She nodded graciously. An awkward pause stretched out as she waited for him to speak. But the politician said nothing, merely waited for her to make the first move. Monsun refused to flinch, a mask locking into place.

"I hope you didn't call this meeting to give me your condolences," she said. "I have other things to do today."

Finon smiled and shook his head. "Unfortunately, there is more troubling news. I arranged this meeting to put an end to the instability in the slums."

Kyra raised a brow at the elder man, sizing him up once again. "The slums have been a problem for as long as Imbra has stood. I'm surprised you're not ready to send in the Eternal Guardsmen."

"Oh, that's a bit below my Guardsmen. The Imbran troops, however, would suit this matter perfectly." His eyes flashed in triumph. "An unknown attacker killed One-Eye Vera last night. And nobody can find the Crime Lady's *otann* supply."

"Nobody?" The Regent leaned back in her chair. So Eli had accomplished his task. Now to see what they knew. "Hyrin? What do our Veils know?"

"We have no idea either, Highness." A single flick of his brows told her he knew exactly who had single-handedly brought down One-Eye Vera. But the Spymaster frowned. "What's strange is how the Leopard's Teeth collapsed. Not fire, or anything like that. The earth rumbled and a single blast destroyed the entire building instantly."

Her world froze. "Survivors?"

"None."

For a moment, she couldn't breathe. Monsun subtly kicked her under the table, and she shifted a horrified gaze to him. A small nod was all he offered her..

Suddenly, she could breathe again. "Are Musadim healers already there?" she asked, and Hyrin nodded. "Good. Send some Royal Healers, unless the Guild wishes to help?"

Yuras hurriedly rearranged his faces into a smile. "Of course." *Got you.* With Yuras in the Order's pay, it was likely they had created the damn thing. Eventually, Kyra stood up, but her eyes connected with Hyrin and Monsun before she left. As soon as she shut the door behind her, as soon as the sentries stopped staring, she allowed herself to sway on exhausted feet.

*Eli.* She had to see him, but as she stepped towards the Vindicator's Spire, the door behind her opened and shut again.

"Highness." She turned slowly to the Vindicator standing there, his uniform as pristine as always.

"Tell me." Kyra kept her voice to a whisper, hardly daring to raise it lest it break. "Tell me he's okay." Monsun raised his brows, something flashing across his face. Spymaster Hyrin emerged behind him, face carefully blank. Kyra flicked her gaze across the pair of them. "We need to talk." She pointed at the meeting room across the way and directed a sentry to stand guard.

Hyrin smiled as she shut the door behind them. "Finally, Highness. I was wondering when you'd at last come to me."

"Why didn't you come to me?" she asked. "You're sworn to assist the Crown."

"I didn't want to put all my cards on the table," he said. "But yes. I know exactly who was responsible for the destruction of the Leopard's Teeth. Your new Vindicator," he nodded to Monsun, "has quite the flair for the dramatic. I'm quite impressed."

Monsun's eyes widened, and his eyes shifted to Kyra. Judgement lay there, judgement he probably thought he had carefully concealed. But she could read him like a book. "You sent Eli to the Leopard's Teeth," he said. If stone could speak, she expected it would have a similar voice to Monsun.

"Yes." She flicked a gaze to Hyrin and bit her lip. But she had to trust someone. "My father gave Eli a list of people loyal to Finon. He's hunting them down."

Monsun snarled. "You sent *my Vindicator* on an assassination mission?"

Kyra turned towards the window, praying he couldn't see the guilt flash across her face. "No. I said nothing about a fireball, or planting Nestham's Will. Something must have gone wrong."

"Highness," the Senior Vindicator growled, "this was not your call."

She faced him, spine as strong as steel. "This was my call. If Finon thinks he can attack my family, then I will see him brought down. And taking down his supporters and his coffers is the best way to do it."

"We cannot even be sure the list is correct!" Monsun slammed his fist on the table, rattling the half-melted candle.

"Yes, we can," Hyrin said, shoving his hands into his pockets. "I gave King Hadrian the list. I'm the Spymaster of Leranion. Try as you might to hide it, my job is to make sure I know everything that goes on in this Kingdom." He paused and let the silence strain for too long. "Six months ago, Guildmaster Yuras increased funding towards weapons development. All well and good, except the Guild never presented new weapons to King Hadrian or the Vindicators." He drummed his fingers along the edge of the chair. "And yet, my Veils have confirmed the endeavour has yielded results." Hyrin held up three calloused fingers, his middle one just a little crooked. "One. Miniature crossbows, which a soldier can hold in one hand. Two, a powder which can flare brighter than an Eternal Torch. And three, another powder which can level mountains." He held their gaze, resplendent in his black leather tunic. "I know it wasn't an act of Nestham that destroyed Mount Sancti."

Kyra sat back, wiping clammy hands on her dress. Finally, an ally coming forth. "What are you proposing?" Careful, so careful.

"You'll need Finon out of the way before you can deal with Temero."

She raised her brows. "You know about Temero?"

"Demon-killing isn't my business," he said, "but I'm aware of it nonetheless."

"And that's where you're wrong. Soon, demon-killing will be everyone's business." She leaned forward, capturing the spymaster in a fierce gaze. "It will engulf all of Ekra in a war soon unless we are very careful. But you're right, I can't fight Temero with Finon waiting to put a knife into my back."

Hyrin adjusted the sleeves on his tunic. "Of course, Highness. I offer you and your Vindicators my support as a Veil and a Councilman." His eyes twinkled. "Three to two."

"Do you know what Rumpre's thinking?"

"Rumpre's an idiot," Hyrin said. "Thinks only of money and food."

"Sounds like most men," Kyra replied instantly, twisting the ring on her finger. Monsun snorted at her side, while Hyrin rolled his eyes and chuckled.

"Possibly. But he's undecided, and worse, he doesn't like being told what to do."

"How did my father deal with him?" Kyra asked the pair. Damn her for not knowing this. She should have paid more attention before she'd left.

Monsun leaned back thoughtfully, and a while passed before he spoke. "Your father once saved Rumpre's life at Raven's Watch. As the story goes, the king grabbed an arrow out of thin air before it hit him. When Rumpre left military service, he followed the king's every decision. It seems such loyalty has not passed on to you."

She chewed her lip, weighing up the possibilities. "Still, if we could convince him, it could turn the tide of the Council."

"I could just have Finon assassinated," Hyrin said. "They'd never find the body."

She shook her head vehemently and felt the weight of her ring more than ever. "I want to do this the right way."

"Still, it's something to consider."

"I can't consider it." That feeling rose in her, the belief that she should be better. "If I stoop to Finon's level, then what does that make me?" A traitorous thought echoed in her mind: she'd already stooped with that list.

"Someone who will go to any lengths to protect her kingdom," Hyrin said.

Monsun's scarred hand rested on the table next to hers. "Say the word, Highness, and it will be done."

Hyrin rose and bowed with a flourish. "I have another meeting, Highness, but I will report tomorrow. I'll find out what Finon's planning." She nodded, her teeth already worrying at her lip.

# Chapter 19

Finon dropped into the rich chair and leaned back, folding withered fingers together. The world was going mad. He reached for an immaculate bottle, pouring delicious brandy into the crystal glass next to it. He took a sip, let the rich flavour roll over his tongue. Giara's holdings made the best drink in Leranion. His gaze fell upon the sword on the wall. A fine weapon of a rare steel, a relic taken from his greatest victory.

Suddenly the drink tasted foul. He drained it anyway. "Sandria?" he called out through the door. Seconds later, she discreetly opened the door. Small, plain, the kind of person who would fade into the background even with the light turned on her.

"Yes, Excellency?" she asked, face unreadable.

"Send for Trayse, please." He could have sworn she trembled as she shut the door a touch more forcefully than he would have liked.

Ten minutes later, the red-haired man lounged against the wall, lean arms folded across his chest. "You wanted to see me, Finon?" The deadly sword hung from his waist, yet his eyes flicked to the beautiful weapon on the wall.

"Have a seat." The Archbishop gestured to the fine leather chairs opposite his desk.

"I'd rather stand."

Finon moved his right foot closer to the pedal underneath his desk, waiting for this meeting to end in bloodshed. He'd walked a fine line with this assassin, one of two he'd trained for over a decade. Trayse he'd found amongst the urchins of Imbra. Even as a street rat, he'd shown no emotion or remorse as he killed his way into becoming Finon's second-most-brilliant assassin.

Finon blinked, shaking his head. "From the way her Highness looked, I see you didn't miss yesterday."

Trayse smirked. "I never miss. And I laced the arrow with Malmir, just like you said. I was right, wasn't I?"

Finon's fists clenched to prevent him from screaming. "Yes, you were right." Stroke his ego, compliment him, or that edge would cut both ways. "She's becoming unstable. With her mother injured, the more she acts rashly, the more vulnerable she becomes."

"What did she do?" Trayse cocked a grin. "You sound like you know something."

Indeed, he did. And the chaos at the last meeting confirmed it. Finon allowed himself a slight smile. "Her pet Vindicator destroyed One-Eye Vera last night." The silver-eyed boy, a memory of a heresy long buried.

"That's a lot of money gone," Trayse replied, though his eyebrow twitched.

The elder man waved a jewelled hand dismissively. "Vera was becoming a liability. My sources say she was planning to betray me, anyway. My allies in the palace are more important." And he had several. Far more than the Antarun bitch would ever see coming. He leaned forward, and Trayse's eyes, full of malice and wicked insanity, narrowed on him. "But blood calls for blood. Tonight, you show Her Highness the price of her little war."

Trayse grinned and clicked his heels together. "As you command, Holiness."

# Chapter 20

Eli knocked on the ancient wooden door and shoved shaking hands into his pockets. He'd at least cleaned up his face, but the scene still didn't stop playing in his mind. How he'd tried to grab people, but they were slow, too slow, and he could do nothing but Rift out of the explosion. The fireball had seared his face, and he'd clawed his way into the castle, and just passed out in his bed without even bothering to clean himself.

The numbness in his hands still hadn't faded, his magic shattered. Normally, it would replenish after a few hours. A day at most, if he had pushed it to the breaking point. Monsun was right. His magic had become a crutch, instead of relying on his years of endless training. He flexed his hand, trying to regain the feeling. Nothing.

"Come in," Syl called out. He peered in, sighing as he found her alone in the room, idly scanning sheets at her desk. She flashed a grin at him as she pulled on a heavy black jacket with a strange flap that rose up to cover her navy tattoo. The jacket paired well with her moon-white hair, strange for one so young.

"So I hear you had a big night out. Care to share?"

"Don't you start. I've already had the lecture from Monsun." He'd deserved it, but it would have been better to deal with the angry Vindicator when he was awake.

"Oh, he was not happy." Syl stacked the paper and shoved it in a drawer nearby.

"Why am I not surprised?"

"He has a point, though," Syl said. "Being a Vindicator isn't just being a good fighter, though we're damn good at it. We have a code that we follow, and if we abide by it and stick with each other, that's what makes us lethal more than any individual skill."

"I didn't do it as a Vindicator, though," he said. "I don't have the tattoo, I didn't show I was working for the Crown."

"Well, that needs to stop. You're a Vindicator now, and you cannot be anything but, or you'll find yourself in a lot of trouble with the big man. But lecture over, let's go." She darted to the door, and he followed her out to the palace gates, out of the Citadel, and into the city beyond.

"Why are we going to the slums?" he asked her.

"I'm the only Vindicator the urchins talk to," she said, tucking that bulky jacket closer to her skin. "I usually go in about once a week to check in with our contacts." She grinned, and it seemed to radiate light like a Marked's star. "Must be because I'm so approachable."

He slouched, deliberately following the lessons Amora had taught him. Just don't be a stranger. Back when he didn't know her, back when he was desperate for answers. Now he had those answers, and he wished he didn't. But it was too late, because they were already marching over the rickety bridge dividing the city from the slums. Smoke still piled into the skyline overhead, and Eli winced, dropping his gaze before Syl could notice.

They headed into narrow alleys, wind whipping through them like a mountain gale. At each gust, the ramshackle buildings swayed side-to-side. An urchin darted between them, and Syl struck like a snake, gripping the young girl's arm.

"Heyo," Syl said, burrowing into her jacket and producing a strip of dried meat, tossing it in the air. "Where's Millin?"

"Out by Big Shack." The girl snatched the meat and sprinted off. "Thanks, gruntah!" she called from a safe distance.

"See? Not so hard."

Eli couldn't stop the grin spreading from ear to ear. "Do you reckon you could get them off the streets?"

"We've tried. A couple of years ago, the Musadim took a bunch into homes, and some of the older ones started working with the Guild. They resettled a few with families, but others just don't want to leave." Syl let out a quiet sigh. "They've seen too much betrayal."

"The Jinnam would have helped. That's what they did for me," he said through a clenched jaw.

"Monsun told me where you came from. I—I'm sorry about what happened to your homes."

"Let's just find Millin." A part of him was eager to meet the boy who had looked after Amora. And then... then Eli would judge if his care was adequate. Syl seemed to know her way around, and led him to Big Shack, in the centre of urchin territory. The Shack itself was slightly larger than the other buildings, slightly less decrepit, and surrounded by almost twenty urchins. The reek was almost enough to make his eyes water.

"They come in during the day," Syl said. "Most of the thieves sleep here. It's safer than the nights, at least."

They sauntered up to the pack, and though none of the youngsters seemed to notice, they knew better. When they were ten metres away, Syl shrugged off her jacket and pulled out bags and bags of food. Nestham above, how did she fit all of that in her jacket? Amidst all the cheers, the food vanished in moments.

"You should have told me you would do that," Eli murmured. "I could have brought some too."

"They wouldn't trust you."

"Millin's inside." A boy of thirteen gestured with a dirty thumb. Syl flashed another of her trademark smiles and stepped past them into the tilting building. They brushed aside tattered drapes, surveying a dusty floor covered with blankets. At the far end was a makeshift desk, occupied by a boy of maybe fifteen. Thin to the point of scrawny, but with a look in his eye that suggested iron control.

That gleam flickered when he glanced at Syl, but returned when he met Eli's gaze. "You know the rules, gruntah. You come alone, or we don't talk."

"I brought extra food this time," Syl said, leaning against a rickety wall. "I'm just showing my new apprentice around."

"Looks a little young." Millin jammed filthy hands into his pockets. In front of him, several utilitarian blades rested on the table.

"Speak for yourself," Eli retorted.

Millin looked at him more closely, a gaze suggesting he'd spent plenty of time analysing targets. "The boy with silver eyes. Amora said you'd come, gruntah."

"Amora's been here?"

"Course, she came back to say hello. Told us all about the boy who got into the Citadel."

Syl turned to him, accusations written in her eyes.

"I was desperate." Eli shrugged. And it hadn't ended that well for him.

"I know, gruntah," Millin said, then turned his gaze to Syl. "Not much to say this week, except someone blew up the Leopard's Teeth. But I expect you already know that."

Syl shrugged slim shoulders. "I did. You got anything else?"

"No." That single word was enough for her to turn away, and she fluffed her jacket and strolled to the door. "Wait!"

"Why do we do this every time," she sighed, even though a faint smile flicked at the corners of her mouth.

Millin grinned, revealing many gaps in his teeth. "Just because I can. Apparently someone attacked Vera's *otann* den before demolishing the Leopard's Teeth. The *otann* ended up on a canoe in the middle of the slums, burnt to a crisp. But there's a new group investing in both Flame and Void."

"Why do you care about the *otann*?" Eli asked.

Shadows reflected in Millin's eyes, and he brushed a hand through greasy black hair. "Anything that stops my kids getting into that is good for me."

Well. "We'll do our best." He smiled, but they were silent as they returned to the palace, the sun just reaching its peak in the sky. Eli couldn't think about anything else.

As they returned to the briefing room, he sighed and turned to Syl. "I need your help with something. Monsun may have already told you, but her Highness and I found something in the tunnels underneath the castle. And—I'm afraid to go back alone."

Syl nodded, her smile gone for once. "Monsun told the other Vindicators. None of us have gone back down since. But would you like to go back down there?"

"No. Five Hells, I'm terrified of going there. But we need to anyway."

# Chapter 21

The palace held many secrets, but the rich quarter held more, with its freshly swept cobbles, its towering mansions, its scandals and intrigues and everything in between. They always had different names to disguise their true nature. For example, they'd granted the Silver Grove the title of restaurant, and in some ways it lived up to its name. It was quieter than the bars in the lower levels, and the men and women sitting at the poorly decorated tables ate with trained grace. But the bar still served the same rough drinks at twice the price. The musician wasn't as good as he claimed, his fingers slipping on the lute every time he tried to play the upper notes of the Queen's Lullaby.

And, of course, the Eternal Order spies were just as obvious as the slum brutes. Hyrin nursed the sturdy mug of ale in his left hand, the right idly passing a coin over his knuckles. He flipped it, once, twice, then left it on the bar, along with the untouched drink. The matron blinked twice as he left, and he winked back as he strolled out into the moonlight. In his rich black outfit, he would be nothing but a nobleman out for a nightly stroll.

The fresh scent of flowers greeted him in the garden outside the restaurant, the blues and oranges and pinks of the wildflowers a dazzling combination, offset by the flicker of torches lighting the stone path. He swung the gate behind him and set off, heading as far away from the river as possible. And as soon as he found an alley, he swung into the shadows. A jewelled hand clasped the hilt of an elegant knife. He called it Verity, and it had seen him through too many interrogations.

But tonight, there would be no interrogation. Not as heavy breathing rasped behind him, and he rolled his eyes.

Five. "Where'd he go?" one asked. The voice was too loud for any properly trained spy. A damn urchin could tell you to mukking whisper.

Four. "Keep your voice down," the other hissed. Some common sense, but still stupid.

Three. "He's just an old man." Like Hells. I'll show you what this old man can do.

Two. "Well, we put him down regardless." They were closer now, just about to come around the corner.

One. "Fine."

His knife flashed out from its sheath, and he leapt into the alley. Slashed once, twice. Two bodies fell to the ground, blood staining his blade.

"Old man," he muttered, cleaning and sheathing Verity. More footsteps, and he faded back into the shadows, until someone clicked three times. He sighed in relief. "I was beginning to think you hadn't made it, Reian."

The young woman glanced at him from under her wide-brimmed hat, concealing her form with a heavy jacket, just as he'd trained her. "Still doubting me, boss?"

"Never," he said. "Got anything?"

She nodded solemnly, her entire body trembling. In all his years of training Reian, she'd never been like this. "You need to warn Her Highness. Finon is sending Trayse after Lady Ajerst."

"Finon's best assassin."

"It's worse. He's the one who poisoned King Hadrian, and the one who shot Queen Taera. He's had it in for the Regent since before she returned to Imbra. They have history."

They fell into synchronised steps, heading out of the alley. "What history?"

"Trayse was the one who found Her Highness long before she returned. He and Finon imprisoned her for several days until she escaped."

"She was the one you told me about—the one Trayse brought in for Finon?" Hyrin swore, vicious and low. "You need to come in. Your position is getting too risky."

She shook her head vehemently, the steelhearted Veil he'd trained. "You posted me here for this exact moment. I'm not leaving until Finon's head is on a spike. Trayse, too." Reian seemed to shrink, almost curling in on herself. "That man is death itself."

"What of Finon's other assassin? The one who calls herself Alondra?"

"Finon never let me see her. But I've heard him talking about her. He hasn't heard from her in weeks." A sly smile. "I think she's done the wisest thing and got the hell out of this country."

Hyrin grinned, but he could feel the sweat beginning to break out on his forehead. "You've done well. Thank you."

"Hyrin?" He turned around to find her brown eyes intent on him. Not Sandria, the small, vulnerable woman, the churchman's trusted secretary. But one of his best Veils. "This is your chance to catch Trayse and put an end to him."

"Once we arrest Trayse, I'll find you a new posting."

They reached the end of the alley, and he turned right. He never heard the arrow as it whistled through the alley.

* * *

Reian choked back a sob, refusing to let him see her emotion. "You said you would let him live." Though she didn't turn, she knew the man who stood behind her. Knew the distinctive flame-red hair on his head. A hand rested on her shoulder, smeared blood on her jacket. She locked the muscles in her back to stop the shudder.

"I said I would let him live as long as you played by the rules, but you contacted him anyway. Give it up, Reian. Your days as a Veil are over." He leaned closer and ripped the hat from her head, spilling her hair over her shoulders. "You work for me now."

"You'll pay for this. The Veils will make you suffer ten times more for what you've done."

"Oh, I don't doubt it." Trayse's smile glittered in the dark. "But since you told him, he had to die." Her hand twitched on the knife at her back. Not the *bela*, but something far more deadly.

Trayse bent to the ground, removed the arrow from Hyrin's back. The body shifted once, and she didn't dare say anything. "If you even think about it, you'll die." The assassin easily slung her mentor's corpse over his shoulder. "Go straight home. If you don't, I'll know about it."

Reian hissed a breath, hot tears falling down her cheeks as his footsteps faded into silence. Then she broke into a sprint, headed straight for the Citadel and Lady Ajerst. Her life be damned. Trayse had destroyed enough of her kingdom tonight.

# Chapter 22

Needle-sharp pain pierced a soft thumb, but Jayne merely pursed her lips and set aside the embroidery, running a practised eye over her work. The outline was nearly finished, but the leopard's ears were already looking impressive.

She sighed and twisted the new golden ring on her finger, replaying the words of her father. "This could begin a powerful alliance with Stallor and Leranion." The ring still felt foreign, too heavy, as though the gold in Stallor wasn't as fine as it was in the Ketan mines.

Ajerst was always, would always, be a part of Amerin, but when the war between Stallor and Fallkirk worsened when she was a child, her father had made a choice. The family had fled the nation, caught between two sides. Even when the conflict had stabilised again, when the Duke of Stallor had risen to power, her father had never picked a side, never looked back. Imbra was her home more than the Plains had ever been. Kyra and Eislyn had her loyalty more than Amerin ever would.

Was that why she was wavering? Or would this actually work?

Heavy thuds echoed outside her luxurious room, decorated in Amerin green, like the fields of the plains. Thuds—and then a dragging sound, a scream. She stood up, smoothed down her dress and opened the door, hand shifting into the slip for her bela.

Her mind fell silent. She couldn't think, couldn't speak, couldn't breathe. A woman lay there, blood spreading from a wound at her neck, smearing over pale skin.

"Lady Ajerst," she coughed out. She should be dead, but this woman had strength unknown. "You must flee. He's coming." But before Jayne could ask more, the woman slumped, her hand dropping from her neck. She spasmed, and fell still. Jayne's hand flew to her mouth, bile rising in her throat. Completely numb, she could do nothing but stare at the body.

More footsteps, this time men in her family's colours. Jirra, a weathered man who'd served her family for so long. "Get inside, Lady Ajerst," he said. When Jayne didn't move, he gently took her by the arm and led her into her room. "Sound the alarm," he called to the other guard. The man nodded and hurried away, but Jayne could do nothing but stare at the closed door.

A soft scrape at the window set her heart flaring.

"Get in the cupboard," her guard hissed. "Do it now." Something spurred her, and she lurched, rushing into the other room. The ancient cupboard loomed, moulded in Amerin's designs. She yanked open the bottom section and curled into a ball, scrabbling to shut the door. It slammed into her foot and she bit her lip to stop from crying out loud.

Her heartbeat pounded, and the breath roared in her ears, amplified in the tiny space. Glass shattered outside, and a singular scream died too quickly. She shuddered, sweat coursing down her back. Footsteps drew closer. Closer, until they stopped outside. Death waited for her, but she couldn't even reach for her bela.

The door shot open, but she didn't even move.

Footsteps faded away, but she didn't move for a long while. When she looked, Jirra's body was drenched in blood. And with that blood, the killer had smeared a single letter.

# Chapter 23

The ancient door screeched open, and Eli pressed his gloved hand over his nose, the foul smell creeping through the tunnel. "Is this the way you came with the Regent?" Monsun asked, and he nodded distantly.

"Alright," Raylene sighed. "Let's just get this over with so I can go to bed. Off you go, boy."

Her words loosened fear's grip and he stepped into the chamber, sinking Nightweave boots into the fetid puddle. Steel whispered on leather, and the Torch's golden light glittered off the polished blade. Vindicators padded behind him on near-silent feet. Tomas brought up the rear, as he always did, an arrow already nocked in his bow.

Flame whipped in the air as he swung the Torch around, highlighting the dim tunnel. At last, they came to the door he'd smashed through. A slight smile tugged at his mouth at the memory, drowned out by the stifling fear rising to choke him. He reached for his armlet, ran a finger over it, and his breathing steadied. "Take this," he handed the Torch to Syl.

"How are you going to see?"

Eli grinned, stripped his glove off his hand and flared his Mark. Ice-blue light flooded the tunnels, shimmering off the water pooled on the floor, highlighting the devastation. Cracked pillars, stone scattered on the floor as if a giant had smashed its way through them.

And there the body of the creature lay, its flesh already decaying. Jagged bite marks covered its legs, as if another predator had already picked over the spoils. Green ichor leaked out of shimmering scales, now mottled black and blue.

"Five Hells," Raylene said.

Eli had to agree as he sheathed his weapon. In the light of his Mark, he beheld the utter ruthlessness of the creature's creator. Monsun poked it with his axe, delicately shifting the body, and all the Vindicators crowded in.

"Looks like someone hit the pincer," Syl said, crouching down by the corpse. She ran a gloved hand across its mottled skin. Her gloves were much thinner than the bulky ones Eli wore. Slim, supple, perfect for thievery.

"Kyra landed a blow with her staff," Eli said. "Steel may not work, though."

Monsun swung his axe in a mighty blow, straight on the creature's pincer. It rebounded without leaving a scratch. "It does not."

"We must find more Nesthamir or some chemical," Tomas said, "if we are to defeat these—these—"

"Mantiks," Raylene said. They all turned to her, and she shrugged. "It was in a legend I read about once. There were three species of them. You could only tell which one they were by the blood they bled. Clearly, this is a green one."

"What else do you know about these mantiques?" Monsun asked.

"Man-tiks. Not much. I think the blue ones survived better in the mountains, but they were weak towards fire. Regardless of the type, Temero bred them to be stronger than whatever magic the Marked had within their blood." It had easily taken Kyra in a fight. But when Eli met Monsun's gaze, he saw something else.

"You said the alpine ones had blue blood?" Monsun said.

"That's exactly what I said," Raylene replied. "Why?"

"Because something with blue blood killed the mother of the Regent's snow leopard."

Raylene hissed, and cold swept over Eli's body. "We need that chemical," he said firmly. Ice-blue light reflected off their tattoos as they nodded as one, but Nestham-blessed hunter's senses pricked and he glanced around. A rat scuttled beyond. Water dripped from above. A faint splash echoed through the tunnels. Eli drew his sword, and the others followed, edging themselves further into the tunnels.

Footsteps. Eli engaged his hearing and held up a hand for silence. The others stopped and assumed outwards gazes, a perfect unit. He held up one finger, then pointed to their right. They moved silently, Eli on point, Tomas in the rear. Eli's heartbeat pounded in his chest, but he kept moving. They rounded the corner, his sword rising into a defensive position.

Nothing. Just a blank wall.

"Fan out," Monsun ordered. He and Syl hefted their torches and headed back into the tunnels, but Eli just stared at the wall. That couldn't be it, could it? He tapped against the wall, poking and prodding. After some time, the others returned.

"All the tunnels are empty," Syl said, but Eli didn't turn around.

"There was someone here. I'm sure of it."

"Hold up," Syl said. "Do you feel a breeze in here?"

Eli glanced at her, and sure enough, her short hair swayed under the gentle wind.

Tomas stalked up to the brick wall, ancient and decaying, then dropped to his knees, face almost pressed to the wall. "That's a symbol I haven't seen for a while," he said. He tapped the brick at the base and the stone rumbled, then swung open.

Another chamber lay beyond. Furnished with a bed, and several weeks' worth of food, and—a ladder. He clomped in, surveying the room, hand dropping to the bed. Still warm. A strange musk filled the air, some kind of perfume. Nothing he'd ever scented before.

"Someone was here recently," he hissed, flaring his Mark and sharpening his vision. Careful fingers brushed the pillow and held out a single strand of hair. One strand of burnished red, like a living flame. Eli swore, more filthy than ever. Monsun raised a brow, but when his gaze fell on the hair, he stiffened.

"Sound the alarm."

Then the screaming started. His body locked up, but only for a moment, and he hurled himself up the ladder, following the deathly noise. He pounded through the hallways until he saw it ahead of him. Blood pooled on the floor as Eislyn moaned softly, a dagger embedded in her side. Eli dropped to her and activated his healing, but it was just as he feared. That shadowy presence lingered in Eislyn.

"I can't heal it." He swore.

"Get her to the surgeon," Monsun said calmly. Raylene and Tomas hefted her gently, so careful not to move the dagger.

"Eli. Look," Syl said. Eli rose from where he had been kneeling, bloodstains spreading across his trousers, and the world tilted.

The blood hadn't pooled. Someone had smeared it into one letter. *T.*

The world became muted, drained of colour. Eli's vision sharpened, his gift flaring to the fullest.

"Not now," Monsun said. He had whispered, but it was as loud as a battle cry. "Not now. Let's go to the Healing House." Every step Eli took behind the other Vindicators he took on leaden feet. They entered the House, a place reserved for peace and healing.

As the Healers took her away, the door slammed open and Kyra was there, breathing heavily, hands shaking. "Who?" she asked.

"Trayse," he said, the very word a knife in his heart. "He's here."

Blood drained from her skin, and she went rigid at his name. Slowly, she spoke. "Did you know?"

He couldn't meet her gaze. She rushed towards him, but Monsun stepped into her path, and she slammed into him, rebounded instantly. "Did you know?" Gold flared in the room, and she was screaming now, the bloodcurdling fury of an angel of death, then fell silent, still shaking.

"I trusted you," she whispered, and marched from the room, like she was forcing her body to move.

Bile surged in Eli's throat, and the world seemed to sway. He slumped to the ground, tears pricking at his eyes.

# Chapter 24

He'd known. He'd known, and decided not to tell her. Kyra's spine was rigid on the bed, just staring over the midnight city. Not a single tear passed down her cheek. Her breathing was a horrible rasp, her nails digging into her skin.

He'd known. Nix sensed her misery and huddled close, seeking warmth. Kyra allowed her hands to brush through the silken fur, letting her mind fall through into Nix's.

*Mistress. What is it?*

*My friend.* That was all she could say, as the silence overwhelmed her. The door opened, and a familiar voice spoke hesitantly. "Kyra..." he said. His voice cracked. "I'm so sorry."

"Get out," she breathed.

"I don't know what else to do."

She turned to him, and though a part of her ached to draw him closer, she couldn't. Not now. "You've already cost me Eislyn. I told you Trayse was too deadly to ignore. But did you listen to me? Did you even for one second think I might be right? *No.* You just thought you could handle him. You thought you could protect us." She let out a dead laugh. "You couldn't even protect your sister."

The blood drained from his face, silver eyes hardening to chips of ice, and she stopped, caught herself, her throat straining with apologies.

None came out of her mouth. Fury burned in his eyes, but he just shut the door with devastating precision, and his footsteps faded away.

# Chapter 25

His bedside chest slammed open and Eli reached in, shoving as many knives into his Nightweave shirt as he could. Each weighed him down. He didn't care. He pulled the Torch out from under his shirt and tossed it under the bed. Light would not serve his purpose. He strapped the sword over his back, for where he would run, he couldn't have any distractions. Finally, his vambraces already humming with power, he shut the chest and the door. As he stalked down the corridor, he felt a throbbing in his chest—the brand, the old wound Temero had given him—as if a part of the nameless malice smiled.

"What do you think you're doing, boy?" Raylene growled from behind him.

"The only thing I can do," he said.

She stepped closer, fury written on every line of her wrinkled face, a smear of blood on her tattoo. "Don't go picking a fight now. Believe me, I know a thing or two about fighting angry."

He held up a hand, not caring anymore. "This ends now." He sprinted into the street, wrath made form.

*Where are you.* He flew over the buildings, his sight that of a hawk, searching for one man.

*Where are you.* He kept running, not caring how many people saw the man cloaked in the night, armed to the teeth.

*Where are you.* He shot through the city, all the way to the tallest building he could find. His gloved hands pulled him up the ramparts and he crouched on a balustrade, scouring the lights.

*Where are you.* His senses hadn't flared like this since the ambush in the city. But what if... he concentrated on that pit of power, flared his sight, flared his hearing, his sense of smell.

*There.* A musk he'd only scented once before in the small bedroom under the castle. Drifting in on an icy breeze, a pleasant scent, with a subtle note of death. It was coming from the slums. He leapt to the lower roof and landed in a crouch, flying across the tiles again. Tracking that scent like a snow leopard.

At last, he found his quarry. The figure darted into a nearby alley, and Eli crouched on the rooftops, a grim smile spreading across his face. He dropped, falling through air, landing delicately on the ground.

"You shouldn't have come back," he growled, unsheathing his sword, fire sweeping through his veins, the fury of a Guardian ready to crush a threat.

"Why not?" Trayse turned, a purple cloak swishing out around him. "Everything I want is here."

Eli snarled and rushed forward, blade blurring in a deadly steel swarm. Trayse's hand dropped under his cloak, but it didn't matter, Eli was moving too fast, almost there.

Almost there.

Pain flared in his abdomen, and he glanced down at the bolt embedded in his stomach, shearing through his Nightweave. Blood spurted out from his wound as he lashed out. The motion twisted the bolt into his flesh, and he screamed, his blow passing just by Trayse's head. The blade screeched harmlessly on stone, and the assassin smiled and flicked a knife out, slicing him on the upper arm. Eli screamed again, hot blood running down his skin.

"You're just in the way now," Trayse murmured. He kicked Eli in the stomach, right where the bolt had gone through, shoving it deeper. The boy's breathing was now a laboured rasp, and he collapsed to his knees, staring blankly ahead. No plan, just mind-numbing pain. Trayse knelt next to him, and the blade kissed his throat. Death was cold tonight. "Goodbye, heretic." Eli gritted his teeth and touched his vambraces together, falling into the Rift.

# Chapter 26

Sometimes silence was peaceful, like the silence of the northern mountains. This silence was like death waiting around the next corner. Kyra wiped reddened eyes and knocked on Jayne's door. It opened, and a blade hovered in her face. It retracted immediately, and Lord Ajerst bowed to her.

"Sorry, Highness. I had to be sure."

She swallowed once, eyes fixed on the scabbard. "Is Jayne all right?" He glanced back, and Kyra followed his eyes. Shattered glass, bloodstains on the floor. Jayne sat amongst the destruction, her expression vacant. "What happened?" Kyra breathed, but Jayne didn't reply, merely gazed at the wall. Kyra bit her lip and sat with her friend. "It will be all right," she whispered. She sat with her friend through the night. But there was a horrible disquiet within her.

Another knock at the door, and Lord Ajerst opened it quickly. Raylene stood there, her face now scrubbed clean of blood, and the harsh lines of her mouth deepened when she saw Kyra. "You need to come with me."

Kyra hesitated, then paced along, her gown swishing around her. They moved in silence, and as she realised where they were heading, she grew terribly cold. The Healing House. Raylene opened the door and ushered Kyra in. Monsun was there, standing tall, broad-shouldered, and guilty.

"Highness," he bowed. But Kyra had no words for him, not as her hand flew to her mouth at the sight on the table. Eli was spread out on it, naked from the waist up, covered in blood, a puncture wound in his belly. The Head Healer removed the last of his instruments and turned to drop them in a bucket. Vaguely, she caught the whiff of a sharp odour.

"What happened?" she breathed.

"He tried to kill Trayse," Raylene said behind him. "And he paid the price." *The price you demanded.*

Her heart stopped, her world flashing, fading—"Will he recover?" she asked the surgeon, hovering beside Eli.

The surgeon turned around, clad in white smeared with red. "I believe so."

"His wound hasn't healed," she breathed. "Why not?"

"I found a slight trace of poison in his wound," the surgeon confirmed. "I do not know what it is, but it may take some time to heal. His wound is similar to that of the Lady Eislyn and Queen Taera, but he seems to respond better. I think he will wake."

She turned to Monsun, the big man's fingers twitching at the hilt of the axe at his side. "Why didn't you tell me Trayse was in Imbra?" she said.

"Because Trayse is your weakness. If you knew, you would put yourself in danger." Truth. She sensed it like an aura around him. "I made a mistake." He glanced around at the Vindicators assembled, each looking at Eli with shame or grief or fury. "I seem to be making a few of those these days."

She breathed once. It all made sense now. "I have to go," she said. Raylene stared at her, an unspoken question, but she didn't answer, just ran. Ran all the way to the library, and to that brick at the back. Alethial. She breathed, letting her power fill her, then spoke in the High Language. It was a tongue that worked like many others. When you spoke it, sometimes you were completely unaware you were speaking it, if you were deep enough in your power. When she had summoned the snow leopard in the blizzard, Kyra could have screamed anything, but so deep in her power, it had become the High Language.

The rulers jealously guarded the High Language, and nobody had ever dared to translate it. But as she stared at the word, as she flared her magic, it shifted.

"Open," she breathed, and it slid open. Alethial. Leaving an unlit space behind, where she reached in, grabbed a leathery cover. She yanked it out, revealing a faded, torn book.

History of the Guardians. She flipped and scanned the text, written entirely in the High Language. As Kyra stared down the page, the scribbles formed words. The book described a Guardian's incredible healing ability. It referenced a specific herb which completely sapped the ability and blocked any healing. "Malmir." She'd never heard of it. She flipped the page again, but the rest of the text was empty, with only a single symbol etched on the last page—a simple depiction of a flame.

# Chapter 27

Light flared, and Eli groaned, a sharp pain stabbing in his stomach. *I failed.* His eyes fluttered open, and they landed on her, and a slow smile dawned on her face.

"You made it," she said, rising off her chair.

He didn't answer, glancing around the empty, stark room. The Healing House. He'd spent too much time here recently. *You couldn't even protect your sister.*

"I'm so sorry," she breathed. "What I said was terrible."

He bit his lip, holding it back. "You threw me out," he replied. "I said I was sorry, and I meant it. I should have told you about Trayse. I made that mistake, and I'm sorry for it." Hurt flashed in her eyes, hurt and guilt. "But then you said the most horrible thing to me."

She glanced down, tears in her eyes. "Never again," she said.

He was just tired of this sick feeling in his stomach. "But I don't think I deserve the high ground here," he said, expelling a lengthy breath.

"You didn't need to hunt Trayse," Kyra said, and reached out a hand. She retracted it immediately, and her fingers twitched at her side.

"I had to." He lay back against the pillow. "As long as he's alive, you'll never be safe. None of us will be safe." As another round of pain washed over him, he breathed in and out, forcing it to leave him. "Why—why can't I heal?"

"Malmir. It's a poison Trayse uses. You're lucky you're not unconscious. Maybe Trayse got the dosage wrong." He doubted it. Trayse didn't make mistakes like that. Kyra went on, keeping herself focused. "The Healer said you may carry that scar forever."

Another scar added to the torture on his chest. But he could no longer find the rage that had boiled within him hours ago. "Can you forgive me?" he asked.

Teary, she nodded. "Can you?" she replied. He closed his eyes and breathed deeply, letting go of the rage within him. The rage that had almost killed him. He reached out his arms, a silent plea. "You're still injured," she protested. He glanced down at his injury, at the wound freshly stitched up, leaving an angry red mark.

"I'll live." He smiled, and she rolled her eyes but clambered onto the bed beside him. The bed was too damn small, but he found he didn't care, not as her scent filled his senses and he drifted off again.

# Chapter 28

Weeks later, Eli fell back into the world onto Kyra's balcony, weapons tucked in their sheaths. Inside, candlelight still burned, and he rolled his eyes, letting out a weary sigh. The glass door slid open with barely a squeak, prompting the massive snow leopard to raise her fuzzy maw. Nix gazed at him with half-lidded eyes, then dropped her head back on the bed, now taking up all the room on the luxurious mattress.

He slid his gaze over to the desk and the source of the light. Kyra was slumped over scattered paper, still gripping the pen. She muttered something in her sleep. To see her in this way...

When he scratched the leopard's chin she purred contentedly, a deep rumble that coursed through the room. Metal chinked as his weapons unclasped from his belt, leaving him just clad in the Nightweave. It took some care, but eventually he plucked the stylus from Kyra's hand and hefted her in his arms. He lowered her onto the bed, clenching his teeth as the movement pulled on his still-healing wound. Nestham above, he missed his healing, blocked by that cursed Malmir. As he placed her on the mattress, her breathing quickened and bloodshot eyes fixed on him as he removed his boots.

"Did you find anything?" she said through a yawn.

"Nothing. I searched the entire slums tonight. Monsun organised for troops to search through the entire city. I've checked the tunnels, the Cathedral and the Order's spire. It's like Trayse has vanished off the face of the earth." The sky was lightening, dawn's rays sweeping in too soon. "You need to rest," he said. "This is the fourth night in a row you've fallen asleep at your desk." He glanced at the book on the Guardians still there, still waiting.

153

"It's also the fourth night in a row you've spent scouring the city," she shot back. "Besides, I need to get up soon, anyway." She glanced over at the book. "I'm sure there's something in there to help."

Malmir was a poison the Head Healer had never heard of, but it seemed to be lost to history. Finon and Trayse were fighting with knowledge on their side. He stalked over and surveyed the last pages, and a symbol leapt out at him, something he'd seen before, but couldn't place.

He sighed deeply, running his hands through his hair. "I should probably get ready as well. Monsun wants to test me again, make sure I'm fit to fight."

"You should rest," she parroted him. "Trayse—he shot you only a week ago."

"I'm fine," he said. "I can feel the Malmir working its way out of my system. Once it's gone, I'll heal fully." Doubt coloured her face. "Also, what happened to Eislyn has made it even harder." He tried to catch himself, but it was too late.

The pain was already flashing through her eyes. King Hadrian, Queen Taera and Lady Eislyn. Trayse was knocking off all the people closest to her, but not killing them. Why? And using Malmir to keep Eli from healing them...

He'd listened to some of Kyra's readings on Malmir. It kept the bodies alive, but constantly weak, never really regaining consciousness. And, of course, any healing magic he tried was utterly useless. She still gazed up at him from the bed, eyes bleary as he paced back and forth, but he dropped onto the mattress and pressed a kiss to her forehead.

The last week, they'd barely seen each other, their bond still recovering as well. It wasn't quite the same, but they were getting there. "How's Jayne holding up?" he breathed.

"She's still shaken," Kyra said. "Her father's trying to help, but she was almost killed. It might take her some time to recover." *She's not like us*, he could feel her saying.

"Trayse didn't try?"

"No. He was in the damn room, killed her guard, but then he just left."

Kyra's eyes moistened, but she narrowed them into a steely glare, the face of the woman who had walked through fire for her throne. The Regent of Leranion, breaking at the seams. Not broken. Not yet.

It crashed down on him then. *Every single thing* their enemies had done was aimed at her. Attacking her loved ones. Releasing a beast in the bowels of Imbra's castle. *All of it* had reduced the strong-willed woman he'd fallen for into a shell of herself, one he couldn't seem to restore.

Trayse could have killed him just by aiming for the heart, but that felt different. He'd sensed it, that Trayse had been toying with him.

*They want Kyra weak for when they take over.*

"What?" she asked, eyes darting over his face, his frozen expression.

"Finon is going to launch a coup."

Her face stilled, as she caught his meaning. "He wants the throne." She lurched off the bed and paced around the room, arms locked tight behind her back. "He started with the refugees. Then the Jinnam. But those were just practice. The Musadim won't oppose him. They're too scared now, and they're weak. The Wildborn are no more."

"And with your parents and your best friend out of the picture..." he trailed off. "We have to move on him. I can tell Monsun, we can just arrest him now."

"No," she said, that wicked cunning he relied on coming to the surface. "No. We proceed as planned."

"Finon and Trayse will keep picking us off," he said.

"The courts will need him to stand trial. If we kill him, we'd just make him a martyr. This isn't just about us and Finon. It's about whether the Order is right." Her eyes grew focused, and a part of him wanted to shout for joy. "Put a watch on our allies. Trayse is no match for a Marked or a Vindicator. Because when he makes his move, we'll be ready." She stood, a new woman, weary yet strong as steel.

"I promise you," he said, wrapping a hand around hers. "I will find Trayse, and I will make him pay for what he's done."

Ocean-blue eyes met his own. "Don't. You've done enough to find Trayse. When the time comes, we will take him. Together."

* * *

Eli fumbled with the keys on his belt and unlocked the Playground's door. It screeched open, and he smiled down at the Vindicator performing a kata with his battleaxe. Monsun didn't look at him as he moved, perfectly balanced, vicious and strong. His muscles rippled as he flipped the axe and brought it down in a final blow. It slammed into the wood with a hollow thud.

"Impressive," Eli said as he stopped at the edge of the ring. His smile died away when Monsun glanced at him. The Senior Vindicator's onyx eyes were hollow, and whiskers had appeared on his chin, his thick braid hanging limp from his head. "Sleepwalking again?" he said. He nodded, his face a shadow, baggy and drawn. "You've never told me what happens," Eli said.

Even shrugging seemed to take all the energy Monsun could muster. "Most nights I do not move. But when I do, and there is nobody stopping me, there's no telling where I go."

"Like the Citadel walls?"

"For that, I am very grateful." He smiled, a blush creeping across his face. He put his axe down and reached for a sword on the rack, rolling his wrist, flicking the blade with deadly ease. Eli did the same as he stepped into the ring, his sword gleaming. He started sparring with Monsun, neither of them really putting that much effort into it.

"I believe Alsair will return today," Monsun commented as his sword landed on Eli's. Eli shoved the blade to the side, stepping to his right.

"And?" he shot back.

"I would have thought you'd be happy to see him."

"I'll have a lot to tell him."

Monsun nodded and lashed out again, a ripping strike which would have cleaved Eli's head from his shoulders had he not dropped. "How's the wound?"

Aching, festering, threatening to tear—"I'll manage."

"If you pull your stitches, you will have more problems."

"I know, I know," he sidestepped a blow and riposted. His skin pulled, and he gritted his teeth, barely keeping the yell down.

"Well then. If you're ready for training, let us begin." Monsun raised a hand and the other Vindicators strode in, trained elegance and honed lethality.

Syl winked at Eli, her hands resting on the hilts of her dual sabres. Tomas and Raylene stopped, the former nodding, his arrows poking out from his shoulder. Raylene's deadly spear gleamed.

"What do you want me to do?"

"Defeat us," Monsun said. "No magic. Prove to me you are worthy of being a Vindicator." Eli smiled and flicked his sword. "Oh, but not here. Get into the maze on the far side. Leave the sword." Eli breathed deeply and headed into the maze, a series of wooden boards forming walls extending past his head. Monsun grinned at him as he pushed him in. "Find Syl and try not to lose."

Eli breathed deeply, already pressing himself to the wall. He moved on hunter's feet, all those years of silent-movement training coming back to him. Honed by Syl's own lessons, how to move through a city unseen and unhindered. He peered around the corner, waiting—just waiting for her to pop out. Syl was a master of stealth, far better than he could ever hope to be. He passed the next wall, turning right, glancing behind him. Nothing.

His heart hammered in his chest, so loud he feared she could hear him. His breathing stilled, as he moved barely a scrape along the stone floor, every sound echoing out. He turned left, noting the carving on the ancient flecked wood. Someone had spent too much time down here, evidently.

There. Just a breath. He waited, waited for her.

Stone scraped, and he moved, flinging an arm out and slamming her into the wall. Meaning to, at least. Syl's moon-white hair flickered as she ducked under his arm and punched low into his ribs. Pain flared, and he moved in closer, pulling her into an armlock. She grinned and tapped the wall. "Good job. Now get up onto the platform. I'll meet you there in a moment."

Eli hesitated, then did as she asked. A minute later, his knees clattered on the wooden platform, gazing at the rope stretching out before him. On the other side, Syl waited, her face a serene mask, clad in her Nightweave, a skin-tight suit barely modest enough for Leranion society. The maze was one thing, but this... "Remind me why I signed up for this?" he called across the gap.

"You wanted to be a Vindicator. This is how you do it."

He placed a foot on the rope. Earlier, with Kyra, it had felt so natural, so free. Now, it was like his legs refused to obey him. "I can't do this."

"This isn't like the Sanctum's bridge, Eli. Do it or you're finished."

He closed his eyes and steadied his breathing. *Picture something you want to see.* And suddenly, Syl was replaced with Kyra, facing him on the rope, staff swinging idly. "Go."

And so he stepped out on the tightrope and stretched his arms out. His magic flared, seeping into every fibre of his being, steadying him. His chest pushed forward, and he held his sword in front of him, reaching towards Syl's blade. He winked at her. Her jaw clenched, and he merely waited. Waited to let her make the first move.

"What's the goal here?" he said.

"Make me fall, and you win."

Eli glanced down at the floor beneath them. "By all means, jump."

She smiled and took a step forward, lashed out with her blade, careful not to put too much effort into it. Eli leaned back. The blade passed by with barely a whisper. He grinned at her, and she sliced again. But he'd learned from her lessons, and knocked it aside, careful not to put a full block in. He wouldn't use his magic for strength. She stumbled, recovered, then aimed a barrage of blows at him. He parried each one, as if his muscles took over, and he could see ten steps ahead.

He wouldn't land a hit on her today, not when she moved like this. He blocked her sword and skipped back, just out of reach. In a blur of motion, he swung downwards and slashed the rope in two, stretching out a hand and grabbing hold of the falling piece. The rope snapped taut and he swung in a wide arc, while Syl landed straight on the ground. "I'd say you fell," he called, the sound echoing in the chamber. Monsun smiled faintly off to the side.

"Creative," Syl said weakly.

When he faced Raylene, he met her spear, blurring, never once touching the roiling storm of power inside him. Raylene's eyes flared as she increased the tempo, but he matched it, and in a heartbeat, it was over, the flat of his blade resting on her side. Approval glimmered in her eyes, and she stepped back, prompting Tomas to draw an arrow from his quiver.

"Next test, Eli," Monsun clapped his hands. "Your bow is up on the obstacle course. Get to it, and don't get hit with an arrow." Monsun passed him a buckler, which he strapped onto his left arm. Tomas gave a rare smile, shifting.

Eli twisted, gazing up at the taller Vindicator. "He's not using real arrows, is he?" Monsun just grinned. "Is he?" he hissed, but his commander was already striding away. Syl, sitting swinging her legs on one of the many platforms, just grinned at him. Eli rolled his eyes. Mukk. Tomas drew his bow, and Eli hefted his arms, ready for the arrow. The bow thrummed, and Eli dodged, twisting to the side. And he was off, running to the obstacles, grabbing the coarse rope.

It was then he realised his mistake. He'd strapped the buckler to his left arm. Tomas was on his right. The arrow hissed, and he flung out an arm, and steel screamed on Nesthamir vambraces. Dammit, Monsun. He kept climbing, hand-over-hand. He sensed rather than saw Tomas fire again and jolted his body, flinging the rope out to the side. The arrow brushed past, merely a whisper of wind. Eli reached the platform. An arrow stuck to the wood above his head. He broke into a run, one eye on the Vindicator at the base of the ring. Ten arrows left.

Another buzzed to his side, and he snapped. Years of training drilled into him, blocking with his vambrace. It smashed to the side, but the steel deflected, severing the rope. He reached out a hand and grabbed ahold, yanking himself up, and he moved again, faster than ever without his magic. A hiss filled the air, and he ducked, letting it stream over his head.

His bow was so close now. He jumped off the platform, flying, rolling, until he was scooping up the bow, nocking an arrow and drawing it at Tomas. They hesitated, arrows pointed. A stalemate.

His arms ached from the heavy draw weight. And he thought he saw Tomas smile. Smile, as he twisted his aim. The arrow leapt from the bow, straight for—Syl. Eli swivelled and fired, already nocking another.

He didn't need to, as his arrow neatly intercepted Tomas', knocking it out of the air. Silence fell in the chamber. "Are you crazy?" he yelled. "What in the Five Hells was that?"

Tomas shrugged. "An outstanding shot. Now come down."

At last, he was left facing Monsun on the uneven ground. The warrior's axe was once again in his hand, and his muscles rippled as he gripped the polished haft. Eli's bones ached, but he refused to touch his magic. He stepped forth on the platforms and readied his stance. Monsun shrugged and waited.

And waited.

160

"You planning on starting?" But the warrior was silent. Eli grinned and knelt, keeping his opponent firmly in his sights. Monsun also knelt down, mirroring his position exactly. His breathing slowed, and though his magic wouldn't come out to play, it was part of him.

"Are you two going to fight anytime soon?" Raylene demanded, and Eli leapt up, sprang for Monsun, feet darting over the uneven ground. Monsun whirled and parried, sending Eli off balance. Eli jumped in again. His reach would be a problem.

But he recognised this move set. He jumped in, swaying from side-to-side, parrying where needed. There. Monsun lashed out with the overhand blow, and Eli swayed to the side, leapt in, and kicked the back of Monsun's knee. His sword rested on the Vindicator's neck in a heartbeat. He breathed out deeply, his chest heaving. And... and a sharp pain in his stomach. He glanced down and swore at the red pooling on his shirt.

"Get yourself to the infirmary," Monsun growled. "And when you're done, report to the Spire."

Hours later, his face still stung, and more than ever, he wished he had that damn healing magic. But when he surveyed himself in the mirror, his tattoo glimmered in the evening light. Not black, not silver. But two intertwined colours, weaving in and out as they arced back to his neck.

Gold and ice-blue.

# Chapter 29

Flames sparked and crackled over the pages, and the scent of charred parchment flooded the room as Monsun slammed the door shut. He flung his hood over his head, listening to the cheers in the Citadel. Apparently, it was the birthday of a minor city official. The briefing had crossed his desk, but he'd passed it off to the Imbran Guard.

He stalked into the slums, hand resting on the hilt of his knife. Had he drawn it, the blade's glittering runes would be unrecognisable in Leranion. Nor would its design ever be seen in this nation. Every little sound made him spin, ready to unleash hell. The slums were deadly, but if his hood slipped for one second, if his Vindicator's tattoo ever saw light... he might never wake.

As he passed a nondescript alley, he dropped and pretended to adjust his boot. There. Three miniscule lines etched on the tile. To anyone else, it would just be a scratch. To him, to any Biralam spy, it was much more. The bricks were cool against his back as he scanned the rest of the alley.

The spy was talented, and he dropped from the rooftops, landing with barely a sound. Monsun whirled, his forearm pinning the man to the wall. Flesh crunched on stone, and he stared into the operative's scarred face, the beard the only part of him not cloaked in shadow.

"You were supposed to contact me earlier," Monsun said.

"Save it, Al-Iman," the figure snapped. "Have you found the Heir?"

Monsun shoved him away into the wall. "No. You know I haven't. If I had found the Heir, I would have returned home." He glared down at the smaller man, now clutching a dangerous-looking pair of knives, the blades gleaming in the moonlight. "It has been years since my exile. Why is the King so urgent now?"

The man snarled at him from underneath the hood. "Events are in motion which will change history. The Eternal Order's attacks trouble Amaldas and the Elder. She has heard the pleas from our Leranion chapters. We expect you to protect all branches of the Musadim in this hellish country."

Monsun raised a brow, just waiting for a threat to reveal itself. "The Musadim should protect themselves. Your vow of non-violence was a mistake."

"It is the Crown's duty to regulate the balance between the creeds, and you have failed. The Musadim were as brothers to the Jinnam and you let the Eternal Order wipe them out!"

Anger kindled within Monsun, and he took a step closer, relishing the way the smaller man twitched though he would have liked to think he had the upper hand. "You don't get to accuse my King or my Regent of that. Not when the Musadim stood aside and let the Order destroy the Wildborn centuries ago."

"Be glad we did so. The Wildborn were fanatics," the operative said. Fanatics, and yet a necessary part. Was there still balance without the Wildborn?

"But you let the reds get a taste of power," Monsun said. "And once the Order got a taste, they kept coming." He didn't dare move. Not when those knives glinted in the moonlight. A figure scurried past, and he froze, waiting for them to move on.

When the footsteps had faded away, the spy spoke again. "The Wildborn needed to burn. Heretics, to claim they could see the future. On this, we and the Order agreed."

Monsun didn't let the amusement cross his face. "And the Guardian? Was Guardian Shiva a fanatic? The first Biralam Vindicator, and you let the Order kill her." The man hesitated, and Monsun knew he'd won. "Prepare for the return of the fanatics. The Guardian is alive, and he is ready to stand against anyone who threatens this world."

"The Guardian lives?" A small, shaky whisper, like he'd seen a ghost.

"Unless the Elder wishes to see Ekra covered in shadow, she must support the Guardian." Monsun met the man's eyes and threw all his conviction into his voice. "I have seen what he can do. He is a warrior, ready to fight with or without magic. He's already faced Temero once, and he is preparing to do so again."

"The Guardian was destroyed. She was wiped from memory hundreds of years ago. The Mark of the Guardian is no more."

"You can't destroy what is free," Monsun said. A free Mark, not passed down by bloodline, but by a command, and by Nestham's will.

"His Excellency has conferred with the Elder," the operative said, angling his blade up. "The Heir must be found for Ekra to survive. Temero is coming."

"Temero is already here," Monsun retorted. "Biralam must prepare its army."

"We have prepared for the demon's return. Biralam is ready. But we will only move once the Heir returns."

"You selfish fool," he hissed. "You cannot wait for the Heir. They could be dead! The line of Amerin broke long ago." Broken in the civil war that had ripped the nation apart so brutally it was no longer a nation. Just the Plains, just villages under their own rule, protected either side of the Thornwood by Fallkirk or Stallor.

"You'd best hope he isn't. Because otherwise you'll have failed."

"You have other operatives. Use them." He turned away, swinging his cloak behind him. "I want no part of Biralam anymore."

He took one step, but the voice spoke again, in a chilling rasp. "Oh, Monsun. You can't just walk away now." And that rasp sounded so like Athsin that he froze.

"I have nothing left in Amaldas," he said, not daring to move.

"Nothing? What about your family? Your father? Your mother? Your brother?" Monsun didn't speak. "Your charge can barely walk, ever since you destroyed your life."

"That wasn't my fault. Athsin brought the destruction. Not me." The scar on his hip seemed to burn, and he touched it on reflex.

"You were his commander." A smiling face, young and earnest. Popular with the men. His head had rolled regardless.

"Don't tell me what I live every night."

"His family vanished soon after you killed him." Names, faces he'd tried to forget, but the blows kept coming. "Your family has expunged you. Monsun Al-Iman does not exist." The operative shrugged, a horrible, futile gesture. "But it matters not. The Al-Iman name has been cursed ever since your failure in Amaldas."

"If my family has expunged me, then I see no reason to return. If His Excellency wishes to destroy his kingdom, then let him. The kingdoms will fall one by one unless you stand together."

"Then find the Heir. Or your brother will suffer the same fate as your charge."

Monsun's breath clutched in his throat. Long seconds passed until at last he spoke. "I've received valuable information. I will bring the Heir before His Excellency. As promised." His hands trembled, and he shoved them in his pockets. "Why is finding the Heir so important?"

"That is not for you to question. You took an oath to serve Biralam."

"I also swore to serve Leranion. And only one kingdom has not betrayed me."

The man snarled, and took a few paces, then glanced over his shoulder. "You have three months to find the Heir. Or your family will suffer the same fate as your former charge."

# Chapter 30

Eli and Kyra took dinner in a quiet room overlooking the city, and as they ate in silence, he couldn't stop looking at her blank gaze. It had been half an hour since they'd returned from the Healing House, and she hadn't spoken a word.

But then the door squeaked open and a warm, elderly chuckle reverberated through the room. Warmth spread through Eli, and his chair rocketed back. He enveloped the monk in his arms, and Alsair's good arm thumped him on the back. "When did you return?"

Alsair beamed back as they separated. "Oh, about an hour ago."

Eli grinned and glanced over at Kyra, but his gut twisted at her steely expression. And when Eli looked back at the monk, that face had a story of life and pain etched on it. Jade eyes, once keen and gleaming with intelligence, now were dull, weary with shadows. And as Eli stepped away, the monk staggered, as if his age had caught up to him. Once, a man with the strength of a lifetime of soldiering, who had sparred with warriors and Guardians alike and always been one step ahead. Now, he was just a tired old man, bowed beneath the weight of his years.

A wan smile flickered on Kyra's face. "I'll leave you two to catch up." Eli opened his mouth to protest, but she shook her head, still maintaining that court-trained smile. As she passed them, she brushed her hand against Eli's, and he sucked in a breath.

"My room, later." Heat rushed to his cheeks, and she grinned.

"I'm yours to command, Highness," he purred. She quickly exited the room, leaving the two men behind. "Alsair, what happened?" Eli asked.

The monk snapped his gaze to him, shadows dancing in vivid green eyes. But as Eli gestured to a seat, Alsair glided his way to the royal chair. He slumped into the seat and reached for the untouched pitcher. An unhealthy amount of wine stained his beard. Eli frowned, eyes straining to see more, more than what was occurring.

"Alsair," he hissed.

Alsair dropped the cup and turned to him. "I thought I would spend a peaceful time out of Imbra," Alsair said, a far-seeing look in his eyes. "I needed some time to recover after what happened in the North. So I went south, a few days past the Kinar River."

"You were missed. We could have used you back here in Imbra." He glanced at the door. "So much has happened since you left."

"Tell me everything," Alsair said.

So he did. When he finished, Alsair leaned back thoughtfully, a manner of his peaceful intelligence returning.

"Malmir," he murmured to himself. "My, my. Malmir and mantiks, you have had quite the adventure here in Imbra." He leaned forward with a smile, resting his stump of a left arm on his leg. When he did, Eli flicked a glance. It seemed grey, lifeless.

"These past few weeks have been nothing but blundering from one slaughter to another. If you would call it an adventure, you're even crazier than I thought," Eli said. He let the wrath bleed into his eyes, the strength and magic he kept locked up.

Alsair's bushy beard shifted as he smiled. "Look at you," he said. "A Guardian, a Vindicator and a Healer. I'm proud of you." Eli's hand fell to his armlet on instinct, but the monk caught that too, and Alsair's smile widened as his eyes traced the beautiful metal. He let out an exaggerated yawn, stretching one hand to the roof.

"I think I need to get some rest," he murmured. "And it sounds like you do too." He waggled his brows and slunk out of the chair, grabbing the wine on his way out.

* * *

167

The leopard let out a rumbling purr as Eli rubbed Nix under her chin. The creature now took up all the double bed, longer than he was tall. She'd been growing faster by the day. Whatever magic connected her to Kyra seemed to increase her size and strength.

"You can't stay on the bed much longer," he murmured to her.

"Well, she got there first, so I guess you're on the floor tonight." Kyra cracked a wicked smile, her eyes dancing with a light he hadn't seen in a while. Nestham above, even with Alsair's condition, he was grateful for that light, brighter than the Mark that glowed on her hand.

"How did your meeting at the Guild go?" he asked. "We never had time to talk at dinner."

"Well." She let her smirk grow, even knowing how much it stirred him. "Yuras did not enjoy having me there one bit. But he had to put up with me, particularly with Raylene growling every time he moved." She shifted, that beautiful evening gown twisting with every move. "He wouldn't tell me what they were up to, but I spoke to Raylene and she noted the same thing. There's a Vault underneath the Guild Hall. If there is an operation making Nestham's Will, then I'd bet that's where they have their supply." For a moment, she was almost downcast. "The Guild has always been making wonderful inventions. They've always made Imbra better." Her gaze refocused, and that smirk came back. "But I wasn't there just to talk to the Guild," she said. He frowned, but she was smoothing down that gown, then assuming the picture of royalty. "Wait here," she ordered, and then skipped off to the wardrobe. Actually *skipped* away. He trembled, refusing to show how close he'd come to doing something stupid.

"The line," he murmured. "The damn line." He sucked in a breath and settled down in the armchair, his Vindicator's uniform creased. She emerged minutes later in a black suit. It fit her body perfectly, snug yet modest. He raised a brow, not

168

daring to move. "When... when did you order a Nightweave suit?" he gritted out.

"This morning," she said with a smile. "You Vindicators get to fight in this all the time?"

He matched her grin, running his hands along the fabric. "Fun, isn't it? What did you have in mind?"

"Gear up and you'll find out."

Ten minutes later, he grinned at her, fully clad in his Nightweave, wearing his sword and a couple of decent knives. His bow he'd left in his chambers. Despite the longing to bring his favourite weapon along, the mission he expected would not be suited to such a clumsy weapon in close quarters. The last item he carried was a blanket strapped to his back.

They crept through the tunnels, finding the one that led all the way back to the grotto underneath the Citadel's walls, just to where the waterfall fell over the cliffs of the palace. A little canoe bobbed where he'd left it tied up, and he silently propelled them to the upper merchant's area, where she'd requested. He tied up the boat as they donned their hoods and gloves, and he reached a hand to help her up.

"Now I can't see your tattoo," she complained. He glanced at her, knowing his expression was pointless underneath the thick hood.

"You like it?" His breath hitched.

"I love it," she purred. He tensed, but stretched out a hand, and together they Rifted to the nearby roof, a short jump of a few metres. Barely enough to matter at this point. His magic writhed, fully replenished. Though his healing magic dwarfed his fire, with it still smothered by the lingering effects of the Malmir, he doubted he'd be able to access it. The wound still ached under his shirt.

They crouched on the sloping roof as footsteps tromped past. Not a march, but more a gaggle of ducks. Eli frowned underneath his hood. Not even the undisciplined Imbran Guard moved like that. Yet as he peeked over the roof, he glimpsed a new set of armour. And the sigil of Treasurer Rumpre

169

emblazoned on it as three men weaved in and out of the lantern's light.

"We've got some work to do," he murmured and pointed.

"What's Rumpre doing in these parts?" Kyra wondered out loud. Eli didn't answer as the men continued past, talking amongst themselves. Not a patrol, then. No way would they be so lousy otherwise. Two wraiths followed the men over the rooftops, until at last they stopped. One sat down, removing his helmet to reveal thinning blonde hair on a sweaty, ruddy face. He breathed heavily, a wheeze that sounded poor even for Treasurer Rumpre.

"I want to find out what's going on here," Eli said. "Do we have time?" She hesitated, but nodded, and he produced the blanket he'd been holding just for this moment. He threw it over them, smiling as it drew memories of a chilly night overlooking a northern crevasse.

"We'll be here for a while. May as well get comfortable."

"So this is what you do every night," she murmured. "Napping without me."

"Hardly. Spying is more boring than you'd think," he shot back, still keeping his voice below a whisper. The roof was flat, and they leaned against the wall, backs in the shadows, trusting the men to alert them with their constant chatter. Eli glanced up at the moon glimmering brightly, the full body of Nestham's light shining on them, and noted its gradual movements, until footsteps paced along the path. The chatter died away, and Eli went to nudge Kyra, but she was already moving forward on her belly, eyes peering over the edge of the roof.

A slim man strode into view, gliding smoothly in a way that seemed to draw no attention, yet was utterly familiar. He wore dark yet expensive clothes, and a small pack lay on his back.

"For heaven's sake," Eli said. "I know that man. He was one of Vera's men."

"Do you think Vera is alive?"

"No. No, she wouldn't have made it out of there alive. Nestham above, that chemical—it blew the entire place sky high." He reached towards the armlet again and twisted it. Twisted it again.

They started talking, and he flared his magic, the words becoming clear. But the conversation didn't need to be followed with words. Not as one man tossed the bag at his belt to Vera's lackey, the contents chinking. The lackey caught it in one slender hand, and reached into his own bag, handing over several bricks of Void.

"I spared you, and that's the thanks I get," Eli said. He glanced up to Kyra, and found her kneeling, surveying the four men below. He could sense the coiled strength curled up inside her, ready to spring, seeing it in the muscles tensing beneath the Nightweave.

"No weapons," he breathed. She nodded and fell into the open air. He did so a split second later, plummeting onto Vera's man and bringing him down with a thud. "Good to see you again." As Eli glanced up, his eyes widened at the clash before him. There were three of them, so Kyra had them seriously outnumbered.

She didn't even bother to use her magic, not as she ducked a clumsy swipe and lashed out with a punch to his belly, right beneath the half-armour. While he reeled, she snapped out with a kick to the throat, then rolled, sweeping another's legs out. She followed by knocking them unconscious. The fight took less than five seconds. Eli snatched up the bag of Void and found Kyra rummaging in their pockets.

"Let's see if there's anything good here," she murmured. One after the other, she checked their pockets. "Nothing." She glanced back at him. "Rift us back up, please." They landed with a flash of light. "This is getting worse. Rumpre buying Void from Vera's men?"

"Who knows what he's been doing," Eli said. "But it makes things more complicated."

171

She nodded and chewed her lip. "All right, let's get out of here."

"Any more gruntahs?" a young voice piped up. Eli whirled, Mark flaring under his gloves, but he lost his voice at the sight that awaited him.

"What on earth are you doing, Amora?" Kyra asked, horror on her face.

From her perch on the rooftop, the girl shrugged with all her impetuousness and bravery. "Followed you. You still can't move good."

"Why did you follow us?" Eli bit out, anger—and fear—coursing through him. Not anger at her, but—she'd already placed herself in too much danger.

Kyra seemed to be thinking along the same lines. "This isn't safe for you, Amora. Go back to your chambers. We'll come back soon."

"No," the girl said defiantly, narrowing night-black eyes. "I can help."

"Maybe she can," Eli said slowly, turning to the princess. Ocean-blue eyes, the only thing he could see under the hood, flashed at him. He shrugged, then knelt to Amora. "Here." He unsheathed a knife and passed it to her.

"I've got one," she withdrew an ancient knife from a sheath at her hip. Belatedly, he realised she was wearing street clothes already. Nestham above, she'd been waiting for this.

He grinned despite himself and ruffled her short hair. "Fine. Follow us, but when we get there, you stay as a lookout. Alright?"

She beamed, and together they turned to Kyra. But the young woman was already shaking her head, letting out a defeated sigh. "You two are dangerous." But Eli could hear the smile in her voice, and he led the way across the rooftops. Any worries he might have had about Amora's ability to keep up with them were quickly dashed, and soon they found themselves outside the magnificent stone building soaring into the sky, the centre of the merchant's quarter. No less than seven Imbran guards waited out the front of the Guild's hall, all facing the street.

The three crouched together, Eli surveying the building. "I'd rather not storm the place by force," he breathed. "Imbran troops are usually friendly enough. All the other entrances are guarded, aren't they?"

Amora nodded, and he sighed, but Kyra tapped his foot. "You once told me you don't need to see a place to Rift us there," she said.

"Maybe," he frowned. "But the Rift is strange. The more I practise with it, the more it changes. Seeing it is best, but if I get a good enough picture of it in my mind, if I can hold that image, I might be able to take us there if I'm in range." He amended it. "If I'm not, we'll just pop out into thin air."

"And fall to our deaths," Kyra finished.

"You wouldn't die," Amora said. "Falling off this building only crippled Rik. They had to drag him away." Kyra drew the girl closer for a brief moment, and Eli continued.

"Carrying people into the Rift drains me faster. I should be able to do it, but we might need to think about another way of getting out. Anyway, do you have a way in?"

They paused, Amora hanging onto every word, as the princess laughed softly and nudged the youngster. "How would you get in, Amora?"

"I'd pop through that window there." A small, dirtied finger pointed to the east wall, about halfway up. A window open just a small crack, gentle candlelight on the walls.

He sucked in a breath. "I should be able to. Describe the room for me?"

"It's wooden, with four walls," Kyra faltered.

"That's more than I had in the slums," Amora added.

"And it's most likely half the rooms in that building," Eli said. "Anything else?" He grinned, but he could sense her stillness, her battle concentration.

At last, Kyra spoke again, her voice slow and clear. "There's a blue vase resting on a side table. It's full of flowers. Roses." She smiled. "You should get me some."

"Take a note of that, Amora," Eli said over his shoulder. "The princess likes roses. What are we aiming for?"

For a moment, Kyra wavered, then she lifted her chin and looked like a queen of old. "I want Nestham's Will. I want whatever we can find in there linking Yuras to Finon, and I want whatever other secrets we can find."

"We could do that as Regent and Vindicator," he said. "Then we'd have Monsun's support, and we could just storm the place."

"Regent Kyra has to appear clean. Regent Kyra can't really order the Guild Chief around." She gestured to herself. "But the Ghost can break into the Guild's base and do whatever she likes."

"The Ghost? You're bringing that title out of the cellar?"

She nodded, and he turned to Amora. "Now," he tapped the young girl's shoulder as she squared herself and looked at him like she was about to rob the world blind. "Stay here. Keep out of sight, and for Nestham's sake don't follow us in." He sucked in a breath, Kyra grabbed his shoulder and he clashed his vambraces together in a flash of light. The roaring blackness consumed Eli and Kyra, and for the first time, he didn't sprint headlong into the dark. He drifted, fixing that image in his head.

The blue vase. Roses.

He was about to let them back out of the Rift, back into the world, but at the last second, he whipped his head around, his skin prickling. They weren't alone in the Rift. Eli pulled them back out into colour and sound, and he gasped for breath, drained from the extended time in the Rift. He slumped against the wall, his breath a shallow rasp. He waved Kyra off when she tried to approach. "I—I'll be fine, I just need a moment."

She marched to the door, listened closely. "Nobody. Let's go."

174

They crept along the passageways, alongside the ancient art littering the walls. Beautiful landscapes mixed with imperious people staring at Eli down their noses. He rolled his eyes and gestured to Kyra.

"How much further?" he breathed.

"Just to the end of the corridor."

He kept pace with her, and eventually they reached the end—and found themselves blocked by a steel wall. "Someone's got a lot of stuff to hide," he said.

"All the more reason to find it."

Footsteps echoed behind them, and a guard's voice rang out. "*Intruders!*"

Eli turned and rushed the guard, quickly knocked him cold. He patted down the man's belt, fumbled for the keys and tried them in the lock. Steel jangled as at last the door slid open and they rushed inside. The room was gloomy, poorly lit, and they descended endless stairs. After what felt like hours, they found the base of the chamber. That acrid stench filled his senses, and he retched. Two small barrels lay on a table and he hefted them under his arms, before turning to Kyra.

But the Regent was picking her way along the tables of treasures, weapons and armour. Her hand fell upon a miniature device, intricately carved. A crossbow, but designed for one hand. Beside it, a small bag of lethal-looking darts. She swept both up and turned to Eli.

"Let's get out of here." With barrels under his arms, it left him unable to fight, so Kyra took point and rushed ahead back up the stairs and down the passages. His breath rasped in his ears, the magic slowly eating him up, begging to be let out. The feeling faded in his fingers, and his light flickered under his glove.

Kyra ducked back to him, swearing quietly. "There's twenty soldiers out there. Can you Rift?"

He frantically scanned the room, and his gaze rested on the small table in the corner, then the window. Perfect. The barrels gingerly settled down on the carpet. "No. But there is another option." Senses roaring, strength limitless, the table flew through the air, straight through the window. Glass shattered, and he picked up the barrels and hurled himself into the night. He thudded into the grass, the breath knocked out of him, and lay there for a long moment, pain blossoming all over his body.Kyra rolled and stood to her feet, extending her hand.

They shuffled into the welcoming embrace of the shadows. His blood pounded in his ears as they crept along the streets, barrels under each arm. At last, they halted and pressed themselves against the wall. Kyra yanked off her mask, hair tousled and her cheeks flushed. They should have been running, but she gave him one look and he was trapped. Agonisingly slowly, he placed the barrels on the stone. Her lips quirked as he slid a hand around her waist, cupped the back of her neck and drew her to him, closer, closer...

"Actor. Gruntah. You done?" Amora whispered from above. Eli sighed quietly and glanced at the figure hanging upside down from the roof, a bunch of vibrant roses in her hand, the thorns helpfully removed. She tossed them to Kyra with a beautiful smile.

"Come here," Kyra grinned and yanked the urchin into the hug, ignoring the shouts in the night. "Let's not tell Monsun what happened," she said. "Want to sleep in my room tonight?"

# Chapter 31

The bells pealed in the city, and Kyra lurched up from her bed, jolting awake. *Invasion!* Golden light flared, the world sharpening.

But—but that wasn't the attack bell. No, it was something different. Almost like—a welcoming? Regardless, she rushed to put on something suitable for combat. Not the Nightweave, that wouldn't be best. She donned a light tunic, suitable for under her armour, and spun to the other side of the wardrobe. The humongous leopard leapt off the bed, landed with a thud that set the floor shaking. Kyra reached for a polished set of armour, but the door swung open, Jayne bursting in, dark circles under her eyes. Her face was pale, set with taut anticipation. Kyra opened her mouth. Though it had been weeks, Jayne was still regaining her strength. Eyes of night swept up and down in an assessing gaze, and she shook her head.

"That won't do. You need something much more formal."

"Why?"

"Just get the white-and-gold gown," Jayne said.

Kyra almost shot her a glare, but trusted her judgement. She always had. The gown wrapped around her and highlighted her athletic figure. As she sat at the table to her right, sweeping a dash of liner on her eyes, Jayne twisted her hair up, and passed her the circlet. Kyra surveyed herself in the mirror. A queen stared back, ready for whatever awaited her.

"So, why am I dressed up nicely?"

"Look outside."

Kyra strode to the balcony and gasped as she gazed out at the city, her power mirrored in the Eternal Flames on the walls. But beyond those walls...

The flow of the Kinar River split at the edge of the city. Tributaries flowed through the slums, but the mighty course of water flowed to the docks, deep enough to bring a warship through. Imbra's small dock was dwarfed by the monstrosity moored there. A double-masted ship, displaying an eagle on a sea-green banner.

"Why the mukk is a Valmor ship in our harbour? And why did we not receive any word from Prian?" The town on the edge of the coast, the fort that controlled the Kinar River. "How did we let a foreign ship right into the heart of our kingdom?"

"Word arrived this morning," Jayne replied. "Apparently, the messenger claims one man waylaid him, tied him to a tree, brewed him tea and released him a day later."

Kyra frowned, but kept staring at that damn ship.

A Sea-King had arrived in Leranion. Maybe even one of their Marked. She'd heard many things of the Sea-Kings, the only real naval power in Ekra. Tales of pirates and monsters in those southern seas around Biralam and Valmor.

"Well," she said under her breath. "This just got much more complicated. Can we kick them out?"

"You can," Jayne said, "but that would be a terrible idea. We—we need allies."

"True. But I'm not sure how far I want to go to make them," Kyra said, dread pooling in her gut. An unmarried Regent was a dangerous thing. Any nation could ask for an alliance—with her hand as the asking price. She would do anything to defeat Temero. But she'd been imprisoned once before.

"Amica, protocol requires that you acknowledge their request. As Regent of Imbra, only you can give them permission to come ashore." Still, the Lady was watching her back.

"Then why were you rushing me? This is diplomacy, not some barn dance. They can stay on that tub for as long as I want."

"Kyra, they arrived at dawn. They've been there for three hours."

"Five Hells." There was subtly reminding a visitor of who was in power, and then there was just plain rudeness. "Fine,

I'll hear what they have to say. Send for my carriage, an escort of soldiers, and Vindicator Monsun please."

She expected her friend to grin and leave, but the willowy girl just shrugged. "They're waiting for you by the palace entrance."

Kyra grimaced and dropped her head. "Honestly, why do people find no joy in sleeping in? Even Eli hates it. He's always gone before dawn." She glanced up, clamping her lips together, but Jayne just laughed softly. It transformed her, from harsh and maybe a little severe, into a genuine beauty whom some men would sell their lives to claim.

"Better you don't speak of that out loud. But I have to say, that armlet looks good on him." Kyra flushed a little, and the Lady rolled her eyes. "Try not to blush in front of the Valmor envoy. Whoever the mukk they are."

"I'll do my best." Kyra exhaled softly and reached for the staff. Again, it faded into her hand. Instead of moving, she tossed the weapon onto the bed.

"What are you doing?" Jayne asked. Kyra didn't answer, and instead stared at her staff, and stretched out her hand. It faded into thin air, and reappeared in her hand, solid as always.

"Useful," Jayne deadpanned.

Kyra grinned, and strode from the room, looking nothing other than the warrior-Regent she was, no matter what the Musadim said. She was the commander of Vindicators. She'd faced a demon. She'd fought alongside a Guardian reborn, and was the first person to wield all of Leranion's gifts since Queen Eshe. Nix slunk along at her side, tail lashing back and forth.

"I doubt she'll fit in your carriage," Jayne said.

"Then we'll need a bigger carriage. Or make Monsun walk."

"You could just let her run outside." Jayne rolled her eyes, clasping her hands behind her back.

"Truth be told, she needs the exercise. They're feeding you too much, Nix." She mussed the leopard's silken fur. Nix

179

rumbled, but twisted her head from side to side, scenting the air. The natural predator exactly where she was supposed to be. At last, they arrived at the entrance. Six soldiers snapped to attention, their royal-blue-and-white uniforms clean and well-pressed, blades at their sides.

Monsun swept into a graceful bow, his Vindicator's uniform and cape as sharp as always, as was the axe gleaming over his shoulder.

"Your Highness." She accepted the proffered hand and climbed into the carriage, Nix squeezing in with her. Monsun somehow squeezed his bulk in across from her. Jayne curtsied and walked back into the castle, her green skirt perfectly straight, the board holding her papers in her hand neatly tucked under her arm.

She turned to Monsun as the carriage clattered into motion. "Do we know who the envoy is?" she asked.

A wealth of emotions clashed on his face, his tattoo shifting as he grimaced. "It's Prince Jalek." At that name, she groaned quietly. Jalek Veturan's reputation preceded him. A notorious warrior and womaniser, he'd fought his way around Ekra and the waters surrounding Valmor, even coming close to Renegade Haven. Monsun handed over a piece of paper to her. "Here's everything that Jayne organised on him."

"Jayne knew? She didn't tell me."

"I believe her words were, 'this is your problem. I have to get her out of bed.'"

Kyra grinned as she perused the document, her teeth worrying at her lip. Once she finished, she mindlessly tapped the parchment against her cheek. "So, Raylene's served with him."

He gave her a terse nod, every inch the warrior. "About two years ago. I sent her to Valmor on an assignment to learn from their warriors." He shrugged. "It's something I have tried in my time here. After all, all of my training was in Amaldas." Kyra raised her brows appreciatively as he continued. Jayne had included Raylene's notes in the report, but it was worth listening to, anyway. "Raylene was on his ship as they tracked down a Renegade fleet coming back from across the sea. He's a hell of a warrior. And, apparently, quite the charmer with the ladies."

"Spectacular. I can't wait to see for myself." This was not what she needed.

At last, the carriage clattered along the road to the river docks. Jalek's ship had pulled up in prime position. It was a magnificent thing, double-masted and heavily gilded.

"It'll be fast," Monsun said. She raised a brow at him, and the Vindicator shrugged. "When Raylene returned from assignment, I had her tell me what she knew about the ships she worked with. I also read whatever I could in the library." He grinned, and it transformed him. "They always fascinated me. This one is a warship, and we have no heavy weapons. If there is a fight, we might struggle."

"We should have brought Raylene along for diplomacy," Kyra said. "If she knows Prince Jalek, it would be handy to smooth things over."

"Even if Raylene knows Jalek, *Raylene* and *diplomacy* should never be uttered in the same sentence," Monsun said. "But it would have been useful. She is on patrol at the moment, and Syl and Eli are co-ordinating some crackdowns in the upper quarter. Several of Treasurer Rumpre's men were found dead last night. The Veils are working on it." He shot a glance at her. "Have you seen Hyrin recently?"

"Hyrin? No, but that's usual. He'll be hiding in the shadows, I'm sure." She blanched, nails pricking the inside of her palm. *Rumpre's men, dead?*

Kyra's carriage lurched to a halt at the docklands, the gentle lapping of waves filling the air. She inhaled the scent of the river, the taverns along the edge of the wharf. Beyond the city walls, the water flowed swiftly, and she had another chance to glance out the carriage windows at the massive warship. Monsun opened the door, ducked under the compact frame, and climbed out, Nix slinking after him. Kyra smoothed down her dress and followed the Vindicator and leopard onto the street, tapping her staff on the cobblestones. A crowd gathered, men and women in stained jerkins, the workers on the docks likely seeing the Regent for the first time. She acknowledged them with a smile and turned her gaze to the ship as her guard assumed defensive positions around her. The ship bobbed up and down, but was completely silent. Kyra raised a brow.

"Ahoy the ship!" Monsun bellowed, a sound which thrummed through her, causing her to flinch slightly. She flicked a glance at him and had the sight of giant shoulders shrugging. "I hear that is how they say it on the docks. I would not know."

"Ahoy below!" the call returned, a youthful voice ringing with strength. Monsun grinned at her, and she sighed quietly. The Vindicator bounced with a new enthusiasm as the unfamiliar voice spoke again. "Do we have permission to come ashore?"

"I guess." She shrugged, and Monsun seemed to take that as encouragement. Either that or all the sailor-speak was going to his head, because now he was doing his best heraldic impression.

"By authority of Regent Kyra Antarun of Leranion, you may come ashore!" he yelled.

Silence. And finally, someone on the ship dared appear. One figure stepped up to the gunwale, leaned on it nonchalantly. Tall, olive-skinned, lithe, hair that swept in the wind whipping around the dock. He glanced down and flashed a grin edged with earned arrogance.

Kyra fought the shiver that swept over her. "Here we go," she breathed. The figure leapt over the railing and executed a perfect flip. He was all controlled power as he landed on perfectly balanced feet, his right hand on the hilt of a gleaming rapier. His left glowed sea-green, a power she could almost feel running through him. *Nestham above.*

The young man blew the hair out of his eyes. "Greetings, Highness," the Prince said.

"Prince Jalek," Kyra said. "You have come a long way without warning."

"But your Highness, it was you who sent for us," Jalek said, his groomed brows flicking down. Monsun shifted beside her, but he said nothing. Jalek flicked his gaze to the massive Vindicator and his eyes widened for a split second, but he glanced back to the ship. "It seems my men will take some time to come ashore."

"Unlike you," Kyra shot back. "Does using a plank bore you, Prince?"

"Exactly! I see someone understands." He grinned. "My apologies, Princess— Regent, I am puzzled. Did you not send for Valmor's aid?"

"I did," she said, fighting to keep control of the situation. "I was not expecting you to arrive so quickly."

"The *Tempest's Wrath* is the fastest in the Casalis fleet," Jalek boasted. "We could not have arrived any sooner. I doubt any of Leranion's ships could have matched this speed. Valmor's armada is unmatched in all of Ekra."

"Except for the Renegades," Kyra replied. Heat crossed Jalek's face, and his eyes flashed, but he kept that bland smile.

"The Renegades are running scared thanks to our fleet. They have retreated to their Haven like rats. These waters are safe once again."

"Wonderful," Kyra said. "I feel safer already." Jalek blinked twice, but she continued as if she'd never insulted him. "Bring your retinue ashore. You and your courtiers will be granted rooms in the palace for the time being."

She made to turn away, but Jalek spoke quietly. "Highness." She turned back, and his lips were thin. "I have no courtiers. My only companions are my men. I request that they be given lodgings."

Kyra's appreciation for the Prince grew. Bold and arrogant as he was, she could respect that. "We'll treat them even better than courtiers, Prince. If any wish to stay aboard the ship, that is fine. They have permission to organise a carriage to the Citadel."

Jalek's smile was as flawless as usual, displaying every one of his perfect teeth. "Thank you, Highness."

"You may attend court this afternoon," Kyra said, before turning curtly and striding off, leaving the Prince of the Sea alone on the docks. As soon as she was alone with Monsun, she looked him dead in the eyes. "Someone invited Veturan here in my name," she said. "And we need to know why."

# Chapter 31

Kyra's knuckles whitened on her staff as she returned from the Healing House. If Trayse crossed her path, if anyone crossed her path...

"Highness." Syl strode up to her, light on her feet as ever. The pristine Vindicator's uniform looked good on her, but it clashed with the hollowness in her eyes. "I got this from one of the Prince's men," she said, extending a slip of paper.

"How?" Kyra asked idly, eyes on the proffered letter.

"I have my ways." Syl grinned, flicking her white hair over her shoulder. "I needed something to do after Eli and I returned from the investigation." Anger flashed over her face for a heartbeat.

"Any progress with that?"

"Nothing. We passed it over to the Veils, so hopefully they will turn something up. They're good people."

Kyra nodded, eyes fixed on the paper. Heat flushed along her neck as she noticed the seal, a roaring snow leopard. Her personal seal, which was still on her desk. This was either a fake, or whoever had done this was a damned good thief.

The paper shook in her hands. "Whoever did this thinks Jalek and Valmor can help us. Well, Jayne was right. Allies are what we need. But..." As she read, she let out a curse that would have caused her mother to throw something. "'Majesty, I am in desperate need of aid, and willing to...' *mukking hells. Five mukking bleeding hells.*"

Syl's eyes were grim. "Yes. You're willing to offer your hand for an alliance with the Sea-Kingdom."

Kyra's muscles locked up, but she refused to allow this. Never again would she become a prisoner. "Whoever did this is a dead man."

"Can I tell Eli?" Syl grinned, that irrepressible mirth finally springing to the surface.

Kyra swallowed once, twice. Suddenly, it became hard to speak.

"Don't—don't you dare." She pressed a hand to her forehead. "I'll deal with this."

Syl dropped the act and stepped closer, concerned for her Regent. A tentative hand brushed her shoulder. "Highness, you don't look well."

"I'm fine," she said, and blinked rapidly. "Just tired." She waved a flippant hand, anything to resolve this. "Get Jayne and Tomas in a room and see if they can find a solution. And make sure Eli is in the room when Jalek shows up."

"That'll be a sight worth seeing."

Two hours later, she couldn't calm her racing heart. The world was spinning out of control as she paced in a side room behind the court. It was like she was losing her grasp on everything. She could feel it slipping away. Her breathing was quicker and quicker, and she felt sick to her stomach.

"Kyra." That voice washed over her, and she inhaled deeply, her heart slowing down, calmed by the scent of the earth after spring rain. *Thank Nestham.* She turned, and he stood there in his blue-and-silver uniform, the half-cape over his left shoulder. "Syl said you might be in here." His hand remained on his sword, the perfect picture of a Vindicator. His tattoo weaved across his cheek in an elegant dance of blue and gold.

"Did she say anything else?" She wrung her hands together, again and again and again.

"No. Why, what's wrong?" he asked, stalking closer.

Kyra stepped back, braced a hand against the wall, breathing deeply. Then she just let it out. "Someone forged a document claiming that I would marry Prince Jalek if he promised us military aid."

Eli's mouth opened, and he reached for the bracelet at his wrist, touched it once. Power glowed in his hand, and war flashed in his eyes. Gone, gone in an instant. He would know what this meant for her without her needing to explain it. Not after seeing what Trayse had done.

186

"You're not going through with it," he said incredulously.

"Of course I'm not going through with it," she said, the last remnants of the plan clicking into place. "I just need you to do one thing for me."

"Do you want me to claim you in front of the court?" He grinned. She could feel the back of her neck growing warm. His smile died as she didn't respond, but she matched his grin, her fear fading.

"Very territorial of you," she purred. "Are you getting jealous?"

"Maybe," he said, stepping closer, hands on his hips. "But I think it's your situation we need to worry about."

The moment held, as her gaze flicked from his eyes to his lips. "Damn right," she said. "But I do need you to put on a show."

She motioned for him to follow her into the court and onto the dais, where she sat on the leopard throne. Eli stood a few paces away, the Vindicator by his Regent. As her eye swept over the chamber, she found her prey, chatting with his men. All olive-skinned like him. Their tunics were practical, yet well-made. As he noticed her, he bowed again, his men doing the same. Well, she couldn't fault his manners.

The four heads of the Houses also stood in the room. Lady Rurik looked particularly unimpressed, considering she owned Prian. Lord Ketan's face was pale, waxy. She'd heard he had barely left his daughter's side. *Don't think about Eislyn right now.* But just for a moment, she remembered the girl lying unconscious, wasting away in the Healing House. Kyra's knuckles whitened again on the carved armrests.

"Highness," Prince Jalek said, his dark eyes sweeping her figure.

She repressed the urge to rise off the throne and punch him. Instead, she started speaking. "Thank you for coming, Prince. I know the journey was long."

"I'm sure it will be well worth it." He grinned. *I'll bet. A Queen and a Kingdom. I'm surprised you're not drooling.* She refrained from smiling. "How would you like to proceed, Highness? The letter was very clear. And while I'm well aware of Your Highness's personal beliefs, we all need allies."

"Indeed, we do." She smiled, but she let wrath bleed into her gaze. Jalek smiled, but the way his dark-brown eyes shifted showed his confusion. He wouldn't be good at playing cards. *Yes. I'm not desperate enough yet to sell myself to a foreign prince.*

"However, in Leranion, we have an ancient tradition at court. We wish to see if the Prince of Casalis, the Bane of Pirates, can live up to his reputation." Kyra smiled, locking her hands together. "In the ancient days, to strike a pact, you would still prove yourself worthy."

"You're talking of a duel," Jalek said.

"I am."

Jalek shrugged, hand on his rapier. "However, I stand ready to uphold my end of the bargain. In your city of Prian, I have a thousand men on ships ready to march for your banner. For our banner. So I fail to see why I should accept any challenge from you or yours." *Mukk, he's good.*

"Scared, Prince?" she purred. Beside her, Eli went rigid. "If mine loses, then I will accept the terms." She swallowed her fury at the very thought. Eli stared ahead, though every muscle in his body had just tensed.

Jalek weighed up her terms for a second. "Agreed. Then who am I facing?" No talk of a champion. Brave. She, however, would sacrifice a bit of bravery for pragmatism.

"My Champion," she said, savouring the moment. "Eli Serae." She hadn't told anyone *that* little detail.

Jalek cocked his head, even as he swung his shoulders to loosen them. "I would have expected you to face me. Are you not a Marked, as I am?" He grinned. "Can you not feel the power that flows within?"

188

The crowd stirred, and Kyra glanced at them. They hadn't understood a word that had just been said, from what showed on their faces.

"In my court, Prince, we speak so that all can understand," she replied in the High Language. Beside her, Eli snorted. Kyra refrained from glancing at him, though it confirmed everything she suspected. "Magic isn't everything. Sometimes a man's training can outweigh any Nestham-granted powers." And he had no idea what Eli was capable of when he was pissed off. "Shall we say, first blood?"

"Agreed."

The crowd stirred, and Lord Errant grinned, the ancient warrior expecting a spectacle. Monsun, however, stepped to Eli, and the young Vindicator shrugged off his cape, stripped himself of his scabbard. Kyra noted he left the armlet on. Silver eyes lit with flame as he turned to her.

"I serve at your pleasure, Highness," he mouthed.

Kyra fought to keep her face from heating, her heart skipping a beat. "Fight well, Champion."

Her allies pulled back to make a circle, and Eli stepped in, dark gloves flexing around his sword's hilt. Jalek had similarly stripped himself, his elegant rapier gleaming in the afternoon light. A gleam of Nesthamir. Kyra went to say something, but restrained herself. Eli had seen Nesthamir just as much as she had. She wondered if Jalek had seen his vambraces.

# Chapter 33

Eli tensed, sword held in both hands, circling to the right, never removing his gaze from his opponent's eyes. Deep, sea-green eyes. Around him, all the other Vindicators looked on. Eli could feel their gaze burning into him, the weight of all their combined lessons. Stealth, cunning, ferocity, strength. Veturan smirked, his admittedly handsome face twisted into raw male confidence. The bastard certainly knew what he was doing, but Eli couldn't be bothered with measuring up. He raised a brow and breathed a quiet sigh, raising his sword into a salute. He dropped into a fighting stance, and the Prince did the same. *Let's get this over with.*

For a moment, pity flashed over Veturan's face. That alone made Eli ready to start swinging. "I have to warn you," Veturan said, "I am a Marked. Don't feel too bad when I beat you."

The court didn't move. Eli could feel the nobles staring at him. The four heads of the Houses. Trade, weapons, food, soldiers. Things which could turn the tide of any war fought over Ekra. Things they would need.

"Put on a show," Kyra had said. Not to entertain. But to show the court she was a figure they could stand behind. Someone to restore the shattered throne of Leranion. Someone to fight for. Veturan's sea-green Mark flashed on his left hand, while his sword remained in his right. The Prince grinned, and the world stopped. Eli pursed his lips, shifted his stance.

*Put on a show.*

He breathed once, twice. "Ah, *mukk* it." He glanced to Monsun. The Vindicator grinned and raised his hand. Eli yanked off his right glove. And as his commander's hand flashed down, Eli plummeted into his magic and let the ice-blue light pulse throughout the luxurious chamber. Screams and gasps rang out as the Nestham-blessed power flickered off the chandeliers, off the countless glass windows, off the finery of the courtiers. And, most importantly, off Veturan's jaw, currently hanging wide open.

Eli smiled at his opponent as he unleashed himself on the Prince.

He launched forward, sword reaching towards Veturan. But the man was already spinning away and batting away Eli's blade, once, twice, three times. They clashed quickly, then withdrew. Veturan lunged swiftly, and Eli flicked it to the side, stepping away. Veturan mirrored the move, his cheer and arrogance long gone.

Eli winked and snapped into a rapid combination, all fast, brutal strikes. Veturan countered them, matching Eli's inexorable style with one of smooth elegance, favouring lunges over slashes. Eli's move finished with that overhand cut, faster than he'd ever done it.

Somehow, the Prince reacted faster, and dodged before leaping into the air. He flipped lazily, and his blade crashed onto Eli's at the apex. The blow was almost enough to send Eli to his knees, and he hissed as his opponent landed smoothly, not even a hair out of place. The court muttered amongst themselves and he almost turned around, ready to yell. *Do you doubt me? Doubt her?*

At the power of this Prince, he could understand why. Veturan's blade reflected his power, and for the first time, he pushed Eli back and put him on the defensive. Eli stepped back and back, parrying as every single strike got closer and closer to his flesh. They locked blades, and the Prince shoved him back, tossing the rapier into his left hand. His Mark's light travelled through his blade, the entire length of the sword glittering with the sea-green power. Nesthamir—no doubt about it. Eli pursed his lips and flipped his inferior sword in his hand. He could only hope it didn't shatter on the Sea-Prince's blade.

They duelled again, but this time fighting against a left-handed soldier made it even more unpredictable. Veturan's smile was back. He'd got the measure of Eli now and found him

191

lacking. Eli spun to the side and smashed his blade against Veturan's. The Prince's rapier careened away, but he flipped back and extended his hand. The rapier reappeared in it immediately, and he stepped forward.

Eli dropped into his magic, letting the power overwhelm him. The chamber gleamed with his light until he was radiant with it, a beacon, a star lighting the day. He barraged Veturan, swinging and swinging and swinging until their swords were to the side, and then Eli moved in with a kick to the knee, then his fist crunched on Veturan's mouth. His opponent sailed back ten metres before he slid on the floor to a stop. Eli closed the distance in a heartbeat and raised his blade to his neck. "Yield, Prince."

Veturan's mouth twitched, blood spilling on his lips, and his eyes flashed green. At last, he sighed. "Very well."

Eli sheathed his sword and hauled his opponent to his feet, nodded once and stepped away, gaze sweeping over the heads of the Houses. Lord Errant nodded at him approvingly. Lady Rurik—her gaze was assessing, practised. He bowed to them, then turned to the throne, bowed again. When he raised his gaze to the woman seated on it, he winked. Kyra merely tilted her head in acknowledgement. No more than one would expect of her Champion. *At least one of us is being formal.*

Grinning, he took a place next to Monsun, settling his breath. As he glanced around, he noticed several eyes on him. "You fought well," the Vindicator rumbled. "Thanks to my teachings."

"I would thank you..." Eli said, "but it seems you beat me to it."

"You stole my move."

"I would say I perfected it."

"Why did you reveal yourself?" Monsun asked. "You could have kept your glove on."

Eli shrugged, keeping his eyes straight ahead. "Finon already knows who I am. So does Temero. May as well let everyone know."

"That was a dangerous move."

"I know," he said. "But it's too late to do anything about it now."

"Prince Jalek." Kyra's voice cut off all conversation. "Please bring half of your forces into Imbra to strengthen our garrison. The remainder can camp outside Prian."

"Highness," Veturan protested. "This hardly seems fair."

"The way I see it," Kyra said, "you had your chance against my Champion and lost."

"Oh, I love the way she does that." Eli smiled. He had the sense that had they not been standing at attention, Monsun would have buried his face in his hands.

"That's my Regent you're talking about," he said. "I don't want to hear about it."

"Embarrassed, Monsun? I didn't think that was an emotion you could feel."

"Enough, or you'll be on slum duty next week." As Veturan shuffled out of the chamber, Monsun added, "He could be a valuable ally. Just try not to get into a measuring contest with him."

"Monsun," Eli mock-gasped. "I never expected that from *you.*"

\* \* \*

After Veturan had been publicly dismissed, the five Vindicators bowed to the throne and stalked their way to the Spire. Clustered in the powerful group, Eli felt awe at how they moved—and how he moved with them. No magic, just pure lethality. Concealed in some, like Syl and Tomas, yet Raylene couldn't help but make noblemen jump out of their way. As they shut the door of the Spire meeting room, Monsun laid the map of Leranion flat over the massive, scarred table.

"Raylene," he said. "Report on the patrol?"

"Nothing. I checked back on the investigation with the Veils. They suspect a new assassin is loose in the city. And no one's heard from Hyrin in a couple of days."

193

Monsun frowned. "In another day, we might need to start looking. The next Council meeting is soon. We'll need Hyrin to swing the vote against Finon and Yuras."

"I'll have a look round tonight," Syl said. "Maybe check in with some of my contacts in the slums. Is it okay if I take Amora?"

"I don't want her going back into that place," Monsun said, a thunderous frown crossing his face.

"Monsun, I'm good in the slums, and you know that. But she was born and raised there much more recently. I'll get information that I never even dreamed of."

His face tightened, and wrath coursed over it, until at last he sighed. "Ask her. If she doesn't want to go back, don't take her."

"What's with the map?" Eli asked.

Monsun nodded to Tomas, and the eldest Vindicator took over.

"Jalek says he has a thousand men ready to sail on twenty ships. It's an impressive armada, and now that we've finally re-established our communication with Prian, it's being confirmed. I've had supplies sent to the harbour to provide for them."

"A thousand men will get restless soon enough, but we don't want them to be let loose in the town. Soldiers are the worst in peacetime," Tomas said.

"Agreed," Monsun said. "We can send half to Talon Reach, to supplement the hundred I've already sent. That should be enough to strengthen the garrison."

"Is that our strategy? Protect the pillars?" Eli asked. "That's a delaying action at best."

"For now. But you remember what happened last time. Only Jaser could defeat Temero. It takes a Marked to do it. You, the Regent, Veturan—Alsair said you were the only ones who could stand against him."

"But there are other Marked out there," Syl said. "King Hadrian and the royal families of Biralam and Valmor."

194

"Biralam will not send aid," Monsun said. "Neither will any of their Marked come." His knuckles whitened on the table.

"Why not?" Tomas asked. "You could reach out to them, with your history in Amaldas." But as Eli watched, the very mention of Amaldas seemed to crumple the Senior Vindicator.

"I have nothing to bargain. They will not listen to me," Monsun said.

"Biralam has three Marked. Valmor has four. Leranion has two. And we have a Guardian," Syl hissed, hands on her hips. "Why, with ten Marked in Ekra, can we only use three?"

"We could have more, if we could find the Heir of Amerin," Monsun said. They all looked at him like he was crazy, but he squared his shoulders. "I believe the Heir still lives—in Imbra."

"Monsun," Tomas said, "that line died out two hundred years ago."

"The Guardians died out five hundred years ago," Monsun said. "Yet here one stands, as a Vindicator of Leranion." His voice quietened, and the powerful warrior pleaded with them. "I have to hope that one still lives."

"Why trust to hope?" Raylene said. "There's no hope in this Nestham-damned world."

"Nestham hasn't damned the world yet." Eli sucked in a breath. "Not while we have strength left." Raylene smiled at him for the first time. "Regardless, we need more Marked. We've now got Veturan. Will the others come?"

Raylene shook her head, diving into the recesses of her memory. "Prince Jovan isn't a warrior and Princess Liljana is too cunning to risk her life for this kind of thing. Queen Eurydike, who carries the Marked bloodline, is failing."

Tomas whipped his gaze to her. "If she dies before this is over, and Jovan or Liljana take the throne, the Prince will lose his Marked abilities. Raylene, you said Valmor appoints inheritance rather than by order of birth. Does Veturan stand a chance of being Heir?"

"Not a chance in any of the Five Hells. Jalek," she sighed, "has been the black sheep of his family ever since he was little."

"What happened to him?" Eli asked. Was there more to the Prince than met the eye?

Those clouds grew over her eyes again. "That is not my story to tell. Regardless, Valmor is clear. Jalek and his troops will be our only aid."

Eli's eyes fell on the map. "What of the Plains? We're moving troops through there to get to Talon Reach, aren't we? Could we get aid from there?"

"Maybe. If we can persuade Stallor and Fallkirk to set aside their differences."

"Maybe see if the Ajerst family can do something," Tomas said.

"That should be the Regent's decision. And the Lady Ajerst's," Syl said, and Monsun nodded his agreement.

"Back to the pillars," he said. "Talon Reach will be secure. Wherever Temero is, he must fight his way across Fallkirk and Stromfield Marsh to sack it. But Aurimia is the hard one. We have no idea where it is."

"Not surprising," Syl said, "since it was a myth. Still is, to most people."

Eli focused on scanning along the map of the Severed Peaks. "Well, dealing with myths and legends is what we do most days."

"For now, there's not a great deal we can do about Aurimia until we find it," Monsun said. "Raylene, you're on point dealing with Veturan's forces. Any issue between them and our men, you sort it out. Tomas, I want you working on Aurimia. Find us a location. Get Jayne and Alsair if you need some extra research help. Syl, deal with the source of the forged document. Whoever promised the Regent to the Prince knows both of them well and knew what would lure him up here."

"Do we still want him up here?" Eli asked.

"You're going to need to work with him," Monsun said. "He's a Marked, that should mean something."

"He seems like hot air with an annoying smile," Eli said, cracking his neck.

"Don't be so quick to judge," Monsun reminded him. "Did I not surprise you?"

"Fine. I'll deal with Veturan."

"No," Monsun said firmly. "You're dealing with the Order."

"Oh, well, I'm way ahead of you." He grinned, relishing his achievement. "I obtained two barrels of the Order's chemical." Silence fell across the room for just a second.

"When in the Hells did you do that?" Raylene barked.

Monsun sat down heavily, with the air of someone who had just had a puzzle solved for them. "What else have you been up to, Eli? Tell me. Why is it you aren't sleeping? Why does your Nightweave smell of smoke? Did you kill Treasurer Rumpre's men?"

"Are you serious? Of course not. But they were buying from some of Vera's former colleagues." The room seemed to shift, and they all focused on him, muscles tensed—this was a room full of killers.

"Syl, check the doors," Monsun said. A lump caught in Eli's throat as the white-blonde Vindicator checked for listeners, then locked the great doors.

"The night that Rumpre's men died," Monsun said, "the Guild reported a break-in. Two figures garbed in black. I should have seen it." Stony faces all around him. "You wore Nightweave on that break-in."

"To get the chemical! We needed that."

"That is not how we do it! We need to fight in the light of the day. That's why we mark ourselves with this tattoo, to prove we are above that." Monsun's expression dropped even further. "Your companion. The only person who can keep up with you. It was the Regent, wasn't it?" Eli's silence was confirmation enough. Raylene looked angry enough to kill him.

But Monsun just looked disappointed. "You swore to be the Torch of the North. What changed?"

He turned a broad back on the young Vindicator and left the room. The others soon followed.

* * *

The waterfall's roar still wasn't loud enough to drown out the roaring in his ears. The stone scraped on Eli's back, pressed against the wall of the grotto. He couldn't stop staring at those innocuous barrels, the simple design belying the destruction contained within. Nestham's Will. He knew he should be scared. Shouldn't be anywhere near these blasted barrels. Shouldn't have brought them underneath the damn castle. And yet, he just couldn't care less. Besides, he'd survived the powder before. Twice, it should have killed him. Twice he'd survived.

And yet, these barrels had cost him the burgeoning trust of the Vindicators. Had undermined any faith they might have had in him. They trusted him to fight Temero. They needed a weapon. He laughed bitterly, sick of pretending. Those barrels weren't the reason they mistrusted him. He'd done that himself by going out into the city at night, fighting unsanctioned missions and all but screaming to their enemies *HERE I AM!*

*"You're making a mistake,"* Jaser had tried to tell him. His head dropped into his hands and he groaned.

"Oh mukk you, Jaser." How had he stuffed that up? Now they wouldn't be able to look him in the eye. Gentle footsteps pattered behind him, but when he turned around, nobody was there. "What are you doing?" Amora piped from beside him. He jumped, then forced a smile on his face. It felt unnatural, like it didn't belong there.

"Just thinking," he said.

The young girl waggled her eyebrows. "Sounds boring."

He huffed a laugh. "It usually is."

But she still twitched, boundless energy in that tiny frame. "You annoyed Monsun earlier," she said, still with that grin on her face.

198

"He told you?" He pursed his lips. Monsun had no right. That wasn't for Amora. They had an unspoken vow to keep her out of all of this. She'd survived enough. He'd protect her from this war, he swore it. She would be nowhere near the battle.

"He didn't need to. I could hear him yelling throughout the palace." Her voice quietened. "He frightened me." Eli wrapped an arm around the girl. She tucked close, no longer the stick-thin creature he'd met. She'd finally stopped carrying that hollowness after weeks of eating good food.

"He didn't mean to, I'm sure."

"If you're not frightened, then why are you hiding down here?" She giggled.

"I'm not hiding from Monsun!" He grinned despite himself.

"Seems like it." Her fingernail tapped on his vambrace, and she gasped quietly. "Ow!" She pulled her hand back like she'd been stung, shaking her fingers loose. She relaxed once more and slouched beside him, curling up into his shoulder like they'd done when they were first on the run.

"I made a big mistake," he said. "I do that more and more, it seems."

She shrugged bony shoulders. "I think you're doing okay." Somehow, that lifted his spirits.

"I'm sorry that I never asked you," he said. "Do you like it here?"

He couldn't see her face, but could hear it in her voice. "Yes. It—it's very different. Everything changed when I stole your money. But when I met you, and met the actor, I knew what you two were fighting for. And the gruntah, even the smoother. I knew I could make a home."

He squeezed her shoulder, a smile creeping over his face. "Thank you."

"For what?"

"Giving me an idea. Do you like chocolate?"

# Chapter 34

Kyra sighed as she leaned on the door to her chambers, barely finding the strength to touch the golden handle. Her side flared with a sudden ache as Nix butted her furry head into her waist, and Kyra sighed again and ran a hand down the leopard's body, feeling the strength within. She avoided falling into the thoughts of the mind bond. Such a power drained her more than she could bear right now, but the love within the leopard's violet eyes was overwhelming, a raw power she hadn't yet witnessed.

A muffled thud echoed from inside her chambers. Nix let out a growl but stopped, her eyes inquisitive, bright. Kyra's hand dropped to the back of her dress, to the hidden pouch contained there. Steel rasped quietly, and her knife glittered in her hand. Kyra's other hand landed on the door handle, and she twisted, heartbeat hammering, opening the door.

She froze, eyes swivelling, and a smile crept over her face as she listened to the giggles. Amora, balanced on Eli's shoulders, the small girl straining to replace the massive glass jar of chocolate she kept on the top shelf of her room. Kyra grinned and leaned on the door frame, arms folded. Something had alerted them, some instincts honed in the forest and the back streets of the Imbran slums, for Amora let out a little cough, and Eli was already turning slowly, cautious of the precious weight he carried.

"Well, it seems we've been caught." Eli smiled, and damn her if it wasn't the best thing she'd seen all day. His eyes twinkled, yet her trained gaze noted the red lining the burning silver eyes, the blotchy patches on his face. Amora let out another little giggle as she plopped yet another piece of chocolate into her mouth, her lips already stained with the residue of the sweet treat. Eli shifted from side to side, swaying Amora around. A warm feeling lodged in Kyra's heart, and Nix immediately sprang on the bed and closed her eyes.

Kyra flexed her fingers, trying to bring the feeling back into them. "I'm sure Master Chum wouldn't have minded giving you some."

"Ah, but where's the fun in that when you can steal it?" Eli grinned. The Guardian leaned forward, and the urchin jumped off, landing lightly on her feet, her beautiful dress swaying elegantly. The girl looked radiant.

"I think it's time the young rascal went off to bed," Kyra said.

Amora rolled her eyes. "Really, actor?"

"Really. Come, I'll take you to bed." Kyra reached out a hand to the girl, and she immediately grabbed it.

Amora's hair had grown out to her collar now, brushed and gleaming, her eyes glowing. "Can I stay with you? The big gruntah snores too loudly."

"Of course, you can stay in the other bedroom again." She led the girl to the chamber and tucked her in, despite her cries that she didn't need someone to put her to bed.

"Can I have Nix?" Amora piped up as Kyra reached the door.

"Stay in bed and I'll see," Kyra said without glancing back. As she exited, she still couldn't keep the smile from her face, as she beheld two hulking figures on the bed.

Eli was already face down, in his uniform, with no weapons in sight for once. Even more surprising were the boots neatly placed by the bed. A gentle whiffle echoed through the room. She couldn't tell if it came from the human or the massive snow leopard sprawling beside him, her head on his back.

When she re-emerged from the bathing suite, finally changed and exhausted, the predator raised her head, violet eyes fixed on her. *Don't you dare touch him*, Nix seemed to say.

"I'm the one you're supposed to protect, Nix," Kyra breathed. She poked the broad back of fur and muscle, then placed her hand on the leopard's head, speaking directly into her mind. This time, the feeling was easier, the cub's thoughts

201

no longer that racing madness she'd had a few weeks ago. Increased intelligence, maturity... and apparently disloyalty.

She placed an image of Amora in the cub's mind and let it remain there until Nix shuffled off to the other room. Muffled laughter and giggles warmed her heart, and she finally settled down under the covers, her eyes running over the man across from her. She'd honestly been looking forward to talking, but he'd practically passed out.

Rumbles echoed from the other chamber. She traced a hand over the elegant tattoo arcing over his cheek, and he stirred, breath catching, warmth shining in his unnatural silver eyes. He smiled, but he wasn't that hard to read.

"What's wrong?" she asked.

He shook his head. "Nothing." She didn't even need the ring to work out the answer to that. He tried to bury his face back in the pillow, but she wouldn't let him.

"Don't do this. Don't shut me out."

He sighed and faced her, and his lip quivered. "Monsun found out about the night missions."

She raised a brow. "Monsun knew you were in the Leopard's Teeth the day after it happened. The day I—never mind." She went on, "Why does it matter?"

"They're not just pissed I dragged you into it. They're pissed because of what I did."

"You only did those things because I told you to."

He rolled onto his back and stared at the ceiling. "I made a choice," he said, then paused, and she could hear his breathing stop. "It all felt too sudden. First, I attack the Leopard's Teeth, then Jayne and Eislyn are attacked? It was retaliation."

"You think so?" she could barely get the words out.

"I know so." *You started this.*

Eli eventually drifted off to sleep, but it never found her.

\* \* \*

Kyra sighed in frustration and peeled off the covers, careful not to wake the sleeping Vindicator. She didn't need to worry, as a rumbling snore emanated from him. She smiled as she dressed and put on soft-soled shoes.

She padded her way through the darkened corridors to the Royal Library and peered in, inhaling the familiar smell of musty parchment. Lights still burned in the study section. Enhanced eyes peered ahead at the onyx hair gleaming in the candlelight. Jayne barely acknowledged her as Kyra slumped down in an ornate chair beside her.

"How goes the research?"

Jayne glanced up at her, her eyes sunken yet focused. "Terrible. Aurimia is a damned fairy tale." She gestured at the scattered sheets around her, including a massive map of the Severed Peaks. "All I know is Aurimia is supposed to be somewhere in this mountain range, but some books say it's east, some say it's west, some say it's at the top of the mountains, and some claim it doesn't exist at all. I can't find a single source that corroborates anything." She glanced at Kyra. "But I know you wouldn't have asked me to do this if you didn't really need to. So what's in Aurimia?"

Kyra hesitated, then lowered her voice. "It's supposed to be a massive pillar of Nesthamir. We need to make sure it's safe. If Temero—or Finon—get their hands on it, we're doomed."

Jayne leaned back and stretched, rubbing the back of her arm. "I feel like the more we learn about Aurimia, the worse it gets. What if he learns about it from us?"

"That's a risk we'll have to take. Can you do it?"

"I'm grateful for the task," Jayne said. "It helps keep my mind off—" She fell silent, but she didn't need to say anything. Not just the attack on her, but the one on *Eislyn*. The third member of their trio. They'd always seemed inseparable growing up, heirs to a throne, a House and a shattered plain. But now everything was pulling them apart.

They both fell into silence, Kyra's heart sinking. She hadn't even checked on Eislyn in a while. Hadn't seen her parents. What kind of friend, daughter, princess was she?

"I tell you though, your friend Alsair's a strange one," Jayne whispered, and Kyra immediately focused in as she continued in a breath. "It's like he never sleeps. Or maybe he sleeps standing up or something. Regardless, he's been reading everything on Aurimia, Temero, the Wildborn, you name it."

"He's been looking into the Wildborn?" Kyra asked. A shadow crossed her heart at the name of the first faith to fall, the traitors.

"Yes. Not sure why, though. I asked him, and he seemed to pass it off as a personal interest." Jayne shuddered. "He's former Jinnam, isn't he?"

"Yes. Soldier-turned-monk, is what Eli told me."

Jayne tapped her lips thoughtfully. "Why would a Jinnam want to know more about the Wildborn?"

A scholar's curiosity, perhaps—but the very lights seemed to quiver as the names were spoken. "They have something in common, don't they? Extinction?"

"I'm not sure why anyone would want to look into them," Jayne said with a shudder. "It was brutal."

Kyra stood up, mind churning. "Get some rest, *amica*. We've got a lot more to do." But the young woman had already turned back obsessively to her book, scanning through and jotting down notes on the paper beside her, flicking over to the map of the Severed Peaks, now littered with symbols.

She almost left, but something nagged at her, and her voice seemed unnaturally loud in the library's silence. "If I wanted to get a history of Leranion's legions and records of individual soldiers, where would I go?"

"Military records are over there," Jayne pointed to her right. Kyra filed through the narrow gap of teetering books, stopped and grabbed one.

A long night's work began. All of Leranion's military kept these records in ongoing volumes. Each legion had a record, as well as the Royal Scouts and Vindicators had their own. She flicked through the history of the Seventh. When Monsun had arrived in Imbra, he'd enlisted at twenty-four, risen to Third and then Second over the following three years, then appointed Commander at twenty-seven. He'd left the Seventh structure to become a Vindicator at thirty, with Commander Aran taking his place. Monsun was appointed Senior Vindicator not two years later, the youngest in history.

But she kept scanning. Commander Aran and the Second and Third were sent on leave, suspected killed by Vindicator Cedwin. A knife twisted in her heart. Cedwin, whom Monsun had said was his greatest failure. Commander Omun—Aran's replacement—had never returned from the Seventh's patrol in the north. No idea where he'd gone, but also no knowledge of Cedwin's strange squad of soldiers, the men in white and gold. Satisfied, she flicked to the list of soldiers. Every soldier who had served in the Seventh recorded there. Nothing.

Two hours later, she lifted her head, the histories of all seven legions before her. All the Kingdom had on every soldier who had ever served in Leranion's army. No record of Syl, but that was unsurprising. Raylene's medal of Armentine was very impressive, considering she never wore it. But Alsair's name was not in any of them.

"Who are you?" she breathed.

Kyra pushed aside the books, left them where they lay. She'd be back for them later. She muttered to herself as she stumbled out of the library, past the librarian who raised a brow, her delicate features shifting. She needed to think, so she headed to the garden. As she entered, the familiar scents wrapped around her, the roses most of all. Grass pricked at her as she lay on her back. The royal garden's glass ceiling let in all the shimmering stars, away from the rest of the palace. Secure. None would dare go near here, and besides, she had the only key. Her balcony was good, but this, this garden, was perfect. Belatedly, she realised he hadn't even seen this yet. Her arm drifted over the grass, relishing the feel of it dragging over her skin, and for the first time that night, sleep drifted over her, beckoning, and she was too ready to fall into its depths. But she couldn't let herself do that, and she blinked twice, forcing her eyes open.

Not a soldier in Leranion, not a Veil or a Scout—yet he'd seen combat. Mercenary? No, definitely military service—he was too disciplined. She hissed a frustrated breath—the answer was so close, she could feel it. Soon, she'd have answers. They had lost too much for anything but the truth. Satisfied with that, she closed her eyes.

A cry rang out over the city, an eerie echo of a lost memory. Kyra lurched up and brushed past the roses of red and white, past the lovely lavender, and peered out into the city from that glass door. Nothing.

A tap on the ceiling, and she glanced up, gasping, hand stretching out. Her staff appeared in it and she flashed the blades out instinctively. A single figure in Nightweave perched above her on the glass, at home on the heights and in the castle. Feminine and fully armed, the masked woman crouched, eyes boring into her.

The woman above her had dual sabres and a wicked assortment of knives strapped to her suit. "You," Kyra breathed, a chord of memory chiming through her. Somewhere, sometime, she'd seen this woman before. But—Kyra blinked rapidly as the memory, dulled by the trauma, resurfaced. When she and Eli had fought Temero in the guise of Cedwin, Eli had taken her far away from the real fight. But she'd surfaced from nightmares and fought this woman. Fought her to a standstill and ripped off her mask. And then—nothing. A hole in her memory where the face should be. The last thing she remembered was Eshe reaching down for her, to get Eli up, to fight regardless of her blood loss.

"Who are you?" she whispered for the second time that evening. A name floated back to her, across time. Alondra. "Alondra!" she called, as if she could actually communicate with her. But as the name rang out in the garden, the figure tensed, cocking her head. Kyra stumbled out onto the balcony, staff smacking into her hand. As soon as she stepped into the chilly air, Alondra leapt off the side of the garden roof, straight into freefall. Her gloved hand caught a trailing bit of rope, and she swung and flipped, landing below in a move Kyra wasn't sure she could pull off. As she gazed out at the retreating figure, something struck in her heart again and again and again.

Even when she returned to her rooms, Kyra didn't sleep well that night.

# Chapter 35

The Chosen frowned through his grey beard at the red-headed man slouching across from him. "You were supposed to be here an hour ago."

"I'm here," Trayse shrugged. "Considering how the Vindicators want to kill me, you're lucky I'm as good as I am."

"Yes, I'm sure we are all eternally grateful for your incredible skills. Do you have any information, or are you just wasting my time and money?"

"It's money well spent. As you would have guessed, or you would have still had Sandria—Reian—feeding all of your secrets to Hyrin."

Finon carefully kept his face blank. He'd known Hyrin had put Veils in the Order—he had his own in the Leranion military. One he'd groomed perfectly to become a Vindicator before Monsun and Raylene had picked Cedwin and then the wretched whelp. But he hadn't seen Sandria coming, had thought that she was just a secretary who Trayse had scared into submission.

"Sandria was never a concern."

"She was a mukking Veil. She was Hyrin's protegee."

Truly, this assassin was infuriating—and yet he was Finon's creation, plain and simple. "I haven't seen Hyrin for a week. What did you do with him?"

"Wouldn't you like to know?" Trayse grinned.

Finon flicked a brow, and the assassin sighed. "They'll never find the body. Happy now?"

"No. Now I need to replace my assistant and find a suitable candidate for Spymaster." The Veils were too damn insular. He'd never been able to penetrate their ranks. "Did you at least get any other useful information besides killing a few Veils?"

"You pay me to kill people," Trayse said, stretching his arms over his head. Finon didn't reply. "The Regent is at breaking point. If you nudge her again, she'll crack. Maybe you won't even need to go after anyone else."

"Then start pushing," Finon said. "Use the trick with the Musadim. She thinks her past is hidden. Let her know it's not. There's a Council meeting planned for the day we strike."

"Why bother? We have an army," Trayse said. "And I can just kill her." No, you can't, Finon mused. He could read the flickering gaze. Either Trayse didn't think himself capable— or didn't want to do it.

"You can't just assassinate everyone," Finon said, and he caught the small sigh of relief the assassin breathed. "I have an army. So does the Regent. These aren't pushover Jinnam monks, Trayse. She's got five Vindicators, including that wretched Champion."

"You can just say his name." Trayse slashed a crooked grin. "He's a Guardian, after all."

A loud bang resounded as the Archbishop slammed a hand on the table. "I refuse to say that! The Guardians were heretics. They belong where they are. Erased from history, just like the Wildborn."

"If you had your way, the Musadim would be gone too." The accusation seemed to flicker the torches in Finon's office, the flames guttering in fear.

Finon raised a withered finger. "Not yet. Damned pacifists—they're a pushover. Don't know why Antarun swore to them."

"Maybe because they're the only faith left that's still alive and isn't totally corrupt," Trayse deadpanned.

"This isn't corruption. This is a fight for the very soul of Ekra." He resumed his pondering. "Besides, the bitch on the throne is not as peaceable as they think." He snorted. "A Princess comes marching down the aisle with a staff in hand, and they think she comes in peace. No, Kyra Antarun comes with war on her lips."

Trayse licked cracked lips, and a shiver went down Finon's spine.

"Did you hear she broke into the Guild's headquarters in the city? Stole two barrels of your powder."

Finon leaned over his paper, surveying the report. "Yes. That was the same night Rumpre's men died. Was that you?"

Trayse shrugged irreverently. "They were in the way. Besides, the Vindicators think they're too good for back-alley stabbing, even that Veil Captain. They'll turn on Serae. Actually, I think they already have. My source says he's already outcast." He shifted the blade at his side, pursing his lips. "Considering he tried to kill me the last time he got rejected, I think I'll lay low tonight."

"You can't take him?" Finon challenged him, held his gaze.

"Only a fool would cross a Vindicator twice," Trayse said. "I'm no fool."

"He's barely old enough to shave." Even with those silver eyes, he was still a boy.

"He's a Guardian. And he's not the Vindicator I'm afraid of," Trayse breathed. Fear bled into his eyes before he cocked that familiar grin. "Do you want anyone dead?"

"No," Finon said. "This can't look like any plot. Put the word out that she killed several Eternal Order soldiers in the south." A pause as he savoured the moment. "The truth will set us free."

Trayse smirked and threw a sloppy salute before vanishing into the night.

# Chapter 36

Every single night for the next week, Kyra again left the sleeping Guardian and found her way into the garden. Nothing had changed. It was there she could at last find a little peace from the things clouding her mind. Just breathing in the rich scents stilled her heart, and she breathed easier. Enemies pushing at her from every corner, the Vindicators tearing apart, Eli on the ropes. Nothing she could say would console him. Nix's tail lashed back and forth, the leopard having accompanied her on every trip, and a low growl rumbled from her throat.

"Hush," she breathed. Nix stilled, though those violet eyes remained steady. Kyra raised her gaze straight at the masked figure above. They sat in silence, neither moving. Alondra remained steady. The first time Kyra had tried to move towards her, she'd leapt away, so Kyra hadn't dared try again. She pointed to the balcony at the edge of the dome, heart hammering in her chest. Alondra hesitated, but perked up and slid to the balcony. She landed gracefully, with poise trained by a harsh master. Kyra couldn't have mastered those moves—but she'd already proven that Alondra was a far more capable warrior than her, anyway. If they came to blows... she didn't want to think about that. Couldn't think about that.

But maybe she'd got further than they had all week. Perhaps she could finally get through to this—warrior? Assassin? Whatever she was, she would be a powerful ally.

"I'm Kyra," she smiled, tapping a hand on her chest. "You're Alondra." The figure didn't move. She tried again. Alondra nodded, and her heart leapt. Finally! She stepped forward, palms raised. Alondra tensed, hand dropping to the vicious sabre at her side.

"Don't worry," she crooned, "I won't hurt you." Alondra stilled, resumed her wooden posture, stiff as a marionette. Yet

Kyra had no doubt she could kill her in a heartbeat if she so wished.

She stepped forward again, close enough to see the whites of Alondra's eyes. The assassin leapt over the balcony into the night again, and Kyra sighed in frustration. But when she glanced down into the night, she found Alondra sitting on the stones. And when Kyra waved goodbye to the figure, slowly, hesitantly, Alondra stretched a hand back.

Kyra tucked that glow in her heart as she checked on Eislyn and her parents. No change. Nix prowled with her into the library, the leopard padding in on silent paws. Again, those two lights still burned in isolated corners. Some people, it seemed, never slept. Just like her these days.

"Don't you have stuff to do?" Jayne sighed. "Courtly things?" She'd always been grumpy when people intruded on her reading space. But this time, Kyra wasn't here for her.

"Probably. But this is something I have to do first." Her tone made Jayne's gaze catch, but she merely raised a brow. Kyra chewed on her lip as she drifted between the massive shelves in the library, darting between the shadows. Her very warmth seemed to have been sucked out of her bones. Goosebumps rippled across her skin. But she couldn't wait any longer. She extended a hand, and the staff reappeared. She dismissed it with a thought and it vanished into thin air.

She didn't know why she'd waited this long, but she couldn't wait any longer. To do so, if she was right, might doom them all.

She rounded the next shelf and there he was, his piercing green eyes flickering over the page. She stopped and waited. He muttered to himself, his lips moving, but she couldn't make it out. And with her gloves off, she couldn't use her heightened senses without revealing herself. But this was strange. She'd always found him hyper-aware of everything, perfectly in control. And yet, he still hadn't noticed her. She coughed pointedly. Alsair jumped, his wiry body shaking, but he forced a smile.

"Hello Kyra," he said distractedly, his hand shifting a piece of paper under another book. She caught a brief glance—it seemed to be a drawing of some kind, but it was gone before she could get a good look.

"Hello Alsair." She plopped down across from him onto the hard wooden chair and peered at him intently, maintaining her courtly smile.

"Is everything alright?" the monk asked. His jade eyes, once focused and clear, were now clouded. His left eye twitched, and his right hand couldn't stop shaking. Slowly, ever so slowly, he dropped it under the table.

She flashed a bland smile. "I wanted to ask you something." She leant forward, hands gripping the table. Alsair said nothing, but his eye twitched again. "Which regiment did you serve in before you joined the Jinnam?"

"The Fifth." A cloud of unease circled him, and Kyra could taste the falsehood ringing in his words, but she kept her face blank, kept probing, as she drew her chair in closer until her torso pressed up against the desk.

"Under which commander?" She shifted, her hand dropping to the small of her back.

"Commander Jennison." Another lie. Surely Alsair knew what he was doing, just as he'd known what he was doing when he'd sent her to die.

She shook her head sadly, and though her heart was hard, she knew Eli's wasn't. This would destroy him. Golden light flickered through the room as she lashed out with her foot, smashing into Alsair's chair. The monk flew backwards and fell onto the ground, letting out a grunt of pain. Kyra leapt up and crouched on the desk, her light shimmering over the shelves, and stared at the dazed monk. Strange. He'd normally reacted quicker than this. He could usually match Eli.

"What happened to you, Alsair?" she breathed. He didn't answer, as the staff appeared in her hand, and she flicked it to rest the blade at his throat. "I've searched every military record, and there is no mention of an Alsair in any regiment. Or

213

a Commander Jennison. But you knew that. I should have just asked you a week ago. Damn it, my damned ring would have told me." He blinked, and his eyes took on a far-seeing look, but he let out a small gasp as she pressed the knife harder. "Who are you? Order? Someone else?"

His eyes flicked on her knife, and she withdrew, slowly, enough for him to croak out, "I am a Jinnam." Truth, but she could almost scent a tiny—just a tiny—trace of bitterness.

"Maybe you were once. But you were something else as well," she said. She stood and made her way back to the desk, probing through the scattered papers. At last, her hand rested on what she sought. She pulled it out, keeping the monk— whatever he was—in sight, but still the drawing drew a shiver down her spine. A massive tree in the centre, its branches covering most of the sky. A small bird, a dove, sheltered in the tree's mighty protection. At the base of the tree was drawn a flickering torch—like an Eternal Flame. In the sky, the last part of the drawing, Alsair had drawn five stars, set in the pattern of Nestham's Shield.

"It's impressive," she said. Alsair didn't respond, his eyes flashing with hurt. She filed that away for later, dropping the drawing back on the desk.

"Let me ask you one thing more," she said, standing over him, golden blades flickering in her hand. Alsair's eyes widened, and she thought she could detect a small smile as he fumbled with his dove necklace. "Whose side are you on?"

"Leranion's," he answered. Truth. She sighed and dismissed the staff.

"You're a good fighter, Alsair." She turned away, but in the corner of her eye, her gaze fell on that necklace. Honed eyesight revealed something she'd never laid eyes upon. An engraving of a torch on the back, now twisted over as he tucked it back in. Her heart hammering in her chest, she turned back to the drawing, her body thrumming with tension, keenly aware of Alsair's presence behind her.

Every part of her itched to draw her staff and strike. But she forced herself to stare at that drawing. The majestic tree—the symbol of the Musadim. The dove resting in its branches—the Jinnam. The constellation in the sky—Nestham's Shield—the Eternal Order. And the torch at the base. "Alsair," she breathed, "why were you looking into the Wildborn? Jinnam are sworn to peace."

"I wanted to know if there was anything in there about how they were destroyed."

*You know how they were destroyed.*

She whirled on him, her staff reappearing. "You're a Wildborn." His eyes widened, but he knew there was no denying it.

"I am the last of my kind."

"You lied about everything. Why?"

His eyes were mournful, and he held out his hand, still prone on the floor. "Because I need to. And I can't tell you why." Truth.

"Try again. Because the next time you lie, this won't miss."

"You wouldn't dare hurt me." He smirked. "Eli would never forgive you." Truth and lies mixed together. Was that all this man was? Just a melange of truth and falsehood, lies and facts, until you couldn't work it out anymore?

"If I told Eli how you betrayed his trust, he'd probably throw you out himself."

Alsair pursed his lips. "Fair enough. So what do I need to give you to keep our little secret?"

"I should tell Eli." She shouldn't even be negotiating with him. He'd lied to her, he'd lied to Eli for ten years—

"You can't. Trust me. If you do, it will all go wrong."

Truth—unmistakable, horrible truth, as he lay within the scattered papers like a man weathering a storm. "Who are you to speak about trust, Alsair? You sent us to face a demon. It nearly killed us."

215

"You didn't die," he pointed out. She growled, and he hurried on. "I understand my actions may seem strange, but I am doing this for the greater good."

"Whose side are you on?" she hissed that question again.

"I am on the side of Nestham. Always." Truth.

A broken, bitter laugh as she spun the staff in her hand, shimmering her light over and over again. "That's not an answer. And considering how the Wildborn fell from Nestham, that's another irony."

Alsair's eyes glistened. "Kyra," he said, but fell into silence.

"I—" She tried to speak, but couldn't. "I've had enough of your lies. I hope you find whatever it is you're looking for." Her jaw clenched, blood pounding in her ears. "But if I *ever* think you will betray us, or hurt Eli, I will throw you out the window myself." Her Mark gleamed, illuminating the acceptance on his face.

Kyra turned and stalked away, seeking the warmth and comfort and strength that she would have found in bed.

# Chapter 37

As the first rays of dawn crept through her window, she sighed and reached over the other side of the bed, and settled on his warmth.

"Morning," he said. She turned her head and found him smiling with his eyes half-closed, that tattoo arcing over his cheek.

"Morning." She inhaled deeper, and a delicious aroma filled her senses. "Is that bacon I smell?"

A sleepy grin twisted his beautiful tattoo. "Anne brought up several servings a few minutes ago. I didn't want to wake you." She smiled at what the servant girl would have made of a half-dressed Eli sleepily taking the tray of food. "There's plenty for Amora as well. Do you want to wake her?" The door opened, and Amora shot in, grabbed a plate of food and sprinted over to the table in the corner, tucking in immediately.

"Good morning to you too," Eli said. She waved a piece of bacon in the air and grinned, some of it still hanging out of her mouth.

Kyra rolled her eyes, still barely awake. "At least bring some over to us," she said.

"Get it yourself," Amora mumbled through chewed-up food.

Sheets rustled as Eli made his way over to the table and grabbed the other two plates of food, still steaming. He handed one to Kyra, and she sat up, greedily tucking into the food, another trace of warmth stealing through her heart. But every time she looked at Eli, all she could see was Alsair's face. Hastily, she turned back to her food and focused on finishing every morsel. Eli made several blissful sounds as he devoured his breakfast.

"That good?" she asked, nudging him with her elbow.

"It's not every day you get to have breakfast in bed." A second passed, two, until his eyes clouded over and she sensed her peaceful morning had just ended. "I need to go talk to Monsun." Her core tightened as he pressed a kiss to her cheek and stepped out onto the balcony, his upper body bare save for the vambraces on his arms. For an instant, he was silhouetted in the sunrise, until he vanished into a flash of light.

"Weird how he does that," Amora commented. "He's still terrible in the slums."

Kyra smiled and went to freshen up. When she exited the bathing suite, garbed in a rich blouse and pants, she extended a hand to the girl wiping bacon grease from her lips. "Do you want to come see Lady Eislyn with me?"

Amora scooted off the seat to join her, and together they left for the Healing Wing. When they entered, they found Jayne already there, her eyes hollow. "How do you do it, Jayne?" Kyra asked. "You were up all night researching, and now I find you back here with Eislyn?" Amora let go of her hand and swept over to Eislyn.

"I'm fine," Jayne said, hands tensed at her sides.

A wave of guilt crashed over Kyra as she gazed at her parents, lying together, barely breathing. Her father's days of lucidity were long gone, and her mother was almost perfectly still. The attendant bustled around, checking pulses and breath rates. He marked it down on a piece of paper, then shuffled off. So clinical, so cold, as if they reduced her parents to numbers on a page. The people who had raised her and taught her almost everything she knew.

She swept her gaze down to Eislyn, and the young woman's arms lay stiff at her side. Her skin was pale, almost bloodless. Golden hair spilled around her like a breaking crown. Kyra's heart cracked, but something caught her senses. A faint hiss of air, almost as if—she turned her head and saw Eislyn's chest rise further than it had done since she'd fallen asleep.

"Did you see that?" she asked, hope rising in her own chest. No, it couldn't. She wouldn't let herself take this false hope—

Eislyn's breathing increased, and her eyes fluttered. Kyra and Jayne gasped in unison, and Jayne yelled for the attendant. The young man clad in white burst in, pressing a finger to Eislyn's wrist, listening to her breathing. Then he called for his superior.

"Send for Lord Ketan," Kyra said. "He needs to see this." Eislyn's amber eyes were clouded, but they were *open.* The Regent stepped forward and laid her hands on Eislyn. The Lady panicked, her breathing coming faster.

"Shh, it's okay. You're safe, *amica.* I'm here, and so is Jayne. Your father is on his way." Eislyn kept gasping for air. Calming her hadn't worked.

"Hold her down!" the head Healer said, a stern woman with grey hair falling to her shoulders. They pushed Eislyn back down onto the bed, but a bloodcurdling scream wrenched itself from her throat.

"No! That reminds her of what happened!" Jayne pushed forward.

"Kallon, get the Voidling," the older woman said. The young man passed a vial to her, and the Healer pressed it to Eislyn's lips, pinched her nose to force her to open her mouth. When she did, she poured it straight into her mouth and clamped her hand over it to prevent Eislyn from spitting it out. At last, she swallowed the liquid.

"What in the Hells was that?" Jayne breathed.

"A mild sedative. It's derived from Void, but we use it here sparingly. It'll keep her calm, and when she wakes, she'll be less likely to panic."

At that moment, Kyra heard raised voices outside. Lord Ketan, arguing with the two guards posted there. Kyra opened the door, and Ketan was too panicked to bow, sweeping into the chamber, his doublet crumpled and stained. It was like the man hadn't even bothered to take care of himself.

"They told me she was awake," he rasped, a horrible light shining in his amber eyes.

"She was," Jayne said. "She's just drifted back off again, but she seems to be recovering." Ketan slumped into a nearby chair, and Kyra turned to Jayne.

"I'll tell the others the good news." She left her friend and her parents, and told herself there was nothing more she could do with them. Strange how easy lying to herself had become.

Her footsteps led her back first to her chambers. She found the bed still messy, but Nix and Eli were gone. She checked the Vindicator's spire and found Monsun and Syl deep in conversation. They rose from their chairs and bowed, but Monsun couldn't mask his anger.

"Lady Eislyn awakened," she said.

Hope rose in Syl's face, yet Monsun remained unmoved. She peered at him and felt the weight of his disappointment. "Oh, for Nestham's sake, say it." She brushed a hand over her face, blearily rubbing her eye.

"We've found the first reports of what we think is Temero."

Her heart dropped all the way into her stomach. "Where?" The world seemed to stop as she stood in their office, the vista of her country stretching out around them.

But Monsun's dark eyes remained steady. "Mount Sancti." Where the first pillar was located, before the Order had smashed it to rubble.

"If Temero knows about the pillars, maybe he knows where the others are located," she said.

"No." Syl shook her head. "But I think he knows *you* know."

"Send more forces to Talon Reach," Kyra said, bracing a hand on the table. "As many as it takes to fortify it."

"Already done. We've begun reaching out to allies, but there are worse things to think about."

She snapped up, watching him carefully. "You reached out to allies without my approval?"

"It had to be done. What's worse," Monsun said, "is his position." Mount Sancti was in the centre of the continent, between Imbra and potential allies.

Jalek's fleet had just become more valuable than ever. "Then we need to act fast against him, or he'll trap us in the north."

They studied the map. Mount Sancti's ruins occupied the middle of Ekra. If Temero could build a big enough force, he'd cut off the rest of them from help. "Imbra should be safe enough behind the Kinar River," Monsun said. "Spring is when it's hardest to cross. He'll have to wait until summer when it calms down."

"Or he could just sit and wait, or even go after some of our allies." Syl turned to Monsun. "Are you going to reach out to the Emperor of Biralam, to warn him and request aid?"

Monsun's eyes darkened, and the muscles tensed in his forearms. "I told you, he won't listen. But we have some alternatives." His finger rested on a castle marked on the southern part of the Eastern Plains. "Dukes Stallor and Fallkirk have claimed ascendancy over their halves of the Plains. If we could get some of their soldiers, or have them hold a line stretching to the Plains, we might contain Temero."

"Stallor would never do it. If he deploys any of his own troops elsewhere, his enemies will attack." War had divided the Plains for years. Kyra had learned of its original name, Amerin, before it fell into civil war.

"What if we sent Jayne back?" Syl asked. "She'd be your ambassador. Maybe she could speak to Stallor."

"What we really need is the Calethim," Monsun said. "They're sworn to serve the Marked of the Plains, but if..." His voice trailed off.

"If we could convince them to fight, they'd be good scouts and secret warriors." *Nestham above, we're really doing it. We're planning a war.*

"Monsun," she said. "You can't fight a war without all five Vindicators." An angry light gleamed in Monsun's eyes. Only his respect for her title prevented him from giving her a dressing-down, as he had done to Eli.

"Permission to speak freely, Highness?"

She sighed, waving a flippant royal hand. "Granted." She braced herself as the Vindicator took a wide stance, almost like he was preparing to fight.

"Eli came to see me this morning," Monsun said. "What I told him is what I will tell you now. The one thing I do not tolerate in my Vindicators is dishonesty. What Eli did, what you sent him to do, was ill-advised. It was not a part of a Vindicator's Code. The ruler does not use Vindicators without my approval."

She raised her brow. "Maybe not. But oaths and tattoos aside, you cannot claim Eli as just a Vindicator. He's a Guardian, which surpasses the claim you—or I—have on him. And you need him, whether you admit it."

Next to him, carefully hidden from the towering Vindicator, Syl raised a brow and nodded imperceptibly.

"I'll consider it," he said coldly.

"Can I count on your support at the Council meeting?" Kyra said. "I need you on my side."

He heaved a breath. "Your will, Highness."

Kyra nodded, concealing the surge of relief that threatened to buckle her knees. It had taken him a lot to say it.

Kyra finished up the planning, and marched back down to the court, seeking Eislyn. She found the girl sitting up, drinking tea, her father on one side and Jayne on the other. Kyra beamed, but Eislyn just ignored her. *What?* Jayne shrugged, her gaze cautious. Lord Ketan glared at her from the comfortable chair.

"It's good to see you've recovered, *amica,*" Kyra said, just hovering there.

The Lady didn't speak for a long moment until she finally shifted and raised her gaze. "Why's that?"

Why? "Because you're my friend, and I was worried about you." Even that sounded pathetic.

Eislyn let out a low hiss, her amber eyes molten, her teeth bared in a snarl. "Worried? You did this to me!"

"What? That was Trayse!" Her heart stopped. Surely Eislyn was imagining things. Surely she was just confused.

Eislyn shivered, clutching a red blanket to her chest. "He told me. Right as he stuck the knife in, he told me what you'd done." Tea spilled onto the sheets, spreading a black stain across the cloth. "He said that you—you ordered him to do it."

"And you believed him? This is Trayse!" Her voice echoed in the quiet halls. "The first time I met him, he slaughtered my friends and tortured me. The second time, he poisoned Monsun and drugged me!"

But none of that made an impact, not as the tea cup wobbled in Eislyn's hands. "This happened to me because of *you.*"

Kyra bit her lip to stop it from trembling. "I tried to save you."

"You can't save anyone. I learned that when your friend tried to kill me. Now get out."

"Eis—"

"I said *get out!*" The mug blurred as it shot towards her face—Kyra ducked underneath the flying object, her Mark flaring into motion. Tears fell from her eyes as she stumbled from the door and down the stairs.

A familiar scent filled her senses, and she choked back a sob, but her vision blurred as he spoke. "Kyra—*Nestham above,* what's wrong?"

To her right lay a closet, and she blindly reached for the handle. "Nothing! I—I just need a minute." She slammed the door shut behind her and forced her breathing to even out, dried her tears. The meeting would start any minute, and she couldn't afford to show weakness.

When she emerged, he was still waiting there, still there, still there for her. She kissed him desperately, wrapping trembling arms around him. "I'll explain later, but I have to go."

"All right. But when you get back, I'm making you go to bed." He smiled wryly.

The words she'd wanted to say rose to her throat, after weeks of being repressed, scared of losing him. "I'll see you in a few hours," was all she said.

# Chapter 38

As Kyra approached the meeting chambers, two men's voices echoed in the corridors.

"I'm sorry Rumpre, but it must be done."

"You truly believe she did this?"

"I have proof. She and her Champion killed your men." Just as Kyra rounded the corner, Finon and Rumpre entered the chambers. She followed a minute later, mind racing.

She was the last to arrive. Yuras was as angry as ever, and an empty chair showed Hyrin was still missing. But Rumpre was the worst. He frowned, not angry, just... not on her side. Kyra found her failure there. The Treasurer had teetered between her and Finon, now no longer. Unless...

"Gentlemen." She nodded. Only Monsun rose, and when he glanced at the rest of them, an angry light gleamed in his eyes.

She raised a brow at the disrespect. "Is there a reason for this?"

Finon at last displayed a smile, and it was not a pretty one. "Certain matters have come to light, Highness, which we cannot overlook."

"Yes. Lady Eislyn has awoken. We know her attacker, and we will catch and execute him promptly," she said.

No reaction from Finon. "I'm afraid it was another matter." The masterful actor was putting up an excellent impression of the concerned citizen acting in her best interests.

The door opened, and Kyra was about to turn and scathe the entrant for interrupting them, but she stopped. A priest in grey, the symbol of the towering tree on his brooch.

"Khadim Leon." She bowed. The priest looked at her in loathing and shouldered past her.

"It appears your indiscretions have been revealed, Highness," Finon said.

Leon spoke, and he was no longer the gentle soul with whom she had served. "You have spilled blood without regard for human life, Kyra Antarun." His voice grated on her ears, and a chill descended on her.

"Khadim, I'm not hiding that I've spilled blood. But always—always in self-defence. You know as well as I do that our code allows it."

"Not when you attacked my men a year ago," Finon said.

And in that instant, she remembered.

*One of them had held a staff. Her first target. He'd gone down fast, with one punch to the gut, and a second to the throat.*

"Your men? They were about to murder a helpless woman!" Her gaze flicked back to the other religious leader. *When their leader had laughed as the woman screamed, red had blurred her eyes. She'd swept up the staff, and seconds later, the other three were down.*

"Khadim, hear me. I have never spilled blood selfishly. The Musadim exists to serve!" *And when she'd met Luca's gaze, blood splattered on her cheek, it was the first time he hadn't smiled.*

Leon shook his head sadly. "Kyra, you have broken our most sacred oath. I have no choice but to dismiss you from the Musadim."

*She'd stood bloody-handed, watching, as a cloaked figure raised his hood, revealing an elder man with an intelligent gaze.*

"Let it be known that Regent Kyra Antarun is a faithless ruler," Finon said. "The Council believes you are not fit to rule."

*"What's your name?" he had asked her.*

"This is an outrage!" Monsun slammed his chair backwards and towered over the others.

*"I have no name," she had replied.*

Finon produced a scrap of parchment from his robes and slid it across the table. "A Regency requires the assent of the Council. I'm afraid that the majority no longer supports you."

Kyra studied the document, pretending her entire world wasn't collapsing around her. The writing was brisk, to the point. And at the bottom, three signatures. Finon, Rumpre, Yuras. Suddenly, Hyrin's absence made a lot more sense, an unmistakable chill sweeping in—the Spymaster had finally fallen. She'd mourn later.

Kyra glanced up, keeping her breathing steady. Monsun was still standing, his gaze darting between everyone he saw as a threat, his fists clenched. A frozen calm descended over her, the strength of the stone-faced warrior. She'd survived killing fields, and she'd survive a room of spiteful old men.

"Stand down, Monsun"—she waved two fingers. "He's been planning this a long time. Council chambers are a sanctuary." Her gaze fell on Leon, who at least had the grace to look down. "Know this, Khadim. I have served Nestham all my life, and I would never dare spill blood for selfish reasons. And when you realise I will do anything—anything—to protect my kingdom, then I will forgive you. But for now, get out of my castle. As for you," her eyes swung to Finon, the old snake smiling slightly, "you know the laws. Sanctuary protects members from arrest while inside chambers."

"What makes you think we will arrest you here, Regent? We are merely acting as we should—for the people."

"And I assume you wish to take command," Monsun spat.

"Of course he does." Kyra leaned back in her chair, willing that swaggering arrogance she'd seen on other warriors, though it did not suit her. "That was the first move when he poisoned my father." Rumpre's gaze widened. "Oh. So you didn't know that, Treasurer? Yes, he had his pet assassin do it. The same person who attacked Lady Eislyn and who probably killed your men." Rumpre's face pinched, but he said nothing. Coward.

She'd failed everyone. Kyra rose from the chambers, and Monsun followed her out into the passage. No one in sight. "The attack is coming tonight," she said. "Make the preparations."

# Chapter 39

The rapping came at Eli's door five minutes later. Monsun burst in, eyes narrowed, a predator in every inch of his being. Eli met his gaze even as he threw the parchment into the desk drawer.

"What do you want?" he asked, his chair grating on the floor. He drew himself up to his full height, but even then, he was dwarfed by the towering warrior. Monsun's face twitched, that silver tattoo shifting. Eli stared up into that face, normally handsome, etched with raw fury.

"Her Highness has been removed as Regent."

The world shattered. "*What?*" he hissed. No, no, it couldn't happen, he wasn't ready, he hadn't planned enough for this.

"Finon swayed Rumpre. The Regent thinks the coup is happening tonight."

"But that's too fast," Eli muttered. "I'm not ready to—" He met Monsun's gaze. "I'm sorry about disobeying you. I was doing what I thought was right."

"I know. I know you know it wasn't right."

Eli rushed to arm himself, shrugging on his weapons, strapping on his vambraces. "What are your orders?" he called over his shoulder, scanning through the room for anything he'd missed.

"Now, there's the Vindicator I trained," Monsun said. "We draw Finon in, and when we do, we capture him with evidence. This is our chance to catch him in the act."

\* \* \*

Hours later, the sun fell over the rooftops in a blazing display of flame. Eli shifted on the rope attached to the roof, hammered in hours ago. His senses remained keen, heightened by the Mark. He clung to the wall of the Cathedral, pressing his face into the wall as the Eternal Flame blazed above. A whisper of wind, and he heard one of the most hated voices in Ekra.

"Have you prepared the troops?" Finon asked, that smooth voice honed by years of whispering secrets and deaths and betrayal.

"Yes, Chosen." A younger voice, bristling with male arrogance, leashed by training. *Chosen.* Yet another blasphemy. And they called *him* the heretic...

"Good. Begin the attack. Capture the Regent, but all of her allies must die."

"And the King and Queen?"

"They've been moved out of the city. We're searching for them now."

Boots clicked once, then marched out on the floor. Eli ached to Rift right into Finon's office and end him, but that wasn't the way. He'd learned his lesson. He was a Vindicator, the Torchbearer, the Light of the North. Eli Rifted to a safe spot and ran into the castle, sprinted to the Vindicator's Spire. He burst into the office. The room stank of stale sweat and nervousness, though it was well-hidden. A room full of professional killers.

"Anything useful?" Monsun asked.

"They took the bait. They think the King and Queen have been removed. They're attacking now, and they want all of us dead." He rolled his shoulders, forcing his breathing to slow. "Her Highness," he winked at Kyra, "is the only one they want alive."

"I'm honoured." Kyra rolled her eyes and flashed a smile at him.

Monsun raised a brow. "Then we have our mission. Syl, you and your men are on patrols. We have evacuated the court. Finon probably already has men in the castle, so you will play cat-and-mouse with the assassins Finon will send." Syl nodded, her hair braided back.

"Raylene, I want you on the front-line in the Citadel. I've given Commander Wurn instructions to follow your orders. You also have men from the Seventh. If any Eternal Order soldiers attempt to enter this castle, you send them back. Jalek," he met a lazy gaze, "you're with her."

"It'll be my pleasure, Lady Raylene." Veturan smirked from his position by the maps. The older woman rolled her eyes, yet a faint smile curled her lips.

"Everyone else will remain in here," Monsun continued, bracing himself on the table. "Seal yourselves in the Playground. If we play this right, we capture Finon, maybe Trayse, and wipe out the Eternal Order's command structure."

"However," Syl took over, "if we get it wrong, we could start a civil war. Thousands of Imbran citizens are members of the Order's congregation, and they don't know what Finon is doing. The other half are Musadim and won't fight, especially if word gets out that Her Highness was defrocked. This must be as quick as possible. As soon as Finon rears his ugly head, we lop it off, metaphorically speaking."

"Get to your positions," Monsun said. "And may Nestham be with us all."

Syl and Raylene snapped off a Vindicator salute, thumping their right hands over their hearts. Veturan flicked a casual forefinger in Monsun's direction and slunk out, and the others turned back to their papers. Eli marched over to the Senior Vindicator.

"Why are you keeping me in the Playground?" He pitched his voice low. "It better not be because of earlier."

"No, Eli. You're the Regent's Champion. They'll expect you to stay with her, and when they come looking, that's exactly what we want them to see. You've got Nix. Protect Amora until your last breath."

"And the King and Queen?"

"We moved them back into the Royal Spire. It's one of the most defensible places in the palace. Nobody will get up there."

Hope, a fire, stirred in Eli, and he thumped the armour on his chest. Glittering steel, complemented by his Nesthamir vambraces. Monsun embraced him, their armour clashing together. Monsun turned and spoke to Alsair, hovering by the windows. The old monk raised his hood and left.

"And what will you do?" Eli called after the hulking figure.

"I'll do what I always do," Monsun said. "Be the anchor."

* * *

Eli shut the massive iron door, its screech in the stone room the only sound. His breath misted as silence settled in. Every single flame in this room they'd doused, but as his eyes adjusted, the hanging ropes and platforms came into view. The only one was the covered Eternal Torch by Tomas's side. When he needed it, he could remove the cover and have it flare immediately. Amora needed no light. Neither did he nor Nix. Tomas had left his maps behind, and now idly checked his bow and quiver, his knives. Eli reached the platform where Tomas waited. He grabbed his bow and strung it, keeping an eye on the door.

"I don't like this," he muttered. "I would have preferred to protect her myself."

"I know," Tomas said. "But it's like you said. They want to capture her. The rest of us don't matter as much."

"I'm still not a fan of dying horribly."

"Well, you'd better shoot properly," Tomas replied. "Because it's the two of us, an urchin, a one-armed monk, and a giant snow leopard against whatever comes in that door."

"I hate the waiting," he muttered.

"Get used to it," Tomas said.

"War is just a lot of waiting," Alsair cut in, amusement in his voice. The two elders grinned at each other, like recognising like.

"Aren't you the General of Leranion? Aren't you supposed to be out there leading the charge?" Eli asked, shoving his hands into his pockets.

"That's Monsun's job. We figured out pretty quickly that I make the plan, and he executes it." Tomas shrugged. "So yes, technically I have equal rank, but he's better in the heat of the moment. I'm not spectacular in a close-quarters fight."

Amora said nothing, but Eli had already seen her eyeing off the ropes with interest.

The silence was still worrying. Had Monsun and the others stopped the conflict? Or was there something waiting in the dark for the perfect moment to strike? He shuffled against the wood for better support, tested the ease of drawing his sword. It slid silently, easily, with barely a whisper of steel on wool, a lethal weapon fit for a Champion, one that had seen him through so many conflicts. He flicked his gaze around, almost tempted to engage his sight just to get a glimpse of their faces, but he settled for brushing Amora's shaking fingers with his own, finding them cold and clammy. He squeezed them, and they squeezed back. Amora smiled, pressed next to the rumbling snow leopard, twitching.

And for a single second, he almost believed they could be okay. But then the building started rumbling, a roar rushed through their ears and all the blood drained from Eli's mind. He recognised that sound; he recognised that feeling, that sense of death.

"Nestham's Will." The earth trembled, but he could see nothing in these depths. He leapt off the platform and sprinted to the door. Eli glanced back, nodded at Tomas ready to unleash an arrow. He threw the door open. Nothing.

But in the windows beyond, the sight made bile surge up into his throat. Flame billowed into the night sky, spewing orange and red death. He rushed back inside.

"They're not targeting the castle," he said, his voice unnaturally loud in the chamber. "They're going after the people."

"It'll be a trap," Tomas said. "One to draw in our troops before they strike."

"Either way," Eli said, "I can't risk it." There was no time for preaching, nothing worth saying. "Stay with Amora."

Amora pulled him into a hug before flinging something into his hand. "Go, gruntah. I'll look after them."

Eli grinned, his teeth glittering in the Eternal Torch's golden glow. He slammed the door shut and sprinted through the castle, the Torch casting strange lights on his armour. He rushed past Raylene and Veturan, guarding the door. "They're moving into the city. We need to go!"

Raylene snarled and pulled the Seventh's Second to her. "Keep your men here. I'll take mine in." She waved for troops of the First to follow, and a Vindicator, a Prince and a Guardian charged into the chaos.

# Chapter 40

Syl ghosted through the darkened castle, pacing past the beautiful ornaments, stalking through the shadows. Around her, the men and women extinguished torches, leaving a trail of darkness around them. Her own force. Former and current Veils, Royal Guards, and a young thief she'd once caught trying to steal her purse. Brun flashed an affable grin at her and stepped closer, revealing a fresh scar added to his face since she'd last seen him.

"How you going?" he breathed.

She waved a gloved hand. "Is this really the time to ask?"

"Sounds like the perfect time. You still pining after that pretty Vindicator?" When she hissed and looked away, staring down the endless passages, she could practically feel his grin pricking her neck. "You didn't deny it."

She flicked her finger in a rude gesture. Around her, the others gathered, not in Nightweave, but in their own clothes. Assassins, spies, exiles, thieves—the future of Leranion rested on these shoulders.

The idea of black and white was a new one for her. Monsun couldn't see the world as anything but. That was the Senior Vindicator for you. But Syl was born in the shadows. Orphaned early, dragged up in the slums. And when she'd broken into a house of an elder man who she'd thought was away for the weekend, he'd returned home to find her raiding his pantry. And he'd looked at the shaking knife she pointed at him and laughed.

"Take as much as you need," he'd said. "I'll be back in an hour." The next night, she'd returned to find dinner left at the window she'd broken.

He'd saved her life. Put her in a Musadim home, with wonderful foster parents who'd raised her. He'd given her a year of peace, then sought her out once again, offering her a choice of a new life. He'd never laid a hand on her as he trained her to become a Veil. Taught her to walk in the darkness while still keeping the light inside her. She'd learned she was not only born in the shadows, but was born for them too. And when she turned twenty-five, Spymaster Hyrin had hugged her once as he approved her transfer to becoming a Vindicator three years ago.

And that was when she met the handsome warrior from Biralam, the famous Monsun Al-Iman, former commander of the Seventh and the future Senior Vindicator. She shook her head, clearing her mind. Yes—born for the shadows. She wore light leather boots and reinforced Nightweave. Strong enough to walk into the melee and emerge covered in everyone else's blood. Her twin sabres poked out from over her shoulders, and she held her knives in harnesses across her thighs. Her outfit wasn't anonymous, but it was battle-capable, a walking armoury.

She held up a hand in the pitch-black castle, and the nobodies paused without a thought. Footsteps approached from around the corner. Order? Leranion? Nobility? She pressed up against the wall and waited. Seconds later, three Order soldiers glided through the passageway, barely even making a sound. She pursed her lips and her Second, Aileen, glanced at her questioningly. *Do we take them down?*

She shook her head, and they remained on edge until the Guardsmen paused. The tallest one, the leader, stood upright, and almost *sniffed* the air. Syl froze, her hand on one of the throwing knives strapped around her waist. If he looked at her, he'd find it sticking out of his chest.

And then the earth rumbled, and the Guardsmen started laughing. A flash of light ripped through the air, and for a second Syl glimpsed the emblem on his chest. A dove, impaled by a sword.

"That's the signal," one muttered.

"Now we move on the Princess," the leader said. Well, that changed her plans. Syl whipped the knife from her belt and flung swiftly. It whizzed through the air and struck the leader in the neck. Blood spurted out, and he went down with barely a cry. A crossbow bolt impaled a second, and the third had a blade shoved through his heart. The bodies crumpled to the floor, dead before they even hit the ground.

Syl glanced at her troops. One nodded at her, ocean-blue eyes concealed beneath a Nightweave hood. Syl winked back. "Hide the bodies," she ordered. "Split up in pairs. Spiral around the Vindicator's Spire. Anyone wearing red or looks like a threat, kill it." They all nodded. *I only hope the others can keep the city under control.*

* * *

His heart thumped in his chest, his Mark shining under steel gauntlets. Every step, his armour fitted perfectly to his body, practically an extension of himself. Vindicators didn't do things by halves. In one hand, a sword glittering in the light of his ice-blue light, in the other, an Eternal Torch glowing with its Nestham-granted power. A beacon to rally around. To his left, Veturan's rapier glowed green, the entire blade pulsing with the power of his Mark.

Eli's senses snapped into being, eyes sharpening, his hearing increasing, his smell picking up the blood and refuse and death emanating from the city. His feet fell into a quick rhythm, easily eating up the metres. He didn't need to look far. The flames from beyond the Citadel walls were enough. Flames and smoke and screams.

Nestham's Will had struck again.

"Where was that explosion?" Veturan yelled, not even out of breath.

"The Imbran Guard barracks," Raylene wheezed from behind them, her footsteps accompanied by the tramp of boots of the First, the last regiment left in Imbra. Eli's stomach plummeted, and he cursed, dodging citizens scrambling to get out of the way. "Likely they were ambushed. The Guard aren't soldiers."

"Then we search for survivors!" Eli roared. The acrid stench clogged his nose, his throat, and he coughed wretchedly. That smell haunted his dreams. It seemed it would never stop.

237

The screams were getting louder. More citizens seemed to run with buckets full of water, drawn from wells throughout the city. The smoke cloud neared until they rounded the corner.

Eli's parched throat dried even further. The stone building was nothing but rubble, as if pebbles brushed aside by a god in a careless game. The same for the bodies, utterly wrecked, just like at Mount Sancti.

"There won't be any survivors," Veturan said.

Bile rose in Eli's throat, tears fell down his face. His sword he sheathed. No matter what he could do, he would always be too late to save these people. He dropped to his knees in the mud, his hands seeking purchase on anything. His fingers caught under the stone, and he grunted, dropping into his strength.

Rock groaned, and he heaved at it, grunting under the weight. "Help me!"

"It's too late, you idiot!" Jalek yelled from behind him, his voice cracking. "It's too late!"

The stone scraped on his armour, pressing down, bowing him under its weight. "These are my people!" he said. "I don't care if it's too late. I swore to protect them! Now help me!"

Veturan stepped closer, and his rapier rasped into its sheath. His face gleamed in the Torch's light. "Fine," he breathed. He dropped beside Eli and pulled, and together, they grunted and lifted the stone, throwing it to the side. It landed with a thud that resonated through Eli's heart. The grisly moan beneath them pierced his soul.

"Get a healer here now!" Raylene yelled. "Soldiers, fan out and secure the area!" The troops spread out and surrounded the area, helping to lift the bodies where needed.

"Help..." a voice echoed from the rubble. Eli dropped to the ground, and more bile rushed into his throat. A face. At least, he thought it was a face. Charred, blistered, destroyed. "They—they struck without warning..." the man sighed through cracked lips. Fresh blood dribbled out of his mouth. Eli clutched the man's hand, screaming inside. He tunnelled into his magic, seeking that light, that light, but that shadowy veil of Malmir, an unholy shield, blocked it, blocked any way of accessing it.

"Break," he ordered it. "*Break.*" With all of his will, he imagined that veil shattering, piercing light through. He swarmed it with attacks of fire, of his magic. It splintered, and light—his healing magic—pulsed through him again. His sob of relief as he pushed it into the man—it recoiled, refusing to enter him, refusing to restore him.

Eli opened his eyes again, and fresh tears dribbled down his face as the Guard's eyes sightlessly stared at the sky. "For—for what you have given, we thank you," Eli said. "May we always remember your sacrifice." To Jalek, he merely said, "Keep looking."

His heart started thrumming; red flashed in his vision. That fire rose to the surface as he roared at the sky, not caring who heard, who looked at him and thought he was insane. He had failed again. More screams filled the air, penetrating the fog of fury in his mind. Footsteps filled the alleys. A troop of Eternal Guardsmen, in gleaming red uniform and armour, faced off against a group of the First.

There was no hesitation, no tense waiting. Weeks of tension boiled over as arrows shot out of the darkness, from the rooftops. Eli ducked as an arrow shot overhead. Raylene tensed, but Jalek gracefully shielded her, swatting the arrow out of the air with his blade. The First was not so lucky. Within seconds, most were downed. Raylene screeched, a horrible keening sound and made to sprint towards the fallen, Eli with her. Powerful hands gloved in armour yanked them back.

"Don't," Veturan said, arrows and screams almost drowning him out.

Beside him, the tall woman screamed, her spear raised to the skies. "Those are my men!"

239

"Not anymore." More arrows came, and they threw themselves to the ground, raced for cover, dragging Raylene with them. Silence.

"You're dead, rats," the shout rang out. "There's no escape!"

"Rot in hell!" Eli yelled back over the rock, his entire body quivering. "We'll fight until you're all dead!" He extended his arms to Raylene and Veturan, who looked at him in confusion. "Grab my shoulders," he said. He snatched up the Torch, and when two hands touched his shoulders, he slammed his vambraces together, vanishing into the Rift.

The space between spaces was even louder than before. Screams everywhere in the inky blackness. They fell out onto rough tiles, and Eli gasped for breath, drawing air into his shattered lungs.

"Since when—since when could you do that?" Veturan asked.

Eli looked him in the eye, the handsome Prince fighting with them. "There's a lot you don't know about me, Prince."

"Well, whatever it is," he said, "do it again." The soldiers climbed onto the roofs, arrows coming close. Eli pulled them back into the Rift and gagged as he exited, his powers draining. Maybe he'd have one more jump in him. Then the earth shook again. But this time, it erupted in a tremendous explosion.

"The Guild headquarters," Raylene said. Safe for a moment, they watched the flames climb high into the sky. More soldiers pushed in, and this time, they could only run. Deeper into the slums.

# Chapter 41

Monsun waited in the main entrance to the palace, his men around him. Together, they raised their voices inside the castle. Monsun waited with a troop, his axe bared and hungry for blood. The door rattled once. Twice. "Stand your ground!" he roared. "They are just men!" He forced himself to grin, to be the legendary commander. "The Seventh eats Guardsmen for breakfast."

Muffled laughter came from around him. He could only hope the rest of the castle was secure, but he trusted Syl. She would do her job, killing off the assassins at his back. In the meantime, it was the enemy in front he had to worry about. That was fine by him. If he could see it, he could cut it in half. He flipped his axe in his hand and banged it on his shield, a crash that echoed throughout the room, echoed by the men behind him. Together, they screamed battle cries at a door shuddering with a mass of Eternal Guardsmen.

He knew the worst. Eli, Raylene and Jalek had gone out and hadn't returned. And when you had no guards and suddenly the gate started banging, well, best to arm up and get ready to kill. The door burst open, metal shards splintering through the room, and Monsun faced a hundred soldiers in that red jerkin. Eternal Guardsmen, ready for war. Well, a war is what they would find when they challenged the Senior Vindicator. The Shield of the North. Armies clashed, and the darkness enveloped Monsun.

Muffled thuds echoed in Syl's ears as she wiped the blood off her blade on the noble silks of yet another Order assassin. They were getting better, and Syl's force had a hard time putting this one down. Brun flashed another grin at her, but she couldn't smile back this time. Not as the very air chilled, and a boom shuddered through the entire palace. A familiar voice roared orders over the din, and her heart stopped. No. She swallowed, finding her mouth dry.

"There shouldn't be many more," she said. "Keep pressing them back."

Brun looked at her, and his gaze was too adult, too grown up, too mature from the boy she'd found in the slums years ago. Barely older now than she'd been when she left. Damn it, she should never have brought him along. But he was a Veil, just like she had been. Born and raised for the shadows, walking that line between light and dark, that knife edge of duty—and doing the right thing. And she'd always preferred being a Veil.

"You're leaving, aren't you?" he said.

She closed her eyes and nodded. "He's in trouble. I have to help."

Brun smiled and jerked his blade clean of the second assassin. "Then good luck."

"Get to the others. Find the other woman in Nightweave. If she dies, I'll never hear the end of it." He shook his head. "Get going." He slunk down the next corridor. Syl, however, broke into a sprint for the main hall, her fingers kissed with death.

* * *

An hour later, Eli watched Veturan shift from his place on the wall, his stance weary. "So, they've funnelled us away from the castle and killed all our men." Somehow, the run for vengeance had turned into a slaughterhouse. Raylene's breathing turned into heavy snarls. Eli glanced down the alleyway as Eternal Guardsmen strutted in, swords at the ready. Brave or foolish to enter the slums fully armed. This was never their domain.

"They played us," he said. "But for all of their planning, they are still just soldiers." Raylene's dead eyes met his own. "I've got no Rifting left. But if we can cut through their lines and head to the bluff near the rich quarter, we can make it back to the palace." He risked a peek up the wall, all the way to the Citadel walls. In the light, he thought he made out red jerkins on the walls. His stomach coiled in knots. "No, no, no." They'd done it. The Order had taken the palace.

"Calm down," Raylene said. "Monsun will hold the palace."

Kyra. She was somewhere in there.

"Doesn't look like your man's doing well," Veturan observed. Eli glared at him, but the olive-skinned warrior was already backing away. "Look, I'm not a fan of fighting through another army. Please tell me there's another way in."

*I can only hope we're not too late.*

His heart beat frantically, concern for Kyra practically tearing at him to go back to the Citadel. "There's a cave behind the waterfall that connects to the tunnels where we found the mantik. They flow all the way underneath the castle."

"That's a terrible security risk," Raylene said.

"Well, I only started this job a few weeks ago. So that was your job, not mine." He glanced at Veturan. "How good is your swimming?"

"Better than yours, norlander. I was born on the water," Veturan said.

"Enough measuring," Raylene growled and pointed an armoured hand at Eli. "Take us there."

He nodded and, somewhere inside him, an ember glowed. He willed it to rise into a raging flame, one that would see him through. Something caught, and he lifted the Eternal Torch, the immortal flame.

Raylene sprinted out into the night, and cries followed her. Eli grinned fiercely and followed. An arrow hissed out into the night, and he batted it away. He raised the Torch higher, because he *wanted* them to see. Wanted them to know they weren't afraid of dying. Because he'd made a promise. And he intended to keep it.

*I will come for you.* The armlet on his bicep gleamed, a sacred oath he had yet to give, but he'd live to give it. She'd live to receive it. Raylene hit the soldiers like a battering ram, and Eli lashed out with his sword, shearing a man at the waist. Veturan's rapier impaled a man in the throat, and he fell with a wet gurgle.

Eli kept running. Kept tracing a path through the soldiers. *Keep fighting.* His Mark dimmed, his fire burning out.

\* \* \*

Tomas rose from his position on the platform. Alsair did too, his sword twitching as he tested its balance. The old soldiers didn't need to speak, Amora pressing herself into the shadows. Nix growled and slunk to the side, her tail flicking as she moved, a born predator in motion. The door burst open, and assassins flung themselves in. The first fell to the ground immediately, his chest impaled with a blue-fletched arrow. Tomas drew and sighted again, falling into the familiar rhythms of death and bloodshed. The assassins withdrew for but a moment; the flow stopped by his constant rain of arrows.

He waited a heartbeat. Two. Then they returned, and his answering shot stuck into a shield. Tomas swore, but more piled in, filing onto the massive stone floor, encircling the waiting monk with his head bowed. He didn't acknowledge them as they surrounded him in the dark.

"Get him!" one barked.

Tomas would never see such a fight again. In fact, it wasn't a fight, so much as a slaughter. One lashed out, but Alsair was already moving, neatly dodging, wielding his massive broadsword to cleave the man's arm off. His sword sunk in the man's chest a moment later. He parried the next swing, and within ten seconds, five of them were on the ground. He moved with the grace of a much younger man, even one-handed.

Alsair withdrew, blood coating his blade, and smiled at the last assassin. The attacker instantly ran, but Nix roared, and the man's head fell to the ground a second later. Another soldier fell through the gap, aided by the knife in his back. Nix purred as a woman in black gracefully stepped through the doorway.

"Everyone alright?" she asked.

Tomas bowed, his bow at his side. "Never better." As her eyes landed on Alsair, they tightened, the monk still standing in the ring of executed assassins. Her fingers curled into fists, and her whole being seemed to shift, a creature of the night ready for more violence. Tomas coughed in the dark, his body a prison of old age.

* * *

Monsun gave one step back. Then another. He hewed the head off an Eternal Guard, but more just kept coming. His shield arm had lost most of its strength. He'd have a hell of an ache tomorrow, if he lived to see the sunrise. The soldiers kept coming, screaming their cries.

A towering Guardsman slammed into his shield, knocking Monsun over. A breach opened and his men fell, slashed left and right around them. A sword raised up above him, and Monsun kicked out at the soldier, but it was too late. A foot smashed into his ribs, crushing the air from his lungs. The sword descended.

But a knife lodged itself into the soldier's wrist, and he screamed. And then Syl was there, a figure cloaked in the night, a streak of light, of bloodied, battered hope. She dropped into a roll and came up slicing, dual sabres appearing in her hands. One took a soldier in the side, and she thrust into a second's throat. For a moment, the breach sealed and two of his men heaved the door shut. The panting figure turned to face Monsun as he groaned, levering his axe to push himself back up. Syl strolled up to him, all feline grace, as something coalesced between them. Shimmering, crackling energy. He'd felt that before.

She peered through her lashes; her molten gaze entrapped him in its depths. "I might claim that one day," she murmured, her hand grazing his side.

Monsun's muscles locked up, but the cries began again and the moment shattered. "Thank you." Syl made to stand at his side, ready to face another wave, but he shook his head.

"Enough death," he murmured. "Enough. Get to Finon in the Cathedral. See if you can get him to stop this fight."

"You know I love doing the impossible. Where are the others?"

A bolt of fear ran through him, surrounded by the bodies and carnage. "They haven't returned."

Syl's eyes flashed, but she nodded without words and sprinted for the Cathedral. Blockaded by who knew how many soldiers.

* * *

Finon sipped some of that Giaran wine again, relished the full taste of the expensive drink. He closed his eyes and sighed, rubbing his forehead. Too many late nights. A thud outside made him raise his head.

"Sandria?" he called, but winced. No, Sandria was gone. He almost felt remorse, but these things had to be done. A scream quickly cut off.

The door opened, and he leaned back in his chair, waiting for the inevitable. He did not expect the masked woman strolling in, her garb and blades covered in red. She ripped the mask from her face, revealing hair as white as the moon, gleaming in the luxurious office. What was more prominent was the navy tattoo on her right cheek. A sabre levelled at his face, as that tattoo contorted in fury.

"Tell your troops to throw down their weapons. This fight is over."

"Or what?" Finon stretched his hands above his head and inched his foot closer to the pedal.

"One more chance, Finon!" the Vindicator—Syl, he thought her name was—barked, her eyes burning. "Yield!"

"I don't think so." His foot stamped down on the pedal, and the mechanism clicked. The bolts took the woman in the stomach. The first one rebounded off Nightweave, the second punctured her flesh. Weapons clattered to the floor, and the Vindicator staggered, letting out a fatal gasp.

"By all means. Sit," Finon gestured at the vermilion chair. Now at least he'd be able to tell someone about it. Syl hissed, her hands cupping the wound, but she knew it was a matter of time. He saw the admission in her eyes.

"You won't get away with this," she hissed.

"I already have. Two of your Vindicators are outside the walls with the Prince, and unfortunately their strength is drained."

"They'll get back inside," she said, clumping onto the chair, gloves pooling with red.

"Into the Citadel, which is surrounded by my Guardsmen."

"I know they'll find a way."

"Yes. The path under the waterfall, isn't that correct?" Syl's eyes widened. Triumph rose in Finon's chest as he delivered the death blow. "The same place where you stored two barrels of Nestham's Will? You should take better care of your belongings."

She tried to rise, but she slumped back in the chair. "I—I am going to kill you."

"You can try."

# Chapter 42

Eli summoned a breath and leapt off the edge. For a timeless moment, he was weightless and empty, ice-blue Mark on one hand, golden Eternal Torch in the other, spiralling flame into freezing water. The familiar cold was still a shock as he punched through the raging surface. This time, however, there were no silver eyes to watch him, nobody to help him. That was fine. He grimaced as he pulled himself out of the water under the roiling curtain of the waterfall into the familiar grotto. Beside him, Raylene and Veturan sighed as they lay on the rock beside him.

Nobody dared speak for a long moment until someone had to open his damned mouth. "Well, that light will give us away," Veturan drawled. "Can't you keep a lid on it?" *Oh for Nestham's sake, can you just shut up!* A warning glare from Raylene made him shove that thought deep down.

"Let's move." Steel glimmered in the Torchlight as the three drew weapons and paced towards the tunnel. That familiar mark glittered on the wall again, but something nagged on Eli's mind. He stopped and flicked his gaze around the cavern. One way, the path to the Citadel walls, and the other, back to the tunnels and the maze underneath the castle. But there was something he wasn't seeing.

"Mukk!" he swore. "The barrels are gone."

Raylene staredat him, horror etched on her face. "Didn't you move them?"

"No. I never touched them after I put them here."

"Please tell me you didn't put barrels of that stuff underneath your castle," Veturan groaned.

Fear lodged in Eli's gut. It amplified as footsteps tramped down the passageways. He snarled and readied his sword, the others doing the same.

From the passage leading to the Citadel walls, twenty soldiers filed down, steel overlaying vermilion jerkins.

"Surrender, and you will be executed swiftly," one said, an elder man with a twisting scar down his face.

"That's an ultimatum," Veturan said. "Never liked them."

"Can you Rift us?" Raylene hissed, her eyes frantic, even as she readied her spear.

"No. I'm empty." All Eli could do was fight, and even then, his magic was flickering, drained from all the soldiers earlier. He'd relied on it like a crutch. The soldiers fanned out, their blades held at the ready. The commander looked at him, a woman with blonde hair swept underneath her helmet. He would have thought her honourable except for the medal on her left breast. The dove lanced through with a sword.

"Well," Eli said, "I guess we start praying."

"I've never been one for praying." Raylene shouldered him aside, levelling her spear at the soldiers. "But I'd like to see them on their knees."

Veturan chuckled and moved to stand at her back. The Guardsmen tensed, and at a nod from the commander, stepped closer. Tears moistened Eli's eyes as he prepared to sell his life dearly, a face overlaid on his mind, ocean-blue eyes alight with laughter and joy and passion, a blazing golden Mark and a beautiful smile.

A roar sounded off the stones. Another. The soldiers glanced around in fear, trembling weapons in shaking hands. Eli let out a maniacal laugh, ringing with deathly mirth. The last time he'd heard that roar, three Eternal Guardsmen were eviscerated.

A low, rumbling snarl rang from the pitch-black tunnel. All the soldiers turned to that entrance. Raylene hissed and lunged forward, but Eli held her back with an outstretched arm. Violet eyes opened in the abyss.

"Nix?" he crooned towards the leopard. "Kill."

Nix unleashed herself on the soldiers, shredding a spine before tearing open a throat. Gore covered her fuzzy cheeks, and she turned gleaming, wild eyes on him. Eli shivered, but

249

drew his knife and slashed at a soldier's belly. He ducked under a blade before a rapier impaled the Guardsman in the gut. Veturan swiftly withdrew the blade and advanced on the soldiers. He grinned, his sea-green Mark flashing in the dark, and twirled his blade, a challenge to all. Eli cut down the last few soldiers, and the rest ran back to the walls.

"We might still get inside," Eli said. Nix trotted over to him, and the huge leopard rubbed mottled fur on his bloodstained armour. A trembling hand caressed her matted fur, crusted with blood. None of it hers, fortunately. "You'll need a bath once we're done," he murmured, and Nix purred happily. He turned to Raylene and Veturan. "I need you to take the castle back. Meet up with Monsun and clear the rest out. Then we can push them out of the Citadel."

"Oh, you're giving us the easy mission," Veturan said.

"I'm going after Kyra. I need to make sure she's safe."

"She'll be fine," Veturan said. "She's probably killed off more soldiers than you tonight."

No, he could feel it. That aching in his bones, that long-held dread. Those nightmares back in the Sanctum. No, he could not shake it that easily. They filed into the tunnels, past the rotting corpse of the mantik, past the devastation, climbing up the ladder into the hidden area of the castle.

"Something's not right," he said. A phantom hand jerked his chin, forced him to look up to the royals' suite.

"What is it?" Raylene asked.

"I don't know, but whenever Jaser does this, he usually has a reason." They stalked to a nearby window, and he pushed his way out onto the ledge, glanced at the Royal Spire. No lights lit the Vindicators' suite, but lights still burned in the royals' chamber. A figure moved in the light, and he engaged his sight, homing in on the image until he could be sure. That familiar orange hair. His vision tilted.

"Trayse is in the Royal Spire." And the lights were on. He wanted him to know. That old wound burned in his gut. A shame and a failure he was eager to repay.

"Mukka!" Raylene swore. "Get to him now. Jalek, go with him."

"*Maria*," Veturan said, too much history conveyed in a single word.

"I'm old and slow. You boys are quick enough to catch him." Eli and Veturan traded glances and threw themselves into a sprint through the palace. Eli's pulse ran wild in his veins, his torch already held high, sword sweeping out. Veturan sheathed his sword, mercifully not saying anything. The smell hit him first, a coppery reek of blood. The bodies were next. Most were Order, but some were Leranion troops. At each one, Eli muttered a silent curse on Finon's head. He would pay for this.

Muffled shouts echoed through the room, until the doors burst open and an Eternal Guard flew through the open air, thudding on the ground. Eli met a gleaming silver tattoo on a bloodied face, and he lowered his blade, heart thudding in his chest. "Nice throw."

"Where the mukk have you been?" the Vindicator asked.

"Outside," he said. "You and Raylene need to clear the Order from the Citadel. Trayse is in the Royal Suite." And just saying it again, his insides roiled again.

Monsun paled, genuine fear flashing on his face. "Go kill."

Eli saluted, and they rushed up the stairs, taking two at a time. Veturan moved ahead of him, lanky legs taking the stairs with a fluid ease. Eli snarled and moved up, dropping into the dregs of his magic. His fingers grew numb, that familiar signal he was draining himself dry. This was going to hurt.

They finished the stairs in silence. Veturan glided to the left, and Eli to the right, blade poised for any attack. The faint squelch underneath his shoe made him cast his Torch down. Golden light illuminated blood underneath his shoes. Veturan stepped behind him as Eli approached the ornate door, the peak of the Royal Spire. Where before the lights were on, it was now as dark as the tunnels. Eli nudged the door open, and it rolled back without a squeak. Were they too late?

A faint hiss sounded from behind him, and he coughed once, inhaling a sweet scent, promising comfort and peace. He opened his mouth to suck in more, but a gloved hand clamped over his nose and mouth. Eli clutched at the hand, his blood pounding in his ears. He strained to breathe, strained to thrash against this traitor—Veturan coughed out one word: "Void." Eli stilled immediately, and Veturan removed the hand from his face.

*Void.* In a vapour form, released when they opened the door. Eli clamped his lips shut, refusing to release the life-sustaining air. An inky mist of Void carpeted the room, flowing like the fog above a death swamp. He raised his gaze to the bed. The Void hadn't reached it yet, and the King and Queen lay side-by-side on their bed, breathing steadily. Their attendant was unconscious beside them. Eli hissed and flicked his gaze around the room, the skin prickling on his neck. Trayse. A faint breeze blew in from their right, the open window allowing in the cool night air and battle screams. Had he already left?

A shadow landed between them and hands squeezed around Eli's neck, tighter and tighter. He gasped and opened his mouth on instinct, desperate for air. Immediately, the sweetness flooded in, sending his world spiralling. "She's mine," Trayse breathed.

*No.* He brought his hands up, shoving Trayse back with panic-fuelled strength, spinning to grab his weapon, but Veturan was already pushing him to the side. His rapier flashed out and sliced up Trayse's back, a shallow wound at best. He moved closer, hand out for balance, but Trayse sprinted to the window and hovered on the edge like a raven. As he turned, only malice was in those ice-blue eyes. "Too late, Guardian."

The assassin leapt out and vanished. Eli rushed to follow him, but his head swam, and he collapsed to the ground, the world spinning in front of his eyes. Internally, he let out a screech of frustration. *So close.*

But then a light flared, and something hissed. He twisted his head, and dread pooled anew. A single flame sparked under the bed, and beside it were two familiar barrels.

* * *

The footsteps at the door caused Kyra to jerk her head up and grab her staff. Already, she moved into a defensive stance, blocking the others in the Playground.

But it was a young man who arrived, one she recognised from Syl's team. "We've regained the castle, Highness."

"How do you know who I am?" she asked.

"Long story." He flashed a boyish smile before turning to the others. "Come on, you lot. The big guy wants everyone to kick the reds out."

Kyra glanced around, checking. "Where's Nix?" she asked. No sooner had she done so than the leopard sprinted in, nuzzling her waist. Kyra smiled and scratched the leopard behind the ears.

"Who did you go after?" she said fondly. "Let's go," she ordered. Tomas and Alsair nodded.

"You stay here until I come back, right?" she said to Amora, ignoring the men that shouldered past her. Amora nodded and curled tighter. "Hey, I'll see you soon," she said. "Nix, stay with Amora." The leopard padded over and flopped down next to the urchin, and the girl grinned at her. Kyra led the way through the passages towards Monsun, recoiling at the death strewn across the hall. Bodies and blood and destruction—but Monsun was there, and his eyes tightened when he saw her. "What?"

"Trayse is in the Royal Spire. I sent Eli and Jalek to deal with him." Her breath tightened. No. No. This whole thing had been a distraction. She turned and prepared to sprint to the Spire, but Alsair was already there, his calm green gaze impaling her.

"Highness. Don't do this."

"Get out of my way, Alsair!" She was shrieking now, heedless of the men who watched.

253

"We can't lose you." Truth, unmistakable and hated, slammed into her, as much as she wanted to scream.

"I can't lose them!"

His eyes filled with tears. "I can't let you go up there. Trust me."

She turned back to Monsun, freshly broken, her staff snapping into her hand. "Fine." She'd make the Order *pay*. With Monsun at her side, she pushed a charge for the door, clearing a path through, their soldiers behind them. Kyra's eyes faded from the battle as it just became noise. She couldn't hear anymore, only focusing on what lay ahead. Finally, she stood amongst a ring of bodies, Eternal Guardsmen dead at her feet in the square outside the palace. Monsun was already barrelling off to the Cathedral; she could only run back to the tower.

But her fatal mistake was being alone.

"I'm sorry, Highness." A fist descended on her head, but before her vision faded to black, she heard Alsair say one more thing. "I still need four."

* * *

Eli pushed on his hands and knees, staggered to the barrels, tried to yank them from their spots. Fixed tight. The spark flickered quickly, licking at the wick, and he tried to pull the wire out, but it wouldn't budge. Not even with his strength, weakened as he was from the effects of the Void. Veturan rushed to his side and added his force to it. Eli shook his head, defeat sapping his might. He raised his gaze to the bed, to the royals on it.

In unspoken communication, they staggered to the King and Queen, pale and shrivelled. Veturan hefted Hadrian and shuffled to the door.

Encumbered and weakened, his mind clouded by the Void, Eli lost his balance. Numbness settled in his hands, the last of his Gift ebbing away, drained. Taera slipped from his grasp, and they fell together, the thud winding him immediately. He gasped for air and drew in only more Void. Eli let out a wretched cough, his vision fading. The spark just kept hissing.

The lithe figure paused at the door, a king balanced on his shoulder.

"Please," Eli mouthed. And then the Prince was gone.

*No.* No, but he couldn't rise. The Void cloud had him now, spiralling into a blissful sleep. He tried to move, tried to fight it, but there was nothing left. Until the clouds parted, and Taera's weight fell from him. Veturan stood above him, easily balancing the Queen on his shoulder. Then he reached for Eli.

The hissing stopped.

\* \* \*

Kyra heaved a sigh and rolled over. Alone, rising from a pile of bodies. What had happened? *Trayse.* With her parents. She staggered up, wincing from the blow, flaring her golden Mark, her magic like a coiled snake, ready to strike. She heaved herself along through the courtyard but a rumble ran through the palace. Her stomach dropped. *No.* She rushed for cover, rushed to protect herself, but she was too late.

The Royal Spire, gleaming glass and shining light, erupted into the skyline. Shards of glass whipped through the air, lancing through the city like arrows. Twisted stone fell to the ground, shattering parts of the roof. Kyra crumpled to her knees.

\* \* \*

Monsun staggered into the Cathedral, bloody and battered. Around him lay Eternal Order corpses covered in gore. Syl had done her work well. He pushed open the door, expecting to see the Archbishop cuffed and Syl's beautiful face smiling at him. A weak, feminine groan sounded from beyond, and his heart dropped as Finon's wizened face grinned at him.

"Ah, Monsun. You're too late, I'm afraid."

"Where is she?" he snarled. Finon shrugged and pointed, and it was then that he saw the white-blonde hair falling limply over the chair. No. No, she couldn't be gone. He rushed over to Syl and gasped in shock. A crossbow bolt had taken her in the gut, blood pooling around the wound.

"It is unfortunate, however—"

Monsun heaved the old man by the throat, pinning him against the wall, his blood pounding in his ears. "It is only because we want you alive that I don't crush your throat now," he snarled. He dropped the Archbishop like a sack of potatoes and scooped up Syl. Energy crackled in his bones, the life debt in full force. His body moved of its own will, finding strength from somewhere. Syl moaned, her face white as her hair, her lifeblood drained.

He cradled her in his arms and took his first step. Slowly, carefully—but the debt forced him to run, to jolt her, to carry her over the corpses in the Citadel, through the palace, straight to the Healing Houses. The men parted as he stepped through, pushed his way to the front.

The Head Healer nodded when Monsun placed her on the last bench. "I'll need honey and fresh bandages. But you— you shouldn't be here for this." The crow's-feet at his eyes crinkled with worry.

"I cannot leave her." Monsun's voice cracked.

"You must." The Head Healer placed a hand on his shoulder. "It is hard to leave those we love, but your Kingdom needs you, Vindicator. Now, leave me so I can save her." Monsun snarled, casting one last look at the small woman on the bench, covered in blood. The door slammed shut behind him, and he checked on the men, looking over their wounds, hearing their stories, being the Senior Vindicator once again. Amongst them, one woman staggered up, bloodied and battered. Her greying hair had been flattened by her helmet, and blood smeared across her face. Yet her spear remained in her hands, and she stood freely.

"We won," Raylene said, not quite believing it.

"We won." They had more to do. No doubt this night had forged many life debts. He'd need to see to it the holders treated their debtees properly, as he had been treated. They deserved nothing less as survivors of this battle.

Then the earth rumbled. His debt roared back full force, and his muscles contracted. He jerked like an animal on a leash. He sprinted back through the room, crashed in the door. The Head Healer glanced up, ire on his face, but the bond pushed, as the wind roared throughout the building, a shattering war cry. He leapt forward onto the bench, onto Syl's body. He cradled his Vindicator as rocks plummeted through the room, leaving nothing but rubble behind. One smashed into the ceiling, narrowly missing him, but the men screamed behind him. He could only hold tighter as the world caved in.

A rock struck him on the head, and he fell into unconsciousness.

# Chapter 43

The rumbling stopped, but the screams were just beginning. She dismissed the staff and picked her way through the bodies, too shocked to cry. Not when everything was pressing her towards the shattered remains of the Spire, and the damaged castle which she would protect. Rubble and blood coated the ground. *Mother. Father. Eli. Monsun. Jalek.* All her friends, all missing.

She glanced up through a shattered ceiling. Glass shards lay on the ground, and she used her staff to clear a path through the gleaming wreckage. It shifted and clinked underfoot, but she didn't notice. Not as the smoke curled into the sky, not as the remains of the Spire littered the ground. She ran for the stairs of the Spire, picking her way through the rubble.

"Mother! Father! Eli! Jalek!" she shouted until her voice was hoarse. The haze grew in the ruins, the smoke curling, choking her, forcing her to wrap her scarf around her mouth.

"Mother!" she kept searching, heart thumping wildly. Every breath, that flame in her chest, that small ember of hope, dimmed, stifled by the knowledge that no one faced Nestham's Will and walked away.

"Father!"

She kept searching, scrambling over rock, picking through the debris. A portrait lay broken in two beside her.

"Jalek."

Her Mark flared, she fought to gaze through the smoke and the haze, the dust which coated the air.

*Eli.*

A weak moan sounded above her, above the ruined stairs. She ignited her Mark and sprang up there, and gasped. Her father's body was propped up against the wall, his eyes closed. Yet his chest rose and fell. Beyond him, her mother lay on the floor, still breathing. Her world returned—almost.

*Eli.*

A shadow filled the ruined doorway, silhouetted, with a sea-green Mark, one which not even the power of the Order's weapon could break. A single figure, young, lean, proud and shattered. He coughed for breath, nodded at her. But she could barely speak.

"Where is he?" she breathed. Her heart hammered in her chest. Please. Please Nestham, not now—he merely gestured over his shoulder, and she pushed past, a hand rising to her mouth, a choked sob, the hope she had stifled now returning full force—Eli lay propped against the wall, eyes barely open. She dropped to her knees and threw her arms around him, felt the familiar beat of his heart. It pulsed strong and steady, stronger than everything which had tried to break it, to destroy him, to destroy them—it couldn't. A reminder of what he had fought for.

*Eli.* He coughed once, and she drew back, planted a kiss on his cheek, her tears sliding down her face.

"Are they safe?" he breathed into her ear. She nodded frantically, the sob clutching her throat again.

"They're safe. Thanks to you," she sobbed. "I thought you were dead."

"So did I," he coughed. She huffed a laugh and pressed another kiss to his lips. A reminder of the strength within them.

"Let's get you up," she said, and hauled him to his feet. He leaned into her strength, as they had done when they first faced Temero. How different were they now? And yet, they were still Eli and Kyra.

Another cough forced her to turn. Her mother spluttered once, then opened her eyes. "Kyra?"

Eli leaned off her weight, back to the wall, and Kyra dropped to the ground, took her mother's hand. It was cold, clammy, but she was awake and talking. "I'm here, Mother," she breathed. Nestham above, *thank you, thank you for saving them.*

"I love you, Kyra," Taera's eyes pulsed with warmth and peace.

"I love you too." She clung tight, fearing what would happen if she let go. Tenderly, she brushed the dust off her mother's face as best she could.

"Where are we?"

"Someplace safe," was all she could choke out.

"Your father?"

"Also safe." She peered through the haze. "We're going to take you now to the Healer's House."

Jalek hefted up her father, once so strong, now reduced to a shell—and they moved in a slow procession. Eli limped behind her, a force to be reckoned with, while she supported her mother.

They reached the Healing Houses, but Jalek stopped. The door was already shattered. Eli shuffled past her and nudged the door open. His muffled curse reached deadened ears, and he fell forward.

A pile of rubble was all that remained of half of the Healing House. Much of the debris was scattered throughout the room. The shattered remains of the Head Healer, crushed under a pile of rock. And on the table...

"Monsun. Syl." Eli pushed forward. He reached for them, touched their hands. Glowing light flared on his Mark, and hope stirred in her. Ice-blue light cut through the dust floating through the room, settling on the three Vindicators.

"What's he doing?" Jalek asked.

"He's healing them," Kyra said quietly. She settled her mother on the ground, caressing her cheek for a heartbeat, then approached Eli, glowing like the sun.

But his eyes were closed, his lips moving—almost like a prayer to Nestham. His Mark flared once, then dimmed again. "I tried my best," he whispered. "They should be okay." Within moments, Monsun stirred. The gash on the back of his head closed, leaving no scar behind. The big Vindicator tried to move, but flailed, arms lashing out. Eli was there immediately, limping to the bigger soldier.

"It's alright, sir. You're safe."

260

Monsun heaved a breath and looked at Syl, tracing a hand down her face. "Is she all right?"

Eli nodded, a gentle smile on his face. "She'll wake up soon. You saved her life, you know."

"The debt. It's gone," he said shakily, his hand trembling.

"Yes, Monsun. You fulfilled it," Kyra said, squeezing his shoulder.

"And Amora?"

"Right here," the urchin said behind her. Kyra whirled on the girl standing in front of Tomas and pulled her into a bone-squeezing hug. Amora squeezed back tighter, almost as strong as a Marked. But then she was gone, and hurling herself on Monsun. The big Vindicator held her close, tears streaming down his cheeks. He grunted as he sat upright, but she didn't stop clinging to him.

A lump formed in Kyra's throat as she watched, and shaking fingers interlocked with her own. She gripped them tighter, blinking furiously. Tears tracked down Eli's face, and when he held his arms open, she stepped into his embrace, laying her head on his shoulder. For a moment, it was enough. But then she opened her eyes and found Jalek leaning against the doorway, looking anywhere but in their direction. Tomas nodded to her and slipped out.

"Jalek," she called. "Get over here." The Prince grinned, but it didn't reach his eyes. She held out her arms, Eli doing the same, and they drew the warrior in. She just let the tears fall, let them wash away the dirt and blood on her face.

Whether she was Jayne Farer or Kyra Antarun, it didn't matter tonight. They'd survived, and for tonight, that was enough.

# Chapter 44

From the moment she stretched out a weary arm and found the bed cold, she knew where he had gone. The unkempt sheets rustled as she blearily sat up, noted the shirt still on the floor, the weapons hung in their rack, now with her staff resting beside them. Nix rumbled from her place by the fire, content to slumber in peace. She threw on another robe and stretched, opening the glass door as the sun's rays glittered on the horizon, mingling with the Eternal Flames. His powerful arms were braced on the balcony, his tattoo curling over to the back of his neck, the intertwining of blue and gold he could never lose.

He'd let his hair grow longer since returning to Imbra, and it ruffled in the wind as he inhaled, the corded muscle of his back shifting with every motion. She leaned on the wall, just taking a moment to drink him in. Because, Nestham above... she could spend a lot of time like this. Even in the week since the attack, she'd felt like they'd had no time.

He murmured something under his breath, but it wasn't for her to hear. Whatever he had said was between him and Nestham. Bare feet passed over the polished stone, and she wrapped her arms around his trim waist, pressed her lips to his bare shoulder. She grinned when goosebumps rippled along his skin.

"Morning," he said. He turned to her and let her into his embrace, tucking her into his chest, next to his carved pendant. One of the two things he never took off. She sighed as he pressed a kiss to the top of her head, and the glitter of gold gleamed on his wrist, a promise she had made him and intended to keep. They didn't speak, only the sound of their breathing mixed with the wispy wind. Her eyes traced the horrible brand and the scar on his belly. Even when he'd used his magic, it still hadn't healed. Not like the one she'd received, the lethal wound in the north. It didn't seem fair that he should carry his scars and heal hers, like she couldn't take his pain away though she ached to do so.

But sometimes scars didn't show on the skin.

She didn't know what awoke her power, but suddenly gold was flashing out across the city, and he responded in kind, ice blue rising to meet it, as she gazed out over the city in springtime. Normally, she'd look at the blooming flowers, the trees blossoming in pink and white and red. But now all she could see was smoke. It still curled into the sky, marking where the rubble lay. The City Guard's barracks and the Guild Hall, both obliterated. Protection and progress wiped from the city.

Her breath hitched as her gaze fell on the Kinar River running from the north, where it split completely, to the waterfall, into the city, and forming the southern fortification, the docks. Jalek's ship had long gone, returning to Prian after the attack, though the Prince had remained in the city. The bells tolled seven times, and she sighed, glancing at the man holding her. His silver eyes tightened on the city.

"What are you thinking?" she asked.

He forced a smile, creasing the skin around depthless eyes. "I'm thinking we could use a holiday."

She huffed a laugh. "More training?"

"Yes. Monsun has pulled more of the Seventh into guard patrols, and we still need to guard the Guardsmen imprisoned in the Cathedral. We're organising a draft as it is, but there's already too few of us."

"Your healing magic?" she said, and when he winced, she poked a nail into his chest, holding him at her mercy. "Don't tell me you haven't been burning yourself out. I know you can't stop using it."

"I need to. It's already back at full strength. I'll be fine."

She couldn't be bothered arguing about this. Not today, not when she had so much else to do. But for now, she pushed that aside as she spent every moment drinking him in. As her heart continued to gnaw at her.

Her father still hadn't woken from the Malmir-induced sleep. No word from Eislyn. Three days after the attack, House Ketan had simply vanished. Jayne was spending as much time as she could researching Aurimia. Amora—she was probably still sleeping downstairs. Alsair—Nestham damn that man. Alsair *Wildborn.* Eli glanced down at her, trust and caring gleaming in his silver eyes. Guilt flicked through her heart, and she prayed it didn't show on her face.

"You know I can be with you today, if you want," he said. "You don't need to do this alone. Particularly if Trayse is out there still."

She shook her head. "You've got more important things to do today."

He smiled at her, but he let the strength, the ferocity, into his face. The warrior he had been born and bred to be. He kept the Healer for her. "If he hurts you, he'll have me to answer to."

"I know. What's Jalek been up to?"

"He's actually been quite useful," Eli sighed, "even if he is a mukking idiot."

"See, I told you so." Her nail briefly skimmed his chest, and his breath hitched just once.

"Of course, Highness. Because you're always right."

She grinned and stood on her tiptoes, brushing his lips with her own. "Is he causing any trouble with the life debt?"

"Thank Nestham, no, but we owe him one. At least he was nice enough to absolve your parents." Yet he'd left Eli there, still hanging on that life debt. She had considered forcing him to revoke it, but who knew? It might come in useful. Besides, she owed him more than that for what he'd done for her.

Eli's expression went vacant again, and she tensed. "If he hadn't got us out when he did—we'd be in a lot more trouble." When the hollow look in his eyes refused to fade away, she poked him again. He winced and shook his head, trying to clear it. "I need to brief the rest of the Vindicators."

"Monsun won't be up yet," Kyra said. "We've got time."

"Monsun's always up. He's still trying to figure out where he stands now." Eli stopped—there was more he wasn't telling her. "He'll be in the briefing room." He kissed her one last time, and she was already counting the hours until nightfall.

* * *

Kyra swept along the chasm, garbed in a grey tunic and pants, her staff in her hand, as she listened to the roar of the water. Strange how timeless this place was. No matter the darkness and the madness outside, the abyss below was eternal. Torches glittered in their brackets as she passed, her staff tapping a regular rhythm on the stone floor, and as her vision sharpened, she noted the guards standing at attention at the widening of the bridge. She stopped in front of them, and they offered a salute. She dismissed the staff and it faded away into nothingness. Her throat caught, but she refused to show it, to show this monster what was inside her.

"I want to talk to him," she said. They nodded and reached for the plank by their feet. In a practised motion, they heaved it across the gap, the wood thudding into place across the abyss. A rickety bridge at best, certain death at worst. She cared not. With her supernatural balance, stepping across the wooden plank was easy. She'd crossed worse in a northern winter. Still, it didn't pay to look down if you could avoid it.

So she stepped up to the cavern in the wall, cut into ancient stone, laced with bars of the finest Leranion steel, straight from the mines of the east. Her Nesthamir ring tapped on the bars, the note chiming through the cell.

"Wake up." Even by flaring her magic, it was still hard to make out the wrinkled face hiding in the shadows.

"Ah, Highness," Finon purred. "Forgive me if I don't get up." That wretched voice washed over her, and goosebumps rippled across her skin. And she hated it, hated herself for letting him get to her. He was now at her mercy, not the other way around. The man who had destroyed the Jinnam, attacked her parents, tried to have her killed—now at her mercy.

*He can't hurt them anymore.* She flashed an icy glare at him, but he seemed to be undeterred. Just kept smiling. Here in his little hole, with nothing but a cot and a bucket.

"I hope they're not treating you well in here. You deserve to suffer a lot more."

Finon paused, his snake-like eyes twitching. "You've got your throne back, Princess." Indeed, she had, since she'd so spectacularly destroyed her own Council. "Why are you here, then? Just to gloat?"

She shrugged, forcing that irreverence back, that swaggering royalty she knew he despised. Every glance, every twitch, part of a game across the hellin's board. And she would be damned if she lost to a hypocritical priest. "A little, perhaps. I am thrilled to see you locked up in here." She rolled her eyes, letting him see every inch of her royal disdain. "Where's Trayse?"

Silence as she waited for the old viper to speak, but he only smiled sadly. "Then that is unfortunate. I don't know where he is."

"He's *your* monster. You should know where he would go."

"He's a monster, alright. But he was never mine." She raised a brow, and he went on, "Do you really know Trayse?"

"I'll be happy to get to know him once his head is rolling across the floor."

"He was orphaned at a young age. Grew up in the back streets of Imbra. In the same slums as the Veil-turned-Vindicator who unfortunately ran into a crossbow. He joined the Order, and I realised he had a special talent for killing." Finon smiled, lost in his memory. "He was one of my best."

"Everyone has a sad story, Finon. And frankly, I don't give a damn about where he was born. I care about where he's going to die. He's going to pay for what he did. Your excuses mean nothing."

"And do you have an excuse? You're no longer a Musadim." Finon smiled. His eyes flicked over her clothes and he grinned. "I'm surprised you wore those colours."

She glared at him, putting all of her wrath in her gaze. "You took that from me. You knew exactly why I killed your men in that town."

"Oh, I know," Finon said. "But you still violated your tenets." He laced his fingers behind his head. "Warriors never did make for good little servants. Particularly not spoiled little princesses who think they know how the world works."

A low hiss escaped her lips. "I ended your reign. I can be a Musadim again." Desperate, maybe, but it was all she had.

"You'll *never* be a Musadim," he said. "You think you know what it is to serve? You think that's all Nestham is? Nestham is power, and passion, and it's only through passion we can achieve greatness."

"You're insane," she spat. "I'll make sure I destroy all your lies."

His voice dipped even lower. "They think they know you. The precious Princess, wielder of the three relics. But I see the real you. *Cheat. Liar. Coward.*" Each word slammed its way into her core. "I know how you watched your friends die and did nothing to help them. You didn't even try to escape Trayse. I know you."

"Enough!" She slammed her hand against the metal, and the bars rattled in their sockets. "Where is he?"

Finon sat back and folded his arms across his chest. "I don't own him."

"You own nothing! You released the demon into this world by your selfishness!"

He cocked his head, refusing to let this surprise move him. "Surely you aren't talking about Temero." He huffed a laugh that turned into a spluttering cough. "I thought you were done with this."

She didn't care anymore. Didn't care about Trayse, or Finon, or anything. She was just tired of all the lies, the deceit

267

and manipulation. "Everything that happens from here, I lay on your head. Every drop of blood that spills in Ekra will be your fault." She marched away, her spine like steel, forcing herself to level her eyes on the exit. "Prepare to rot in here."

"Your lover will burn in the First Circle," Finon said.

"Then I guess you'll see him there," Kyra called. She wiped away traitorous tears from her face as she strode away from the chasm.

# Chapter 45

Kyra entered the cathedral of the Musadim, unarmed and alone. No guards. The Musadim actually trusted the people, rather than relying on steel. Still, she could see several unfriendly glances directed her way.

Sure, the Eternal Order cathedral was grand and beautiful, but even before they'd tried to kill her, before she had been brought there a prisoner, she'd always preferred the simple design of the Musadim cathedral.

"Highness." A young woman bowed. Kyra bowed back and proceeded on, but the woman moved to block her, black hair flowing over her shoulders like a wave.

The Regent frowned at the near-sacrilege. "Is everything alright?" she asked.

"Highness, you—you shouldn't be here."

Kyra raised a brow, but before she could reply, an elder man approached them, wearing the necklace of a Khadim—a Servant, one of the highest ranking Musadim in all of Ekra, answering only to the Elder. "Khadim Leon," she bowed, hands behind her back.

"Highness," he said. "You shouldn't have come back."

Kyra pointed at the office door, and together they entered. As expected of a Musadim, it was simply furnished. Nothing would show its owner was one of the most powerful religious figures in Imbra. But she took the seat—of course, the visitor's one was padded, unlike the one behind the desk. After the door shut, he walked gingerly over to the empty desk.

"Why did you return?" he asked, dropping into the uncomfortable chair.

"Am I not a Musadim anymore?"

"No. I thought I made that clear when you were pronounced faithless. Did you not understand the one tenet—do no harm?"

"Oh, I understood that part perfectly. However, you know the commandments better than me. Self-defence is allowed, isn't it? Or do you expect a woman cornered to just sit there meekly and wait for the inevitable?" Kyra flung her hands into the air, using her strength to dominate her opponent. "At least she did no harm. At least she didn't break your precious commandments."

A grimace crossed his face. It was true. Self-defence, though frowned upon by the Musadim, was allowed. After all, the women of the court kept a *bela* in their gowns for a reason.

"What you did was an unprovoked attack on Eternal Order Guardsmen."

"Khadim," she said. "I'm going to tell you a story. And it would do your Kingdom a great service if you shut up and listen."

She told the story of the Order. How, over a year ago, they'd attempted to assassinate her. She'd survived them. And she told him the truth of what happened in that backwater town. How she'd seen the woman threatened. And she didn't regret it.

"I know you as a Musadim will look at me and see a killer," she said, "and I don't want your forgiveness. After all, it's not yours I need."

He frowned, and uncharacteristic anger crossed his face. "Then what do you need, Highness?"

"Your support. The Musadim is the last faith left standing in Imbra after the Order's attack." They still hadn't named the shattering events of the last week. The city had fallen silent since they had held the defence, and survived Finon's push to topple them. "And your help in rebuilding."

"Ah yes. Is that all we are to you? When you need help building a bridge, find a Musadim to get over it?"

"Partially. But I don't see why we need to be enemies. I still want to be a Musadim. This faith—being a part of the community meant so much." Her throat tightened, and she dropped the connection for a second. She had to say this. "I returned to unite Imbra. I'd sell my soul for this nation. But I can't sell it for this faith. If the Musadim can't have me as I am, I understand. But this city still needs your help."

* * *

Late that night, Kyra yawned and reopened the *History of the Guardians,* the candles burning brightly on Eli's desk. All in the High Language, ready for a Marked to read. *Something like this would have been destroyed.* There was no way the Order would have let it survive had it not been hidden. Thank Nestham Eli had taken it to his room the day before the coup.

She flicked back earlier. *The history of the Guardians can be traced back to the first Guardian, Jaser Cathom. Since then, there has always been one. Every so often, a Guardian can heal themselves or others. Never has there been more than one Guardian.* But the words... they just stopped, with several blank pages after. Which meant... there was more. But that symbol. She'd searched for it, never remembered it.

It—it had been under the Eternal Flame's Wellspring when they had escaped the Cathedral. She jumped out of the chair, wrenched the Torch out of its socket, and held it over the book. Golden flames rippled above the page, the heatless fire casting long shadows. As the light touched the pages, they shifted, revealing beautiful calligraphy and ancient words. A slow smile spread across her face.

*The Mark, symbol of Nestham's reign*
*The Life Debt, to uphold the balance of our world*
*The Soul Trade, for those willing to sacrifice*
*And for the preservation of our world, the gift of Sight.*

A flash of light on the balcony, and her smile widened. Seconds later, the door slid open, and the scent of earth with fresh rain hit her. Powerful arms wrapped around her, and Eli pressed a kiss to her head.

"Where have you been?" she mumbled.

"Hunting," he said, his voice rough with exhaustion. She bit her lip, toes curling. Seconds later, there was a thud, and when she turned around, Eli was making his way to the dressing room. He emerged dressed in a comfortable tunic and pants,

271

showing off his powerful torso. "I know that look," he said. "What did you find?"

She grinned broadly and showed him the page. His breath tickled her ear as he scanned it. "More mysteries," he said. "Have you ever heard of a gift of Sight?"

"There were rumours," she said, "that the Wildborn could see the future. That was why they fell into ruin long ago."

"I remember Alsair telling me about the Wildborn," Eli said. "He said they'd all been destroyed."

Kyra winced, but hurried on. "So we know about the Mark and the Life Debt. But the Soul Trade?"

"I guess that's something else to ask Alsair."

# Chapter 46

Syl coughed subtly as she entered the meeting room. The Senior Vindicator glanced up, a deep smile creeping over his face. "Morning," he slurred, shuffling the papers around with his left arm. His right, he cradled in a sling. Eli had healed him enough to save him, but Monsun had protested using more on him when there were others in worse condition. Damned noble bastard. Even if she had done the same. Even if the bandages still stayed on her after so many days. She'd carry the scar for the rest of her life.

She raised a brow at his state. "Sleepwalking again?" she asked. He blushed, and she just shook her head. "You sure you don't want someone to stick around and make sure you don't walk off a cliff?"

"I'm fine," he replied. "Considering what happened to you a few days ago, I'm surprised you're making jokes."

"Eli healed me just as he healed you. I'm fit and healthy." She shifted, the wound aching under the bandages wrapped around her ribs. Her little gasp wasn't missed, as his bushy brows drew together, a thundercloud threatening to burst under the weight of the judgement.

"I just don't want you to hurt." She knew why he cared, more than she wanted to admit. It had been growing on her for a while now.

"Going to the Cathedral was my choice," she said, waving a flippant hand at her abdomen. "It wasn't your fault."

Pity crossed his face, pity and shame and guilt, and as soon as she saw that, the fire built in her. She wanted no man's pity, ever.

"It was my decision," he said. There it was, that classic bullheaded manoeuvre. He carried the Kingdom on his shoulders. He wouldn't understand. He saw only right and

273

wrong. Whatever had happened to him in Biralam was affecting him again.

"Oh, shut up," she hissed, blindly reaching into her pocket. She didn't know what she was doing. All she could do was reach into her pocket, and suddenly her arm was lashing forward, propelling something—something black, flashing across the room.

She opened her eyes to find Monsun's gaze wide, holding a ring in his hand. Her ring. He rose, every inch the lethal warrior stalking towards her, even when injured.

"Did you throw this at me?" he breathed, looming over her. And for the first time in her life, she wasn't the bold woman she'd been. Hesitantly, she nodded. His handsome face grinned, utterly sure of himself, the silver tattoo twisting in his mirth. "And do you mean it?" Her jaw locked, but she nodded nonetheless, heart hammering in her chest, setting the wound afire, but she didn't care.

And suddenly his lips were on hers, and she couldn't speak, couldn't do anything but kiss him back harder, rising onto her tiptoes, doing anything to get closer, arching into him...

# Chapter 47

For the first time in his memory, the meeting room door was closed. Eli hesitantly opened it, and something twinged in his mind. Nix, beside him, let out a whuffle, her tail flicking to the side. He glanced around, noted the papers scattered all over the floor, as if brushed off carelessly. He activated his Mark, let his senses sharpen, scented the room. "Oh, absolutely not." He patted Nix on the head and quickly left, shaking his head.

Fifteen minutes later, he reopened the door even more gingerly than before, ears pricked for any sound. He found all the Vindicators waiting for him.

"Late as usual," Syl sighed. He flashed a glare at her, then took a seat at the table beside Monsun. He subtly tapped the Vindicator on the foot. Muscle tensed beside him and he quietly grinned. Nix, beside him, rumbled quietly.

"You don't want to run outside and play or something?" Eli whispered to Nix. "You're going to embarrass me in front of the others." Nix whuffled quietly. *That's the idea,* her violet gaze seemed to say. He didn't have that bond with her that Kyra did, but he shivered anyway. Her eyes were filled with a human intelligence. Nix yawned and pushed her paws down in front of her, settling down with a quiet purr. However, two hundred kilograms of snow leopard took up a lot of space.

He glanced at Monsun and Syl. They seemed more injured now than before. Syl, in particular, winced every time she moved, which was often. And, whenever she glanced at Monsun, heat rushed to her pale cheeks.

"Now that we're all here, I guess let's get on with it," Monsun said. They had too much to do these days. "Firstly. Eli." Instantly, he felt the heavy weight of the stares of four lethal warriors pressing down on him. "The wounded?"

"Still several hundred," he said. "At least the Musadim have opened up their Healers. Considering how we lost about

275

half of the Guild's healers, and we lost some of our own, that's something. Some of the Order's healers didn't want to treat the wounded. I had to—persuade them."

Tomas flicked his brows up. "The fanaticism ran that deep?" At least the rest of the congregation hadn't followed suit.

"Somewhat," Syl said. "The Guardsmen were mostly the fanatics. The others apparently were just following orders."

"Excuses," Raylene spat. "All soldiers will say that."

"True," Monsun said, "but for now, we have the soldiers under lock and key. The Veils are sorting out who willingly took part in the slaughters."

"Just look for anyone wearing that medal," Eli said. "That'll help." He shrugged and resumed his brief. "Once the meeting concludes, I'll check on all the Healing Houses and burn off my magic."

"Just be careful. Though we have quelled the Order threat, we've lost half of our troops on a civil skirmish," Monsun said. "Syl, the mood in the city?"

Syl shook her head. "The slums are worse than ever. Without the Order and the Imbran Guard, crime is growing again. My contacts amongst the Veils and the urchins say more people are disappearing from the slums. And they think Hyrin—they think Hyrin was murdered."

Instantly, the mood sharpened. "Do they have a suspect?"

"No, but it had to be a master assassin. Most likely Trayse, who we haven't heard from since the attack."

Monsun frowned and placed a hand on hers, wrapping it in his massive paw. She smiled, but removed her hand instantly.

Raylene took over. "If that's it from the internals, we have more to discuss on the externals. The scouts have informed us Temero has done what we've feared. Mount Sancti's ruins have been turned into a fortress. He's building an army on the plains around there. We can't get a count of the forces. Most have probably been underground, in the caverns around there."

"Mount Sancti's caverns didn't go underground," Eli interjected.

"They do now."

"What's worse is not the men," Tomas said. "We think he's breeding monsters like those mantiks. Our scouts heard screams and roars that did not seem human." He turned his attention to his notes, far more at ease.

"Our walls hold strong, both the Outer Wall and the Citadel. Trouble is, we have barely ten thousand troops across all of Leranion." He grimaced, stretching a withered face. "I, for one, dislike the idea of sitting behind the wall and waiting. Temero is between us and the pillar. If Aurimia is in the Severed Peaks, then we will have a hard time getting to it unnoticed. Jayne and I have narrowed down the last few potential locations for Aurimia. We should have a confirmed location soon."

"Does anyone really even know what is in Aurimia? There could be nothing there beside a big pillar of Nesthamir," Eli said.

"Then that makes our job even easier," Raylene said. "If we can find it, we can defend it."

"That still brings us back to the problem of allies," Tomas said.

"I've sent word to Biralam," Monsun sighed. "I doubt they will respond, however." He glanced at them. "I think it's time we held a full war council. The Vindicators, the Regent, the Houses and our allies from Valmor."

Tomas steepled withered fingers and glanced at the map of Leranion, at the Ketan holdings. "Has anyone found where House Ketan went?"

"It's like they vanished off the face of the earth," Raylene said. "We cannot find them."

A chill settled in Eli's bones. They were planning a war, and they were missing a House.

"One more thing," Syl said. "I want to recruit from the urchins."

277

"We shouldn't use them as troops," Monsun said.

"No. We use them as messengers, pages," Syl said, sitting to her full height. "We can give them a home, get them off the streets."

Monsun shrugged. "Agreed. I'll leave you to put that to them. If you can convince them, then do so."

"If that's it, then we should adjourn," Eli said. He winced as he glanced at Monsun. "Sorry, sir."

But the Senior Vindicator waved at him to continue. "By all means." They all rose, and Raylene and Tomas stumbled out.

Eli turned to Monsun and Syl, still sitting there quietly. For once, Syl's boundless energy had been curbed. She seemed tired, yet happy. "How are your wounds?" he asked.

"Never better," Syl beamed. "Thank you."

"It's nothing," he shrugged.

"Eli?" Monsun stared him down. "When was the last time you slept?"

The young Guardian shrugged. "Maybe two nights ago?"

"Please don't tell me you're hunting Trayse again."

Eli's blood boiled. "He's escaped us too many times. I'm going to bring him in, if only for Kyra's sake. Look at what he did! He destroyed the entire Royal Spire. The King and Queen are still recuperating in the Healing House, and Kyra has to share a Vindicator's room."

"I don't think she *has* to." Syl did a terrible job of hiding her smile. "I think that was her choice. And she chose well." Blood rushed to Eli's cheeks, and he couldn't keep her gaze. "You're a good man, Eli. You'll run yourself into the ground for the people you love. But soon, you'll be no use to anyone in your condition."

"What about you, Monsun? You seemed tired earlier."

Monsun shrugged, and the collar of his uniform shifted, revealing a very new bruise. Eli's jaw dropped, and Syl cracked up laughing.

Eli gingerly removed his hands from the table, wiping them quietly on his pants. "I'm impressed. So who started it?"

Monsun grinned and pulled out a necklace from his shirt, where a simple black ring gleamed on a chain. *Finally.*

Eli pushed away from the table and rose, his sword bumping into his thigh as he did so. "After the healers, I'll head to check up on the new guard." He placed a hand on the doorknob, and glanced back. "If you're going to get to know each other on the meeting table, don't do it *before* the meeting. Oh, and congratulations."

* * *

Eli's gut clenched as he exited the Citadel and stepped out into the devastated city. The streams of the Kinar River finally flowed freely, but it wasn't crystalline as it had once been. The streets were littered with debris across the entire city. The once-pristine noble quarter was still dirty, stones and blood scattered over the flagstones. He cut through the peaceful park on the banks of the Kinar, where as he stood on a grassy hill, he could see across the city skyline. All the way to the Guild Hall's smoking ruins, a once-proud building now ashes. Soldiers were still picking over the ruins, trying to salvage what they could.

He finally found his destination, elegant towers soaring high into the sky. That at least was unchanged. Where the banner had once moved with vigour, now it hung limply in the breeze; the silver pickaxe on a black field seemed like a death shroud. He crossed into Ketan Castle, into the main hall. Once, it had been a ballroom. Kyra had told him stories of magnificent parties held there, where she and Eislyn and Jayne had danced until dawn. But now it was only cries and death wheezes. Makeshift beds covered every spare bit of the floor, some nothing but piles of rags, providing the bare minimum of cushioning. Blankets covered too many faces, the bodies yet to be retrieved by the white-garbed men and women, calm in their bearing, but exhaustion on their faces.

One, a young woman, stood from a shuddering man and smiled, washing bloodstained hands in a bowl beside her. Eli waved and walked over, careful to portray the same calm.

"Vindicator Eli," she piped up, earnest green eyes flicking to his and blushing.

Eli smiled gently. "Sister Deidre. Who can I help today?"

Deidre paused. Concern, guilt even, crossed her face as she glanced around, weighing up who was most likely to die without his help.

"Barian over there," she breathed. He nodded, understanding how she'd come to that decision, and let her lead the way, a uniformed and fully armed Vindicator following the diminutive healer. All around them, other Healers glanced up and nodded. A Vindicator, come to visit the dying.

Eli hated places like these. They reminded him too much of the healing ward back at Mount Sancti. Where his mother had died. But it was too late to think of that, for they finally stood beside Barian's cot. Eli winced as he studied the man, noting the charred face, the burns all over his body, and the entirety of his left arm missing. Bandages covered the end, staunching the bleeding.

"We had to amputate his arm," Deidre said. "Debris crushed it in the Guild's collapse. The wound hasn't healed as much as we hoped, and infection set in."

"I'll do what I can," he said. Barian stirred from sleep, his breathing nothing but a weak rasp, one that quickened as Eli leaned towards him, sat cross-legged by the man's side. Deidre sat the other side, her steady hand reaching to grab Barian's good one.

"Barian," Sister Deidre said. "The man I told you about will make you better. I just need you to breathe slowly and relax." The young, soothing voice washed over Barian, and the bearded man blinked at Eli. The young Guardian smiled, and Barian let go of Deidre's hand.

"Help... help me," he gasped. Eli nodded and reached for Barian's hand. It gripped him with surprising strength, desperation clinging to life. The Guardian sucked in a breath and closed his eyes, reaching for the light within him. What had felt limited earlier now felt bottomless, as if fighting through the Malmir had revealed more of his power. He had been right that day on the snow. The fire, the fighting gift—that was dwarfed by his light. He grabbed hold of that light.

And suddenly he could see it all. He could feel Barian's presence like a song. A steady, powerful rhythm, like the folk chants they sang at Mount Sancti. He saw the infection which coursed through his veins like a creeping parasite. He reached within Barian's life source and went up against that corruption. It snapped at him. So close, so close to claiming him—he lashed out, and it withered in holy fire. He turned his focus to the other injuries, sealing them up, then withdrew. He realised he was still glowing; the Mark bursting with light. Deidre sat wide-eyed, but Barian breathed much easier, his face restored to a healthy tan. New, pink flesh stretched over the wound on his arm. It hadn't regrown, but it wouldn't face infection.

The glow faded away, and he breathed slowly, performing another check on his magic. To his surprise, it still roiled inside him, so much left untapped. Indeed, that fire was nothing compared to his healing.

"An angel," Barian breathed. "Nestham's blessed."

Eli bit his lip as Deidre glanced at him and blushed.

"I may have spread some rumours," she said to the floor. "This, what you're doing—it gives people hope."

"I'm no angel," he said with a heavy sigh. "I'm just doing what I can." He'd failed countless times. Failed to save the Jinnam. Failed to protect the city.

"But that's it," she insisted. "You're blessed by Nestham Himself!"

He smiled fondly, shoving his hands into his pockets. When had his optimism turned to this endless weariness? "If you think this will give people hope, then keep going. But I'm not Nestham, and I can only heal so many."

"Vindicator! Over here!" another called, and Eli rose on shaky legs and staggered over to an elder woman with a gaping chest wound, a vicious slash down her sternum. This wound was easier to heal, and his Mark flared, his magic poured into her, and soon her breathing steadied. The wounded stirred, and his heart hammered faster, aching for the solace of the woods, the peace and comfort. But he forced himself to remain, to dole out every piece of his power, to everyone who called for it. The Healers were smiling, but he was gasping for breath as he left the keep.

The sun was low in the west as he exited, promising to return as soon as he could. In the city centre, men were drilling whilst others rebuilt the ruins of the Imbran Barracks. A lean man showed off a flourishing stroke, his sea-green Mark gleaming, his blade glowing.

Eli leaned on the wall and watched until Jalek finished. The Prince flashed a practised smile at him, brushing the hair out of his eyes. "I'm not the one you should be watching like that," he drawled.

The Guardian rolled his eyes. "I didn't expect to see you here. You didn't seem the type."

"Well, I missed this. And since my men are back in Prian, I thought I'd work with yours." He shrugged, placing his hands on narrow hips. "Your troops aren't too bad. Course, mine'd take them in a heartbeat."

Somewhere in there amongst the deflection and insults was a good man—maybe. "Thanks for sticking around," Eli said. "After we almost got killed, I didn't think you would."

"Well, your city is an exciting place." They fell into step, heading back into the palace, passing the soldiers tromping through the streets. "You made a lot of enemies very quickly. I'm the same, but the ones who want to kill me usually use forks and fingernails."

Eli raised a brow, and Jalek flashed that smile again. "Thank you. For saving our lives."

"I got a life debt out of it, so I'm fine." The Prince hesitated, slicking his long hair to the side. "I know I can be a bit irritating, but I'm glad to be here. And if you ever need a hand..."

"I'll get it somewhere else." Eli winked, and Jalek chuckled. A shout rang out farther along the training ground, and they turned, hands dropping to swords in an instant. Jalek took half a step closer to Eli, and turned to cover his back.

"Shall we?" Eli gestured, and the Prince rolled his eyes. Together, boots crunched on the compacted dirt. They passed more soldiers drilling, each saluting as they went past. Ahead lay a soldier on the ground, hand on his chest, wheezing hard.

Eli squatted down beside the man, dropping a hand to his shoulder. "What's the matter, soldier?" he pitched his voice low.

"Nothing, sir," the man replied, his arm shaking.

"That doesn't look like nothing," he said. "What's your name?"

"Oryn."

"Oryn looks like he's under a life debt," Jalek observed. "You had that same look about you earlier."

Eli didn't glance away, kept his eyes on the soldier's face. When the man's face contorted in anger, it was clear the blow had struck true. "Who holds the debt?" Eli asked. The man shakily pointed to another, removing his helmet and tossing blonde hair around.

"Tennison," he spat.

Eli nodded at the soldier and Jalek stepped over to retrieve the other man, drawing him over to them. The Prince cheerfully clapped him on the shoulder.

"Word is you hold a life debt," he said, grinning. "Care to tell us what happened?"

"Nothing happened," Oryn said, his face going red. "Got in a scrap with some reds is all."

"Sounds like you don't want the debt," Jalek said. "Well, rules are rules."

"It's not fair!" Oryn protested. "I have to do whatever he says!"

Eli glanced at Jalek, and the Prince rolled his eyes. Spare him from whiny soldiers. Jalek raised his brows, a message clear in his eyes. *Do you want this or shall I?*

The young Guardian sat on the ground next to Oryn. "Oryn, here's the problem. Tennison here saved your life, and you're not only ungrateful, but being a mukka as well." The soldier's brows drew together, but Eli was undeterred. "Life debts are strange, but Nestham saw fit to create them, and we should not argue about it. If you feel like Tennison is treating you unfairly, take it up with your commander, and we'll deal with it. Alternatively, you could politely ask Tennison to absolve it." He huffed a breath, and savoured his next words. "Otherwise, with the greatest respect, shut up. You survived the Red Night. Many of your comrades didn't."

He left the soldier in the dirt and rejoined the Prince.

"You don't know what it's like!" Oryn shrieked.

"You're talking to your Vindicator like that?" Jalek whipped around, his Mark flashing. Fear pulsed on the soldier's face. "Eli Serae is under a life debt to me." The lithe young man clapped him on the shoulder. "He'll find out what it's like soon enough." They strolled away side-by-side.

# Chapter 48

Finon pushed the scraps of food away, back onto the plank and curled his lip in disgust.

"Comfortable there, your Holiness?" one of the guards mocked him, a wicked grin on her face. Finon stared, but she just kept talking. "Course, I would have preferred the chicken. They had this big roast in the barracks last night. Kept spares and everything." She cackled.

Finon slumped back into the cell. He glanced up as a young boy, clad in the silver and blue of the royal household, brought two waterskins to the guards. They each took a hefty drink, then strapped them at their waists. The boy headed off into the distance, and Finon stonily stared ahead. And he waited.

Time didn't matter in this cell, but if he had to guess, it happened roughly an hour later. They were in some inane discussion about the clothing in the streets. Apparently, Biralam silk would be the height of fashion this year. What were they to know fashion? And discuss it in front of him, the one man who wore Nestham's Shield.

The woman wobbled slightly, then pitched forward. The man staggered back and would have fallen into the abyss had he not been caught one-handed, then lowered onto the stone bridge. Finon gazed at the hooded figure rummaging for the keys. His heart hammered in his chest. Escape at last.

The door unlocked, and he rose, but he was too slow. The man slammed him back into the wall, an elbow at his chest, and a knife at his throat. "Archbishop Finon," the man growled, and underneath his hood, jade eyes glowed.

"Who are you?" he spat out. This was no man he recognised. But the man was so much stronger than him, even though he was shorter.

"I am the last of my kind. You saw to that."

The knife fell away, and a medallion was held up to his eye. A wooden dove, intricately carved, displayed in the stranger's hand.

"A Jinnam," he said, then smiled. "A traitor to your name. Forgiveness is in your nature."

"I am no Jinnam." The stranger flipped the medallion.

"Impossible. We stamped your heresy out. Your fanaticism endangered all of Ekra."

"Our fanaticism endangered the Order. Your predecessors couldn't stand it. And you couldn't either. But try as you might, you can never stamp out the fire." The stranger grinned, and it was not a pretty sight, filled with vengeance pent-up for years. "But you failed. You let us survive, and I found the Guardian. I found him before your assassins could get near him." All those years of hunting the Guardian. He thought he'd extinguished the line for good, yet it seemed it hadn't broken. "I raised him in the last place you would ever look for a warrior. I forged him into the greatest warrior Ekra has ever seen since Jaser Cathom."

"Jaser Cathom was a failure," Finon spat on the ground. "He failed all of Ekra."

And the man got even closer, and the distinct scent of coffee lingered in his breath. "Oh, he did. But my Guardian will save it. After you doomed us by releasing a demon."

"Oh, not this horseshit again," Finon said. "Temero is a fairy tale."

But the hooded man didn't relent. "Temero was your responsibility. Temero was the Eternal Order's responsibility. That was the reason you formed your cursed Order."

"Don't lecture me on history, wretch," Finon said, frantically trying to wrench himself out. "Guards!"

"Oh, there's nobody to hear you." White teeth flashed under the hood. "And why shouldn't I lecture you about history? I've waited for this for *twenty years*. I'm just savouring the moment.

"You're a failure, Finon. A failure and a traitor. The Order fell long before your time, but you, you destroyed it by attacking the other faiths. We all served Nestham. What made us different was *how*. You upset the balance of the faiths, and you could have doomed the entire world with your greed and lust for power."

"Oh, you're so high and mighty. You know as well as I do how this ends. The Guardian's power should never have existed. The Marked should never have existed." Finon scoffed, "They're just tools for kings and vagabonds to believe they have a chance."

"The Marked are our only chance. Particularly the Guardian. Ever since I armed him with the Eternal Flame."

Finon struggled, but it was worthless. Even with one hand, the man still held him easily. "You stole the most sacred relic of the Order!"

"Well, you stole ours first." The knife quivered, inches away from his face. "This is justice for my brothers and sisters. This is for the soldiers you slaughtered. The Seers you tortured. The children you orphaned. You destroyed our home, you burned any trace of our history. And you will burn in Hell for all of it." He paused, and Finon closed his eyes. His pants grew damp as he waited.

"But I have one question," the man breathed. "What was in Laif that you wanted? Why did you send soldiers garbed as bandits to slaughter those people?"

"When a little girl told me of her brother with silver eyes." He grinned, his last victory in the open. "I think you lost one."

The figure slammed the knife home... and then nothing.

An hour later, the guards would stir, and they would see the blood blended perfectly well with his robes. They would also see the single blood-soaked initial on the stone of his cell.

*T.*

# Chapter 49

Those damn vambraces were inches away from him, and yet utterly untouchable. Eli gritted his teeth and focused on his Mark, dwelling on all that Kyra had told him. The plain metal hummed, a pure, resonant sound. And they started flickering, fading away to somewhere between Ekra and the Rift, and then stopped, became solid again. He sighed and ran his hand through his dark hair.

"Nice work," Kyra called from the bed. He turned and flashed a grin, but she didn't look up, engrossed in the book held in her lap, Amora turning the page. They'd been at this for hours now, as soon as Kyra found out that Amora only knew the basics of reading. Though Monsun had already taught her more, the pair was reading one of Kyra's favourite adventure novels she'd loved as a child. The tale of an adolescent girl and the mysterious crescent necklace she wore.

He turned back to the desk and exhaled slowly, focusing on that fire and light. His magic roared, he tensed his forearms, and the connection clicked. The vambraces vanished from the table and reappeared on his arms, humming, rife with power. He slammed them together and vanished into the Rift. And for the first time, he paused.

The Rift was still a strange place. It lingered like a sanctuary sheltered from the sands of time. This time, the void was peaceful, undisturbed. Though last time he'd sensed another presence, now he felt—felt like he could stay here forever. And his power wasn't being drained as he hovered in place, not bothering to visualise Ekra's colour. Perhaps it was the distance he moved in the Rift which sapped his strength.

Peace washed over him, and he let go of the Rift and drifted back into the world, right in the chair where he had left. Sight and sound returned, and he chuckled, unclipping a vambrace from his forearm. Kyra raised a brow, but as she opened her mouth to comment, she was too late. He propelled the vambrace forward, shimmering Nesthamir flashing through the room.

Gold gleamed as Kyra's Mark flared and she ducked, but he tensed his arm and it reappeared back on his wrist. Wrath gleamed in her eyes, and Amora was grinning beside her.

"You're dead meat, Serae," Kyra said, and thrust out her arm. Her staff obliged, and twin blades of Nesthamir flew for his face. His heart stopped, but she simply curled her fingers, and it vanished just before it impaled his skull. He raised his brows, sweat trickling down the back of his neck. Kyra blew a kiss and settled back with her book while Amora leaned on her muscled arm. The girl grimaced as her hand briefly touched Kyra's ring.

Eli rubbed the arcing lines of his Vindicator's tattoo and unfolded the parchment he'd carried across battlefields and icy wastelands. The copy of the poem written by Prince Cayce, son of Queen Eshe, who fell at the Sanctum centuries ago. He let his Mark shine, dropped deep into his power.

"What are you doing?" Kyra asked.

"Trying to translate this poem," he said.

"You're doing it again," Amora chided him.

He spun around, blue light gleaming, reflecting off the ancient furniture. "It worked?"

"Did you just try speaking in the High Language?" Kyra asked, and he spoke again. Amora just glanced between them impatiently, but he could see how Kyra swallowed and failed to prevent the blush on her cheeks. She glared at him again, but he merely grinned at her and glanced at the poem. The words, once gibberish, shifted in his mind. Beautiful, ancient poetry, enough to make his heart melt.

A single, hesitant knock on the door. "Enter," Kyra called.

The door opened to Jalek's lean form, clad in a navy tunic. The Prince flashed an easy smile. "May I come in?"

"I think the Lady just said you could," Eli said.

Jalek rolled in and surveyed the room, which was beginning to get cramped. Kyra's clothes had taken up most of Eli's space in the wardrobe, and he'd resorted to stashing his armour by the desk. She'd dragged up a comfortable armchair to sit between the bed and the desk.

Amora grinned at Jalek, and Nix glanced at the Prince, then her head thudded on the floor again. Jalek stepped around the snow leopard, pausing to scratch her chin, drawing out contented rumbles. "Is that *A Traitor's Crescent*?" he asked.

Kyra raised the book, displaying the cover. "You know it?"

"Gaud Quo lives in Casalis. It's one of my favourite books!"

Eli sat back and watched, smiling, as the two immediately began an animated discussion. An hour later, he had finished translating the poem, and was seriously considering picking up the book after Kyra and Jalek had enthused about it.

But another knock came at the door. Monsun's face was a thundercloud, and Eli braced for the downpour. "Trayse killed Finon."

# Chapter 50

Eli brushed a kiss over the slim shoulder facing away from him and rolled out of bed. He stood up with simple grace and donned the Nightweave suit, laced up his boots, trod around, testing the silenced soles. A sword on his back and a knife on his chest, he surveyed himself in the chipped mirror—one thing Kyra had scavenged from the wreckage. Amongst the mess their room had become, a hollowed man stared back.

Just one more night.

He stepped out onto his balcony, sidling past the small cot containing Amora, and glanced out across his city reshaping itself. Even in the night, the city didn't sleep. The City of Light, he'd once heard Imbra called. And for the first time, it looked like the name was justified.

A spring breeze arced over the Citadel, down into the lower districts, where it brought comfort to all, rustling the trees, and flickering the Eternal Torches. Above the Cathedral, the massive Eternal Flame danced over the beautiful building. Eli savoured the cool night air, and at last looked up at the glimmering stars above him. Five stars in the shape of Nestham's Shield. At least, that was what the Eternal Order had called it.

Only the Musadim remain. The Eternal Order, devastated after the coup. The Jinnam, destroyed in their monastery. The Wildborn? Who knows. True or not, the faith that Imbrans had in Nestham was slipping. The wind rustled, coalescing into a human form, perched on the balcony beside him. He didn't need to even speak before Eli glared at him. "Can't Nestham send Eshe? Kyra says she's a much nicer dead person."

Jaser returned the withering look. "Her Majesty, Queen Eshe, had several choice words for you, mainly considering your conduct towards her descendant. But she's—like you said—a much nicer person, so she's forgiven you since your Queen has. I still have questions."

"Out with it. The sooner you ask, the sooner you leave."

"What the mukking hells are you doing?" Jaser said.

Eli frantically waved for him to keep his voice down, even though he knew no one could hear. "I'm going out one last time."

"The last time you went out, you almost got this entire city destroyed."

He deserved that. Still, he wouldn't admit it—not to this dead man. "Jaser, get to the part where you're useful."

And for the first time in a while, Jaser's eyes softened. "Be ready, Eli." He vanished, and the wind howled at his departure. A small stone swished through where his shadow had been.

Amora sidled up next to Eli, elbowed him in the side. "He's not nice, is he?"

Eli chuckled quietly. "No. No, he isn't." The urchin girl climbed onto the rail, and part of him wanted to tell her to be careful, but she balanced expertly and he held his tongue.

"Let's go, gruntah."

He laughed and turned around so she could climb on his back, clinging around the blades on his torso. "Grab on, amica." Small arms latched around his chest. He glanced back once at the bed, then leaned forward. "Ready?"

Amora clung tighter, so he stepped up on the railing and stretched out his arms. The wind whispered across his Nightweave before he pitched himself forward into the drop. The air rushed up at him, screaming in his ears as his body tensed for impact. Amora whooped with delight as he crashed his arms together and fell into the Rift. They drifted through the world of darkness, slowing their momentum, before flashing into sight and sound on the empty street. "How was that?"

She giggled in reply, and they exited the Citadel in the pre-dawn light. After a glide through the rich quarter, amongst the gentle parks near the Kinar, he launched them up onto a nearby roof. Boots thudded onto red tiles, and they waited in silence, Amora swinging her legs over the edge.

This time, he was sure. Every note, every time he'd spent poring over the records, the strategy he'd devised, the times he'd fought him, even some base-level hunter's intuition, he was sure he would be here.

The figure appeared soon enough. Tall, caped, wearing a sword despite Imbra's laws. Beside him, Amora shivered, drawing into Eli's warmth. The man sauntered down the street, a bottle of wine in one hand, a sack over his shoulder. His hair was a dirty blond, but Eli summoned his Mark and let his senses sharpen. That familiar musk was a clear sign.

Trayse.

As the assassin paced down the street, Eli nudged Amora. They kept pace with the assassin on the rooftops, but some part of him trembled, ached to leap forward and cut down the man for all he had done. For beating him last time. Yet a wiser part resisted. This wasn't his fight. He'd suffered from Trayse, but he hadn't suffered as much as Kyra. She deserved to be there when they took him down. And besides, he'd need help. Odds were, Trayse was ready for them.

Trayse vanished into a nearby building on the edge of the poor quarter, a dilapidated shack, the porch sagging on the right pillar. Soon, a flicker of flame appeared within the window.

"It's his house," Eli breathed.

"I've seen better," Amora sniffed.

Eli leaned forward, staring intently at the shack. Men like Trayse were like rats, so he probably had a few holes to hide in. And yet, he didn't seem like he was expecting company. Maybe, just maybe, if Eli and Kyra attacked in his home, they could overcome him.

But the rays of dawn were finally stealing over the horizon. Eli tracked his way back to the Citadel and Rifted back up to the windowsill. He ducked into the wardrobe and dressed himself in a flowing shirt. When he emerged, he smiled at the still form of the princess beside him. Still a heavy sleeper. He leaned on the balcony, face turned to the east, waiting for the golden rays to appear.

The sun rose, and his heart with it.

Then the familiar glow vanished from sight.

# Chapter 51

Monsun leaned back in his chair, intent on the woman across the table from him. Bleary eyes blinked rapidly, took a long drink of lukewarm coffee. "Ugh. I've had nicer tasting poisons," he spat. He gingerly replaced the mug on the scratched desk and returned his attention to Syl's last words. "So you've heard nothing?"

Syl yawned, fluttering her red-rimmed eyes. "Nothing at all. It's like they've vanished off the face of the earth." Her face dropped. "If Temero captured them, they could break. Or worse, what if he turns them? The men Eli and the Regent fought in the north were not human."

Monsun swore and stumbled out of his chair, clenching his injured fist. He marched over to the desk littered with maps. Symbols and scrawled notes covered a map of the Severed Peaks, evidence of Jayne's research. "We have had no more reports on Mount Sancti. Nobody has been close and survived. And we are just waiting for an attack."

Syl rubbed her eyes. "At least we know that Talon Reach still stands. The last report came in yesterday."

But in his anger, he pushed too far. "But what's the point if we're all dead before the pillars fall?" She said nothing, but her beautiful brown eyes just closed for a second. He sighed and wrapped his arm around her back, and she leaned into his side. "I want to believe it will be okay as well."

"It will be," she vowed. "I'll make sure of it. And Temero will not see it coming." *Keep telling yourself that.*

He couldn't help but remember Alsair's words to him. The monk had seemed tired, erratic. His skin had paled, and his jade eyes were dull. The elder's strength seemed to fade a little more each day as he spoke in ragged sentences.

*I can't see it anymore. It's like the pressure never stops. There's something waiting, I can feel it. And I know that I'm powerless to stop it.*

But why? He hadn't even tracked down the Heir of Amerin yet, for Nestham's sake! Nothing he tried seemed to work. Alsair had told him the Heir was in Imbra. Yet he'd scoured the streets, looking for anyone who might fit the description of the Heir. Anyone with Plains heritage. If he was to succeed, he needed that child.

"Monsun?" Syl snapped. Monsun blinked, felt liquid running over his hand, glanced down. Rivulets of blood mingled with coffee, the shards of mug slicing deep into his hand. He swore again and reached for bandages to clean up his mess.

Syl just shook her head. "What is it with you?" she asked. "You haven't been yourself for a long while."

"You want to know?" Why would he tell her this? But she was already nodding, and really there was no choice. There was no one he'd rather tell. And so he told her why he left Biralam, and why he came to Imbra. When he finished, Syl was staring at him with silver-lined eyes.

"I'm so sorry," she said. "No wonder you don't want to talk to Biralam. Do you—will you go home?"

"I am home," he said. "I miss my family, but I couldn't imagine returning to Amaldas." He let out a bitter laugh.

"But what you said—if you don't return with the Heir, they'll hurt your brother."

"I've been trying, but I have heard nothing. Alsair promised me I'd find the Heir in Imbra, but I can't seem to do anything. And if I fail—" He choked.

"You should have told me earlier," she said. "I'll help you. And I won't rest until you find the Heir."

The door slammed open. Syl half-rose from her seat, but Jayne was already there, black hair a tangled mess. Her eyes were bloodshot and her face pale, but she looked *alive*. Alive and euphoric.

"I found it," she let out, and dumped a pile of papers on the table. In the midst, she unfurled a map on the table, and slammed her finger down on a small X, halfway along the Severed Peaks. So tiny, so insignificant. Yet that was where their future would lie. Two pillars to safeguard, and a Demon to kill.

"Now we strike," Monsun vowed. "Right when he thinks we're weak. We send more of the Valmor armada to reinforce Talon Reach and take our troops to Aurimia. And then we kill Temero."

Syl beamed, fatigue melting from her lithe body. "We could actually do it."

He laughed, a real belly laugh, and for the first time he was lighter, strength rising through him, shedding all the doubt and the guilt and shame. He scooped her up and she actually *let* him, laughing along with him, a bright, musical laugh that made the world spin. She was so small in his arms, yet she had the strength of steel in her spine.

The door clicked shut, and Monsun realised they were alone. He glanced down and met Syl's breathtaking smile. Her full lips stretched into a wicked grin, then she claimed his own.

The first rays of dawn crept into the room, the sun's gold stretching over him. Monsun turned, ready to meet a glorious sunrise. Yet where there should have been beautiful light, only darkness remained.

# Chapter 52

Eli staggered back, hand rising to his mouth. The golden sun, which was creeping over the horizon, was engulfed by shadow. And in the distance, a cloud of gloom appeared, just a thin line, marching in from the south. Marching quickly. It flew north as if propelled by the breath of Nestham Himself. Eli pushed off from the railing, rushed back into the bedroom. Quickly, he shook Kyra awake, and she groaned.

"What?" she murmured sleepily.

"Trouble," he breathed. "Get up."

Something in his voice alerted her, something hinted by their months of running and planning and fighting, and she was instantly awake. Those old habits, learned in her days as Jayne Farer, were hard to forget. Kyra straightened her robe and stalked out with a warrior's stride, but froze at the window.

The cloud flew towards the City, thickening, swirling on an ominous breeze. A cold, clammy hand latched onto Eli's, and they stood there in silence. The world grew darker, night falling on them again, but not a single star glimmered in the sky.

The bells pealed, clamour and chaos ringing across every single street, into the Spires, into the slums. The call to arms, to repel an invasion. But what they faced was not of this world. The only light that remained were the golden Eternal Flames ringing the city walls, the trail pointing south, burning brilliance, a beacon of hope and Nestham's strength.

"Wherever you are, Jaser, I hope you can see this," Eli breathed. The flames marched south, the trail leading up to their glorious city. But in the distance, the furthest Flame flickered once, as if stirred by a quiet breeze.

Then it stopped burning. The shock smashed through Eli like a fist, and beside him, Kyra raised a hand to her mouth to cover the shaky gasp. The next Torch winked out. Each one flickered, then died. Again, and again, and again, until there only remained the ring of fire around the City of Light, the bastion of the North. As if Nestham had grasped them in his fist, they all sputtered and died. The screams of men and women shattered the air, and steel screeched as guards rushed to the walls, hoping and peering and praying.

In the almost-perfect darkness, a sea-green Mark ignited. Jalek, somewhere on the walls. The tug of the life debt confirmed it, almost *pulling* Eli to the window. He struggled, and eventually it let him loose, leaving the crackling bond in his chest.

He turned his attention to the last Flame burning, the roaring inferno at the Cathedral's peak. It reached towards the darkness, flailed, thrashing in the night, pushed back on the wall of death. And for a second, hope rose in his heart, as the gift of Nestham rallied against the shadow.

The darkness tore it apart.

Eli ignited his Mark, and golden light joined his ice blue. But he glanced back into the room, and their golden Torch still burned bright, a beacon of hope, somehow missed by the darkness. Kyra threw it under the bed and met his gaze. He turned away as she dressed, arming himself.

"Get to the walls," she commanded. "Help Jalek." He risked a glance back over his shoulder. She'd dressed herself in a tunic and pants fit for battle. Not armour, but in the meantime, this would do. She'd pulled her hair back, and donned her circlet, the sapphires of her House gleaming on head and hand. Kyra extended her hand and the staff faded into it, and as she snapped her fingers, the massive leopard raised her head, growling at the darkness. Violet eyes gleamed in the new night.

The Queen of Leranion, the thrice-blessed, ready for war.

* * *

Once Eli reached the bottom of the stairs, he sprinted into the night, and ice blue flickered on horrified faces as he raced through the streets, using his speed and reflexes to keep from

299

bumping into frantic citizens.

Armour glimmered ahead, three men in Imbran garb. "You lot, with me!" he pointed at them, but slowed as he neared them, almost skidding to a stop as he surveyed them from head to toe. Ill-fitting uniforms, hands that shook on their swords. Nestham above, they were barely boys armed with swords. He jerked his head, and they fell into a run behind him. One boy was larger than the others, and soon his breathing rasped in Eli's heightened ears, burning with his magic and senses.

He pressed on through the shadow, this unnatural darkness. But as he ran, the hopelessness of their situation was dawning on him. Were these boys truly all Imbra offered? They'd barely seen sixteen summers. But with the legions still scattered across Leranion...

He pressed on, keeping them close as they clattered up the steps on the outer walls. Beyond, the Kinar River drifted past, the docklands down to their left. Silence, as Eli turned to them, the three trembling and wide-eyed and covered in a sweaty sheen. He forced himself to smile, to draw his shoulders back, to stand proudly above them. He placed a hand on the lead boy's shoulder, and the boy—no, the soldier—straightened, his skin gleaming in the light of Eli's Mark. That light flared brighter and glinted off steel. Sea-green joined it a second later.

"You're going to be fine." Jalek grinned. "We can take whatever it is." The tall one nodded sharply, his training reasserting itself. "Now get yourself over there."

They filed off, and Eli met Jalek's gaze. "Good work," he said. "How many have reported in?"

"At least three hundred. We've filled the walls, but we—we can't light a single flame. It's like the very air refuses to obey us." He waved a flippant hand to the shadow, and it almost seemed to hiss at him.

The Prince hissed back, and his perfect teeth glinted in the light of his Mark. Eli chuckled and slapped Jalek on the back. The soldiers drew their strength from the glowing men at their centre, and in Nestham's name, he was going to give them nothing to be afraid of. Fear killed a man just as well as steel. Monsun had taught him that.

"Are the others coming?" Jalek pitched his voice low.

"Kyra will be here soon, and the other Vindicators will—I expect—be working on something." His own damned plans might have just been thrown out the window with this arrival. Unless...

Jalek pushed his raven hair out of his eyes and stared into the mist-like shadow. "For now, it's just us. So what say we go take a look?" Jalek's fierce gaze met Eli's, and he didn't even bother to unsheathe his rapier—it just appeared in his hand.

Eli tensed his arms and his vambraces snapped into place. Murmurs around them, but the two Marked marched to the edge of the fortification, peering into the night. The silence settled on him like a weight.

"We'll jump, and I'll Rift us up if needed," Eli said.

"Agreed. One."

"Two."

"Three—"

A flash of white cracked through the sky, shattering his vision, and he cursed, staggering back. Around him, men screamed. Seconds later, the light faded away, and a single figure emerged from the stillness, at home in the mist. A stunningly handsome man, shadows dancing at his fingertips. But as a Marked, Eli could sense something different. Some part of him glowed—like the peaceful glow of the hearth. Yes, that was it—that elusive peace.

"People of Imbra," the stranger said, too-white teeth flashing in the darkness. "I come in peace, and yet you prepare for war!" He did not shout, did not even seem to raise his voice. But they all heard it, as if he was right in front of them. And to Eli, it seemed as if the stranger was the one with the high ground.

"Who are you?" Eli roared back.

The figure snapped his gaze to him and smiled. *You know who I am.* The voice blasted through his mind, its sweet,

301

cloying scent filling his nose. A soldier dropped to the ground and retched, but Eli just unsheathed his sword. And still the stranger kept speaking. "All I ask is one thing. Give me that one thing, and I will leave this beautiful city in peace."

"You'll do that anyway," Jalek said. "Or you leave in pieces!"

The stranger smiled again, a knowing, winning smile. One that had surely charmed many opponents. "Jalek Veturan of Valmor. Prince of the Sea, Bane of Pirates. You have many titles, yet your family never recognised them. That's why you left, isn't it? That's why you begged—begged on your knees to be given the sacred sword of Valmor. Left your family behind to seek glory on the seas?"

Jalek trembled with rage, but the Prince did not respond.

The Guardian did. Eli stepped in front of the lithe man, sword outstretched. "Last chance!" He raised his hand, gleaming with his Mark, and a hundred bows trained on the stranger. "Leave us!"

"As soon as I have what I want." The silence settled down on the walls again. Nobody dared ask the question, and the mists surged, spilling over the walls, coursing around his feet. Eli's heart thrummed, and he prayed his Regent would arrive soon.

"What do you want?" a soldier yelled out.

The stranger smiled and spoke the death sentence. "I want Eli Serae. I want the boy who calls himself a Guardian. Hand him over, and you will all be spared. If not..." He snapped his fingers once, revealing the army behind him. A horde of soldiers on the other side of the Kinar River. The bridge, already secure. Three siege towers loomed, easily the height of the wall. "You have one day to comply before we raze the city."

Darkness descended upon them again. Eli slumped to the ground, and shouts rang out across the battlements.

\* \* \*

302

Eli didn't know how he made it back to the castle. Perhaps Jalek had carried him, but he couldn't think properly as he gazed at Kyra, his mind blank.

Hand him over.

"No." Kyra's face was ashen, her eyes stark. She whipped her gaze back and forth between Eli and Jalek, and Eli's breath rasped in his ears. Temero had come, and despite all of his planning, all of his careful manoeuvring, Eli was still helpless, still powerless. He'd failed.

He could not summon the words, could only stare as she collapsed in front of him. Crumpled to her knees in her armour. Around them, their allies were grim. Alsair's eyes lined with silver, Amora clutched at Monsun's hand. The big warrior held her to him, but he didn't meet Eli's gaze.

There was no choice, and none dared argue with him. Not as he blinked away the traitorous tears. Kyra's nails scraped on the floor as she spoke. "Can you give us a moment?"

His friends nodded and withdrew until it was only the two of them left. They'd started this on a snow-covered battlefield in the north. They'd started it together. It seemed fitting it would end that way.

"You can't go," she choked. And now, it was written across her face. The iron will, the strength that had carried her across killing fields and icy mountains, was failing. It had cracked. The woman he had fallen in love with was breaking because of him. He fell to his knees, gathered her in his arms and held her tight.

"It should have been me," she breathed into his shirt. "You know what he wants from you." His heart cracked more, and he retreated, now careless of the tears on his cheeks.

"I know what he wants. He won't get it. I'll stall as long as I can and do what needs to be done."

Those perfect ocean-blue eyes welled with tears. "I need you to survive. Do you understand me? I can't lose you too."

"You won't." He kissed her hard, and she pressed closer to him, as if every piece of air between them was a world apart.

When they at last pulled back, he tucked a stray hair behind her ear.

"It's better this way," he whispered. "You have a people to lead." He was a symbol, but a living Princess might save them all. "I'll come back, I promise." He pressed his lips to her forehead. He stared into her eyes, gripped her hand tight. She knew her duty, he knew his, and he would have it no other way. "When I leave, look on my desk for the notes with the red seal."

Eli kissed her one last time, and as he locked hands with her, he passed the scrap of paper from his pocket. He forced himself to turn away, stripping himself of his weapons, his armour and his jewellery. Temero would have none of it.

Eli closed the door on his shattered queen and didn't look back.

As he stepped out into the lush surroundings, he found his friends there, old and new. He knelt down on one knee, and Amora threw her arms around his neck, clutched him tight. "Look after them." He grinned. Inside, his stomach roiled, thrown by fear and cowardice. But he choked down that fear, willing her never to see it. Amora let go and turned away, hands shoved into her pockets.

Monsun and Syl approached him, two figures in the night mist. Two Vindicators. The shield in the light and the knife in the shadow. They could not be more different. Monsun clasped his arm, and they embraced, the bigger man's armour crushing into his chest. Syl's arms were rigid as they locked around him, and slowly, ever so slowly, he returned the hug.

"Live for justice," he said.

Monsun sucked in a breath. "Die—without fear."

And as Eli moved past them, his words choked in his mouth. He didn't know what to say. There was so much history, so many words unsaid—but Alsair was there, wrapping his one good arm around Eli. The young man embraced harder, wishing he could never let go, clinging to the one who had raised him.

"Nestham be with you, son." There were tears freely cascading down his face, but he smiled at Eli, stretching the age lines around his mouth. "I'll see you soon."

The Guardian left the palace and paced out into the silent city. Only Jalek paced alongside him, a silent question on his lips. The life debt between them cracked with energy, just as it had with Monsun. They passed the darkened Cathedral, and kept down the main road lined with soldiers and frightened Imbrans in the darkness. Each gave him a salute, a wave. Eli kept his head high as they approached the outer gate. The snarling leopards offered him scant protection this time. The empty brackets of the Eternal Torches loomed above.

They stopped outside the gate, and Eli's hands shook at his sides, his knees growing weak.

"Good luck, brother," Jalek said. "Give that bastard hell." They clasped hands, and as they did so, Eli pulled him into a hug, briefly whispered in his ear. Jalek paled, but nodded and left with his head bowed.

Eli marched to the gate and saluted the sentries, hundreds of eyes on him. The steel gate screamed as it opened, like a condemned before the butcher's block. It slammed to a stop, leaving nothing but twisting mist. The shadow parted as if recognising him, escorting him like an honour guard. Eli took one step outside the castle walls, cold settling in his bones.

Eli Serae had entered this city searching for answers. He could leave, knowing it was safe. The gate slammed shut, and a shimmering form appeared next to him.

"I'm proud of you," Jaser said, the older warrior flickering beside him, his armour polished and looking as composed as ever.

Eli didn't have that same strength as he spoke his death sentence. "I failed. You told me to unite them, and I couldn't."

The apparition smiled wistfully, and warmth gleamed in his face for the first time. Warmth—and guilt. "Didn't you? Together, a Prince of Valmor and a Princess of Leranion plan war. The Princess of Biralam stirs, ready to fight."

"We've three Marked in Imbra. Two, now."

"Don't count yourself out yet, Eli. You've survived so much."

Silence. Then— "Please. Don't leave."

"I'm sorry, but I cannot stay." Jaser glanced away, quivering in the darkness.

"Jaser!" Eli roared, but the spirit vanished, leaving only darkness around him. He turned to the Citadel, his eyes peering at the spire he knew so well. A single golden light flashed in the gloom. Blue reflected until the night swallowed it whole.

# Chapter 53

Kyra choked back another sob as he vanished into the darkness. That ice-blue light, that beautiful blessing of Nestham and the unwavering strength it symbolised, faded into the night. The Princess stumbled and shuddered-in a breath, tried to control her flickering heart, her fist scrunching the scrap of paper in her hand.

Tried. She honestly tried to keep herself from falling back into the darkness, the one which had consumed her when she was captured. She refused to let herself crumble under this attack. Trayse hadn't broken all of her, and if he hadn't killed her, hadn't shattered her soul, then Temero couldn't either. Kyra had reforged herself in the fires of the Hells.

"This will not break me," she whispered into the mists, but she stared over the twisting darkness that enveloped her city. Somewhere over there was the nobles' quarter, the mansions of the Houses and the merchants. The Guild's smoking ruins. The slums. And across her entire city, the only light was a sea-green Mark belonging to the Bane of Pirates. The Prince paced the wall, rallying the men.

She'd seen enough. She'd lost everything three times. Never again.

Kyra slammed the door shut and marched over to the desk in Eli's room. Tried to ignore how his scent still clung to the pillow, tried to ignore how the Torch still flickered under the bed, tried to ignore the shirt carelessly hung over the aged chair. She shifted through the stack of papers on the desk, the ones she'd attempted to tidy each day.

He'd sealed a red mark over the top of a small stack of pages. And as she read them, she couldn't stop the tears sliding down her face. Pages and pages of notes in Eli's messy hand, a scrawl she could barely read. A last gift to her, instructions she would follow to the letter, and the complement to the scrap of paper in her hand, the last piece of the puzzle. She read every single instruction again and again until she'd burned them into her memory, then folded them and replaced them in the desk. But as she turned to leave, a second sheet caught her eye, written in that same scrawl. A poem. As she read it, she started crying again.

But she would accept Eli's last gift for her, the only thing he could offer: closure.

He understood her too well, understood she wouldn't be content to sit idly by, not again. Not when there was something she could do. Kyra threw open the wardrobe she'd stolen from her Guardian and changed again. The Nightweave fitted snug over her body like a second skin, barely modest enough, but thanks to Eli, she had a few extra surprises. He'd shown her how to hunt, and that was a good thing. Her prey would not die easily.

Just one more time, she'd let herself use this identity. She was Kyra Antarun, the thrice-blessed Regent of Leranion, heir of Eshe herself. It was time to leave Jayne Farer in the past. She was dead, her secrets now released from the grave. She stalked out of the Citadel, justice garbed in shadow, face set in stone.

Jayne Farer was dead, but you couldn't kill a Ghost.

# Chapter 54

Trayse stroked a hand down his clean-shaven face, and as he leaned back on the stained couch, he swore bitterly. His mind raced too quickly, flickering through all options as he stared out the window onto the darkened street. It was well past time to leave Imbra. In fact, he should have left the moment Finon died. Whoever killed him had done a marvellous job of framing Trayse. He could respect that, at least.

But with so many hunting him, with so many new enemies... Yes, he should probably flee the city. Particularly with a demon lurking outside. He'd never liked Finon's way of pretending the past didn't exist. Even if he'd enjoyed slaughtering the refugees. Finon had paid him, but he'd paid her more. He'd never spoken of her, but he'd heard the whispers of a second assassin. And though Trayse was paid well, with all the money going straight into his account in the Order's treasury, he'd never received the good assignments. For many years, he'd searched for this woman, the so-called greatest assassin in the Eternal Order, and he'd only learned her name. Alondra.

Trayse wiped the dagger clean and glanced around the room. To his left, the grand pianoforte sat gathering dust. This house had once been that of a musician attempting to gentrify the slums. He'd run up enormous debts and had his throat cut for the trouble.

But as Trayse tucked the cloth back into his jerkin, he smiled. There was still one reason to stick around. One flawless and untouchable reason. He knew her, knew her better than she probably did, knew that she'd be frantic soon. That girl was not a leader. She had no judgement even worth considering. A warrior who couldn't even separate her feelings from the job. She was just a stupid royal brat, falling head over heels for a boy barely old enough to shave. A boy who, despite all of his magic, couldn't fight him in an alley.

No. Trayse couldn't leave yet. It was time for one last hunt. He stood, brushed pastry crumbs off his pants, and sheathed the knife. After hooking the cylinder onto his belt, he reached for the crossbow.

A loose plank creaked outside. Joy shot through him, a thrill which raced up and down his entire body. She was here. In a fluid movement, he grabbed the crossbow and flung himself over the couch. He slammed a Malmir-laced bolt into the weapon and paused, his body shielded by the furniture. His breath rasped in his ears, the crossbow trained on the door.

The door creaked open, and a figure in black stood there silently. To anyone else, she might have been mistaken for another Nightweave warrior. Not to Trayse. His eyes, accustomed to the pitch-black, homed in on the young woman. He smiled and pulled the trigger. The bolt leapt from the crossbow.

Blinding golden light lit the room with incandescent brilliance, and he barely contained the scream.

The light faded away, and there she was. Her eyes peeked above a scarf wrapped around her face, a strange metal staff in one hand. The other clutched his bolt in between reddened nails and snapped it single-handedly. The crunch shuddered through his bones, and the bitch threw the splinters to the side. Trayse stood, tossed the worthless crossbow to the side, and smiled.

"Welcome, Highness." Her deep-blue eyes tightened, gleaming with power, but she said nothing. "I can't wait to have you stay." *That* got a reaction. She twisted the staff once, so fast he could barely see it, and wicked blades flashed out of the end, glowing golden just as her hand did. Trayse's heart sped up, and his blood thrummed with the thrill. *Finally.*

He reached for the wooden staff behind him, felt the familiarity of it, and stepped back, keenly aware of the cramped space. The bulk of the couch rested between them. Kyra took another step closer, and he waited. Her whole body was taut, like a string ready to snap. *Just one more.* His fingers twitched towards his belt.

The princess stepped again. Trayse whipped the canister off his belt, squeezed it and held his breath. Dark smoke poured out, vapour seeking a target. Gaseous Void, perfect for circumstances like this. He grinned at her. Any second now, and she'd be his.

The seconds passed, but she remained standing. And with a strange, sinking feeling, he finally understood why, and pieced together the purpose of the fabric she'd tied around her face.

"Clever girl," he hissed. Her gaze snapped to his, frozen fire in ocean eyes. And just for a second, he thought he could see the animalistic rage in there, a roaring predator aching to get out. He smashed his staff down on hers, overextending past the couch, and she easily threw him off, that damned golden light gleaming through the room.

"Just think of what your lover is going through," he said. A muffled scream echoed through the room and she seemed to *shift,* blurring between the fabric of the world as she rushed him, leaping over the couch, but he ducked and placed the bulk between them again. Oh, he knew. He knew how she fought. While her lover fought hot-blooded, Kyra, Jayne, whatever her name was, she fought cold. Because she'd become unbalanced if she even tried to embrace emotion. It weakened her, and she'd make a mistake if she ever tried to feel.

"His pain is nothing compared to what you're living in."

She screamed again and sprang for him. But this time, he didn't dodge, but he blocked her, and each strained for dominance, pushing and shoving. And as he stared deep into her eyes, strained and shifting, he realised the truth. "Oh," he breathed, as a euphoric smile spread across his face, barely a hand's width from hers. "He actually did it. He *broke* you." A bitter laugh, cold and rimmed with dark mirth. "In a way I never could." He leapt over behind the couch and grinned triumphantly.

Fire smouldered in her eyes. And then, it vanished, as she lashed out with her leg—the couch screeched backwards, shoving into him, causing him to stumble. He blinked, wiggled free, but his blood turned to ice as her right hand dropped to the small of her back and reappeared. A loud crack echoed through the room, and fire scorched through his lower half.

* * *

Kyra's mind screamed at her to *go,* to end it, as Trayse stumbled forward, blood pooling from his stomach, grabbing a sword from the wall. She tossed the miniature crossbow to the side and engaged, her blades slicing through the air. There was no honour, no glory, no victory. She swung and swung until her blade shattered his into splinters. Her mind sharpened, as Trayse lashed out with the stump of his sword, screeching with the pain, her dart still embedded in his abdomen.

His blade clanged off Nesthamir vambraces. His sword spun and shattered her ring's sapphire, flashing shards of blue. Kyra snarled and slashed down with her staff. Bone shattered, tendon severed, and Trayse's right hand fell to the ground. "That was for my friends."

She didn't hesitate, twirling the staff and slamming a glowing blade through his heart. Kyra *pushed* until she impaled him on an arm's length of Nesthamir. "That was for my family." She pulled the staff loose with a wet squelch, blood clinging to the metal. Trayse fell to his knees, mouth open, any flicker of humour long gone.

"And this is for me," she breathed, and swung one last stroke. Tears ran down her face as Trayse's head toppled from his shoulders.

When she looked down, blood covered the pieces of her sapphire. Kyra wiped her tears and strode from the room, leaving the body of her tormentor behind. As she strode through the darkened streets, the world seemed different. Something had shifted. She found her way detoured through the nobles' quarters, and glanced at the keeps, their standards fluttering in the breeze. The silver pickaxe hung forlornly, and she bowed her head. She'd loved that mansion, but there was nothing there for her now.

As she stumbled into the castle, a tall, broad-shouldered figure met her, frantic and wild. Monsun took one look at her, at the staff drenched in blood. At her hands, covered in red.

"What did you do?" he breathed.

She narrowed her eyes at him, craned her neck up at the towering warrior, at the silver tattoo stretching over his cheek. "I ended him." She couldn't recognise her own voice. But Monsun didn't judge her, thought of nothing else other than their mission.

"The people need to see you, Highness. Show them you're willing to fight."

"I—I can't just yet." She moved back into the ensuite and let the water run over her hands, over the ring, the pitted Nesthamir ring. The bloodstains marred cream skin, and the red slowly dripped into the basin. As she stared into the mirror, she found a hollow gaze staring back at her. Kyra shook that off and dressed herself with shaky hands, marched out to the wall in perfect blackness. Her golden light shone, but it guttered, drained of warmth. It mingled with the light of sea-green. It should have mingled with blue.

"He's just waiting," Raylene grunted beside Jalek. "It'd be the perfect time to strike, but we don't have the numbers to commit. And there's no telling what else he has up his sleeve." She hesitated. "Are we extracting Eli?"

Kyra bit her lip and lowered her voice. "No. There will be no extraction. Eli made his choice."

"The Hells with that, Highness. You two"—she pointed at Kyra and Jalek—"you could get him out. If you wished." Her face burned in the light of their Marks, and the soldiers shifted uncomfortably. They lived and died believing their leaders would save them if they were in trouble. And now, a Queen refused to rescue a Vindicator?

Kyra didn't back down. "I made myself clear. There will be no attempt to extract Eli. He's a Vindicator and a Guardian. He'll be fine." The words rang hollow, even to her own ears.

"You threw him to the wolves," Raylene hissed. "What is it with you? Why do you always seem to kill the young men?" Fury lingered in every harsh line in her face. "You slaughtered Cedwin in the North. And now you condemn Eli to Temero."

Kyra could add one more to that list. *And I let Trayse kill Luca.*

"*Maria*," Jalek pleaded with her. "Now is not the time. This is your Queen."

"To Hells with that," Raylene slapped his arm away.

"Raylene," Kyra said evenly, though her heart raced. "I need you to trust me. Can you?" The woman wavered, a vein in her neck pulsing rapidly.

But a piercing cry rang out in the night, cutting off all of their conversation. That sound... that was the voice of that creature in the Citadel tunnels.

"I trust you," Raylene muttered, and stepped closer. Hot breath curled in Kyra's ear, like another whose blood had stained her hands. "Just make sure he survives." The creature—mantik—roared again. One had almost destroyed Amora. And now it could destroy her own home.

Not today. She raised her fist and let the golden light flare brighter than it ever had before. Men muttered and stirred next to her, and she could feel hundreds of eyes swivel on her.

This was a moment for a speech worthy of history. But while history may have cared about her words, Jayne Farer had never been one for dramatic speeches. Neither was Kyra Antarun. Dramatic speeches were for fools who cared more about their words than their people.

So she didn't preach about glory of battle, or honour in death. This was war, and honour and glory were for men who thought killing a game. She'd lost too many to think of it as anything but a waste.

If it was as she wished, Eli would have been here in her place. She might have avoided this speech and taken his place on the table. He might have flashed a grin on these battlements, his teeth glinting in the light of his gift. Kyra didn't smile as she slammed her staff on the ground. Once, twice, three times, until all was still.

"This enemy we face steals what we hold most precious." His vambraces on her arms were a constant reminder. "And yes, he makes you—makes me afraid." Soldiers shifted, but she hadn't finished. She wouldn't—couldn't stop until Temero was gone and Eli was safe. "But someone once told me we can never let fear control us. If we do that, we've already lost." Her grip tightened on her staff, and her blood thrummed, a song, a call to the others like her.

And Jalek stepped forward, placed a hand on her shoulder, and winked. "We never fight alone," he called. "We'll walk into this darkness and we won't stop fighting until the sun shines on us again." The Prince of the Sea, Bane of Pirates, bowed to the future Queen of Leranion. "All hail the Regent!" he roared.

"All hail the Regent!" the army screamed back, and Kyra at last allowed herself to smile.

"Get everyone who can't fight into the Citadel. Get everyone who can to the walls." She turned to leave, but Jalek tapped her arm.

"I'll make sure he returns," he said.

# Chapter 55

Eli peered into the blackness, the twisting night. Jaser had long gone. And he kept walking. At last, the shadows parted, and three soldiers stepped forth. "Eli Serae?" one asked. Eli nodded. But when he noticed what they bore, he couldn't stop the tremble that raced through him, as the metal shackles jangled, heavy and gleaming.

But he wordlessly let himself be leashed as irons went around his ankles, his wrists, and finally, his neck. Then they pushed him into the night, hunched over and bound by steel. Pain flared up his body as the shackles bit into his skin, and blood beaded at his wounds. His Mark flared as he engaged his heightened sight, but he never looked up. Eli stumbled twice, each time being kicked until he rose, clenching his teeth together.

He couldn't tell how long they walked until dim shadows came into view. No light. Just hundreds of soldiers marching purposefully, with no sign they struggled to see as he did. Each one had a silver bracelet glimmering around their wrist. And in this war camp outside his city, the crest on the tents was a silver pickaxe on a field of black. So he had been right after all. They jerked to a halt, and he glanced at the lead soldier for the first time in the entire trip. The soldier grinned and unsheathed his knife. And plunged it into Eli's gut and wrenched it out just as swiftly. Eli screamed, and fell to his knees, black pushing into his vision. They would just end him now?

No. Not kill him. His magic rushed to fill the wound, uncontrollable, seeking to mend and replace. And when he couldn't control it, it vanished immediately. Instantly, the light fled his body. Used up, just like that. They wrenched him off the ground and pushed him to a larger tent. A growing presence filled his senses, like a raw throbbing power. He'd felt something similar once before, when Kyra had been furious.

The power then... that was nothing like what waited for him inside. He stumbled in, and his eyes fell straight on the handsome man from earlier. Without a doubt, he was the source of that power. He stretched, his blonde hair falling to his shoulders.

"See, my lord? He would come, just like I said." The blonde man gestured to Eli, bound in chains, and a beautiful smile stretched across his lips. "Her Highness is pragmatic. He's only one man, after all." Eli snarled viciously at him. The man turned a laughing smile on him. "Good evening, Vindicator. Or is it Guardian? So many titles, Eli Serae."

"Shut up and get on with it, Temero." He shrugged, difficult to do in the chains. "I'd rather not die bored." His skin crawled at his own words.

"Oh, you would like to die, wouldn't you? Payment for all your sins? Failure to save the ones you love?" Eli's heart turned to ice, and he almost roared at the demon. "Don't worry, you won't die until I have what I want." Temero gestured at the soldiers, and they pushed Eli down on a chair. "And I think you know what that is. Where are the pillars?"

"What pillars?" Eli feigned nonchalance.

"Boy, I've picked over the ruins of Mount Sancti. That was your home, wasn't it?" He waved dismissively. "I've found the shards of Nesthamir from that pillar." He smiled. "Where did you think I got my new bracelets from?" Eli quietly sucked in a breath. "Where are the pillars?"

"I don't know."

Temero raised a hand, and Eli's chest glowed red. That horrible feeling, the smell of burning flesh, the searing agony—it crept back again until he was screaming for breath.

"The last time we were together like this," Temero murmured, "I thought you were just a thief. I branded you to control you, but it didn't work. Bracelets are far more effective."

The pain subsided, and Eli gasped for air. He glanced at Lord Ketan, the ageing man with a furrowed brow. "What did he offer you? The throne?" But Ketan said nothing, and the pain started up again, and Eli drifted into unconsciousness.

This went on for some time. How long, he did not know. Temero wasn't always there, but Ketan was. The same knife, every time. And always he bit down, clamped his lips shut, refusing to scream. He would not falter. He would not cower. He would not break. Lord Ketan wrenched the knife out, wiped it clean, and placed it gently on the table beside him. "It'll go easier if you tell him," he said, striding to a large bowl of water where he wrung the red out of blood-stained hands.

Eli gasped for breath, sweat coursing over his brow. He barely shifted on the table, almost screeching again, as blood covered his legs. The knife had entered his calf this time, neatly severing the tendons. His magic flared, wiping away the pain, but he could still feel the phantom knife there, the cold bite of steel worming its way through his flesh.

"Easier for me until he kills all of us. I'll never tell him," Eli said. "But—but there's still a chance for you. Throw your support to Kyra. Help us fight him."

The old man barked a laugh. "Why would I ever ally with her? Or you? The two of you are the bringers of chaos." His grey beard was wiry and matted, and it twisted with his words. "My daughter is the only thing I have left. I cannot put her in danger."

Eli bit his lip as the phantom knife dug deeper. "So you brought her to a camp full of demons."

Ketan stopped and stared at him. "What are you talking about?"

"You're not serious," Eli said, surprise and grief washing over him. "He's destroyed your men. Twisted them into something else. You were once one of the brightest lords in Imbra. Tell me you haven't believed his lies." He could tell, when Ketan's eyes shuttered, that he had fallen for it.

Ketan turned away, his hands falling to a table behind them. Maps rustled in fingers that trembled slightly, droplets of water still clinging to aged flesh. "It's too late for me," he said.

Eli raised his head as much as he could, strapped to the table. "Personally, I believe that it's never too late for anyone. Even grumpy old men." He flashed a grin, pain-wracked as it was. "I've dealt with a few of them, after all. But it's not too late for Eislyn. You can still protect her."

"Not with Antarun. That *bitch* is the reason my daughter was hurt."

Eli snarled a warning, low and full of death. "That's my Regent you speak of. And Kyra would never hurt Eislyn. She was her *best friend*. There is a way out of this, but I need you to trust me."

"Why should I? Ever since you arrived in Imbra you've brought nothing but death."

"Temero will bring even more if you don't help me. Just hear me out. Send for Eislyn, and make sure nobody else is in earshot. And if you don't like it," Eli said, "then you can go back to torturing me."

It was hours later when Ketan could do as he asked. Familiar footsteps glided in, and Eli craned his neck around to look. Familiar golden hair floated down, and she was as stunning as he remembered. And still as displeased with him.

"What happened to you?" Eislyn gasped.

Eli smiled, but something twinged in his leg. The memories flooded back, Lord Ketan shattering his kneecap with a dull hammer. It was an effort to keep smiling at his tormentor. His ally.

"Ask your new friend," Eli drawled.

Each breath was an effort until his wounds healed. They always did. Ketan waited for Eli's healing properties to refill, then started again. Every time, as long as he stopped before killing Eli, he would do it.

Lord Ketan stopped, assumed a stonelike stance. But his daughter, the firebrand, she would burn in whatever way she could. She glared at Eli, but something gleamed in her eye.

"I bring a message from my Regent," Eli said.

Eislyn smiled slowly, and he breathed into her ear. When she drew back, she slapped him across the face. "Get away from me, filth," she spat, a drop of phlegm coursing down his bare chest.

And finally, the Guardian flinched, sagging against the chains that bound him. She turned away, her dark trousers ready for combat, her blade on display.

"I never want to see him again," she said to nobody.

"Don't do this, Eislyn! Temero will betray you!" he bellowed, raging, thrashing in his irons, bound, helpless.

Eislyn turned, and her amber eyes turned molten again. "Well, your lover did it first."

The power returned to the tent, a pulsing, throbbing strength that crawled over his skin. His magic sang to it and he cursed himself for doing so. But that beautiful golden-haired man returned, strength in his very stride. Eli could barely raise his head where it was sticky with blood, Ketan still forced to keep up his pretences.

"Good morning, child," Temero crooned. "I have a proposition for you."

Eli sucked in a breath, preparing to resist whatever mind power Temero used. He'd faced it once before. Hallucinations, manipulation... he'd faced it head on and emerged victorious. But more footsteps glided in beside the demon king.

"My love," Temero crooned, stroking something behind Eli. "Take off your mask."

A faint rasp of fabric, and something prompted him to look.

And the world fell silent.

Somewhere, Eislyn was gasping, but it was lost in the roaring in his ears, lost in the spots appearing before his eyes. His silver eyes matched by those of the woman in front of him, set in a face that mirrored his, framed by light brown hair.

"Miriel," he breathed. His sister, dead these eleven years, cocked her head, and turned to Temero.

"Who is 'Miriel', Luce?" She brushed her hands along Temero's side, gripping the muscles there. Eli shuddered once, and his breath stopped. His limbs refused to obey him.

"Someone he used to know," Temero said. "Nobody important."

Eli's hands shook at his side, and the magic roiled in him, snapped, but he was too weak, drained by the knife spilling his lifeblood on the board.

"*What have you done to her?*" Eli found his voice, his magic and his muscles ripping at the shackles. They clanged against each other, and he found some purchase, straining at the metal. Temero wrapped a hand around her, but his other rippled with power. Shadows pulsed at his fingertips and blasted Eli back onto the table.

"I awakened her. Since the day you lost her, she has been mine. And when I returned to Ekra"—he smiled—"I found her again. Waiting for me. After so many years."

Eli couldn't take his eyes off the beautiful woman across from him. Her face was solemn until she looked at Temero. Love bloomed there.

Love built on a lie.

Temero turned back to Eli. "And now, my proposition," he said. "Tell me where the pillars are, and I will release Alondra and let her return to your lover. Refuse, and she dies." Eli couldn't move.

"My lord," Ketan said, "this isn't right."

Temero glanced at him. No. No, this wasn't the plan. Eli had waited. He'd passed on the message. He'd done his duty. It was all up to Kyra, now. No, he tried to blink. Run. Get away. But the dreaded words came. "I've had enough of you, Ketan." And from a hidden sheath, he flung a dagger into Ketan's heart.

"*No!*" Eislyn shrieked. Eli couldn't think or move, Eislyn's screams settling into the haze. She sank to the floor, and soon her father's blood covered her tunic. Soon, Ketan breathed his last.

Eli sagged back against the table. He'd failed. Their plan had failed. He'd miscalculated so badly.

"Last chance, Serae."

And as he gazed at Miriel, something cracked within him. "Talon Reach and Aurimia."

Temero grinned and Miriel giggled as he pressed a kiss to her lips. "Alondra," he said. "I have a special mission for you." He breathed into her ear and, though Eli strained, he couldn't make out the commands.

His sister smiled and sped off into the night, moving like a Marked—she was a Marked. *At least Miriel's safe.* Tears fell down Eli's cheeks, tracking paths through the blood. "You have what you want, Temero. Now get out of my city."

"In time," Temero said. "But only once the bells toll for your lover. Alondra against Antarun. That's a fight I wish I could see." He reached into his pocket and produced a strip of gleaming metal—Nesthamir. Eli's limbs lost all their strength, and he slumped back on the board, the rough wood digging into his bare back. A faint hiss, and Eli's mind went blank.

# Chapter 56

One rap at the door was enough before Monsun wrenched it open, clad only in billowing trousers. His eyes fell on the shorter man twitching there. He'd wrapped his missing forearm in his tunic, the sleeve twisted over at the end. "What is it, Alsair?"

"No time to explain," the monk said, barging into his simple chambers. Just two bedrooms, one for Amora on the far side, though she'd been sleeping in Eli's room recently. Thankfully, Alsair didn't comment on the Syl-sized shirt hanging over the chair, or the perfume flooding the room. "I need you to keep Amora and Syl in your room for the next few hours."

Monsun raised a brow and stepped forward, looming over the older man. He gave nothing else away, but this monk—even in his current condition—was uncanny. "I will do it," he murmured. He trusted this strange little man, had relied on him in the north.

"No matter what you hear outside, no matter what comes, keep them safe, and do not interfere."

"Alsair," he growled. Anger coiled in him, strength and passion that had seen him through battles and destruction. That same strength which had seen him across the continent. Whatever came, he could fight it.

But the monk surged on. "Once the siege breaks, get out of here. Take Amora to Amaldas and contact the royals. One of their Marked is the Chosen of Biralam, and they must come forth."

Monsun swore loudly, his insides churning. "I can't go back. If I return without the Heir of Amerin, I'll lose everything."

"We have bigger problems to worry about than your ego," Alsair said.

Monsun sucked in a breath, prepared to punch the monk for that, but he had a point. They did have bigger problems. "Biralam has three Marked, two of whom are Heirs. How should I know who is their Chosen?" And what their Chosen even meant.

Alsair shifted from side to side, his hand clenching and unclenching around the hilt of the sword on his back. "That's the thing," Alsair said, his eyes glazing over. "You don't know. It will destroy your soul, but it must be done nonetheless."

Monsun's soul would wither within hours of arriving, but he put that aside. He silently swore he would protect his family when he arrived. "How intact is your soul, Jinnam?" he breathed.

Alsair didn't respond immediately, and when he did, he ignored the question. "There are six Chosen. Six Marked, out of all of the blessed who walk Ekra. One of them must do as Nestham requires. My task is—was—to assemble four of them."

Eli. Kyra. Jalek. "Who is the fourth?"

"She is making her way here as we speak. I must prepare to meet her now."

"What will you do?"

"Something for which I have prepared before Eli first came to Mount Sancti." His jade eyes, once piercing, glazed over. "Farewell, old friend. We will meet again one day. When you return from Amaldas, give this to Eli. Not before." He handed him a scrappy book, the cover faded with age.

The monk turned to go, but Monsun grabbed his good arm, the skin wrinkled and saggy. Alsair turned baleful eyes on him, but he seemed smaller than ever.

"I know about Finon. And it was justice."

As if a crushing weight lifted from his shoulders, Alsair breathed again. "Thank you." Alsair turned and marched away, and to Monsun, it seemed as if he was a soldier again.

# Chapter 57

The clock on the wall had to be wrong. It couldn't have been an entire *day* since she'd let Eli go into Temero's clutches. Since she had sent him to his death, or worse.

Stick with the plan. The one they'd created together, hoping and praying and gambling. One throw of the dice was all it would take, perhaps, and they could break the siege. All of it for her people, she'd once thought. But she'd fought and bled and sacrificed herself and those closest to her, and for what? This foul darkness hadn't lifted, and an army was still outside her city. She'd made several trips to the walls, comforted the men, let her light shine. Even then, it seemed pointless. What were two Marks against the endless dark?

She didn't really know why she paced through the Citadel's silent streets to the Eternal Order's Cathedral. The door squeaked open, unlocked and unguarded yet in pristine condition.

Her boots sank into carpet she'd once stained with her blood. There was nothing but silence as she sank onto an abandoned pew and stared at the walls. The artworks were majestic yet, without light, they were powerless. The demons seemed too real, the angels too fake.

Since time itself, people had lived in a world of darkness, and though they tried to project humanity on divinity, she knew the truth. No one was coming to help them. And they certainly wouldn't help her, a follower of Nestham rejected by her own faith. Scorned by the very congregation to which she'd once pledged.

Leon cared about the enemies she'd killed. That was nothing compared to her friends she'd killed with her failings, her lack of judgement. Eshe's hand brushed her shoulder. A warning? It didn't matter, much more blood would spill before this war ended.

Perhaps it would be her own.

She stood and walked to the end of the Cathedral, glaring at the sentry waiting outside Finon's office. She wondered what he thought he was guarding. The Archbishop was dead, his empire shattered. The bishops hadn't exchanged correspondence since Red Night. She would have to help elect a new Archbishop soon, if the faith survived the next few months.

The Archbishop's office was just as she remembered. A priest, an assassin and a prisoner had met in that room, and she alone still survived.

The hellin's board rested on the pine table between luxurious chairs. The flame token lay on the centre square, surrounded by shadow tokens. Her bitten fingernail idly tipped over the flame.

Why was she here? Finon was dead, but she found herself in his sanctuary, anyway. To hide? *You're better than this,* she told herself. Yet, she couldn't go outside. She couldn't face it. Why not?

Finon's desk was ancient and grand, polished wood gilded at the edges. She dropped behind it and paused at sight of the hidden mechanism, ready to trigger the crossbows that had wounded Syl. Each so similar to the one strapped to her back, its quiver on her belt. A fine weapon. Pragmatic, not glorious.

"Well, we can all use a little more pragmatism," she muttered. Her fingernail tapped an irregular rhythm on the elegant chair as she spun her gaze around the room. Gold light cast long shadows as her Mark flared over the rich decorations, the books, the sword on the wall, the scabbard mounted above it.

*The sword on the wall.* Finon won with cunning and deception. Despite the Order's military heritage, he wasn't a warrior. Her entire body went rigid. *If Finon isn't a warrior, then why does he have a sword mounted on the wall?* It was a fine weapon, perhaps a decoration. And yet... something rang differently about it. She stepped over the lush carpet, replaced since she was last here, and reached for the magnificent weapon. One hand rested on the hilt, the other on the polished blade.

And her Mark flared brilliantly, a signal of the power that washed over her.

"Nesthamir," she breathed. "Jaser's sword." *But how did Finon have it?* Later. She would deal with that later, she told herself as she hefted the mighty blade and its sheath.

Besides, she suspected the man she'd never trusted had manoeuvred it here for this very moment. Alsair, the last Wildborn, the last Jinnam. He seemed even more erratic lately, pacing the halls and muttering to himself. Monsun had tried speaking with him, but to no avail.

Her mind was foggy, no longer the planner she had been. But when she held that sword in her hand, her senses cleared and her burdens fell away. Kyra swung it twice, and marvelled at its balance, at the way it cut through the air. An ancient, unbreakable symbol. Eli would love this weapon. For it was his, as much as the vambraces she wore on her wrists. They protected her, but she couldn't touch the Rift, for relics only had loyalty to their gifted Marked. The bell tolled outside, and she returned to wait in Eli's room. She could do nothing but wait until the agreed time.

Down by the walls, Jalek's Mark kept shining. She should go down there again, but it was so easy just to sit up here. Too easy to let Jalek handle it, too easy to let Monsun and the other Vindicators deal with the siege. She'd already had to deal with unrest in the city, the fights that were breaking out. Their food stocks were already running low. Twice she'd been in the slums, trying to convince others they would get through this. The injured in the Musadim's Healing House were crying out for their Saviour, the man with healing in his touch. Eli.

But when light flared in the city beneath her, she sensed that the time for waiting was over. A single figure sprinting to the Spire at superhuman speed. And glowing faintly at their wrist, she thought she saw a glimmer of ice blue.

# Chapter 58

Alsair used to always clasp his hands behind his back when he walked. Impatient, his old mentor had called him. It was better than zealot or fanatic. He'd lost his impatience with his hand, and he'd seen the truth of the world in an instant.

And as he paced through the castle, as those doors loomed in the Vindicator's Spire, he blinked away tears. One of the young people he'd cursed waited within. His heart railed against him, and his vision ebbed, fading.

"I'm sorry, Alsair." He'd last heard that voice over ten years ago. Solemn, yet commanding. That voice belonged in a different age, to a warrior who had slaughtered his way across the continent. The Solemn Warrior, Ekra's failure.

Alsair inclined his head to the Guardian gliding beside him. "Jaser Cathom. I'd be lying if I said it was good to see you, harbinger."

"I'm sorry," Jaser repeated. His silver eyes—Eli's eyes—were downcast, and Alsair wondered if it was the first time doubt had crossed the bullheaded Guardian's face. He didn't seem the type to recognise it.

"I know. But you can't just apologise for this. At least not when he finds out." The monk stretched a hand to his back, testing the draw of the sword strapped to his spine. "Ten years, Jaser. And I'm wondering if we made a mistake."

"Don't do this, Alsair," Jaser grimaced. "This will only make it worse for you."

The monk barked a laugh nobody was around to hear. "Oh, it's too late for that. You weren't there to watch him grow. You didn't teach him how to shave, how to hunt and fight, how to be a man. You didn't watch him fall in love with a princess, and you didn't leave him alone to fight a demon." Alsair dashed a hand over his eyes and marched off.

"I was always watching," Jaser replied, striding beside him.

As if that mattered. "Always watching, but never seeing," Alsair said.

Jaser twisted a transparent neck to glare at him. "I never liked your kind, even when you pledged to me. I found few worthy."

"Most were more worthy to carry the Mark than you were. Shira was a Guardian that anyone would follow. She united the nations."

"What are you implying, monk?" Jaser paused, showing considerable fury for a dead man.

Alsair smirked, but it wasn't out of amusement. "I think you giving Eli orders is a cosmic irony, considering how you damned this world to hell a millennium ago." Anger—anger and shame crossed Jaser's handsome face, and the spirit's outline rippled. "Or isn't that why you never became a Riftsinger?" Alsair pushed in the final blow, as he'd taught his young protégé to do.

"How—how do you know of them?"

The Wildborn's smile was dark and cunning. "I suspected they were watching me for years, long before you made me what I am. So I found one. She was kind, generous, and the only person to ever best me." He'd never forget her.

She'd laughed softly when he'd begged for her name. *You could never pronounce it,* she'd said, brushing a glowing finger across his chin. Her armour was like nothing he'd seen across all of Ekra. Her mahogany skin shone radiant when she was joyful, and her eyes blazed like the Hells' fires when she was angry.

When he saw her, glorious wings of pure night enraptured him. But when she spoke, that was when he had lost his senses. Her voice was like Nestham's, and yet when she sang, she could make the most beautiful singer in Ekra sound like a drunken sailor. In their time by the river, she'd told him every Riftsinger had that power. Jaser swore quietly, and Alsair snapped back to the present.

"Do you have anything useful?" Alsair demanded.

"Eli got that from you, I see."

"Eli got a lot of things from me." Alsair folded his arms, tapping a finger on a stump. "Good judgement when talking to spirits was one of them."

Jaser snapped his teeth at him, shifting and shimmering. "That was for his own good, and for that of the girl."

"The girl has a name. And they are both more than lambs bred for the slaughter." Even if she hated him, he could still offer her that grace.

"That was the price." Yet in that moment, Jaser—the first Guardian of Ekra, a man who would have been revered a hero had the Order not expunged his history—looked away.

"The price that you should have paid." Alsair braced a hand against the wall as the headache threatened to overwhelm him. "Jaser, it's failing. I can't see like I once could."

"Not much longer." The Guardian pressed closer. "You still have fight in you, with what you have left to give."

Alsair closed his eyes as his forehead touched cold stone. "Look after the boy." The headache passed, and all that remained was an old man talking to a dead warrior. "Will we win?" he breathed, a decade of plotting and planning and shredding his heart in a single question. Because if they didn't, his life was in vain. He'd lost so many of his friends to the Order. All turned towards one question. One goal.

"I don't know," Jaser said. He'd have to be content with that and buy them a chance. Alsair sucked in a breath and nodded at the dead Guardian. "For what it's worth, I hope you can find peace," the apparition said.

"Well, those who live by the sword..." Alsair grinned, quoting from the Nesthamara. Jaser vanished, and like a prisoner awaiting execution, Alsair rested outside Eli's chambers.

So many sunrises. So many bloody days. He'd faced each one as a servant of Nestham, as a Wildborn, as a Jinnam, as a mentor, as a friend. He'd do the same tonight. Alsair closed his eyes and breathed deeply in the meditation he'd learned over twenty years ago, well before the battle that had spelled his fate.

Before then, he'd been the Wildborn's greatest warrior. The men and women of the shadows, the loyal servants of Nestham, the fourth faith of Ekra, and the first to fall. Crushed under an army's boots.

They didn't have the Order's idealism and passion.

They didn't have the Musadim's healing touch and servant's heart.

They didn't have the Jinnam's peace and patience.

The Order had called them vigilantes, long before they'd purged the continent of his kind. The Musadim had called them hypocrites, to claim they served Nestham, but also went to battle. In the end, few had mourned their destruction. But as he exhaled again, his battle meditation was complete. A technique learned as a Wildborn and perfected as a Jinnam. It would restore him to do his duty.

"My soul is prepared, Lord." A faint hand brushed his shoulder in farewell.

In his mind's eye, he saw the warrior clambering up the tower. A wraith in the shadows, merely just another speck in the blackness that Temero had used to cover the land. A faint light gleamed under her dark gloves. Not ice-blue, but pure white. Silver eyes glimmered under a hood, and a Nesthamir bracelet covered her wrist. Alsair checked his sword, forged for him in the Wildborn's monastery, a broadsword balanced for one hand. A weapon fit for a king, his master had said.

It was time to kill an assassin.

*  *  *

Kyra glanced back at the sword and staff scattered on Eli's—on her bed, but her heart thudded in her chest as she stared at the man carrying that shimmering light. Guardian,

Vindicator, Saviour. Eli. She stepped back from the balcony and stretched out her arms, just waiting for the warmth that would fill them. He vaulted onto the balcony, rolled in a fluid motion, then stood, Nightweave covering his muscled form. And for a split second longer, she thought it was him.

He had Eli's beautiful eyes, but it wasn't him. He stood with innate power, but it wasn't him.

"Alondra," she breathed, and the woman froze. The silence lengthened, longer, longer, until every breath was an eternity. Kyra stretched out a calloused hand and took one step forth. Her teeth sunk into her lip, but that hand extended forward, a silent offer.

Protection, safety, and more, that was what she offered to the assassin. "Come with me," she whispered. Alondra hesitated, then stepped forward. Her left hand—gloved, unlike her right—landed in her own, and Kyra sighed, a smile spreading over her face. She shuffled closer, her heart opening up. Maybe she could give this assassin a chance.

It was in the eyes. They flashed once—and Kyra barely dodged the sword arcing through the air.

She rolled back through the balcony doorway and slammed it shut, locking the assassin on the other side. Alondra's wrist glowed white, her sword dangling loosely in her hand. And blood roared in Kyra's ears. A Marked. Alondra was a *Marked*.

The assassin slammed her fist against the glass, and shards shot into the air. Kyra leapt for the bed and rolled onto the other side, the wood digging into her knees. A spray of spikes embedded themselves in the pillow. She rose, her staff fading into her hands, whirring, pulsing with light.

"Not again," she breathed. The assassin drew a second sabre. "Alondra, stop!"

Alondra didn't. She lashed out with the sabres. Kyra blocked and riposted, her blade aimed squarely at Alondra's ribs. The girl sprang back, her sword swiping everything off the shelf.

Alondra swung high and low, and Kyra dodged, but she retreated a step. She thrust forward, but it carried her too far, and she had to recover. Each time, conceding ground to the assassin, gliding on the polished wooden floor.

Until her back pressed against the wall hanging, and her heart stopped. The sword slammed into the wall and stuck there, and Alondra's sabre pressed to her throat. Kyra willed herself to show no fear, but as she stared into Alondra's eyes, she wished she had more time.

The door crashed open, and a shoulder slammed into Alondra's chest, hurling the assassin away. Kyra sucked in a breath and glanced to her right. Alsair's broadsword pointed at the assassin.

"Stay out of this," he roared. And something twinged in Kyra's chest, but she obeyed. The monk closed his eyes and assumed a ready stance, and Alondra rushed him, always alternating her swings with her sabres. Alsair duelled smoothly, blocking strike after strike after strike. Never as quick as her, but always with his sword in place at just the right time.

Kyra tried to keep watching, and even as they fought, she could sense the trap, could see the way Alondra's overhand blow went in, but the other swung towards Alsair's remaining wrist—but the monk was already moving, batting away one strike, then the other. Like he had seen it coming. Like he was ten steps ahead of her.

And in that moment, Kyra understood. She'd seen Alsair fight just once. But even then, Eli, one of the best swordsmen she knew, couldn't beat Alsair though using his Mark. How could an ageing, one-armed monk be faster than a supernaturally superior warrior?

Only if he knew every move they made before they did. Alsair moved calmly, letting Alondra strike with everything she had. Alondra's attacks were storm-tossed waves crashing on unbreakable stone.

It wasn't enough. As Kyra watched, Alsair seemed to slow, and he staggered as he parried her attacks. Whatever he had, he had just lost. Alondra sensed it and renewed her push. Her boot pressed Alsair in the chest, and the monk stumbled back, back to the bed, where he collapsed against the frame, the sword tumbling from his grasp. Her sabre swept up, readying for a final strike. Alsair twisted, reaching for the bed, reaching for the Guardian's sword.

Alondra's blade shattered against Nesthamir. The assassin staggered back, shards of steel around her boots. Alsair's hand propelled forward with a strength summoned from outside of this world. The assassin was silent as she toppled to the floor, the Guardian's blade embedded in her heart.

\* \* \*

Alsair sighed as Alondra collapsed to the floor, blood pooling around her chest. Kyra had done as he had asked, even with the mistrust that still burned in her eyes. The shock and horror, the disgust, so like the people who'd tried to break him. But he wasn't finished yet. The sword slipped from Alondra's torso with a wet squelch. She let out a painful scream, but he was so gentle as he slipped the hood from her face. Behind him, Kyra let out a strangled moan.

"Miriel," he breathed. The face that stared back at him was almost identical to the one he'd raised. Eli's shadow, missing for so long.

Kyra dropped to her knees beside him. "You can save her," she begged, and there were tears gleaming on her face, tears for a woman who'd tried to kill her. "Please. Get a healer in here!"

"There won't be a healer who can fix this," he said. And suddenly, the weight of all those years crashed on him. The decade as the master of the hellin's board, moving all his friends as pieces, crashed on him. He'd been the flame surrounded by shadow, and it was time to come home. "Temero controls her. He can't have her."

"What are you talking about?"

"Forgive me," he said. "I know you don't trust me, but everything I do, I did for Ekra." He reached back for the girl.

Her faint gasps of breath mirrored the innocence Temero had taken and corrupted. The human was still in there somewhere. He knew it.

"With Nestham as my witness, I make this claim. My blood for her blood, my life for her life... my soul for her soul."

Light pulsed on Miriel's wrist, and her wound closed. Her face a deathly pale, she still slumbered peacefully. His own became a rasp. Her bracelet dimmed, its power destroyed—one last redemption.

"The Marked must stand against Temero. On the Severed Peaks, one must fall to save Ekra." His breathing stilled, and a gentle voice welcomed him home.

# Chapter 59

Kyra's yells summoned the pages who burst into the room. A young woman—Anne —raised a shaky hand to her face, already whitening as she took in the bodies, the blood, the destruction.

"Summon Prince Jalek," Kyra breathed, and the young woman ran as fast as she could. The other, a teenage boy, approached her as she knelt over the blood-stained woman, still breathing. "Help me lift her," she commanded, and together they gently lifted the girl onto the bed. Her face was peaceful in sleep, almost childish, though a small scar marred her cheek.

When that was done, Kyra turned to the monk on the ground. His face was utterly serene, but she bit her lip, trembling. "For what you have given, we thank you," she breathed. "May we always remember your sacrifice." She covered him with a blanket and sat down to wait, her head in her hands.

"Highness?" the page said.

"I'm fine," she said shakily. "Get a healer in here to check on Alondra."

"And what of the man?"

"Let him lie in state until we bury him." He nodded, and she grabbed the ancient blade of the Guardians, mechanically wiping it down, all the while glancing at Alondra—Miriel. She barely registered the four soldiers who took Alsair away. Jalek arrived eventually, the Prince exhausted, filthy. A dirt-covered hand clasped hers, and she arose on shaky legs.

"I'm so sorry," he said, as he followed her into the bathing suite, onto the tiled floor. He didn't need to speak further as he removed his shirt and climbed into the tub. She couldn't look at him, instead grabbing a piece of cloth from the bench and folding it end over end.

"Save your breath and bite down," she said, passing him the cloth. She grabbed the rest, piling up bandages she'd stockpiled ever since her Spire was destroyed. He did so, and she tried not to think about the blood she would spill. "Are you ready?" She'd wanted to give Eli more time, but they couldn't afford that anymore.

Jalek nodded, and Kyra plunged her dagger into his gut, trying to blot out the muffled screaming.

# Chapter 60

Eli swam in his mind, trapped in an endless sea of shadow. Did he have a body? He glanced down, but the night held him captive, and when he focused his power, his Mark didn't shine, the ice-blue light now as familiar to him as his own hand. Temero's essence ebbed around him, no longer just power, but a presence that slithered over him, clogging his very senses.

When he glanced down at his hand, his gut clenched. Clasped at his wrist was a silver bracelet, unremarkable save for the strange, corrupting taste of twisted Nesthamir. A once-holy metal, now used for horrific purposes.

The mists parted and an unfamiliar figure stood before him, wreathed in light. "I'm glad you wanted to serve me, Eli," the angel said. Holy power filled his clothes, every part of him radiating awesome might. His hair flowed around him, drifting on a phantom breeze, and his face shone with incandescent brightness. And his wings—glorious wings like those of a mighty bird, pulsed with blessed light.

"Who are you?" he breathed.

"I am Lucial," he said, and his voice echoed through the mists. "And Nestham has sent me to save this world."

"From Temero?"

The angel laughed softly. "From yourselves. Men lie and cheat, they rob and kill, and nothing changes. You need help. And I can help you."

The angel's voice was so strong, so commanding, yet so peaceful. Eli held out his hand, and the angel neared him, the only source of light in this wicked world.

No. Not anymore. A light flared in his mind, and a tether filled the void, crackling with energy. It wrapped around his torso, and yanked him through the mists, back through that darkness, so similar to the Rift—Eli surfaced in his mind, whole again, back to the pain of the mortal world.

That bond pulsed in his blood, commanded his heart. *Jalek.* The life debt had activated.

He wrenched against the chains, his magic restored. A man under a life debt could do inhuman things. A Marked under a life debt—the metal screeched and shattered in seconds, twisting shackles hanging from his wrists, blood pooling on his skin. Eli resisted his magic's power to heal the wounds, kept the lid on the light. He'd need every spare trace of strength to save Jalek. He bolted through the camp. The baying of monsters rang out, but he raced uncontested through the House Ketan guards.

At the perimeter, two guards loomed in Ketan colours. Eli flared his light and ran barefoot, the rocky ground nipping at his feet. They tried to stop him.

But he punched through, and their bodies blasted into the shadows. A howl echoed through the night, but he hoped he was already clear.

He'd failed tonight, and Kyra had to know. The castle gates loomed, and the soldiers screamed at him to stop. But Eli was already propelling himself through the air into a flip. He landed on the ramparts. He must have looked a sight, bloody, branded, tattooed and half-naked. The soldiers didn't touch him as he sprinted through the darkened city. Even now, the citizens refused to leave their houses, terrified of the darkness.

He followed that debt, urging him to hurry, pressing him onwards, sprinting through the castle, racing up the stairs of the Vindicator's Spire. He crashed into his own chambers, past a pile of blankets on the floor, past a woman in his bed, straight into the bathing suite—Kyra and Jalek. Relief bloomed on their faces, Kyra pressing a rag to the knife still in his gut. Jalek had cloth between his teeth, shaking with agony. Eli, prompted by the debt, leaned forward and wrenched the blade out. Blood spurted out, staining his hand, coursing over his skin. The Prince groaned through the wound, collapsing to the side. The Guardian plummeted into his magic, descended into the roiling storm of power and his hands wreathed with light, connected with injured skin.

His healing—finally restored after so much torture, snapped into Jalek. And just like before, he could see the Prince, feel the energy, the life that coursed from him. Jalek's presence was not like Kyra's. Kyra's was a song of remembrance. A quiet melody that built and built and built into a crescendo that shattered the world. Jalek's—Jalek's was like nothing he'd ever heard. It was loud and proud, rife with bold, triumphant chords. And yet—he could feel the broken notes, the slight tremors that corrupted the melody. Eli reached for that song and poured his magic into it. After what felt like hours, the Prince's breathing eased, and his wound no longer oozed blood. Silence.

"You were supposed to get here earlier," Jalek coughed. Eli winked at him as the bond slipped away between them. He turned, just before he was assaulted by one of the most powerful women in the world. Kyra clutched him tight, and he let himself breathe in her scent, that familiar rose and oil wrapping around her. He was *home.*

And yet, he couldn't stop shaking. "I failed," he said. There it was, that unavoidable, damnable truth. "I failed. Temero knows where the pillars are. I'm so sorry, Kyra. I broke." He couldn't stop the tears cascading down his face. As he wiped them off, they mingled with Jalek's blood. Kyra didn't care, not as she pressed a kiss to his lips.

"It wasn't your fault. It was mine. I shouldn't have put you in that position. I should have gone myself." Maybe. Maybe she wouldn't have broken, maybe she wouldn't have yielded, maybe she would have been able to sacrifice Miriel for the world. Miriel—

"Miriel. She's alive," he breathed into the space between them. Kyra bit her lip. *No.* If Kyra was alive, then Miriel— Miriel— "Oh, Nestham." He sank to his knees, head to the floor. But Kyra fell with him and lifted his chin. A quiet strength gleamed in those grief-stricken eyes.

"She's safe. Safe and free." She hesitated, and he knew. He knew without her having to tell him. Not as sympathy—not grief—showed in her face. "But Alsair is gone. He saved my life, and he gave Miriel hers back."

Eli's hand left a bloody imprint on the tiled floor. "I need to see her."

Jalek rolled to his feet, his strength restored. "Stay a while. I'll get back down to the walls." He grimaced and glanced down at himself, at the blood barely dry. "Glad I took my shirt off earlier." He swung it back on and armed himself with that seaman's swagger, despite the grievous wound he'd just received. Or maybe that was just Jalek.

"Eli," Kyra said firmly. "I need to know. Did you convince Ketan?"

"I tried. Temero killed him, and—I don't think Eislyn can help."

"So," Jalek said. "We're on our own." The sailor shut the door behind him, leaving silence in his wake.

Clothing rustled as Kyra turned to Eli, ageless grace and regal strength, but she said nothing. She didn't need to, and just held him as the tears finally spilled. He let himself break, but she was still there to keep him standing.

After what felt like seconds, Kyra raised him and drew him to the bed, and the figure lying atop it. That face—twin to his own. Miriel looked so small, so innocent. But Eli couldn't stop the tears gushing from his face as he knelt next to the bed, watching her. A small scar ran across her cheek. How had she gotten that? She was so much older, yet eternally youthful. Eleven years since he lost her. The day she had reached for something shiny in the water and had fallen in the river.

Something shiny in the water. The gleaming, utterly unholy bracelet on her wrist.

"*Get it off her*," he growled, unsheathing his dagger and slamming it on the metal. It didn't crack, and his sister didn't stir.

"We should go," Kyra said, draping a hand on his shoulder. "I've got the staff looking after her. They'll remove the bracelet."

"Fine," he sighed, and turned to leave, tensing his arms. The vambraces appeared on them immediately, and he shuffled to the door.

"Eli?"

"Hm?" he stirred and blinked blearily.

She raised a brow, glancing at his chest. "Put some clothes on, love."

He glanced down, and heat rushed to his cheeks, and he hurriedly stepped into the wardrobe. The door shut behind him, but he didn't move.

*Alsair.* The man who had raised him, trained him, been like a father to him. And he'd barely spoken with him in the past weeks.

A Vindicator who couldn't protect his country, a Guardian who couldn't stop Temero, a boy who couldn't care about his father. He wiped away the traitorous tears as he threw on the pants and shirt and whatever armour he could. When he exited the wardrobe, he found a new sword resting on his bed, unlike anything he'd ever seen. The hilt shone with a silver hue, a dim echo of majesty. When he drew it, ice blue rippled through the room.

He'd seen this before, in a vision in the north. Alsair had carried it through Mount Sancti during the purge. When Eli strapped it on his waist, it was comfortable, like it was always meant to belong there.

Lastly, he grabbed the Eternal Torch from under the bed. He turned to the extra sheath he hung for it, but in its place he found a fresh one of polished black leather, etched with whorls of ice-blue and gold. When he lifted it and upended it, a simple ring of gold fell into his palm. Eli pocketed the ring and slammed the Torch in his sheath.

Dressed, armed, ready for war. The Torchbearer once again.

# Chapter 61

Kyra noted that Monsun couldn't keep the relief from his eyes.

"Vindicator," he said. "You're late."

"Sorry, sir," Eli said, forcing a grin for the soldiers around him. "I was a little delayed."

Armoured fingers clasped his shoulder. "No matter. It's good to have you back. Did you find out anything useful?"

"Later." Eli nodded, watching his Regent.

Kyra rose up the steps, her heart racing, pressure rising in her head.

She stared out at the plains beyond her city walls. *Eislyn*—no, she would get Eislyn out, same as Eli. Right now, her city waited for her.

Twisting mists lurked beyond the battlements. Her Mark ignited on her hand, and she extended the blades on her staff, holding it up high. Light flared out over the darkness.

"No matter what comes during this night," Kyra shouted, "we will not yield! You are people of Leranion. You are my people! And we will defeat Temero!"

Beside her, Eli raised his Eternal Torch high into the night and flared his Mark. Jalek did the same, and three Marked stared into the faceless dark.

The cool metal of her staff became slick in her hand, but she lifted her chin higher, forcing herself to keep breathing.

A faint trace of light crept over the horizon. The sun's rays gleamed, melting away the shadow, and—nothing. Nothing but the hills on the other side of the Kinar. Nothing but scorched earth. Nothing but destroyed landscape which once held an army. Somehow, Temero had escaped.

"He got what he wanted," Eli said.

They'd failed. Temero had his army, the location of the pillars—he had Eislyn. "Oh Nestham," Kyra rasped. "Eislyn."

"Temero took her?" Jayne asked. Kyra spun on her heels, heart rising into her throat. The Lady was wide-eyed, trembling, and Kyra stretched out shaking arms. Jayne all but collapsed into them.

"We'll find her," Kyra said, stroking her hair. "We'll find her." She met Eli's gaze—full of fire, and determination.

*We'll find her.*

The sun's rays should have felt warm against Kyra's shoulders, but she just felt cold all over.

Raylene marched up the steps, the soldiers parting before her with salutes. Behind her, Tomas and Syl walked side-by-side, age and youth, nobility's discerning gaze and the street's shadows.

Kyra jerked her head at her Vindicators, nodded for the newly appointed Commander Janus of the First to take over.

He snapped a smart salute, and she folded her hands behind her back—trying to pretend that her world hadn't turned upside down. A hand brushed hers, and instantly Eli was there, a gritted smile on his face. Around them, citizens began to emerge from their homes, smiles blooming on their faces. The siege had lifted—the city would soon celebrate. She couldn't celebrate anything right now. Kyra and her Vindicators reached a secluded spot in the park—it would take too long to return to the Citadel. The wind whispered through the trees as Monsun's looming form stared down at her.

"Report."

Beside her, Eli opened his mouth—but she had to speak. This was her fault. "When Eli revealed his power against Temero, we knew it was only a matter of time before he came hunting for us. We knew where the pillars were, and the surest way for him to find out was to take that information from us. And when House Ketan left, I knew what would happen."

"We gambled on one of us being taken," Eli took up the thread. "We didn't know how, and there are too many spies in Imbra, so she had to act broken—which she did flawlessly." That memory was enough to destroy him, and he didn't dare look at

Kyra. "The plan—the plan was to get close enough to Eislyn to get the Ketan force to revolt. But it didn't work. I broke." His voice cracked on the word. "We didn't factor in Miriel."

"No plan survives the first second of a battle," Monsun said. "The loss of House Ketan is devastating. But Leranion will survive." He swept his gaze around all of them. "But what are you going to do with Lady Eislyn, Highness?"

Kyra hesitated. Nothing but silence. *What can I do?*

"I'll go," Eli said, steel in his voice. "I'll find her and bring her home."

"No. Not home," Kyra said. She met the gazes of all of her Vindicators. "Now that Temero has the location of the pillars, he'll move on them quickly. Monsun, leave as many troops behind as you see fit. Of the rest, half will go to Aurimia, and half to Talon Reach. Raylene, Jalek"—she glanced at them—"you're in command of Talon Reach."

Raylene rustled chain mail as she bowed. "At your service, milady." Jalek just nodded, his mirth gone, dirty hair flopping into his eyes.

"Monsun, we leave as soon as possible." The birds chirped overhead, yet a strange stillness seeped into her. A sense that they were at a crossroads, and not all would return.

"I cannot go with you," Monsun said. A shock pierced the fog in her mind, and she rounded on her Senior Vindicator.

"*What?*" she asked, not daring to believe it.

The bigger man winced, contorting his silver tattoo. "Before he died, Alsair gave me one last mission. Amora and I leave for Amaldas to find support in Biralam. Until we return, Tomas and Syl will command the forces at Aurimia."

Kyra bit her lip—Alsair had taken too much from her. He'd taken his secrets to his grave. He'd take one of her best generals too? She didn't trust him. He'd sent her to fight Temero without any idea what she was up against. He'd manipulated her, lied to her, controlled her like a puppet.

*I am on the side of Nestham. Always.* The one truth he'd told. She had to trust that. If she pretended to be a Musadim, she had to trust that.

"Fine," she said. "My parents will remain in Imbra to bolster the garrison. They're healing well enough, and we should leave at least one Marked to defend the city."

Monsun nodded, pride glowing in his eyes.

"Well," she said. "Farewell, Senior Vindicator. I'll see you at the head of a Biralam army."

"You will have your army, Highness," he said. "I promise."

She gave him a quick hug, wishing Amora was here—but she'd been safely left at the palace, probably causing hell.

She turned her back in the morning sun, wiping tears from her face. And the last of Alsair's words echoed in her mind.

"Farewell, Highness." Two Vindicators filed away, the rest following.

# Chapter 62

The ring clenched in Eli's fist cut into his skin as the tears finally fell. The cold, empty room had just one window, weak light spilling in. On the bed, a black sheet covered the form he knew so well.

He murmured a prayer through the lump in his throat, and rose on shaking legs. "I—I think you would have wanted to see this," Eli said. The clouds lay thick overhead, but the city was rejoicing, for light had returned to Imbra at last. "I'm not sure I ever fully understood you, and maybe I never will. But you took me in when I lost everything, you saved me countless times, and for better or worse, you made me who I am. I owe you everything, Alsair. Thank you."

He turned, wiping tears from his face, and met the ocean-blue gaze of the woman who leaned against the wall. Beside her, a snow leopard sat, violet eyes fixed intently on him. Nix blinked once, then nudged Kyra. His Regent held her staff loosely in one hand—she hadn't let go of it since dawn broke.

"I'm sorry, Eli," she said.

He nodded, shoving his hands into his pockets. "I should get going. I need to get to Mount Sancti. Figure out what Lucial—what Temero's up to, and get Eislyn out."

"Do you want to see Miriel before you go?"

"No," he said. "If I look at her one more time—I'll never be able to leave."

She took his hand. "I'll take care of her. I promise."

He pulled her into a fierce hug before she could respond. "Please." His voice cracked. "The two of you are all I have left."

After what felt like an instant, she withdrew and pressed a kiss to his cheek. "Eli, before he died, Alsair said something strange. *The Marked must stand against Temero. On the Severed Peaks, one must fall to save Ekra.*"

The words chilled him to the core, and the world spun before his eyes.

"Does that mean anything to you?" she asked.

"I had those words in a dream before I met you," he said. "When I was alone on the plains after Mount Sancti was destroyed." He shook his head, fighting to keep himself together. "But I'll figure it out on the way. I'll find Eislyn"—he clutched her hand—"and I'll meet you at Aurimia. I promise."

"Aurimia," she said, lifting her chin high. Nestham above, she was radiant.

It took more strength to leave than he could bear. But soon, the gates of the Citadel shut behind him, a horse by his side, armed and packed for a long journey.

Mount Sancti. Where he'd once again face Temero—he wasn't finished with the demon yet. Temero had won the first battle, but the war was just beginning. Eli stepped into the unknown, the ghost of a hand on his shoulder.

# Epilogue

Lucial glided through the rubble of the fallen sanctuary, descending into the steps below the mountain. The clatter of troops surrounded him, the excavation still ongoing. Even now, an old man raised his hand triumphantly, the glimmer of Nesthamir in his fingers.

Darkness didn't bother Lucial; he'd spent too much time in it, though it had once been light. This body, however—he'd need to find one that suited him better. Shadows trailed at his feet as he nodded at Lady Eislyn. She looked resplendent in a black gown, poring over the maps spread on his desk. She flashed him a smile as he passed through the stone chamber and gazed at the cell in the far corner.

A woman lay on a stone table, shadows holding her in place. Her mahogany skin was radiant, glowing in the underground darkness. She twitched as he neared the bars, and a shadow snapped at her face, pinning down wings of pure night.

"Now, Mahari," he said with a grin, "why don't you tell me exactly what you're doing in my world."

# Acknowledgements

This book has been a journey to write. It's taken over three years from first draft to print copy, but there are so many people I need to thank for supporting me on this adventure!

To my incredible editor, Belinda Pollard, for your patient correction and guidance on how to improve my writing over the years despite everything that's going on in this world.

To Mum and Dad, for encouraging me not to give up on my goals despite all the other endeavours I could pursue. Your support both emotional and practical has been a relief over these last few years.

To Steven White-Smith, who designed the new cover of *Torchbearer* as well as the cover for *Faithless,* your skill blows me away. I cannot wait to see what the next one looks like!

To Komal, for handling my socials when I was in the pit of assignment hell, and for creating better designs than I could ever dream of.

And to Ben, who has been forcing me to *do better* with my design and marketing ever since *Torchbearer* was a first draft.

To my beta readers, especially Amanda, who has read every single manuscript I have produced. Your advice and passion for writing keeps me going when I feel like scrapping the entire manuscript.

To Ryan—it has been a *time.* Since *Torchbearer,* we've seen a lot more of each other—and I'm so grateful for that. Also to Liv, you two have been wonderful comrades in the suffering of law school.

To my particularly chaotic group of friends, thank you for the 'support'—and endless amount of laughs.

To the folks at New Spring, my 'Real Friends' and my friends at uni—you are all amazing people and make my day.

To Joel, thank you for your kindness and enthusiasm throughout the publishing process—and for the art you have been working on!

To the team at the WA Justice Association—thank you for letting me be part of this amazing organisation. Let's keep bringing change wherever we go.

Above all, I thank God for the ability and passion for writing that He's given me, and I am grateful to share it with all of you.

Finally, thanks to you, reader, for sticking through with *Faithless* to the end. I hope you enjoyed reading it as much as I have enjoyed writing it. If you have, please consider leaving a review. It would be much appreciated!

# About the Author

Steven is a resident of the most isolated capital city in the world: Perth, Australia. He is currently working on the finale of the *Tales of the Marked* series. To find out more, visit **riftsingerpress.com** and follow **@srthiele** on Instagram.

www.ingramcontent.com/pod-product-compliance
Lightning Source LLC
Chambersburg PA
CBHW030516120726
47904CB00005B/1490